THE CIRQUE

Martin Van Pelt

This is a work of fiction. Names, characters, places, and incidents either are the product of the author's imagination or are used fictitiously. Any resemblance to actual persons, living or dead, events, government facilities, business establishments, or locales is entirely coincidental.

THECIRQUENOVEL@HOTMAIL.COM
First Edition
Copyright © 2012 by Martin Van Pelt
All rights reserved.
ISBN: 1470098873
ISBN-13: 9781470098872
CreateSpace, North Charleston, SC

THIS BOOK IS DEDICATED
TO THE MEMORY OF MY MOTHER
MARY VAN PELT
WHO ALWAYS SAID
"THERE'S NOTHING BETTER
THAN A GOOD BOOK."

2032 AD
Boulder, Colorado

Junior Coleman pulled into the driveway of the classic 1940s ranch house. It sat on a wooded hillside nestled against the foothills just inside the city limits of Boulder, Colorado, and had been designed by a disciple of Frank Lloyd Wright. The student architect himself had been recognized over the past few decades for his designs, although never achieving the notoriety of his famous teacher. The house shared its two acres with aspen trees and ponderosa pines. The almost ninety-year-old house had been lovingly restored over the years by his parents. He shut off the ignition to his Honda Civic station wagon's fuel cell and loosened his tie. He sighed. Having been an only child, he was really all alone now, he thought. Mom and Pop were both gone: his mother some fifteen years ago; his father just a week ago. Both had eventually succumbed to some form of cancer. His mother's death had dragged out for over a year. His father had gone in less than a month, with leukemia, at the age of eighty-four. Science had been promising a cure for over a century.

Junior took the urn off the front seat, opened the Honda's door, and stepped out. His nickname had stuck to him all these years even though he was now a fifty-eight-year-old, divorced, balding man. He was dressed in a dark suit and top coat bought especially for the memorial service an hour ago at the University of Colorado's chapel. There had been hundreds of people giving him their respect and condolences. His father had certainly been well liked in the English department, more so than he had ever thought. He pulled at the suit jacket. It didn't seem to fit all that well. The suit was the same size he always wore, but the pants were a little too tight around the waist now. His ex-wife had always been after him to start a workout program, but he just never seemed to have the time. The store salesman had smiled, winked, and told him he would like the way he looked—he guaranteed it. Junior knew hype when he heard it.

As he approached the double garage door, he heard the low rumble of the other car's expensive petroleum engine and turned just as the vintage, blue stretch Lincoln Town Car idled up along the curb behind his Honda.

Junior turned back and entered the familiar code into the keypad: his father's birth date. The garage door started up.

Inside, in the suddenly bright, late-afternoon December light, a tarp outlined a familiar shape. He gently placed the urn on a nearby workbench. As he pulled the cover off the car, he thought about having to sell the sixty-year-old, mint-condition Porsche 911T, now that his father was gone. The chrome trim gleamed in the sunlight. The silver paint was flawless—Pop always saw to that. The now classic, white-and-green Colorado license plates had been the same number as long as he could remember. It would probably fetch a good price, Junior thought.

A man's shadow fell across the Porsche.

"You aren't going to sell it are you?"

Junior turned and smiled at the longtime family friend. "I have no use for it. I'll give you a good price though."

The other man smiled and placed his hand on Junior's shoulder. "I just might take you up on that." And then he added, "Your father loved that car."

Junior nodded and laughed. "Yeah, he sure did. But Mom didn't, for some reason. This car always seemed to irritate her. I never could figure that out."

The other man chuckled, "There were some other things that irritated your mother—including me."

Junior had certainly heard that over the years, but out of politeness did not comment.

The other man, James "Jamie" Anderson, had also dressed in a dark suit for the funeral. His well-tailored and very expensive suit contrasted noticeably with Junior's. The man was tall—well over six feet—and lean, and stood straight, despite his eighty-four years; he could have easily passed for a man in his mid-sixties. His hair, which had been blond most of his life, had turned almost pure white and, miraculously, was still just as thick as a young man's. He wore it long and over his collar. His face and hands had many spots and wrinkles, but his youthful eyes still seemed to twinkle with life and mirth as if he was about to tell a good joke, despite the many crow's feet surrounding them. He was cochairman of the board of directors of the fabulous, worldwide Forsyth Hotel and Resort chain, a war hero, and, as he always added, an Eagle Scout. He looked every bit the very successful business man he had become in the past forty-five years. The Forsyth Hotel business, headquartered in Las Vegas, was the flagship, but there were many other interests as well. Experts put his and his wife's net worth at well over thirty billion dollars.

Jamie Anderson reflected, "I knew your father literally all his life—since we were just a few weeks old."

Junior Coleman nodded as they both looked at the Porsche. He certainly knew this fact and some of the other stories his father had told him about the exploits of his father's friend. Their friendship had indeed been lifelong.

Jamie Anderson raised his chin at the urn on the workbench and continued, "He was a good friend and a good man. He lived a full life. Don't be sad." Then the older man paused and motioned to the inside door. "C'mon, let's go inside. We have something to talk about." He pointed at the urn. "Don't forget your old man there."

Junior looked over his shoulder at the Lincoln. The tinted windows masked the interior but a figure could still be seen in the front passenger's seat. "But Aunt Deb..."

"Don't worry. She'll be in later. I told her we had some business. She understands and will give us a little time."

With that Jamie Anderson opened the door to the kitchen and motioned Rod Jr. to follow him inside. The house had not been lived in for a month or more and smelled musty. Junior followed the older man into the kitchen and then into the expansive living room, furnished with early-twentieth-century arts and crafts furniture, including some valuable original Stickley pieces. Junior was puzzled when Jamie did not stop there but instead continued down the hallway toward his dad's study and the bedrooms.

Junior gently placed the urn on the coffee table next to two framed photographs. The color of the old photos had faded, but he could still make out the two, smiling young men: his father and Jamie Anderson. One had been taken on a mountaintop; climbing gear sat at their feet. In the other, the two men were standing next to the silver Porsche on what looked like a mountain pass. After pausing at these familiar sights, Junior followed the other man down the hallway.

Jamie stopped halfway down the hall and looked up. He reached up and pulled the chain on an overhead trapdoor that led into the attic of the classic, four-bedroom home. The door came down and revealed steps—actually a folding ladder—on the backside. Jamie unfolded the steps and climbed spryly into the attic as Junior stood there puzzling over why the old man would climb up there.

In a few minutes Jamie appeared in the opening and indicated to Junior to take a large, brown, weathered, leather suitcase down from him. Junior took the heavy suitcase's weight with some effort.

"I think this is the only one left. Right where your father said it would be," Jamie said, as he descended the stairs and brushed the dust off his hands onto his expensive suit pants.

Junior hefted the suitcase as Jamie squeezed by and walked into the living room. As the younger man followed, he stirred up dust from the carpet, which danced in the evening winter sunlight now pouring into the room.

Jamie looked for a moment at the two framed photographs on the table and the urn. He then moved them carefully to one side and indicated to the younger man to put the suitcase on the coffee table in front of the sofa. Jamie sat on the sofa, snapped open the locks, and opened the old suitcase.

Junior caught his breath. His eyes widened. The suitcase was half full of money. It looked like bundles and bundles of one hundred and fifty dollar bills. Lots of them. He saw that they were the old drab green ones unlike the modern, now colorful currency which ironically were still called greenbacks.

"What the...," Junior mumbled.

Jamie shook his head and picked up a bundle of fifties. "Looks like about four or five hundred thousand. Your dad always felt kind of weird about this money for some reason. Of course most of it was invested for him, but he just always wanted some cash around. I don't know why."

"I don't understand...," Junior mumbled again, as he looked from the money and to Jamie.

"C'mon, have a seat," Jamie said, as he motioned to the other man to sit down beside him on the sofa. "Your father died a rich man. Now you're going to be a rich man, Junior. I'm the executor of his will, and he died with over twenty million. Not bad. I could have made him much more, but he was so damned conservative about everything he did from the time we were kids. And after some charitable donations—mainly to the university—you're going to wind up with about ten million, I figure. And we started out with just a few million apiece." Jamie pointed at the suitcase. "This is what is left of the original money."

"What original money? I always knew dad had some investments here and there. What are you talking about, Uncle Jamie?"

Jamie laughed and looked again at the aging photographs. "Well, it was a long time ago. And, of course, we were younger then. In our mid-thirties." He chuckled to himself. "We sure thought that was getting old, too, at the time. Over the hill. I guess you'd have been about eight or ten years old."

The old man paused and then laughed again at the younger man's puzzlement. He placed his hand on Rod Jr.'s knee, laughed once more, and said, "I guess you don't understand. Boy, have I got a story for you, Junior. Actually, I should start when we were kids. So here goes." He paused one more time as if to reflect for a moment. He looked once more at the old photos. Then Jamie Anderson cleared his throat and resumed, "Now, Junior, you've got to remember that things were a little simpler way back then in the early 1980s. Yes, things were much less sophisticated than they are now—"

Junior quickly interrupted, "What things?"

Jamie Anderson answered with a wink, "Drug smuggling for one."

CHAPTER 1

1960 AD
Indiana

A cold, early-March drizzle fell lightly on the long fallow field. It had been one of those record-breaking midwestern winters in which weary snowmen stand in front yards for months, tin mailboxes on icy country roads get buried daily with piles of dirty, gray snow as the plows make their rounds, and cars remain encrusted with salt until the spring thaw. Although a few buds were bravely beginning to show on the rain-slick branches of some of the trees and bushes at the edge of the field, everything was a dismal brown and, for the most part, still lay dormant, waiting for some sort of signal from Mother Nature that winter was really over for good.

In the middle of the fallow field, the tip of the big blond kid's head bobbed up and down just above ground level as he worked with his shovel in the bottom of the large erosion gully. His feet made sucking noises as he shifted them in the muddy water. The erosion gully ran diagonally across the field like an angry, brown gash. Just a few feet deep at the upper fence line, it was nearly twelve feet deep where it ended in the creek just beyond the lower tree line. Presently, suburbia still lay a mile away on the outskirts of Indianapolis, and the future expanding wave of freeways, theme shopping malls, and fast-food franchises was still a generation away from this spot.

Some logs, their bark soggy and slick in the rain, were piled on the ground near the edge of the gully, where the tall boy worked. He wore a Cincinnati Redlegs hat, a blue Indiana University sweatshirt, which hung heavily from his shoulders, a pair of tan chino pants, and black rubber boots with metal buckles. And he was soaked to the skin.

He thought again of the fast-approaching deadline. He needed just one more merit badge to become a Star Scout, and he was working on the soil conservation badge—Really, a pretty easy one, all things considered. The check dam in the bottom of the gully was the final project. When he finished, the dam would prevent topsoil from traveling all the way to the Gulf of Mexico, keeping it in Indiana where it belonged. More importantly, it was another step down the long, difficult road to becoming an Eagle Scout.

The tall boy rested on his shovel for a few moments. He winced when he heard the intermittent *thunks* of his friend's ax as the other boy worked to cut down one more tree for the dam. He wanted to yell across the field to his buddy to hurry up but didn't dare.

This was the enemy's stronghold.

This was McGuire territory.

Every kid that explored these fields and woods lived in mortal fear of them. They were the dirt-poor hillbilly family that lived in the ramshackle farmhouse just over the hill: husband, wife, and two mean sons. Even meaner dogs—no one knew how many there were. Last count put it at forty—mostly scraggly, long-eared hounds. When a local boy messed around in these woods, he always tried to give their place a wide berth.

And woe to the boy actually captured by them. Everybody at school knew what they did with their captives. Ricky McFadden had told everyone in homeroom last month of his ordeal. He had indeed been taken prisoner one day by Mike and Eddie McGuire while risking a shortcut. They had eventually let him go with a warning to stay off their land, but not before they had actually held him headfirst by his feet over the black hole in their outhouse and made him swear he would never return to their place.

The tall boy shivered at that prospect and glanced nervously around the field. Just last year, he had to run for his life from the older brother when Eddie caught him trying to catch a few tadpoles down along the creek. He had just made it to the sanctuary of his backyard.

Jeez, he thought. He wished his friend would hurry up and finish chopping down that tree.

Seventy-five yards across the field and into the woods, the other twelve-year-old couldn't have agreed more. He certainly didn't want to tangle with the McGuires.

Soaked to the skin and miserable, like his friend, rain spotted his almost completely fogged-up glasses. Every time he swung the big, double-bitted Hudson Bay ax, they fell down on his nose, and he had to push them up. Also, if his father knew that he had taken the ax from his workshop without permission, he would kill him.

He thought his friend was always putting him in situations he didn't like such as this.

It had been the tall boy's idea to join the Boy Scouts last year, and now it was his idea to build this stupid dam in the rain—*adventure* he called it.

Both their mothers thought they were downtown at the YMCA taking swimming lessons—more guilt heaped upon his skinny shoulders. They had started down to the bus stop but then had doubled back to get the ax. All in all, the skinny kid thought, he would rather be home in a warm room watching his favorite Saturday morning show, *Sky King*.

But it had always been like this. For some reason, he always seemed to do what the other boy wanted to do. The skinny kid had never become very popular at school, and this made him value his friend's companionship even more. The other boy was his best friend. In fact, he was his only friend at the moment.

He took another halfhearted swipe at the tree with the heavy ax. This time, to his surprise, it bit deep and stuck.

He pried back and forth and worked it free. Pushing up his glasses, he took another swing and thought about Abraham Lincoln building a log cabin. Some chips flew back at him and a satisfying chunk of the tree fell out, deepening the notch he had put in the trunk. Then an ominous cracking sound ricocheted along the tree; he ran back, dragging the ax in the leaves, fully expecting the tree to fall. He stared at the tree, but it didn't budge. Slowly, he approached it again. Almost done. He pushed his glasses up on his nose once more. Just a couple of more swings would do it, he thought, as he hefted the big ax again.

His arms were getting tired, and he was really ready to call it quits. But if your best friend wanted you to help him, you just had to go along with it.

Neighbors, having been born just ten days apart, there had literally not been a time when they had not known each other. Well, maybe a month—when you got right down to it—before the tall boy's mother had first asked the other boy's mother to baby-sit for an hour or two. After that they had become inseparable, growing up together. They had begun playing in the sandbox together and then advanced to the swing set later. They had started kindergarten together and now were in the sixth grade, with old lady Kennedy as their teacher. They had climbed a hundred trees and built a hundred or more model airplanes and ships. They had explored the woods and fields behind their houses until they knew that territory like the backs of their hands. They pretended to be cowboys at one time and GIs in search of Krauts or Japs at another.

He brought the big ax over his head and started it down with all the strength he could muster. His skinny arms gave a little bit, and for a terrifying second, he knew the swing was not right.

The heavy ax came down and hit the tree below the notch with a glancing blow on the wet, shiny bark. It ricocheted off the trunk, and he tried with all his might to stop its momentum, but to no avail. The razor-sharp edge easily cut through his pants and buried itself down to the bone.

At first, he simply felt utter disbelief and shock as he was swept off his feet—no pain yet—as if someone had kicked his feet out from under him in a touch football game. He fell onto his side on the muddy ground among the twigs and dead leaves.

Then the pain came. Like some river of liquid fire running down his leg. And he screamed.

And he screamed louder when he looked at the damage.

The ax head had struck him mid-calf, peeled back a huge flap of skin, and buried itself in his ankle. He could see muscle and white tendon dangling over shiny bone. It reminded him of something he had seen at the butcher's shop while shopping with his mom. The blood began to well up quickly, and he felt faint and sick at the same time. He knew he would pass out, and just before he did, he thought of all the trouble he was going to be in.

The tall boy heard his friend scream just as he was scrambling up the slick, muddy bank to get the first log and place it in the bottom of the gully. He got to his feet and then heard the second scream. Then as if his mind went to an automatic setting, he knew instinctively what had happened and what he must do.

Years later and thousands of miles away, over a steaming jungle, he would have to call upon this inner reserve of strength and calmness over and over again. Some would call it courage, but the tall boy would later say he was in the wrong place at the right time with the right amount of luck.

He sprinted across the field with remarkable agility for such a tall and gangly boy his age. He gained the tree line in seconds. Pushing aside brambles and low branches, he could see his friend lying on the ground, not moving, his pants leg red with blood. He pushed a branch aside, and it rebounded, striking him across the face and immediately raising a large, angry, red welt on his forehead. But he didn't feel it as he reached his friend, breathless, and knelt over him.

At first he thought his friend had died somehow, but he quickly noticed his chest rising and falling slowly and shallowly. He realized his friend had fainted; he knelt down and could tell the boy had lost a lot of blood in a hurry from the deep wound. The ground seemed to be saturated with it.

The tall boy had obtained his first aid merit badge some months ago. It had been the first he had gotten. He unbuckled his official Boy Scouts of America web belt and pulled it from his pants. He then took off his sweatshirt and T-shirt. Next he pulled his official Boy Scouts of America pocket knife from his pants and opened it to the cutting blade. Gingerly he began to cut his friend's pant leg from the wound.

God, what a mess, he thought.

A large flap of bloody skin, muscle, and tendon hung away from the calf, exposing the bone. Blood squirted from the wound in small jets. An artery, he thought. He would have to work fast. He quickly wound the belt around his friend's thigh, pulled it tight, making sure the serrated edges on the buckle caught. It was a makeshift tourniquet, but it would work. He would have to loosen it in about fifteen minutes, he remembered.

Next he took his T-shirt in both hands and stretched it as far as he could between his arms and then twirled it a couple of times, making a temporary bandage. He gently pushed the flap of skin back in place with his fingers, noticing that the bleeding had slowed. Holding the flap in one hand, he started to wind the T-shirt around his friend's leg, leaving each end of the makeshift bandage free to tie off.

Everything had been by the book up to that point. The bandage seemed to be working. But he knew that now he needed to treat his friend for shock, while somehow summoning help, without just leaving him lying there in the wet.

His friend stirred and then moaned. He was coming back around. Still, the grayness of the injured boy's face frightened the tall boy. He knew he should leave him and get some help now, but he was a good mile and a half from home—a three-mile round-trip not including time wasted getting someone's attention. And you couldn't get an ambulance near here. The old Cadillac the volunteer fire department used would be axle-deep in mud before it was fifty yards off the road.

So he quickly figured he had three choices.

He could leave his friend and get help. He knew he shouldn't move him, but to leave him for who knows how long in the cold, while he tried to get someone to understand what had happened and come back, didn't seem like a good idea. Besides he didn't have a blanket to put over him like all the first aid books said.

Second, he could carry him home and call the ambulance on the phone. This would also take time. Precious time.

Or, he could head off in the other direction and carry his friend right to the firehouse itself. There would be no time lost. One of the volunteers could crank up the Caddy and hit the lights and siren. They would be at the hospital in no time.

The only trouble with the last option was that he had to cut right through the McGuire place. Right into their backyard, past the house and forty dogs, right under the noses of Mike and Eddie, and down the half-mile driveway to town. Not an appealing gauntlet to run.

He looked at the leg. It was still bleeding—not as much, thanks to the tourniquet. But his friend's breathing was becoming shallower. His face was still gray.

Okay, the tall boy thought, I've made my choice. He gently picked up his friend, cradled him in his arms, and started up the hill toward the McGuire's farmhouse. At least it had stopped raining, he thought.

Ten minutes and a half mile later, he was kneeling in the wet, overgrown honeysuckle bushes along the fence line to the rear of the farmhouse as he tried to catch his breath. It had been a long haul, but he had been determined not to stop until that point, no matter how tired he had become. Besides he wanted to loosen the tourniquet.

He peered at the dilapidated farmhouse and the barn next to it. Both had been painted white once with green trim, but most of the paint had faded, leaving an overall gray color. At first glance it appeared as if no one was around. A single light bulb burned through the open barn door. An old Model A flatbed truck sat in the driveway. A few chickens pecked the bare ground in the side yard underneath a clothesline. Best of all—there were no dogs in sight.

He was just thinking that he had never been this close to the McGuire place when he heard a cry from his friend. He turned around just as a dog barked on the other side of the house. He put his hand over the other boy's mouth and whispered, "Shut up; you'll give us away."

His friend was confused for a moment then felt the pain and remembered his leg. He grimaced. The tall boy took his hand away from his mouth. The skinny kid asked, "Where are we? What's going on?"

"We're right at the back fence of the McGuire place. Now shut up while I loosen this tourniquet. You've really got us in a fine mess this time."

"I didn't mean it, honest. It just slipped." The injured boy stiffened and began to cry as the other boy loosened the tourniquet.

Working on the leg, the tall boy felt a moment of guilt for what he had said. "Yeah, I know. Don't worry about it. But keep quiet, I have to get you to the firehouse, and the shortest way is to go down their driveway to the main road."

Then, the skinny boy fainted again.

Good, the tall boy thought, as he tightened the belt. At least he won't be screaming or doing something stupid when I pick him up.

He bent over and gently hoisted his friend up into his arms. After carefully stepping through a gap in the fence, he started sprinting across the yard, aiming for the side yard between the house and the barn.

The chickens scattered and started squawking. Then a big, brown hound came bounding off the front porch and around the side of the house. It started barking and snarling when it saw the two boys, but kept its distance.

Shit, the tall boy thought, and hoped nobody was home.

Then suddenly he heard someone yell from the barn, "What the hell is all that ruckus out there?"

The tall boy stopped dead in his tracks opposite the barn door. In the doorway, stood old man McGuire himself. Unshaven, the man wore an old pair of blue bib overalls, a checked flannel shirt, leather boots, and an old baseball cap, the logo long since covered with grease. He was holding a gigantic red-handled screwdriver in one hand.

He stepped from the doorway and yelled again, gesturing with the screwdriver. "What the hell are you boys doin'?"

The tall boy froze in his tracks. As old man McGuire came closer, the boy willed his legs to move, but they wouldn't. He couldn't run for it this time.

He stammered, "My friend's hurt real bad, mister. He hit himself with an ax."

McGuire could now see the wound. "Jesus H. Christ!" Then he yelled toward the house, "Sarah, get the truck started!"

A tired, gray-haired women in a checked dress leaned out one of the side windows wiping her hands with a towel. In a sweet voice, she asked, "What is it, Donald?"

"We've got a hurt boy here—start the truck!"

The woman disappeared from the window and, in a moment, was walking across the front porch toward the driveway.

The hound was still barking, and McGuire gave it a swift kick in the head, sending it yelping toward the barn.

"Put the boy on the ground and let me look at this."

The tall boy did as he was told.

McGuire knelt over the injured boy. "I used to be a medic in the big one over in Germany." He looked at the bloody T-shirt and the tourniquet. "You done real well so far, boy, but we have to get him to a hospital. Help me carry him to the truck."

Jeez, thought the tall boy, no dogs eating us alive or burials in the outhouse or anything. And old man McGuire is going to drive us to the hospital in his truck.

They gently carried the unconscious boy to the truck, which by now old lady McGuire had started, and lifted him over the tailgate onto the bed. Smoke poured from the tailpipe, and the engine made a horrible clattering noise. McGuire hit the cab top a couple of times, and she let out the clutch. They rattled down the long driveway, over the creek, and into town.

Donald McGuire wasn't the villain all the kids thought. He was just a poor man living with his family on the edge of the new suburbia. Decades later McGuire would retire after selling his broken-down farm for over three million dollars, twice its appraised value, to a large Las Vegas consortium that wanted the land for a housing development.

The Model A had arrived at the hospital fifteen minutes later.

They had gotten the boy to the emergency room just in time—in shock and barely alive. The doctors had to operate on the leg for over two hours but had saved it. The skinny boy would walk with the aid of crutches for five months. He would carry some bad scars there for the rest of his life. And the doctors told his mother there might be a small stiffness in his ankle for a long time. Maybe forever.

The tall boy was given a medal by the Boy Scouts of America for his quick thinking. The whole incident was depicted in cartoon form on the back page of *Boys' Life* magazine a year later in a section on the last page titled "Scouts in Action."

This would not be the only be time his town made him a hero. There would be a Silver Star in his future, earned over a humid jungle nine thousand miles from home.

Afterward, he was never really sure he deserved either.

CHAPTER 2

October 1984 AD
Denver, Colorado
Cubicles

Rod Coleman stared out the forty-second floor window of the Front Range Bank Building. The sun was just setting behind the mountains to the west. At times like this, whenever he worked late, he always stopped for twenty minutes or so at sunset and watched the city lights wink on. The real rush hour was long over, but even so there was still quite a lot of traffic down there, judging by the number of headlights and taillights: stragglers like himself working late, people going out to dinner to celebrate the beginning of the weekend, or shoppers headed for the numerous malls around the area.

He noticed some flashing red and blue lights stopped way out in the valley on I-25, the north-south artery through Denver. Another set of lights was rapidly approaching from the south. Probably the Colorado State Patrol—the CSP, as they were known by everyone—responding to another wreck. It appeared they were near the notorious Mousetrap interchange of I-25 and I-70. A nightmare of short ramps and very sharp curves designed in the 1950s, made worse by the sheer volume of traffic that had to negotiate it every day—it had been given its nickname years ago by an imaginative traffic reporter. Most Denverites used worse, unprintable nicknames for it. Rod himself had to run this gauntlet twice a day commuting from his home in Thornton, a suburb in the northern part of the city. Every week or so, some truck would fail to make a curve and spread its cargo of apples or beer or lawn chairs or whatever—once a few months ago, a shipment of navy torpedoes—all over the road. Accidents could clog the already congested roads for hours.

Rod looked back up toward the mountains—Colorado's pride and joy. It was a clear October evening, with little smog for a change. He could plainly see the sharp, black outlines of the various peaks against the lingering red glow of the setting sun. Due west was the large hump of Mt. Evans, one of the *fourteeners*, so named because its summit was just over fourteen thousand feet, 14,264 feet to be exact, Rod knew. During the summer months, tourists could drive their cars within a few yards of the summit. The road closed for the winter. Looking north he could easily make out the square summit of Long's Peak in Rocky Mountain National Park some seventy miles away—another fourteener. Reaching its summit was another matter. A person in good shape could scramble to the top on a summer day after a long, tiring hike; years ago he had once done it the hard way—climbing the sheer two-thousand-foot east face.

Rod turned his head toward the south part of the city at the muted sound of a siren far below. He couldn't find its flashing source. Probably an ambulance, he thought. Over the last ten years, he had gotten pretty good at judging sirens from his boring perch.

He glanced up, seeing his own reflection in the tempered glass, and tried to ignore it. He noticed the first stars becoming visible in the darkening sky. A set of flashing strobe lights were streaking westward over the city as a jet climbed on its course.

He reached down, opened his bottom right drawer, and withdrew a compact pair of binoculars. He removed his glasses and tried to focus on the silhouette of the airliner as it faded into the night. But he couldn't identify it. Too many reflections on the glass and just too dark. He knew it had just taken off on the north-south runway of Denver's Stapleton International Airport a few minutes ago. Probably bound for LA or Vegas.

Rod tried to ignore his reflection once again, as he placed the binoculars in the open briefcase on the chair by his desk, but was drawn back to it. Was that really someone nearing forty staring back? Impossible. But there was no doubt about it now. The hair was thinner, and his forehead was higher. Silver threads were beginning to show just above the temples. And despite all the exercise, a small paunch was pushing over his belt.

He checked his watch and then tried to train his attention on the paperwork in front of him. He tried to concentrate, but couldn't. He picked up a ballpoint pen and clicked it absentmindedly and then leaned back in his chair. He stared out the window again. Just a few weeks ago, he had celebrated fifteen years with the company: the Evergreen Mutual Insurance Company. Had he really been sitting here at this spot for a whole decade?

Another jet streaked overhead into the distance. He imagined the crew sitting in their seats. Would even their job become boring after a while? He didn't think so. He himself had learned to fly once a long, long time ago, had even gotten his private pilot's license. But that had been before he had married Ann and then the budget just seemed to get tighter and tighter no matter how much you made. He hadn't flown an airplane since his wedding day.

Rod tried to concentrate again. Garbage in and garbage out, he thought.

He looked at his watch. Jamie's flight was due in at 8:15, so he still had plenty of time to drive the few miles to the airport. He would leave at 7:30, which would give him time to fight the traffic and find a parking place in that hodgepodge of levels and confusion the city of Denver liked to call "airport parking."

His mind wandered again as he looked around at the office of the Evergreen Mutual Insurance Company. The company occupied an entire floor of the building and was completely open. Rows of desks were walled off into tiny cubicles by six-foot partitions. The company referred to these as "work areas." The openness of the floor was supposed to promote teamwork within the company, while the individual areas were to allow some privacy. All the walls and dividers had been painted in cheery colors: Rod's area, a sickening lavender. He had protested, but the designer had insisted it had to be lavender to "blend" with the yellow in the next area.

Each person was allowed to decorate an individual work area as he or she wished, even with no control over the color. Due to the decorating rule, the entire floor was rampant with plants, Garfield the Cat calendars, and HAVE A NICE DAY posters. The most recent rage—a bumper sticker made to resemble the familiar green-and-white Colorado license plate with the mountains depicted along the top, on which various messages were printed like the letters and numbers on the real license plate—was plastered everywhere. The favorite message was simply NATIVE—this in a state where it seemed most of the population had been born elsewhere. The fad had spread, and now there were bumper stickers that read SEMI-NATIVE, ALIEN, HIKER, or even WHO CARES? Some brave souls in the office had risked bodily harm with one that proudly proclaimed TEXAN.

Rod had been rewarded with a window desk five years after being hired. Ten years in the same spot. He had not decorated his area yet. What was the hurry, anyway?

In fact, besides a calendar and various insurance manuals lying on a file cabinet, he had only two pictures on his desk. One showed a rather plain-looking, slightly overweight woman standing on a front porch with a skinny, ten-year-old boy in glasses. His wife, Ann, and his son, Rod Jr. The other showed a much younger Rod Coleman wearing a puffy, red, down parka, down mittens, stocking hat, and heavy hiking boots. Standing next to him was another man. He was a good foot taller than Rod and had long, blond hair overlapping his collar. He was also dressed in a red down parka, red stocking cap, boots, and baggy, brown canvas pants. The man had his arm around Rod's shoulders and was grinning beneath a large mustache. Two large coils of golden, braided rope lay on two large, red backpacks at their feet; behind stood a large, triangular cairn of rocks. In the distance, out of focus, could be seen an endless line of snow-capped mountains. An inscription, written later in black marker across the blue sky of the photograph, said simply, "Summit Long's Peak, East Face, July 29, 1968."

Jamie Anderson and Rod Coleman had grown up together just outside Indianapolis, neighbors until Jamie's parents divorced when both boys were fourteen. When Jamie's mother wanted to move back to California, and his father found a new job in Florida, Jamie moved in with the Coleman's to finish high school. The situation in the Anderson household was never very good in the years before his parent's divorce, and Jamie had spent most of his time over at the Coleman's anyway—so it was a natural solution. They became the brothers they never had.

Jamie, a natural athlete, excelled in all sports, especially football. His teammates voted him captain of the high school team in both his junior and senior years. Rod was made equipment manager and usually sat next to his friend on the bench. During Jamie's senior year, he began attracting the attention of many universities eager to recruit a good quarterback. Finally he settled on the University of Colorado at Boulder, which awarded him a full four-year scholarship. He worked a deal whereby they came up with a partial scholarship for his friend and neighbor in exchange for his accepting their full scholarship. He never told Rod this fact.

Just months before the start of the fall quarter, Rod's father was tragically killed in a car wreck. A tearful Harriet Coleman saw both of her boys off to Colorado that autumn. By then, Jamie felt closer to her than his real mother, whom he hadn't seen for over two years.

While Rod was pulling down mostly As in his liberal arts courses, Jamie let his new T-bird and the women of Boulder get the best of him so that by his second year his grades were at a dangerous level. He was the starting quarterback his sophomore year, but his grades continued to plummet, and, finally, the T-bird and the scholarship disappeared.

During these years at CU, Jamie and Rod fell in love with the mountains of Colorado. Following his academic difficulties, Jamie didn't leave Boulder but instead continued to live in the area with various women, and, when they kicked him out, he always moved back in with his old friend. They usually found time in the fall to go elk and deer hunting, and in the spring and summer to go backpacking along the Front Range of the Rockies. Also during these years, Jamie, always eager to try something new, discovered the sport of rock climbing in the foothills west of Boulder. Jamie convinced his friend to at least give the sport a try. Hesitant at first, Rod found to his surprise that he liked it, though he never really got used to heights. He enjoyed the high quality of the equipment and the precise skill needed to accomplish a climb, while Jamie just plain enjoyed the physical challenge. They were a perfect team.

Also during this period, they discovered what would become their favorite destination—Hourglass Lake, set high in one of the lesser known ranges in central Colorado.

By the spring of Rod's senior year, the Vietnam War was really beginning to heat up, and Jamie, supporting himself by working at fast food restaurants and with no hope of any kind of deferment, found the draft board back in Indiana breathing down his neck. Rod, on the other hand, scheduled to graduate with honors from CU, had already been accepted into graduate school with a full scholarship and a university position teaching freshman English classes. After some spirited discussion one night, Jamie decided to enlist in the army. Rod opposed the war. His friend thought it would be quite an adventure.

After testing, Jamie was sent to train as a helicopter pilot at Ft. Rucker, Alabama. A few months later, he was sent to Vietnam.

Rod, now in graduate school, participated in many of the antiwar rallies on campus.

Jamie found he was one of those rare natural pilots and served twice in Vietnam, a total of two and a half years. At the beginning he flew a helicopter gunship, but then during his second tour, he was transferred to a squadron that rescued downed pilots. He made many daring rescues and was wounded twice superficially. Highly decorated, he was proud that he had never lost a helicopter or crewman in all his missions. But even the army thought two tours was enough, and he was transferred to Europe. After Vietnam, Germany bored him. He and the army parted ways a year later, following an incident whereby he was accused of landing his chopper full of intoxicated GIs in the parking lot of a notorious brothel outside Hamburg. Only the fact that a high-ranking colonel was aboard and Jamie's numerous decorations from Vietnam saved him from a court martial.

The two friends did not keep in touch much during these years—only an occasional letter or phone call.

Rod received his master's from CU and desperately tried to find a teaching job, though they were hard to come by and didn't pay all that well. He became engaged to his future wife, whom he had met in graduate school. He took the job with Evergreen Mutual as an underwriter.

Jamie lived for a while on savings after he left the army, before quickly landing a job with an oil company in Saudi Arabia. Despite his excellence as a pilot, he was fired two years later over an incident involving the airlift of twenty cases of beer into the country from an offshore freighter. He barely escaped a prison sentence and was quickly spirited out of the country on a company jet. Upon arrival in New York, he was promptly given his last paycheck.

Rod and Ann married, and she became pregnant. Jamie and Rod reunited for a camping trip to Hourglass Lake—when Ann gave birth to Rod Jr. Ann never forgave Jamie for dragging her husband off, despite the fact that the baby arrived three weeks premature.

Soon thereafter, Jamie found a job with another oil company flying support for the new Alaskan pipeline. He flew in some of the worst weather imaginable—winter temperatures so bitter that machines ran twenty-four hours a day. He and four others spent five days stranded on the tundra in his helicopter after it developed engine trouble during an unexpected blizzard. They were all found alive due to Jamie's survival training and mountain experience.

But he had had enough of the cold and soon quit the Alaskan job. He easily found a job flying workers to oil rigs in the Gulf of Mexico off the Louisiana coast: killer humidity in summer and boring flying, but at least it was warm most of the time.

About this time Rod got his window desk at Evergreen Mutual.

The two friends hadn't seen each other for three years.

Rod pushed his glasses up on his nose and leaned forward in his chair. Reaching over to his briefcase, he shut it and snapped both latches. He put the vinyl cover over the electric typewriter. Standing up, he took his coat from the hangar next to the window and draped it over his arm. He took one last look at his desk to be sure he hadn't forgotten anything and then picked up the briefcase. He walked down the aisle to the hall with the elevators, turning off the overhead lights as he went. He pushed the touch-sensitive down button and waited for the car to arrive.

Jamie had written him in January about a possible week-long trip to Hourglass that summer. They had initially planned the trip in August, but commitments on both sides had forced them to finally settle on the first week in October. Although the fall weather had been fine and the aspen were still in their splendor beneath deep, blue skies, it could be dangerously late to be in the high country of Colorado at that time of year. The first serious storm of the winter season could occur at any time. They both knew they might be pushing their luck. But both were experienced backpackers and climbers with excellent equipment.

The elevator silently arrived, and Rod stepped into the car, thinking about the weather as the door swished shut.

The TV weatherman on channel 4 had said that morning that a high-pressure ridge would remain over the state for the rest of the week despite a low-pressure area forming off the coast of California. The woman on the new Weather Channel had backed this forecast up. They should have great fall weather, but he knew how unpredictable Colorado's weather could be. People joked about long-range forecasts in Colorado, especially after Labor Day, and it seemed that Colorado weathermen mostly made guesses. Two days before the great Christmas blizzard of 1982, they had predicted partly cloudy skies with a small chance for a snow shower. Almost three feet of snow had buried Denver.

Rod pushed the button marked G, and the elevator started its silent descent to the garage level. The doors opened, and he headed for the farthest corner of the empty underground garage. His footsteps echoed off the concrete floor in the dimly lit area, as he neared the beautiful silver Porsche 911 parked diagonally across two parking spaces. Rod went to the driver's side and carefully laid his briefcase on the gleaming roof of the German car. He fished in his pocket for the keys. The car was obviously in mint condition, and he had an intimate relationship with it. It was a 1972 model, now almost a collector's item. He had purchased it new after completing his master's degree and, more importantly, before his marriage. The car stood as proof of the only time he could remember that he had done something on a whim.

Rod unlocked the door and, after opening it gently, took the briefcase from the roof while looking for any scratches. He put the case on the leather passenger's seat and twisted the key in the ignition. The engine caught with a familiar roar, and the six cylinders settled into a sweet idle. He gently closed the driver's door and sat with both hands on the fat steering wheel. The mechanic had warned him to let the newly rebuilt engine warm up a little at first and to take it easy for a few weeks. Rod was still in the habit of doing this.

He and Ann had their last big fight over this car a month before. She wanted a new car—a family car this time. But he wanted the engine rebuilt on the Porsche. Sell the Porsche, she said. Use the money for a down payment on one of those new, popular Japanese station wagons, she insisted. They had an old Oldsmobile sedan that ran fine, in addition to the sports car. He put his foot down for almost the first time in their marriage and had the Porsche's engine rebuilt. Their marriage took a turn for the worst. She tried to sabotage the backpacking trip with Jamie by insisting that he take her and Rod Jr. to visit her mother—this very week—after all the plans had been laid. Again he put his foot down and determined not to change his mind. So she pulled the boy out of school, bought two airline tickets with money from their skimpy savings account, and flew home to Los Angeles anyway. They were set to return Tuesday, when he and Jamie would be far back at Hourglass Lake.

He put the car in gear, drove through the empty garage, up the ramp, and into the crisp October evening, heading toward the airport. He mused that the way things were going he just might have this car longer than his wife. Then he shook off this thought and began to look forward to seeing his old friend and leaving the rat race for a few days.

CHAPTER 3

The Reunion

The blue and silver Air National 727 was cleared to begin its initial descent to twenty thousand feet by the female controller at the Denver air traffic control center. A moment later the pilot gently pulled all three power levers back to idle, disengaged the altitude hold on the autopilot, and then trimmed the nose of the big jet slightly below the horizon. The other pilot reported to the controller that they were leaving flight level 310. The airspeed slowly built and then stabilized, and the altimeter began to unwind on the instrument panel. Denver was still one hundred fifty miles over the horizon, but on this clear night, the pilots were just beginning to see the telltale glow of the sprawling metropolitan area.

The tall, blond man in the third row of the first class section leaned forward in his seat. Pulling against his seatbelt, he cupped his hands on either side of his head to block some of the reflection from the cabin lights and peered into the inky darkness below. He had felt the power being retarded and the slight pitch change. Now he heard the increased rush of air around the fuselage. He looked at the large chronograph on his wrist and knew that they must be starting their descent into Denver. He had instinctively started the stopwatch function of his watch on takeoff from New Orleans, and it now read two hours and one minute. He figured they would be on the ground in about twenty-five minutes.

He also reminded himself to reset the watch to mountain daylight time. He saw nothing out the cabin window but a few scattered farmyard lights far below and a small city about twenty miles distant. He looked back at the dark left wing of the 727 as it swept across the lights and obscured them. He could see the red glow of the navigation light on the wingtip and the pulsing red sweep of the rotating beacon on the belly of the aircraft.

The tall man leaned back into his seat and reclined it an inch or so. He always felt a little nervous in a passenger seat. Some of it was the anticipation of being back in Colorado and the week ahead, he knew, but he just didn't like to be in any aircraft and not be in control. He knew air travel was safe enough, but he had spent enough time in the driver's seat to know it wasn't all that safe, no matter how much propaganda the airlines and the FAA put out. And at this moment, he wasn't up front making all the decisions.

He took a last gulp of his fourth scotch since leaving New Orleans. It had been a long day so far. In fact it had almost been a fatal one.

He smiled at the red-haired flight attendant as she walked past him checking seatbelts and picking up empty cups. She was interested all right. Then his mind drifted back to the upcoming trip.

Julie had been surprised when the tall, blond man had shown her his first-class boarding pass seconds before she was to close the door for the Jetway to roll back. She would have guessed coach, smoking section. He was tall—tall enough to have to duck under the doorway when he entered the 727. She guessed about six five at least. No fat, about 210 pounds. Early forties, but maybe late thirties. Didn't seem gay. It was getting harder and harder to tell these days. And, more importantly, no ring on his left hand. But of course, she had thought, giving him her best smile, she had known guys who routinely removed their wedding rings when they traveled. She had been pleased that he was sitting in first class and that she would be serving him.

He was wearing some type of royal blue jumpsuit, the kind with all the zippers and pockets on the arms. An American flag was emblazoned on one shoulder, while on the other, an embroidered patch depicted a helicopter in front and to one side of what looked to be an oil well— one of those big ones you saw on the news sitting in the middle of the ocean. Across the top of the patch was the name BAYOU HELICOPTERS. Above the left breast pocket, which held a pair of expensive sunglasses, was embroidered the name, J. ANDERSON. He had on a pair of brown, very scruffy cowboy boots. The blond hair came just over his collar, in total confusion. She noticed that he smelled just a little gamy and that there were some grease smears on the jumpsuit. But she had been just devastated by his smile when she had asked for his boarding pass. It seemed to be full of mischief as the crow's feet around his eyes crinkled. Julie had two thoughts after showing him to his seat: this one was no phony; and just name the place, honey. But so far, despite her best efforts, he had shown very little interest.

The red-haired flight attendant went to the front of the cabin checking seatbelts, and after unbuttoning one more button on her blouse—strictly against company regulations—she turned around and started back.

She noticed he had almost finished his drink and, leaning over the empty seat next to him, asked in her best first-class voice, "Would you like another drink before we land, Mr. Anderson?"

The tall man looked up and noticed her name tag and open blouse at the same time. He smiled while picking up the empty glass and handing it to her. "No, thanks…uh, Julie. We'll be on the ground soon, and I don't want to stagger down the concourse too badly with my friend." And he added, "Please call me Jim."

"That's okay, Jim. I'll help you and your friend prop you up if you want." She put the emphasis on the last three words. "She sounds like a lucky girl."

"Well, actually, she is a *he*—an old friend of mine."

She sat down on the arm of the opposite aisle seat. "Maybe you'll need some help finding your car, too."

"Maybe"—he grinned and leaned in her direction slightly—"if you have a friend here in Denver."

"What's that uniform you're wearing?" she asked, changing the subject while trying to think how to hint that she was based in Denver.

She reached out and touched the American flag on his shoulder. "Are you an astronaut or something?"

"I could be if you want me to be one."

She squirmed and began twisting an earring.

He had to cut this out. Rodney was probably waiting for him at the gate already.

"No, I'm not an astronaut, but I do fly for a living. Just a glorified combination taxi driver and truck driver. I fly men and equipment out to the oil rigs in the Gulf."

"Then you're a helicopter pilot?"

"Yeah, that's right."

"Gee, it must be an exciting job."

Sure, he thought, thousands of boring hours flying around pitted out, foul-smelling roughnecks and greasy equipment, with a few seconds of terror thrown in once in a while—like this morning.

"Sometimes," he said. "How do you like this job? I think it would be interesting." He gestured with one hand as if to encompass the entire 727's interior.

"I just hate it usually," she frowned. "If it wasn't for all the free travel, I'd quit in a second. What with all the assholes you have to put up with." She sighed.

26

At the word *asshole*, an older, white-haired lady two seats back looked up from her magazine and scowled.

Julie noticed the lady and lowered her voice. She said conspiratorially to him, "I mean, I get to travel all over the world courtesy of Air National and everything, but it can really become a hassle sometimes, especially back there in the cattle section." She pointed back to the curtain dividing first class from coach. "I mean, can you imagine trying to serve a hundred and five meals and drinks in ninety minutes? We fight to see who gets to serve first class." She reached out and touched the flag again. "And besides, you get to meet a nicer group of people up here."

"Yeah, I see what you mean," he added with mock sympathy, knowing he had a coach ticket in his pocket.

The 727 jolted a few times, and the FASTEN SEATBELT sign came on immediately, along with an announcement from the cockpit about some unexpected turbulence.

Jamie looked out the dark window instinctively but saw nothing but his own reflection.

"Must be some turbulence coming off the mountains."

The flight attendant stood in the aisle.

"Well, I'd better see that everyone is fastened in," she said as she picked up his empty glass. "I'll see you when we're on the ground."

Her last words, more a question than a statement, Jamie noticed, and he nodded as she turned around and walked down the aisle while discretely buttoning the blouse back to company regulations.

Jamie turned in his seat and followed her with his eyes, admiring her slim figure until she disappeared into coach.

He began to think about how he would explain this to Rodney. Once he sees her, he'll understand, he thought. Besides, I can always meet him in the morning.

The flight attendant swished back through the curtain and smiled at him once more as she walked to the forward section of the airplane.

Jamie caught a whiff of her perfume. He watched as she unlocked the cockpit door with her key and leaned in, talking to the crew for a moment. She then shut the door and took her seat.

The jet began to tremble and bank to the left. The crew had deployed the first flap setting, and they were slowing for the landing in Denver.

Jamie sat back and thought about the flight attendant. How many women had there been in his life? They were beginning to blur. He was in his late thirties now but didn't feel any different physically than he did twenty years ago. Or did he? Was this the trick age played on you? Did you go over the hill so gradually that your mind accepted it? The eyesight seemed as sharp as ever, although he did notice things were getting a little blurry up close. There were more aches and pains. And he did seem more fatigued at the end of a long day now. But at his last FAA flight physical, the doctor told him he had the body of a thirty-year-old. He still tried to get in a good workout every other day when his schedule permitted. Sometimes it was tough, though. He had missed the last two days due to the increased flights before he went on vacation. But he had always sensed mortality after the tours in Vietnam and had tried to live life to the fullest. The trouble was that it was more than half over now, he mused. Was this the beginning of the midlife crisis everyone talked about? What was in his future? He rapidly dismissed the thought.

The 727 banked again. The flaps were deployed farther again, and the leading edge slats slid forward. The jet slowed further in its descent and began its characteristic rumble.

Jamie glanced up at the flight attendant. She smiled back.

He thought of his friend Rodney and his family. One woman all these years and a son. A stable job.

No doubt about it: he was a little envious of his friend.

Jamie looked out the window. The lights were closer together as they dipped lower over the southern suburbs of Denver.

More whirring and rumbling followed, and then the solid *thunks* as the landing gear came down and locked into place.

Jamie disliked this part the most. Airplanes after all *had* landed too short or too long. At 160 miles per hour, the margin for error was small, even on a ten-thousand-foot runway. The pilot couldn't stop this 727 in midair and think about it for a moment like the helicopters he flew.

The jet descended lower, and he could make out individual houses and cars. Then they were over the airport boundary. Runway lights began to race by, but he sensed they were too high, and the bright, white lights were moving by too fast.

More runway lights. Jamie began to squirm in his seat.

Suddenly the jet settled onto the runway with a jolt, became airborne again for a moment, then hit again with a thump. The wings' spoilers deployed. The passengers were thrown forward against their seatbelts, as the thrust reversers came on and the brakes grabbed in earnest.

The runway lights, still going by too fast, had now become amber, signaling the last few thousand feet of remaining runway.

The pilot made his approach too high and too fast.

At last the 727 groaned to a crawl and just as quickly veered to the left toward the terminal. From his side Jamie could see the red runway end identifier lights. The jet finally came to a halt on the taxiway. There had been no runway left to come to a complete stop. He thought of some of the landings he had lived through in C130 cargo planes in Vietnam on short, muddy strips under fire. They had been almost as bad, but at least he hadn't bought a ticket for those rides.

The pilot added a little power, and the jet began moving toward the terminal. One of the flight attendants requested all passengers remain seated until they came to a complete stop at the gate, thanked everyone for flying on Air National, hoped their trip was a nice one, and instructed them to see the agent at the gate if they were making any connections. A moment later when the 727 finally pulled into its parking place and the seatbelt signs were extinguished, everyone jumped up at once and began reaching under seats and into overhead storage bins for coats, bags, and whatever else they had carried on board the airplane.

Passengers pressed together in a line toward the front of the airplane. Once the door opened, they began streaming up the Jetway. Jamie remained seated. He looked at his watch and noticed they were two minutes late.

The flight attendant who had spoken to him and had such high hopes was standing at the forward door, bidding all passengers good-bye, telling them to have a nice evening, and wishing they would all fly Air National again.

When the last passenger had departed, Jamie stood a little unsteadily and headed for the door. The flight attendant smiled as he made his way forward holding on to seatbacks.

She was the furthest thing from his mind as he stopped in front of the cockpit door, took a deep breath to steady himself, and, after trying the knob, knocked on it loudly three times.

The horrified flight attendant was taken completely by surprise. Stepping back from the open door, she started to exclaim, "You can't go in there…"

Rod had found the evening traffic light and had no problems arriving at the airport with twenty minutes to spare. He drove the Porsche into the crowded first level of the parking garage and, after negotiating the winding ramps, carefully parked the car crosswise in two parking places on the sparse fifth level near the very rear.

Taking the elevator to the second level, he walked across the elevated walkway into the terminal. Finding the Air National ticket counter and the video displays, he saw that Jamie's flight would arrive on time at gate thirty-six in the B concourse. He entered the small line at the beginning of the concourse for the security check.

A bold, red-lettered sign had been placed to the right. COMMENTS REGARDING WEAPONS, BOMBS, AND HIJACKINGS ARE TAKEN SERIOUSLY! NO JOKES PLEASE!

Rod passed the check with flying colors, but the elderly gentleman in front of him had set the alarm off. The old man, clearly in his eighties, was now emptying his pockets under the terse stare of the black security guard. The keys to his Buick were suspect, and he was being asked to walk back through the screening device. It was a sign of the times, Rod supposed, wondering how it could ever get any worse.

Rod started down the concourse, thinking that all the arrivals and departures he had ever known had always been at the farthest gate. The closer gates never seemed to be in use.

His ankle bothered him a little, and when he came to a long segment of moving walkway, he gratefully got on board.

After finding the correct gate at the very end of the concourse, he walked into the waiting area decorated in the blue and silver colors of Air National Airlines. He sat down in the row of uncomfortable fiberglass seats nearest the window and unconsciously picked up an abandoned Denver morning paper. He glanced at his watch and started to read the headlines, but found he couldn't concentrate, due partly to the anticipation of seeing his best friend and partly because his attention was drawn to the activity beyond the windows on the ramp. He laid the newspaper down on the seat next to him and gazed out the window.

Across at the next concourse, under the harsh, amber floodlights, a new red, white, blue, and silver American Airlines 767 had started its engines and was waiting to be pushed back from its gate by a tug. Rod suddenly remembered a flight instructor years ago saying that a jet only turned on its red rotating beacons when its engines were running and to never taxi a small airplane behind one. Even when its engines were idling, a large jet could blow over a small Cessna. The American Airlines jet was pushed back and, after being released from its tug, turned left

31

and rumbled away from the floodlights into the dark area bordered by a sea of blue taxiway lights.

An Air National 727 was sitting at the next gate, and as he watched, a luggage tug approached, pulling eight small trailers crammed with bags. The jet had been boarding passengers as he had sat down a few minutes ago. Its destination was Chicago. Through the concourse window, he could see people moving about inside the aircraft and getting settled into their seats. The luggage tug and its train stopped near another truck with a slanted conveyer belt mounted on its bed. Three men attacked the luggage train and began to throw suitcases onto the conveyer belt. Two men had disappeared inside the belly of the jet. Rod watched in amazement as the men slammed the suitcases down as hard as possible until all the trailers were empty. Passengers on that side of the jet could also watch the spectacle. Finally the luggage train drove off with a few suitcases and boxes still on the roof of one of the cars. Rod was thinking how pissed off the passengers whose luggage this was would be when they arrived in Chicago when he noticed the red rotating beacons and the green and red navigation lights of a jet in the darkness just beyond the bright ramp lights. It was approaching the concourse. He also noticed activity on the ground near the Jetway in front of him as one of the Air National gate agents unlocked the door leading into the Jetway from the concourse.

He glanced at his watch. If it was Jamie's flight, it was right on time, actually two minutes early. The jet entered the ramp lights, and he could see the blue and silver markings of an Air National 727. This must be it, he thought, and stood up in anticipation.

Rod remembered that it had been almost three years since he had flown down to Louisiana to see his friend for a long weekend. Ann had opposed that reunion also. He thought for a moment about that trip and smiled. As it turned out, she had good reason for not wanting him to go there.

The 727, now parallel to the gate, pivoted on its landing gear until its nose pointed straight at Rod. He looked down and could see a man in Air National coveralls and baseball cap, wearing large, orange, molded plastic earmuffs to protect himself from the three screaming engines. The man held two lighted wands over his head and began to motion the pilot to taxi straight ahead. The nose wheel perfectly straddled the yellow line leading to the Jetway. The man with the wands raised them over his head and crossed them, indicating for the pilot to stop. Rod heard the engines wind down while other men raced to place chocks under the wheels. He wondered if the same professional suitcase throwers would be back for another round.

Since he was now directly over the nose of the 727, Rod stared down into the cockpit and could see the captain in the left seat and the copilot in the right, busy writing on clipboards and flipping switches.

He envied the crew for their exciting careers as he walked over to the door leading down the Jetway. In a few moments, people began exiting the door into the terminal. Jamie was always easy to recognize because he was so much taller than everyone else, but as Rod waited longer and longer, the crowd exiting the airplane thinned out, and finally the Jetway was empty.

Disappointed, he thought maybe his friend had somehow missed the flight, and after waiting for a few more minutes, he began to walk back down the concourse to the main terminal area. He knew Jamie had his work number at the insurance company. He could usually rely on Jamie. Discouraged, he thought his friend could have at least phoned.

The captain and the copilot had said virtually nothing to each other since landing a few minutes ago. The flight engineer had leaned forward and told the pilots their assigned gate. These had been the only words spoken on the flight deck. Now the captain was maneuvering the jet into its parking place at the gate.

The copilot felt he should say something about the bad landing, but the authority in the left seat was just too much to overcome. The captain, due to retire in about two months anyway, probably wouldn't kill anyone between now and then, so the copilot had decided to keep quiet, despite what his new-fangled crew resource management training manual stated.

They came to a halt, and the captain reached down and shut off the engines. The captain hadn't felt particularly well since New Orleans; he hoped it was just a mild case of indigestion. He wondered if his copilot would say anything about the landing. He should have gone around when he had been unable to stabilize the 727's approach, but pride dictated otherwise. Barely two more months—sixty days—and he would be able to put his feet up on the porch railing forever, satisfied with a fat pension. Unlike most airline pilots forced to retire at the age of sixty, he was glad to be stopping forever.

The crew could hear the passengers unloading behind the locked cockpit door and began to automatically go through the checklists after shutdown. The captain thought back to the days when the door was never locked.

Suddenly someone was banging on the door.

The flight engineer—who knew the captain had botched the landing and secretly wished that old pilots would either retire or fail their physicals, so he would be promoted to a pilot's position—turned away from his panel of gauges and switches and reached for the door handle. He hoped it would be the red-haired flight attendant again, who was rumored to be a hot little number. Opening the door, he was taken by surprise by the tall man in the blue jumpsuit. The red-haired flight attendant was standing behind the man and appeared nervous.

Jamie surveyed the flight deck for a moment and asked, "Which one of you jerks made that fucked-up approach and landing?"

The two pilots, still lost in their thoughts, hadn't noticed the flight engineer opening the door. They quickly turned in their seats.

Jamie said, while nodding toward the captain, "I take it your silence means you did it. Because if he did it"—he nodded toward the copilot—"you would have blamed him real quick." As he was turning to leave, he added, "I just wanted to inform you guys that it was the worst one I've ever had the privilege of sitting through since Vietnam."

The captain had recovered from his surprise and stammered, "What makes you such an expert, mister?"

Jamie stopped in the door. "My ass meter, that's what." He bent, twisted slightly, and pointed to his backside. "I usually judge a landing by how hard this part of my anatomy hits the ground."

The copilot leaned against the right side of the cockpit, beginning to enjoy himself.

Jamie turned in the door and stumbled slightly against the red-haired flight attendant.

The captain, noticing Jamie's slightly slurred words and exaggerated speech, rejoined, "You're drunk, mister. Now get off my aircraft before I call airport security." He picked up a microphone as if to use one of the airplane's radios.

"Okay," Jamie said as he held up his hands, "I've never actually flown an airplane, but I have a buddy waiting for me in there"—he pointed toward the terminal—"who barely has fifty hours, but I'll bet he knows enough to go around and try it again on a fouled up approach."

Jamie turned in the doorway, took a step, and stopped. He leaned back into the cockpit and said, "Just so you know, I would have stopped in and said hello even if you had greased it on."

Then he brushed past the flight attendant and her colleagues, who had also gathered at the cockpit door by now, and bounded up the Jetway into the now empty concourse.

Jamie jogged down the concourse. Before long he spied the familiar figure walking away from him toward the terminal and broke into a sprint.

Rod was lost in his thoughts and didn't hear Jamie as he ran up from behind.

Jamie threw his right arm around Rod's shoulders and almost knocked the other man off his feet. Both men stood side by side. Jamie still had his arm around Rod's shoulders. He rocked him back and forth in a big bear hug and yelled a word each time as he pulled him toward him, "Rodney…how…the…hell…are…you…ya…little…fucker!" Rod's glasses almost fell from his face with each word.

Jamie let his friend go but kept one arm on his shoulder. They now stood face to face in the middle of the concourse. Rod was aware of some people at the nearest gate looking his way as he pushed his glasses back up onto his nose. He looked around self-consciously then extended his right hand to his friend. Jamie did likewise, and they shook hands.

Rod was still trying to regain his composure. He poked Jamie in the stomach. "You scared the shit out of me, asshole." He paused and then added, "Aren't you a sight for sore eyes. I can't believe it's been three years. But what happened back there? I thought for sure you had missed the flight."

"Eh, I decided to stay around a few minutes and try to set you and me up with two of the flight attendants. Then I had to talk to the pilot about a bad landing."

Rod noticed the sarcasm in Jamie's last statement. "You had the nerve to tell the pilot he made a bad landing? Christ, you've never even flown an airplane—just those noisy eggbeaters." He looked back down the concourse. "But what about the flight attendants?" Rod knew that part might be no idle threat where his friend was concerned.

Then Rod noticed Jamie sway just a little bit and now smelled the liquor on his friend's breath.

Jamie said, "I almost had us all set up for the weekend—and to hell with this camping bullshit—but to tell you the truth, I don't think those girls had the stamina for us, old buddy."

Rod laughed and replied, "I think you're crocked. And I'm disappointed. I would have thought you'd be in training for this weekend."

"That's a fair assessment, old buddy. I get there at the last minute for my flight, right, just before they were going to shut the door. And it so happens they've filled up all the coach seats. Sold mine right out from under me. So I flirt with the gate agent a little and persuade her to give me a vacant first class seat. Same price and drinks on the house all the way up here." Jamie waved a finger back and forth in front of Rod's face. "But don't worry; I'm sober enough to drive. Just give me the keys to that German piece of shit, and we'll blow the carbon out of her." He swayed slightly again.

Rod started walking toward the terminal again. "Like hell you're going to drive my car. I just had the engine rebuilt, and I know your method of breaking it in."

"How's it running?"

"Just great!" Rod reached out and pinched the sleeve of Jamie's jumpsuit as both men walked along the concourse. He wrinkled his nose. "You could stand a shower. And why the macho suit. Trying to impress the stewardesses?"

Jamie laughed, "I've been up since four and literally flew myself to the airport to catch that flight. The company's going to be pissed about the extra time on the ship, but what the hell. Didn't have time to change."

"What's that in your hair?"

Jamie was puzzled for a moment and ran his fingers through his hair. "What are you talking about?"

Rod continued while pointing to some gray hairs at Jamie's left temple. "That white paint. What've you been doing—painting your apartment?" He laughed at his own joke.

Jamie caught Rod by the neck suddenly and bent him over. He gave him a vicious Dutch rub and exclaimed, "It's the same thing that's giving you this nice little bald spot, old buddy. Old age." He let him go. "In case you didn't notice it, we're getting to be a couple of very old farts."

Rod had let out a mock scream when his friend had grabbed him. He straightened up and pushed him away. Red-faced, he exclaimed, "Jesus, you never change! Here we are a couple of middle-aged guys, and you're still acting like a little kid!"

They reached the moving walkway. Rod got on, but Jamie disdained the convenience and instead took giant steps next to it in order to keep up with his friend. As he walked alongside him, Jamie reached over and poked a finger into his side. "Feels pretty soft to me. If you think I'm going to carry you up a fucking mountain, you're going to face a harsh reality."

Rod knew there was a little truth in this. He had been trying to run a few miles a day on his lunch hour for the past month but had spent the majority of his time just sitting at this desk. He knew Jamie still kept up a very strenuous workout program. But he shot back good-naturedly, "We'll see how a flatlander from Louisiana does at thirteen thousand feet."

Jamie also knew there was some truth in this jab. Rodney did have an advantage by living at the mile-high elevation of Denver. But he also knew that the trip would be difficult for anyone, no matter their condition. He knew that the reward was in the physical challenge, the feeling of self-sufficiency—that you had carried everything to support yourself for days; that you had done so with your own two legs, no machines doing the work.

Rod came to the end of the walkway and stepped off. They walked together toward the terminal, for a few moments lost in their thoughts.

Then Jamie asked, "How's Ann and Rodney Jr.?"

Rod hesitated before he answered, and Jamie sensed things were not good. "Fine," he answered insincerely. "They are both in LA at her mom's for a few days' visit. They come back on Tuesday."

"Too bad, I was looking forward to seeing both of them. Well, I guess I can see them when we get back."

Jamie thought about Ann. He had first met her in Boulder when he and Rod were living off campus, before he had enlisted in the army. He had found her intelligent, but distant and cold compared to the girls he had been dating. He had secretly nicknamed her the Ice Queen. He had never understood why Rod had married her but had shrugged it off as being Rod's business. At least his friend had found someone to share his life with, unlike himself. He knew she had never liked him, despite his best efforts. This had always puzzled him. What's not to like? Well—he shrugged inwardly—this LA trip was no doubt just another excuse to avoid being around and having to be civil to him.

They approached the security screening area again. Rod glanced over the divider and noticed that the guard was giving somebody the business again. This time it appeared to be a woman in her eighties.

Rod pointed to the screening area and asked Jamie, "I wonder if that really does any good?"

Jamie glanced over and answered, "All for show at the larger airports. If I wanted to hijack a flight, I'd hit them from the front and at a smaller airport. Same airplane, same airline, but less security."

"What do you mean by 'the front'?"

"I'd go into the concourse area with a helicopter full of commandoes, land, and storm the Jetway from the ramp area. In twenty seconds it'd all be over."

"You've been giving this some thought?"

"I can't help but notice things. Blame it on my army training."

Jamie noticed the serious look on Rod's face. He laughed.

"Hey, lighten up. It's just a fantasy." He poked his friend in the ribs again.

Rod grimaced and rubbed his side. If this kept up, he'd be black and blue in a few days. They approached the escalator that would take them down to the baggage area. Rod watched Jamie bounding down the steps, not content to let the machinery taken him down to the lower level. Both men walked along the empty baggage carrousels until they found a large crowd standing around one that was turning but still empty. A sign above it indicated it was the correct one for Jamie's Air National flight.

Jamie walked up to the fence separating the baggage area from the rest of the lower level. Along the opposite wall were the various stalls for rental car agencies and shuttles to other cities north and south of Denver.

Jamie said loudly to no one in particular, "Hell, it takes longer to get your damn baggage than to fly here."

A few people standing to one side heard his remark and laughed.

A few minutes later the luggage began sliding down from the conveyer belt to the polished carousel. The third piece off was a large, gray backpack. Jamie stepped into the baggage area and, after wading through the crowd, plucked the pack from the carousel. He hoisted it over one shoulder. He waited a few more minutes and did the same with an olive drab duffel bag. He then turned around and headed for the gate, where an attendant studied the baggage claim to make sure he was the owner. She noticed the big, gray backpack and asked him, "Are you taking a trip into the mountains?"

Jamie answered and pointed over to where Rod waited, "Yeah, my friend and I are going up tomorrow."

"Well, you two have a nice trip. My husband and I were up near Leadville last weekend, and the aspen were just starting to turn. They should be gorgeous this weekend!"

Jamie replied politely, "Thank you, ma'am. We will."

Jamie walked over to the Avis booth where Rod stood and handed him the duffel bag. They both walked out the door and across the six lanes of traffic, dodging taxis, to the parking garage beyond. Entering the garage, they stepped into one of the elevators, and Rod pushed the button for the fifth level. The doors opened, and Jamie, noticing his friend limping a little, followed him to where the Porsche was parked in a distant corner across two spaces.

Rod dropped the duffel bag on the floor of the garage and fished for his keys.

Jamie admired the gleaming paint and had to admit that the car did look as if it were still new. He took a deep breath of the crisp, evening air as Rod unlocked the driver's door.

"God, that dry Colorado air feels good! You can't believe the humidity all the time along the Gulf. I can't wait to get up there."

Rod reached back and placed the duffel bag in the luggage space behind the seats then got in and unlocked the passenger door.

Jamie opened his door and, placing his pack next to the duffel bag, got in as Rod started the car. They both sat there as the engine warmed up. Jamie had been through this before and knew that the car wouldn't budge until its driver believed it was thoroughly ready to drive. No use fighting it, he thought.

"Sounds real good."

"I just had it rebuilt."

"Oh yeah, I forgot. You did say that in your letter. How much?"

"That's kind of a personal question."

"C'mon, how much?"

"Two grand."

Jamie whistled softly, "Jesus, that's a lot for a car that's almost twelve years old. I'll betcha I haven't paid two thousand TOTAL for all the cars I've owned in my life."

"Yeah, I've ridden in a few of those lead sleds."

Jamie's taste in cars ran to old Buicks, Olds, and Caddies with an old Lincoln thrown in once in a while for good measure.

"How much is this 'classic' worth now you think?"

Rod put the Porsche in gear. "I had an offer of eight thousand for it last week."

"You wouldn't sell it for twice that."

Satisfied that it had sufficiently warmed up, Rod put the car in gear, and they started out of the garage, winding down the corkscrew ramps to the bottom level and finally through the exit toward the toll booths.

Jamie reached into his pocket and brought out some crumpled bills. He handed them to Rod. "Here, I'll treat this time."

"The last of the big-time spenders," Rod replied.

They pulled into the line of traffic waiting to pay for parking. There were six toll booths, but only one of them was open.

Jamie said casually, "Have you heard from your mother lately?'

Rod inched forward in the line. "I called her last week. She's fine, asked about you. Said you should call her once in a while."

"Yeah, I should do that more."

"She's was talking about moving again. The same old complaint about the house and yard being too big to handle."

"She probably wants to move out here to be near you, Ann, and Rodney Jr."

"I don't know about that; she still has her two sisters back there." Besides, Rod thought, there might not be a family to visit out here much longer. "She wanted to know when you were going to pay her another surprise visit. She was really excited after that."

Jamie had ferried a new helicopter from Connecticut to Louisiana in late spring and had literally dropped in on Rod's mother, landing in the ample backyard.

"Yeah, I could have gone on to the airport, but I decided what the hell—I've landed in lots smaller areas."

Rod handed the attendant the money and received some change. He handed the coins over to Jamie. "I'll bet you caused a big ruckus in the neighborhood."

"Yeah, somebody called the cops. I guess they thought there had been a crash or something. Officer Bisbee showed up with the fire department."

"Shit, is he still a cop back there?"

"The police chief."

"Jesus."

"He still doesn't like me; I could tell. He'll never forgive me for that flagpole prank. Madder than hell again this time but couldn't find any laws broken. The funny thing was your mom's whole reaction to everything."

"What do you mean?"

"Well, here I come into the backyard, turbine screaming, dust and shit flying everywhere. You know how much noise they make. Well, after I get everything shut down and unbuckle myself, here she comes out the back door, walks up to me with her apron still on, and gives me a big hug. Said she knew it just had to be me. Next thing I know I'm sitting at the same old kitchen table scarfing down milk and cookies as the fire department arrives. Just like a helicopter lands in her yard every day. What a lady."

Rod accelerated into the stream of traffic coming from the terminal. "That's the way she always will be. Still sees us as kids. Helicopters or tricycles—makes no difference."

Jamie, now somewhat sober, glanced at his watch, cussed himself for forgetting, and set it back one hour. He asked Rod, "Did you buy all the equipment I put on the list, especially the new rope? What about the food? Take care of that?"

Rod waited to answer while he changed lanes. "All taken care of. We will eat like kings even if we don't catch anything."

"No chance of that," Jamie said as he relaxed in his seat.

The Porsche accelerated by the large general aviation ramp. Neither man noticed the twin-engine Cessna 414A with its distinctive F and H crown logo on the tail taxiing to a stop on the other side of the fence.

CHAPTER 4

Lines

Edwin Forsyth Jr. squirmed in his seat as the twin-engine Cessna exited the runway at Denver's Stapleton Airport and started its taxi to the general aviation ramp near the passenger terminal. It had been a tiring, three-hour flight from Las Vegas, and he felt slightly claustrophobic in the small aircraft even though he was the only passenger. He peered out his window on the left side of the aircraft as they entered the well-lit ramp area but could see nothing but the automobile traffic streaming to and from the terminal building and parking garage. He reached into the elegant, brown leather briefcase on the opposite seat and pulled out the fifth Almond Joy of the trip. Gently peeling back the wrapper, he took a bite which halved the bar. Flying made him nervous, and when he became nervous, he had to eat although his doctor continuously warned him about his health especially his blood sugar. The next bite almost took the rest of the bar. Other people smoked to calm their nerves, he thought. He had never taken up that filthy habit, so what was the harm in a little chocolate?

Edwin shifted his three-hundred-pound bulk again on the narrow seat and wished again for the wide leather seats of the former corporate jet. He licked his fingers and put down the Almond Joy. He sighed and placed his hands over his ample stomach. That corporate jet even had a bar, he remembered. But after the board of directors convinced him he could no longer afford a four million dollar airplane, the jet—and a lot more—was gone. He had fought just to keep this small airplane and one pilot. The rest of the pilots had simply been fired. But he did need this one airplane at least for purposes the directors would never approve of, although in the long run they would surely benefit, he knew.

Edwin Jr. looked out the window again as the Cessna came to a halt. He reflected on the upcoming weekend at the ranch. It would be a crucial one. Things were getting just slightly out of control, and he didn't know what to do about it. He blamed his father for dying and his sister for being such a slut. It was all their fault. Maybe he should just go into the terminal and buy a ticket on the first flight anywhere, but he knew the people he was dealing with had the ability to find you no matter which remote spot on Earth you ran to.

Edwin was now the head of the Forsyth Flagship Hotel chain, a position he had inherited three years ago when his father, the chain's founder, suffered a fatal heart attack while inspecting the Mexico City Forsyth Flagship. His father's trusted number two man, Bert Wilson, a chain smoker, died suddenly of lung cancer six months later. Edwin Jr. had been relying on Wilson to oversee the affairs of the extensive chain. Now, for the past two years, the business was floundering as Edwin Jr. didn't have the foggiest idea what he was doing and had been unprepared to run the hotel chain.

He sat back in his seat, as the pilot cut the engines, and reflected on his father's rags-to-riches story.

Edwin Sr. had been a waiter at a small hotel and casino in downtown Las Vegas when he started his business empire. His only son was just a toddler then. The young family was originally from Colorado. Caught in the last throes of the Depression, they headed to LA and the promise of a good job through a relative. Along the way, they got stranded in what was then just a small town and railroad stop in the middle of the Nevada desert. Their beat-up, old Ford Model T had given up some twenty miles outside town, and they had been given a lift into the small, dusty city.

Lacking the money to fix the car, Edwin's father found a dishwashing job in a small restaurant downtown and put the family up in a cheap hotel room. Edwin Sr. worked there for a while, trying to save some money for the rest of the journey to California. Always an ambitious and smart man, if not a highly educated one, he soon found a better paying job washing dishes and tending bar in one of the combination hotel casinos on the main street and was able to move his family out of the hotel room and into a dingy one-room apartment. Shortly thereafter the owner of the hotel recognized Edwin Sr.'s organizational talents and promoted him to assistant manager. The salary was good for the times, and California was soon forgotten. In a few months, he was able to rent a nice five-room bungalow for his family. He even managed to save a little money and opened up his first bank account. Hitler had overrun Europe, and the Japanese were about to bomb Pearl Harbor, when he was promoted to manager of the small hotel casino.

When the war did start, Las Vegas began to grow, as servicemen stationed in California and the various bases in the Southwest began pouring into Nevada—and Las Vegas in particular—to enjoy the legalized gambling and prostitution on their leaves. Edwin Sr., over his wife's objections, saw the future and withdrew all his money from the bank to buy fifty acres of parched land a few miles south of the city limits. A lot of people thought he was crazy. The fifteen hundred dollars he spent for this land seemed a fortune at the time.

He continued to save and to gain a reputation as a first-class manager, and he bought still more land on the outskirts of the city.

By the war's end, he had saved enough to launch his plans.

At first, his bank was reluctant to loan him the additional money, but he convinced them of the future, and construction began on the first Forsyth Hotel just south of town. The bank never regretted their decision—at least not for four decades—as the state of Nevada soon afterward issued a gambling license, and the hotel plans expanded into a full-blown casino, one of the first to be built smack in the middle of what would become the famous Strip.

This first hotel and casino got off to a somewhat shaky start soon after the grand opening because people thought it was too far from town. But Edwin Sr. wanted room to expand. More casinos began to go up in the area, and "The Forsyth" became well established along with the other pioneering hotels and casinos.

Soon afterward, Edwin began construction of his second hotel and casino in the little town of Reno to the north. Upon its completion, he changed the name of the hotel in Las Vegas to the grandiose Forsyth Flagship Hotel in honor of it being the first in the chain of two.

In the late fifties, when Edwin Jr. was just starting high school, the family had another child, Debra Ann. He had become used to being an only child and a somewhat selfish teenager. He therefore hated his sister from the very beginning.

The Forsyth Hotel chain continued to expand and prosper under Edwin Sr.'s vision and guidance, adding one in Los Angeles and later in San Francisco. When the hotel was completed in Denver in the early sixties, there were fifteen in the chain, and the family prospered. The father was especially proud of the Denver hotel. He had left that city penniless over twenty years before and had returned a millionaire. He decided to move his family back to Colorado, where he had grown up. Two months after the Denver hotel's grand opening, he purchased the White Elk River Ranch in central Colorado and moved his residence there from Las Vegas.

The ranch consisted of slightly over sixteen thousand acres spread along most of the eastern side of the White Elk Mountains and a magnificent log home built in 1898. The mountains provided a stunning panorama for the house, whose large front windows faced them.

The White Elks, as they were known, were not a major mountain range in Colorado. They stretched roughly twenty miles in a northwest-southeast direction. They rose from nine thousand feet in the north along a central ridge to the high point, Mt. Grant, a few hundred feet short of fourteen thousand feet, in the middle. Other significant peaks in the range, Mt. Sherman, Mt. McClellan, and Mt. Lee., were all named after famous Civil War generals by miners who had served in both the North and South armies and who first explored the range in the 1870s. The miners quickly left the area when no valuable metals were found, leaving the range unscarred except for some timber operations run in later years by the US Forest Service. The area was one of the first granted wilderness status in 1964 and left alone.

From Mt. Grant, the highest point in the chain, the central ridge gradually progressed downward to roughly nine thousand feet again at the southern end. The heavily timbered western slope of the range gradually descended, in contrast to the dramatic steep eastern side facing the ranch. The eastern side had been heavily glaciated and eroded. Three spectacular gorges split it, and the streams within each came roaring toward the ranch. Joining inside forest boundaries, they combined to form the White Elk River, which then meandered quietly for over ten miles through the ranch supplying irrigation water for hay and livestock operations. It also created a magnificent blue-ribbon trout stream for the lucky few invited to fish it.

Edwin Sr. loved his ranch, and although his growing hotel operation forced him to spend much of his time at the headquarters in Las Vegas, he always considered it home for himself and his family and tried to remain there as much as possible with his wife, Elizabeth, and their son and daughter.

The hotel chain expanded to twenty in the early sixties with openings in Miami, New Orleans, Dallas, and Atlanta, and monopolized his time even more. His wife died suddenly of a stroke, and he was determined to be around for his son and daughter. Travel between Denver's Stapleton Airport and the ranch could consume a whole day even in the best weather.

Edwin Sr. bought his first airplane soon thereafter and hired a young pilot, Walt Jameson, to fly it. Since, at the time, even the smallest unimproved airstrip was over an hour's drive from the ranch, in Gunnison, Edwin Sr. had the road directly south of the house straightened, improved, and eventually paved, creating a runway over a mile and a half long. The ranch's elevation of nearly seven thousand feet presented some performance problems in the summer months as airplanes struggled to gain altitude in the thin air, but the approaches were clear of obstructions for miles.

The straight section of the airstrip ended just east of the ranch house and then turned toward it, where the pavement ended in a large oval in front of the house. In the middle of the oval stood a tall flagpole, with an American flag flapping just above the familiar pennant of the Forsyth chain. The pennant was gold with the letters *F* and *H* in gold, too, inside a green crown. On one of the house's roof peaks was a windsock for the pilots using the airstrip in addition to another at the far end, since wind conditions could be totally different over a mile away. It became customary to buzz the house in order to check the wind's direction and also to look for livestock on the road before landing. This also told anyone in the house to either expect company or that Edwin Sr. was returning home.

Famous and powerful people from all over the world visited the ranch as pampered guests the year round to sample the fresh mountain air; they came to fish the famous private stretch of the White Elk River in the summer, hunt elk in the fall, or cross-country ski in the winter.

It was not unusual in later years to see at least one or two corporate jets parked near the house, their owners enjoying the Forsyth hospitality.

But sadly, Edwin Sr., the gregarious genius in business matters, sired a son just the opposite. Edwin Jr., a self-conscious, shy, inward boy, grew up a chubby child, even during the early years in Las Vegas when food had not been plentiful on the Forsyth table. Edwin Sr., a tall, lean man, always thought his son would stretch out and distribute the weight as he grew. But this never happened, and Edwin Jr. remained a short, fat person all his life.

After the move to the ranch, Edwin Jr. spent a tormented youth. To most boys, it would have been a paradise, but he disdained most physical exercise including any hiking, fishing, or hunting on the ranch. He hated it when his father forced him to accompany him on trips into the White Elks to the west of the ranch. The hired help made fun of him behind his father's back, and Edwin Jr. spent many isolated hours in his room reading and eating his favorite junk food, which he smuggled into the house.

He went to high school in the small town of Crestridge ten miles away, with other children from other ranches. They were a tough lot, and he never fit in with them. Most had to be up at dawn to catch the school bus for the long ride into town. Their parents for the most part were barely scratching out a living, in contrast to the pudgy kid whose father owned one of the biggest ranches in the state. Edwin Jr.'s grades suffered, and he became so miserable that after a long talk with his teacher, Edwin Sr. relented and sent him to an exclusive school in Dallas. He remained there until he graduated from high school, coming home to Colorado only on vacations and in the summer months. His grades remained mediocre.

After graduating from high school, his father made one last desperate stab and tried to enroll him in an Ivy League school, but one by one they all turned Edwin Jr. down. His grades were just not sufficient, and his father could not ignite any spark.

Finally he was admitted to the business college at Colorado State University, a public school which had to admit just about any resident of the state. He graduated in the middle sixties and was sent to the hotel in Dallas as an assistant manager. His father still had hopes to groom him to take over the business someday.

But his stint as an assistant manager was also a disaster. Most of the other employees secretly resented his being promoted because he was the boss's son. On top of that, they had to carry him, making up for his poor performance. He made little effort to be friendly, and eventually all despised him—this too in sharp contrast to his father, who everyone adored. No one let Edwin Sr. in on this reality, fearing for their jobs if they leveled with him, so his father falsely began to believe that maybe his son was beginning to come around after all.

Edwin Sr. wanted to believe this so badly that by the early 80s he put his son in charge of the Las Vegas Forsyth, still the biggest and best in the entire chain of thirty-eight hotels now scattered around the United States, Europe, and the Caribbean.

The pattern repeated itself in Las Vegas. His more able and conscientious employees, especially the number two man, Bert Wilson continued to carry Edwin Jr. along. Wilson joined the Forsyth chain just after the first hotel opened almost three decades before. He knew the boss's son for a bumbling idiot, and now in addition to his major duties as the vice president of the corporation, he found himself practically running the Las Vegas hotel while covering Edwin Jr.'s mistakes. Wilson never leveled with the father, out of respect for their friendship, perpetuating Edwin Sr.'s belief that his son had become a decent businessman. He had even begun to talk about retirement right before his fatal heart attack.

Whatever qualities her brother lacked, his baby sister, Debra Ann, possessed fivefold. She excelled in school as a ballet dancer and gymnast. A cheerleader, Debbie was elected class president her senior year and graduated with honors from the small school in Crestridge. She enjoyed exploring the far corners of the family land on her own horse. She bagged her first elk at the age of thirteen, hunting with some of the ranch hands, and caught a six-pound rainbow trout from the White Elk River several hundred yards downstream from the house. She was everything her father could ask for in a daughter, but Edwin Sr. rarely noticed.

Edwin Sr., in his quest to expand his hotel empire and groom his son, never seemed to see these qualities in his daughter. He never really had time for her after his wife died. Debbie tried as hard as she could to sustain a high level of achievement in the hope of receiving some recognition from him. She was the valedictorian of her small Crestridge High School class, but Edwin Sr. had been unable to attend the ceremony having been called out of town suddenly to attend to a crisis in his newly opened hotel in Atlanta. She didn't forget the fact that he had made a special flight to Dallas to see her brother graduate from the posh private prep school, and remembered him clapping Edwin Jr. on the back and telling him what a great future he had ahead of him in the family business.

Despite all this, she maintained her usual high grades at the University of Colorado at Boulder. She was on the dean's list for two straight years, majoring in liberal arts.

But during her junior year, at the beginning of the seventies, she at last became disillusioned and began to question the world around her. She began to participate in the antiwar movement, moving from one protest group to another, finally ending up in an underground organization; she had a close brush with the law involving a terrorist bombing in the early seventies. During these years of turmoil and protest, she discovered drugs and freely experimented with every kind her ample allowance could buy.

Shaken after the terrorist bombing incident, she fled back to the ranch, living there for two years with the fear that somehow the FBI would link her name with the group, the majority of whom had been arrested. But to her relief, no federal agents ever appeared suddenly at the ranch. And to her credit, during this time she tried to get her life back together, though to no avail. She found she had lost all interest in the ranch. She sat around the house most of the time in a depressed state instead of participating in her early activities of hiking, fishing, or hunting. Her father and brother unfortunately failed to grasp the seriousness of her condition, thinking she was just going through some kind of phase like all women do. Debbie eventually left the ranch and spent a year hitchhiking around Europe; but before long she ended up back at the ranch as bored and depressed as ever. She finally confronted her father and asked for a job in the family business.

At first her father was surprised at the request, never realizing that she had felt left out. Then he was delighted that she would take an interest in his business. He found her a position at once as an assistant to the general manager of the Forsyth hotel in Miami. He made it clear to the manager there to rotate his daughter through the various departments, so she could learn all the aspects of running a large hotel with as many guests as a small town. Debbie packed once more and headed for Florida.

Her brother was furious over this new development. He had no doubt she would excel where he could not. For the first time, he began to see her as a rival and began to take steps to correct the situation.

At first she exhibited much talent, but gradually the other employees began to resent her, thanks to the work her brother did behind her back to ensure her failure. She reacted to this hostility by becoming increasingly more depressed and once more turned to the world of drugs for relief.

A year later, and just six months before her father died, she met Juan Rivas for the first time.

Edwin Jr. took a last bite of the Almond Joy and licked the remaining chocolate from his pudgy fingers. The twin-engine Cessna came to a halt between two other aircraft on the general aviation ramp. He thought briefly of his sister and Juan Rivas in Miami. He hated the Cuban, but he had just been the go-between. Don Ortiz, back at the Las Vegas Forsyth, wielded the real power in the shadowy organization. Edwin Jr. knew now he had been stupid to have anything to do with these people, but at the time his intentions had been good. That had been three years ago, and they had spread through the business like a cancer. He tried to believe that his weekend would go smoothly. Then he would try to end it once and for all and take the reins of the hotel chain once more.

Walt Jameson, the pilot of the Cessna, shut down both engines and secured the aircraft. The engines had seemed to be running smoothly for the past three hours although the left engine had felt rough to him during the run-up in Las Vegas. He suspected one of the magnetos and reminded himself to have it checked. At least he hoped it was just a magneto. The engines were dangerously past due for complete overhauls. He had requested new engines three times, twice in person and once in a memo, but had received the same answer: no funds available.

Walt settled back in his seat for a moment and stretched after the long flight. He could feel the airplane moving as his boss grunted and twisted in the tight confines of the rear cabin.

Walt found the part about no money for anything but minimal maintenance for the twin-engine Cessna hard to believe. He had some ideas about what was going on with the business. He had flown that asshole Ortiz to the ranch for "business meetings" on several occasions in the past two years.

He tiredly looked out the window at the beautiful Learjet parked to his left with envy. The reflection of the sodium vapor lights sparkled off its perfect paint. The Forsyth Hotel chain once had a jet bigger than that one, and he had been the chief pilot, with five other pilots under him.

Now he was the only one left. The others had been let go when the jet had been sold, and now in his early fifties, he had a very dubious future. Too old to start over. Well, he thought, at least I'm still pulling down the same salary.

Edwin Sr. had hired Walt fresh out of the Air Force at the age of twenty-six when he had answered an ad placed in the Denver paper. He had been given an interview the following week at the Denver Forsyth and, being new in the job market, hadn't even thought to bring a resume. Both men had hit it off immediately and found their love of the Colorado mountains a common bond. Instead of talking airplanes and salary, the conversation had lapsed into a lively discussion of trout fishing and the right fly, hunting and the right caliber bullet. Walt had left thinking he had really blown the interview but felt some consolation in the dozens of applications he had on file with most of the airlines. But to his surprise, he was hired the next week and given a blank check to purchase a new airplane of his choice. He moved to Las Vegas almost immediately, although he hated leaving his hometown of Denver. He found solace in the fact that he would be spending a lot of time at the White Elk River Ranch with full access to the famous trout fishing and hunting.

The first airplane to bear the Forsyth Hotel crown was a small, twin-engine Piper. Barely a year later, this airplane was sold and replaced by a larger twin-engine aircraft. The second airplane, equipped with turbocharged engines, dealt better with Colorado's high altitudes.

As the business grew so did the distances flown, and finally Walt convinced Edwin Sr. to buy his first jet in the late sixties, and hire three more pilots. But they still needed a more efficient airplane than the jet for shorter distances, so they bought two twin-engine Cessnas and hired two more pilots. They based one of the Cessnas in Atlanta while hangaring the jet and the other Cessna in Las Vegas. This system worked well until Edwin Sr. died and his son took over the business.

The flight department was the first to be cut, leaving only the one twin-engine Cessna—and it was as tired as Walt.

Walt pried himself from the pilot's seat and, stooping over in the small cockpit, slid the curtain back that divided the flight deck from the five passenger seats. He thought maybe he should have taken that airline job twenty-five years ago. He probably would be flying a jumbo jet overseas with a salary almost as big as the airplane he flew. But that was water over the dam. He knew the Forsyth Hotel business was just an inch from sliding over the cliff into bankruptcy. And the sharks were circling. There had been some ridiculous offers already.

Edwin Jr. looked up as Walt slid the curtain back.

"Long flight, huh, Walt?" he said in his squeaky voice. "I'm sorry I had to move it up to tonight instead of the way we planned it tomorrow morning, but I was kind of...uh...anxious to get out of Vegas. But I should have taken your word for it and just known that it would be too dark to find the airstrip at the ranch."

Walt, after adjusting his tie, reached back into the small cockpit and picked up his overnight case and jacket from the right seat. He reflected on his big plans for this night and the new girl he was dating, Rita. But he said, "Don't worry about it. If we hadn't had that unexpected headwind, we'd have made it before dark." But not really you idiot, he thought. There had been no headwind just as there had been no chance in hell of making it to the ranch before dark.

They had arrived over the town of Crestridge long after the sun had set, with sufficient altitude to clear the nearby peaks but rather low on fuel. Walt had cancelled his flight plan with Denver Center. At Edwin Jr.'s insistence, he had tried to find the ranch but was very reluctant to lose much altitude. Flying in and around the mountains of Colorado was a daylight proposition. He had to explain to Edwin that there were no lights on the ranch's airstrip. Of course, he knew where the ranch lay and had flown there hundreds of times, but still he was nervous, knowing the high ridge of the White Elk Mountains was out there somewhere in the moonless night. They had spotted the lights of the ranch, and he had circled over them, but there was no way he could have seen the road much less landed on it. Of course he had known all this before he had even started the engines in Las Vegas.

As Walt made his way down the narrow aisle, he continued, "I radioed ahead to UNICOM about twenty minutes out, so the hotel limo will be here soon. I'm sure they'll be able to find us a room at the inn." He hoped that the last sentence didn't sound too sarcastic. He hadn't meant for it to be, but it had just ended up that way. He knew the Denver Forsyth was probably half empty tonight. The occupancy rate of the entire chain had plummeted.

Edwin Jr. was still collecting his things as Walt tried to make his way past him to the rear door. Edwin finally had to sit down again in order to permit Walt to ease around his bulk. Walt reached the door and turned the handle. The latches gave, and the door folded down into steps. The cool October air flooded the cabin, and he threw his jacket on as he climbed down to the ramp. He turned around and waited for his boss.

Soon Edwin appeared in the doorway and handed his suitcase down to the pilot. He then picked his way down the steps one at a time to the concrete ramp. The thin cable that held the door open sagged under his weight. Walt wondered what load factor the engineers had designed into it.

"Well, Walt," Edwin said cheerfully, "we'll just have to hole up here for the night and fly out to the ranch tomorrow. I hope you didn't have plans. After you drop me off and have something to eat, you can head back to Vegas. Meanwhile, dinner at the hotel is on me."

Walt thought of his ruined plans for the night. Decent of you, lard butt. Rita, one of the waitresses in the casino section of the Forsyth Flagship on the Strip, was his new passion. He had just met her last week, but they quickly hit it off. She was just one of many he had known over the years living in Las Vegas; he was always amazed at how similar they all were. Usually from a big city, in this case Boston, seeking fame and fortune, which usually ended up eluding them. But Rita might go places. She had the biggest tits Walt had ever encountered. He had been promised the night off, and they were planning to see the Wayne Newton show.

Shit, he thought again, we should have flown out in the morning. But instead, he said to his boss, "That sounds okay to me. I would like to stay for a few days and try some late-fall fishing for those big browns, but I have some things to do back in Vegas."

Edwin blew his nose. "Well, you're welcome to stay if you want to, Walt, but I'll probably have you fly Don back here on Monday or Tuesday, the way things are looking. I'm not sure which day. So when you get back tomorrow, stay near a phone."

"Sure, I will." There's one right next to Rita's bed, he mused to himself.

Edwin left Walt to tend to the airplane and walked into the general aviation terminal. He set his suitcase and briefcase down and, after noticing there were no candy machines present, walked over to the pop machine, where he bought himself a Coke.

Walt told the line boy to top off the fuel tanks; he said they were in a hurry, so he would pay by credit card in the morning. He would need enough fuel to fly to the ranch, less than an hour's flight, and then back to Las Vegas. He also told the line boy to check the oil in the engines, especially the left one, which had started to use a little more than normal.

Finished with this business, he picked up his overnight case and joined Edwin in the terminal, where both men waited for the hotel's limo.

They didn't have long to wait. In a few minutes, a tan stretched Cadillac pulled up. Both men stood, picked up their bags, and walked through the automatic doors.

The driver, a teenager named Lonny who worked in the hotel's kitchen, did double-duty as the limo driver during the evening. He was still slightly high on some angel dust he scored earlier that evening. The beat coming from the two-speaker AM-FM-cassette ghetto blaster on the front seat thumped audibly through the car's thick divider glass. He was in the middle of his dinner break when he had been told to pick up the two men, and was pissed off. He didn't think much of Edwin either, though he had never met him until this very moment. He based his dislike on rumors flying around the hotel about impending layoffs. Still though, there was a chance he was going to keep his job, so he had the limo's rear door and trunk open when the two men walked out of the general aviation terminal. His boss was fatter than he had been led to believe.

Lonny put both men's luggage into the trunk and slammed the lid. Edwin heaved himself into the back seat and shut the door himself. Walt climbed into the front seat and quickly fumbled for the volume control on the boom box, thinking all the while that the damn thing had more controls than the space shuttle.

The hotel had purchased two Cadillacs to transport VIPs to and from the airport and to appointments around town while they stayed at the Denver Forsyth. Walt ran a finger through the dust that had accumulated on the dashboard and thought about the maintenance issue with the hotel's airplane. In fact, the car hadn't been driven for three weeks.

Lonny slipped into the driver's seat, put the limo in gear, and, with a small chirp of the rear tires, maneuvered the large car into the traffic leaving the airport. He absentmindedly snapped the fingers of his right hand as if he hadn't noticed the radio was off and drove with his left as he crossed the four lanes of traffic leaving the main terminal's parking garage.

Walt hurriedly fumbled with his seatbelt.

They arrived at the downtown hotel in a record seven minutes, and the teenager quickly retrieved the suitcases from the trunk and opened the rear door for his boss. He then ran up the short flight of steps into the lobby with both men's luggage under his arms. He was in a hurry; as part of the deal for going to the airport, he had been promised the use of the limo for one hour, and he intended to impress his girlfriend, hopefully with the spacious rear seat. Edwin and Walt met Lonny at the front doors as he raced back down to the street.

Both the general manager, who had been hastily called from his home, and the night manager greeted the two as they came through the front door into the sparsely populated lobby. The general manager had high aspirations and hoped one day to be appointed to the staff at the headquarters in Las Vegas. He almost clicked his heels as he shook Edwin's hand. "I hope, sir, that you had a good flight. It's an unexpected surprise to have you here tonight, Mr. Forsyth. The Columbine Room has been prepared, and the chef has been held overtime to prepare you a nice dinner. I'm sure you're famished."

The man finally stopped shaking Edwin's hand, and he said. "Thank you, that was considerate. I am tired and a little hungry, but I think I'd prefer to just eat in my room."

"That'll be fine, sir. I've had one of the suites prepared for you." He snapped his fingers, and another teenager appeared out of nowhere to take the suitcases. The general manager turned to Walt and handed him a room key. "I've assigned room 718 to you, Mr. Jameson. Do you wish anything to eat?"

"No, thanks. I just want to take a shower and lie down. Watch some TV. I can still hear the engines. Maybe I can order up a couple of sandwiches later."

"That will be fine." The general manager beamed, and nodded at the night manager. "Bill, show Mr. Jameson to his room, and I'll do the same with Mr. Forsyth."

Walt held up his hands in protest. "That won't be necessary; and please call me Walt." He picked up his own suitcase a split second before the night manager. "I'll find my room no problem." He turned to Edwin. "When do you want to depart in the morning?"

"I think between ten and eleven o'clock should be fine," Edwin answered.

"Okay, I'll see you then."

Walt left the trio and walked across the large lobby to the elevators. While waiting for one of the cars to descend, he noticed the especially worn and dirty gold carpeting in front of the doors. This never happened when Edwin's father was alive, he thought. More small signs of a failing business.

After the pilot had left, the general manager turned to Edwin. "Sir, er, a Mr. Rivas has been trying to get in touch with you all evening. He called several times and repeatedly said it was very important that he talk with you."

Edwin sighed nervously, "If he calls again, tell him I'm just not here yet and that I will call him from the ranch sometime tomorrow."

"Very good, sir," the manager said, wondering who Rivas was.

The three turned and walked toward the elevators.

After a huge dinner, which consisted of a sixteen ounce steak, two baked potatoes, a salad, and three slices of cheesecake, Edwin rested on his queen-sized bed and worried.

Why had Rivas called? What was wrong now? He knew he should have called him but was afraid of bad news. He would find out tomorrow. After all, he was the president of this business and shouldn't have to run to the phone every time some greaser like Rivas wanted to talk to him.

Edwin cursed his sister once more for the mess he was in as he heaved himself from the bed and opened his suitcase. He reached down into the bottom and brought out a pair of shoes. Gently shaking one of them, he removed a small prescription bottle that had been jammed into the toe. He set both shoes down and took a small, glass tube from his shaving kit. He twisted open the bottle cap and gently shook some white powder onto the nightstand next to the bed. Arranging the white substance in narrow rows with the aid of the glass tube, he bent over while holding one nostril shut and began to inhale the powder through the tube, moving methodically up and down the rows.

Edwin instantly felt better about this weekend as the cocaine rushed to his brain.

CHAPTER 5

The Drive

The electronic beeping sounded familiar but distant. Jamie gradually realized it was his wrist alarm and awoke in total darkness. At first puzzled about his whereabouts, he raised himself up on one elbow and tried to rub the sleep from his eyes. Then he remembered he was on Rod's sleeper couch in the living room. He lay back down with a sigh and brought one arm over his head. He pushed one of the buttons on his chronograph to backlight the digital display. Four thirty in the morning. The house was still. He could hear the refrigerator running in the kitchen. The only light in the room filtered through the drapes from the streetlight in front of the house. He stretched. He found his back was stiff from trying to avoid the support bar in the middle of the sofa bed's woefully thin mattress. His feet dangled over the end of the bed.

After returning from the airport, he and Rod hadn't gotten to bed until a little after one. Even then they had continued to catch up on things by talking back and forth down the hallway until he had drifted off some twenty minutes later.

Jamie groaned and finally forced himself to a sitting position on the edge of the bed. Then he hoisted himself up and stretched again. Three hours of sleep was just not going to be enough today, he thought.

Still rubbing the sleep from his eyes, he walked over to the front door and threw the deadbolt. He opened the door and walked out onto the porch, dressed only in his jockey shorts. The air was crisp and some stars were actually visible straight up through Denver's polluted air. A light touch of frost twinkled on the grass under the streetlight. The lights of the city spread out on the horizon to the south. Dawn was still a few hours away.

Jamie relieved himself on the front yard, yawned, and went back into the warm house. He turned on the kitchen light and walked down the hallway to Rod's bedroom. Pushing the door open, he flicked on the overhead light and shouted, "C'mon, you asshole, rise and shine! We gotta make tracks. Time's a-wasting!" He pounded on the wall next to the switch a few times.

Rod groaned and rolled over, holding a pillow over his head. Jamie advanced on the bed, pulled off all the covers, and threw them on the floor. Rod held onto his pillow and instantly retracted to a fetal position. Jamie jerked the pillow from his friend's grasp and threw it aside. Rod tried to pry his eyes open against the glaring light and moaned, "Can't we wait a few more hours? Jesus, what time is it anyway?"

"It's four thirty-five in the morning, and we have to finish packing. Now get your fucking act on the road!"

Rod made an effort to sit on the side of the bed. He yawned, picked up his glasses from the nightstand, and peered closely at the glowing red numerals on the face of the digital alarm clock. He tried to focus his eyes on the numbers. They looked like 4:38. But Jamie was right; they did need an early start.

"I feel like I just closed my eyes ten minutes ago." Rod toppled back onto the bed.

Jamie grabbed one of Rod's arms and with little trouble pulled him back into a seated position.

"Look, asshole, I want to get to that trailhead by ten, so let's get going. It'll take us five hours to drive there."

Rod stood up with effort and then shuffled down the hall to the bathroom, still trying to rub the sleep from his eyes.

Jamie walked back into the living room and began pulling clothes from his duffel bag. He selected a pair of heavy, brown corduroy pants with lighter, worn areas on the knees and seat. They appeared to be a size or two too large but were well broken in and soft. He threw on a red and blue plaid wool shirt but left it unbuttoned for the time being as he fished out a pair of rainbow colored suspenders, which he fastened to the pants. Next he drew out a pair of battered running shoes and thick wool socks and sat down on the edge of the sofa bed, pulling both on but leaving the shoes untied for the time being. Then he got up and began adding things from the duffel bag to the already bulging backpack leaning against the wall.

While Jamie was attending to his pack a slowly waking Rod appeared in the living room half carrying and half dragging a large, green external frame backpack with a rolled up tent and sleeping bag strapped individually to the top and bottom. He was wearing a pair of tough-looking, tan canvas pants and a blue chamois shirt. Already freshly shaven, his hair was neatly combed.

Rod asked, "Do you want to eat here or later?"

"Let's just grab something on the road." Then Jamie added, "My treat this morning."

"Big of you. I know your idea of breakfast is to grab a pair of Twinkies at a 7-Eleven."

Rod leaned his pack against the wall. "Naw, we'll stop at a restaurant up in Dillon or someplace."

Both men laughed. The years had somehow vanished; both felt that time had been magically stripped away, and they were suddenly in the more carefree days they had reminisced about the previous evening.

While Rod tidied up the house and folded up the sofa bed, Jamie began carrying the packs and other gear into the garage, piling things up next to the Porsche. Two pairs of Vibram-soled boots and two coils of multicolored climbing rope sat beside the two heavy packs. He opened the passenger door and folded the front seatback forward, then began to lift the packs into the luggage area. By turning them crosswise on top of one another, he was finally able to wedge them into the tight fit. The visibility out the rear window would suffer. Then he leaned across the passenger's seat and felt for the inside latch release for the front hood. It popped open; he walked around to the front and, after raising the hood and setting the brace, began placing the boots and ropes into the front of the car.

Rod came out of the kitchen into the chilly garage, carrying his prized Nikon over his shoulder. He walked around to the driver's side, opened the door, and gently laid the camera on the seat. Next he went to the workbench along the back wall of the garage and picked up a clean, red rag. He went to the rear of the car and opened the engine hatch. Jamie was just finishing rearranging the last coil of rope around the boots.

Rod grabbed the dipstick and wiped it clean. He really didn't want to take the Porsche but had no choice. Ann had taken the Olds. "The house is all shipshape so I don't catch hell, and I left a note for Ann."

Jamie stood up and slammed the hood. Rod winced as he pushed the dipstick back into the engine. Jamie asked, "Who's going to pick her up at the airport Tuesday?"

"She took the Olds to the airport and parked it there."

Jamie walked around to the rear of the car. "Is everything okay with you two?"

Rod pulled the dipstick out again and held it up toward the light. He pushed his glasses up onto the bridge of his nose and carefully inspected the oil, which looked clean and golden, having just been changed a few weeks ago. The level was correct. He announced to Jamie, "It's only used about a quarter of a quart in the last five hundred miles—that's pretty good."

"You know how I know my oil's low?"

"No."

"I wait until the lifters start making noise or the idiot light flashes on in a turn. Until then I leave it alone."

Rod, shaking his head, carefully replaced the dipstick and tugged on the fan belt, testing its tension before closing the hatch.

He answered Jamie's previous question. "I guess it could be better."

"Huh?"

"You know...Ann...I guess it could be better." He wiped his fingers on the rag. "Trouble is...I don't know if it's me or her." Then he sighed and said, "Let's save it for later, okay?"

Jamie shrugged his shoulders. "Fine with me." He walked to the front of the garage and started to push the overhead door open. "I've got some things bothering me, too." He was lost in thought for a moment as Rod started the engine. After a sufficient warm-up, Rod backed the car out of the garage.

Jamie went back into the garage and turned the lights out. He grabbed the rope dangling from the overhead door and gave it a yank while simultaneously running forward. The door moved on its springs and began to shut. When it was almost closed, he suddenly caught the bottom edge and yanked it open again then ran through the garage and into the dark kitchen, emerging a moment later with a six-pack of beer. He motioned for Rod to unlatch the front hood. Rod popped the latch, and Jamie quickly slid the beer under the ropes and slammed the hood down as hard as before. Then he quickly shut and locked the big garage door.

Jamie got in the front seat and shut the door. "Best damn refrigerator in the world is the front of a VW on a cold day. It should be good and cold by the Eisenhower Tunnel."

"This is not a VW," Rod said, trying to act hurt as he put the car in gear.

"Same Kraut heritage," Jamie quipped.

Rod backed out of the driveway and accelerated down his street. Jamie suddenly let out an Indian war whoop and then shouted, "Yes, sir, we are on our way!"

Rod turned east onto 104th Avenue toward the interstate. The eastern sky was now a sliver of dark blue. The traffic lights were still blinking yellow for the through streets.

A mile later Jamie pointed to a McDonald's on the other side of the four-lane highway. "I don't think I'll last until the mountains. Pull in, and we'll pick up something."

"I thought you wanted to wait?"

"My stomach's growling now."

"I can't turn around."

"Sure you can, at the next light."

Rod sighed and made an illegal U-turn at the next intersection. Checking his rearview mirror for cops, he pulled into the empty lot. "It's still closed."

Jamie opened the door. "Naw, I saw movement behind the counter." He checked his watch. "It's five thirty; they should just be opening the doors."

Rod got out of the car and automatically locked his door. Jamie had left his partially open.

As they walked past the playground to the side door, a teenage girl was just unlocking it. She was slim with shiny blond hair and green eyes. She was wearing the McDonald's uniform of the day, a pair of blue pants, a smock that matched, with her name tag over her left breast, and a stylish McDonald's hat. She made minimum wage. She smiled as she opened the door. "Good morning, you're our first customers of the day."

"Good morning to you, too, honey," Jamie said, as he and Rod walked up to the counter. The girl disappeared for a moment and then suddenly reappeared on the other side of the counter.

"Can I take your order?"

Jamie winked at her. "I hope you have some coffee brewing 'cause I sure need my morning fix."

She asked Rod, "How about you, sir?"

"No thanks."

She turned around and poured Jamie a steaming cup of coffee, while Rod studied the overhead menu.

The teenager walked back to the counter and set the cup in front of Jamie. He took a sip.

"Hope it's hot enough for you. Can I take your order now?"

Jamie looked directly at her and winked. "Well, honey, I know what I'd like to have, but it's probably illegal in this state, so I'll just settle for three Egg McMuffins and an order of hash browns."

The girl giggled and blushed.

Rod looked up at the ceiling.

The manager, who had now appeared in the rear, frowned at Jamie.

The girl asked Rod, "What about you, sir?"

Rod noticed she always used the word *sir* when addressing him, but not Jamie.

"I'll have some hash browns, an Egg McMuffin, and some orange juice."

She gave Jamie a sly look as she turned to get the order. The manager frowned at her, too, as he slid the fast food into the correct slots.

Jamie and Rod took a booth near the front.

Rod asked, "Why do you always try to give women a bad time?"

"I dunno. She's cute though."

"You could be her father for Christ's sake."

"C'mon, they all like to flirt a little."

"Maybe with you. You're the type; you can pull it off. They'd just as well call the cops with me." Rod unwrapped the Egg McMuffin and took a bite.

"You worry too much."

Rod sighed and took another bite of his Egg McMuffin as Jamie continued, "You know, it was a place like this that was responsible for me going to Vietnam and everything that followed."

Rod looked up. "Huh? What do you mean? You enlisted."

"Well, I was working the counter at McD's in Boulder for minimum wage when that punk and his friends walked in and ordered a strawberry shake. Ten minutes later I would've been off duty and out the door."

"Huh?"

"This kid orders a strawberry shake, and I go get him one from the shake machine. Then I bring it to the counter, and he says he had ordered a vanilla one instead. So I take the strawberry one back and get him a vanilla. So this time he says he ordered a chocolate one. His friends are laughing now and pissing me off. So I fake a turn, reach out over the counter, and grab him by the shirt. Then, while I'm holding him against the counter, I plop the whole thing on top of his head. You should have seen his eyes bug out."

Rod laughed, "But what does that have to do with the army?"

"Next day, I came in for a day shift, and I was fired on the spot. The manager said he understood, and laughed about it, but fired me anyhow. The kid's mother had complained. The draft board was breathing down my neck anyhow. Three hours later I had enlisted."

"You never told me that story."

"If it weren't for that kid and his smartass friends, I might have ended up never seeing khaki." He paused and said softly, "Or the other shit."

Rod sensed a definite, sudden lull in the morning chitchat. He said cheerfully, "C'mon, you would have been drafted anyhow. That kid and his friends wouldn't have made any difference. And look at all the stuff you've done since."

"What do you mean?"

"You've had all kinds of adventures. You've seen the world, not just the inside of an office building."

Jamie swallowed the rest of his sandwich. "I wouldn't call getting shot at for two years much fun."

"What about Saudi Arabia?"

"Too hot. No beer and very few women."

"What about Germany?"

"Too much beer and too much army."

"What about your time in Alaska?"

"Too cold. Still no women."

"How about your job now? In Louisiana. High adventure compared to the drudgery I face each day."

Jamie smiled and wiped his mouth. "Too humid. Too many women. Besides you've got a good, secure job and a nice family. A lot of guys would like that."

"Sure," Rod said as he looked out the window. The traffic on 104th was filling with weekend commuters. "I guarantee your life beats spending the last twelve years in the same office. You've been tested. You've saved lives and proven yourself. All I've done is push around papers and bullshit people about damn life insurance policies." He angrily wadded up his trash.

"C'mon, I was just in the wrong spot at the right time. I'm sure you would've reacted the same way."

"I'm not so sure of that. Besides I'll never get the chance." Rod wiped his mouth. "I lead a boring life."

Jamie changed the subject and motioned over Rod's shoulder. "It looks like it's going to be a really great day. Nice sunrise." The eastern sky had turned a brilliant orange when seen through the carbon monoxide and other pollutants in Denver's air. The sky overhead was turning a deep blue.

Jamie started to rise. "I can hardly wait to get there." He knew something was troubling his friend though. It was one of the first times he had heard Rod complain about anything. But a McDonald's was no place for any deep discussions.

"Yeah, looks like we lucked out with the weather this time of year."

Jamie took the last bite of his third Egg McMuffin and washed it down with the last of the coffee. "Maybe we should've checked the weather this morning, though." Then he shrugged. "But I guess the mountain men didn't have the Weather Channel to depend on; they just took what came and didn't worry about it."

Rod turned around on his way out to the parking lot and joked, "Yeah, and they didn't have nice, snug nylon tents, freeze-dried food, or down sleeping bags either. Maybe if we're not supposed to listen to the weather on TV, then we should leave all that modern equipment behind, too, and just take some old buffalo robes to roll ourselves up into when it gets cold."

They had divided up the food and common gear last night then loaded the packs. Rod had bought enough provisions for six days, eight if they had to make do.

"And that reminds me, asshole," Rod added, "you owe me thirty bucks for the food."

"You'll get your money if and when my palate approves. But did you have to buy so much oatmeal?"

"Fuck you. Buy your own food." They both laughed.

Jamie turned and winked at the teenager before leaving. She smiled and blushed.

They walked across the parking lot and stood next to the driver's side door.

Rod knew this would eventually happen. It always did. He reached into his pocket, unlocked the passenger's door, and handed the keys across the roof to Jamie.

"Take it easy," Rod sighed.

Jamie unlocked the driver's door. "You worry too much."

Jamie slid the seat back with a bang. Rod grimaced as he shut his door.

The engine started on the first try. Rod watched the tachometer as Jamie revved the engine.

"Take it easy; it was just rebuilt."

"Yeah, I know."

"State patrol is on the prowl out there."

Jamie ignored the warning and put the Porsche in reverse. "You have a warranty don't you."

"Twelve thousand miles."

"Well, don't worry," Jamie said, as he pulled out on 104th and accelerated to almost the red line in first gear.

He made a U-turn at the end of the block through the morning traffic and sped eastward. The sun was now fully above the horizon and both men simultaneously flipped their sun visors down against the glare.

Jamie turned left down the on-ramp for the interstate and quickly merged with the lighter Saturday traffic. Soon he dropped the gear lever into fifth with the speedometer just edging past eighty miles an hour.

He raised his voice over the wind and engine noise. "Sure runs good!"

"Jesus, slow down!" Rod shouted over the din, while looking ahead for any sign of a police car.

Jamie changed lanes and applied a little more pressure to the accelerator pedal. The Porsche effortlessly passed ninety miles an hour.

"You need a radar detector," Jamie said, as he let the car slow to seventy, then sixty as they approached the Mousetrap interchange, where they would turn westbound. He looked across at his friend, who was now visibly relieved and had released his grip on the armrest attached to the door. "Don't worry; I was just blowing the carbon out of the engine that builds up from you driving around town like a little old lady."

"I just don't like to drive fast."

"Then buy a '65 Valiant."

They neared the Mousetrap, and Jamie merged right. The city of Denver was spread out before them. The sun had just touched the highest buildings, and the golden light reflected off thousands of windows.

Jamie pulled out his aviation sunglasses from his shirt pocket while decelerating for the westbound I-70 on-ramp. The sunlight that was just touching the large buildings of downtown Denver was also just painting the high mountains west of Denver with pink light. Except for an occasional white spot in the distance marking a small snowfield left from the previous winter, the gray peaks were devoid of any snow. Though still early in the season, soon the billion dollar ski industry would begin its countdown to the first snow, hopefully before the critical Thanksgiving holidays, when skiers would jam Denver's airport.

The sun had risen substantially above the horizon as the silver Porsche left the last western suburbs and began its climb past Golden into the foothills.

The country had endured the fifty-five mile per hour speed limit for years, but now that the speed limit was again a sane sixty-five miles per hour, Jamie decided that seventy was a good compromise to keep the peace with Rod inside the car and also outside with the state patrol. The car, he decided, did run like the thoroughbred it was, and they quickly topped the first grade.

Rod studied the foothills as they entered them. All the shrubs and vegetation covering these lower elevations were brown and now dormant in anticipation of the coming winter. The higher, forested slopes were just ahead, and beyond them, seven thousand feet higher and still sixty miles in the distance, were the stark peaks running along the continental divide. He always wondered what the first mountain men or pioneers in their frail wagons must have thought after months crossing the Great Plains to suddenly face this immense wall of rock. But how great it would have been, at least looking with hindsight from the twentieth century, to be one of the first to see it through clear air and not through the pollution caused by millions of people. In his senior year at CU, Rod had taken an ecology course, which studied the biology and environment of the Front Range area of Colorado. This had been in the late sixties, when concern for the environment had just begun to get serious. The class with its accompanying field trips in and around Denver and Boulder had been a real pleasure to him, not only to break the routine of dull English Lit courses on campus, but also to give him an appreciation for the mountains west of Denver.

He was suddenly distracted as Jamie turned the radio on and twisted the tuning knob from side to side, hoping to hear some kind of weather report. Static, interspersed with an occasional loud voice, sprang from the speakers.

Rod turned and looked back out his window at the sagebrush-covered foothills. Although they were driving west, steadily gaining altitude, he knew that in another way they were also driving north. In fact, driving fifty miles west of Denver was the same as driving thousands of miles north to the tundra of the Arctic Circle.

Denver itself could almost be considered desert-like, situated on the high plains and barely receiving fourteen or fifteen inches of precipitation a year despite an occasional, highly publicized blizzard. Most of the time, the rain shadow of the Rocky Mountains kept the weather in the city mild and very dry. The mountains trapped the majority of the moisture from the Pacific at the higher elevations, keeping it from ever reaching the plains. Rod had spent many boring winter days at his desk watching storms rage in the distant mountains and later went to lunch in his shirtsleeves under a bright winter sun in downtown Denver.

But when the right conditions prevailed, the weather along the eastern side of the Front Range could get very nasty. The TV weathermen referred to this condition as *upslope*, and most of the millions who lived in the area knew the term. Upslope meant a wind laden with moisture that came out of the east, instead of the usual westerlies. When this condition occurred, air was uplifted against the mountains, condensing and cooling as it rose. The weather could quite literally change for the worst in a matter of hours. A low-pressure area in the right spot in Colorado, Kansas, or New Mexico, and its characteristic counter-clockwise flow, was usually the culprit, pushing air up against the eastern slopes of the Rockies and sometimes farther west.

The interstate became steeper as it now climbed into the forested slopes, and Jamie downshifted to fourth.

Rod knew as they climbed they were driving from one plant zone to another. Each zone had its own species of trees, shrubs, and grasses, which had evolved with a very complicated system of factors such as elevation, rainfall, snowfall, temperature, sunlight, and even wind. The class had taught him that if a person knew what he was looking for, each zone could be readily identified by the major specie of tree growing there. The first zone contained Ponderosa pine; the next higher one, lodgepole pine; then giving way to the spruce forest, which finally petered out at over eleven thousand feet. The highest zone was the treeless tundra. It contained microscopic flowers and huge vistas and was Rod's favorite place in the world. Their destination, Hourglass Lake, in the White Elk Mountains, lay within this highest zone at just over twelve thousand feet above sea level.

The summer season was very short at that elevation, and both men knew Indian summer could end any day, and the area would be suddenly plunged into winter. Depending on how severe the winter, backpackers could usually count on the first week in July to begin hiking this high in the Rockies. In some years high elevation lakes such as Hourglass weren't even ice free until the first part of August. Winter usually returned in a few short months, around the first part of October. In between the weather could be fickle and severe. Snow in August was not at all uncommon. But the tundra was the most spectacular area of Colorado, and luckily the state was blessed with hundreds of square miles of it surrounded by peak after peak. Rod thought Colorado was unchallenged by any other state for beauty.

These thoughts were suddenly broken by Jamie's exclamation, "Look at that son of a bitch."

Rod followed Jamie's pointing finger to a large motor home some two miles ahead in the left lane—their lane at the moment. They were well into the mountains west of Denver, and the grade was steep. Despite the grade though, Jamie was still able to hold a steady seventy miles per hour. Rod shrugged. "So, just go around to the right."

"Dammit, he's in the passing lane. Ten-to-one it's two senile, white-haired old farts from Texas out to see America like Peter Fonda and Dennis Hopper." They closed in on the motor home, which was probably doing just under forty. "People in this country just have no lane discipline. Have I ever told you about how the Germans drive on the autobahn?"

It was one of Jamie's favorite subjects while driving.

"A hundred times."

"Yeah, well, the Krauts stay over to the right except when passing. No exceptions. If you're rear ended in the left lane, it's your fault."

The Porsche was closing fast. Jamie was still maintaining a steady seventy. Despite its slow speed, both men could now see the motorhome was painstakingly gaining on an eighteen wheeler in the right lane. The gap between the two was narrowing.

"Just go around, for Christ's sake."

Jamie flashed the Porsche's headlights, to no effect.

"No fucking lane discipline."

"Slow down," Rod pleaded.

The trucker saw the situation in his mirrors and began to pull his rig over onto the shoulder.

The gap was seventy-five yards now.

At the last second, Jamie quickly shot into the right lane, passing the motorhome, and then squeezed left in front of it, missing the truck, whose driver was now hanging on the air horn chain. The outside rearview mirror next to Rod missed the truck's huge front bumper by a fraction of an inch.

Rod was sure they were going to collide with one of the other vehicles and had instinctively ducked, while bracing with both hands on the dash. Before he clamped his eyes shut, he saw and then heard the whine of the huge rear wheels of the trailer, which were taller than the car itself. He was sure he would end up as a feature in one of those gruesome State Patrol films shown every year at high schools around the state. The flattened Porsche would be taken on tour to schools on a flatbed trailer as a lesson of excess speed and recklessness, dried blood still on the seats.

But there was no impact.

Rod opened his eyes. They were back in the left lane, the horns fading in the distance behind them.

He looked over at Jamie, who was now intently looking into his rearview mirror. Jamie studied the receding truck and motorhome.

"I was wrong about those assholes in the motorhome." He chuckled. "They're from Michigan, not Texas."

"Christ, you almost killed us!" Rod stammered, as he sat straight up in his seat again and let out a breath.

"Not even close. I had a foot on both sides."

"What if the truck hadn't pulled over?"

"Have I ever told you that if you rear end someone in Germany, it's your fault?"

"Pull over and let me drive."

Jamie took a hand from the wheel and poked Rod in the ribs.

Rod flinched. "C'mon."

Jamie said casually, "Don't get all upset and ruin the trip. I've never so much as put a scratch on any car or helicopter. Besides, I saw the truck start to pull over, or I'd have gone around the left side. We'll make a piss stop in a little bit, and you can take over."

Jamie studied the road ahead. Shit, that had been close, he thought. He hadn't realized until the last second just how fast he had been closing in on the motorhome. Just as he hadn't realized he was too low and close when he had made his approach to that oil rig yesterday. Somehow his judgment had been off, and he almost put his helicopter into the side of the gigantic platform. There had been ten other people aboard. The landing had been hard, and there had been some questioning looks from men he had flown with hundreds of times.

Rod studied the scenery. He knew he should never have let his friend drive, but all his life he had had trouble saying no to him. Why was he so wishy-washy and so reluctant to disagree with him? Jamie could always exert his will over him. Was it some kind of physical intimidation? He didn't think so. Rod wondered if anybody could say no to such a character as Jamie Anderson.

Jamie switched on the Blaupunkt again and tried the FM band. Receiving nothing but static, he tried the AM band and was able to tune in a Denver station. Stevie Nicks was coolly singing "Gypsy".

Jamie nervously tapped the steering wheel. He turned to Rod. "Look, I apologize for driving like a drug-crazed teenager in his old man's car. I guess I was feeling pretty good about being back out here. You've got every right to be pissed."

"Don't apologize; I'm getting to be an old fuddy-duddy. I've gotten myself in a rut. Maybe I'm too particular about things, too much of a perfectionist, too afraid to try something different. You're always able to grab the gusto—like in those beer commercials—and have a good time, while I just sit around and worry about things."

"Don't worry; everybody feels they're in a rut once in a while—even me."

The incident had passed, and the two rode along in silence for a while listening to the radio. Idaho Springs and Georgetown were now behind them and even the Porsche was beginning to feel the grade and the altitude as the interstate continued its climb to the continental divide. The midmorning sun now shone behind them in the deep blue sky. Although still chilly at the higher altitude, the day was warming up steadily. Jamie shut off the heater and let the sun warm up the interior of the car. Both men cracked a window. The fresh air, smelling of pine and spruce, felt good.

As the interstate wound higher toward the Eisenhower Tunnel under the continental divide, whole avalanches of gold aspen trees tumbled down to the highway along each drainage. And here and there along the dark, forested slopes, flashes of color stood out in stark contrast as an isolated grove of aspen, or even a single tree, tried to outshine its neighbors down the slope. But the very highest aspen were now bare. In a week or so, the splendor would be gone.

The highway still continued to climb, and the mountains on either side rose up even higher against a sky that was now almost navy blue. The trees on either side reached only halfway up the slopes before ending at the tree line. One hundred yards below this clear border, the spruce trees grew normally, but just higher, they suddenly grew stunted as they advanced to this magic line until at the tree line only a few small windswept bushes held on.

The Porsche now strained to pass a semi barely moving thirty miles an hour; a steady black stream of smoke poured from its stacks. The interstate suddenly straightened out and seemingly dead-ended in an immense ridge directly ahead of the traffic.

To the left, the steep grade of old US Route 6 could be seen switch-backing above the ski area to emerge just above the tree line and top out on Loveland Pass, at nearly twelve thousand feet. But the interstate itself now ran straight for the ridge and into the mile-long Eisenhower Tunnel. The first bore had been completed years ago and consisted of just two lanes of traffic. No longer did traffic have to snake up and over the pass. The tunnel cut off miles of twisting dangerous road, especially treacherous in winter. A second bore had been completed next to the original. Four full lanes of traffic now ran through the mountain. Even so, trucks with explosives or hazardous materials still had to use the old road over the pass all year. Rod and Jamie were now passing a very large, black-and-yellow sign directing trucks with these cargoes to take the next exit.

Jamie took the exit.

As they came off the interstate, Rod asked, "Where are you going?"

"Sightseeing—the scenic route."

"I thought you were in hurry."

"We have a whole week. Besides, I haven't been up this way since college."

He downshifted and began the climb to the top of the pass. Most of the vehicles went through the tunnel, and traffic on the way over the pass was thin.

At the last switchback, Jamie downshifted again, and they emerged above the timberline. Soon after the road swung to the south and leveled off at the top of the pass. Just as quickly the pavement plunged down the other side.

Jamie pulled into the small parking lot and parked in front of the large, brown-and-yellow US Forest Service sign, which proclaimed, LOVELAND PASS 11,995 FT. ABOVE SEA LEVEL. Below this, the sign told everyone they were now on the continental divide. Arrows pointed in opposing directions with ATLANTIC AND PACIFIC OCEANS in the middle.

Jamie shut off the engine and pulled the front hood release. The wind buffeted the car occasionally. Ticking sounds came from the cooling mufflers. The parking lot was empty at this time of the year. Opening the door, he jackknifed himself out and stretched in the bright sunlight.

Rod climbed out. Although the sun was shining, the wind blowing across the pass was not warm. He reached back into the car and brought out a bright red stocking cap from his pack, which he pulled down over his ears. Satisfied that his head would be warm, he picked up his Nikon from the front floor. He also stretched the kinks out of his back in the bright sunlight.

Jamie left his door open and walked to the front of the car. He opened the hood and, bending over the pile of ropes and boots, tore two cans of beer from their plastic collars. He tossed one to Rod, who was caught by surprise, but managed to catch it without dropping the expensive camera.

Rod wasn't much of a beer drinker, and freely admitted it, but he popped the top of the can and took a cautious sip. The beer was ice-cold, and he could barely swallow it. "You're right." He motioned to the front of the car with the can. "That is a great refrigerator."

"Only one better," Jamie said, as he tossed his head back and took two swallows that emptied half the can.

"What's that?" Rod asked.

"You don't remember? Well, you'll see," he said, as he bounded up the rock steps to an overlook. He took a quick look around, raised his arms as if to encompass the entire mountainside, and breathed deeply. He yelled back down at Rod, who also made his way up the steps, "It's great to be back out here!"

Rod agreed as he joined Jamie and took in the late-fall scenery.

Thousands of feet below and to the north, they could see the interstate and the tunnel entrance eating up and disgorging cars and trucks. Peak after peak marched north to the horizon along the continental divide. Turning around, at their feet lay the old two-lane highway, which they had just climbed up to the pass on the north side and which now dropped steeply away in a series of switchbacks to the south and the Pacific side of the divide. Just at the tree line, it passed another ski area, its lifts immobile and silent at this time of the year, then ran toward the mountain towns of Dillon and Frisco. On the southern horizon, one jagged peak after another reared up, dotted with small snowfields awaiting winter's onslaught.

Despite his heavy flannel shirt, Rod was beginning to become chilled and started back down to the car, half-full beer can in hand.

Jamie took one last swallow from his can, crushed it in one hand, and flipped it over the railing onto the brown tundra beyond. It rolled a few inches and stopped.

Rod turned around and frowned at this friend.

Jamie held up both hands in surrender. "Just kidding. Lighten up," he pleaded as he ducked under the railing and retrieved the empty can.

"Asshole."

"I can always get a rise out of you," Jamie said as he followed his friend down to the car.

As they neared the Porsche, they began to dimly hear an engine in the distance as it labored up the steep grade on the north side of the pass below them, but neither man paid any attention. Rod walked to the rear of the car and raised his Nikon to eye level while motioning for Jamie to stand near the sign in front of the car. Jamie struck a pose.

"For posterity," Rod said.

"Right. Fifty years from now, we can look back as old farts in a nursing home and remember this trip. And your grandchildren can see the antique car we were driving, which you'll probably still have squirreled away in some garage."

"Cut the chatter and move over a little."

Jamie did as he was told and raised the second beer can he had grabbed from the car in mock salute just as the shutter clicked.

"To your grandkids."

"And yours."

"Yeah, right." Jamie frowned as he thought about pushing forty with no one special in his life. This had begun to bother him more and more in recent months, as he had suddenly felt for no apparent reason little stability in his life or job. Nothing to come home to but a disheveled apartment like the dozens he had rented over the years. No money in the bank to speak of. And now it seemed he was just as suddenly almost on the other side of forty. How he envied Rod and his marriage and kid. He barely kept in touch with his folks, who were at opposite ends of the country in any case.

"C'mon, smile for one more."

Jamie shook himself from his thoughts and grinned. The shutter clicked again. Rod walked forward and handed Jamie the camera. "Now you take one of me."

Jamie turned the Nikon over in his hand. Jamie whined as he feigned ignorance, "C'mon, you know I can't operate anything this complicated. Why don't you buy one of those Instamatics?"

"It's all set. Just press the button."

Jamie put the strap around his neck and stepped back. He raised the camera to eye level and began to frame his friend in the bright viewfinder. The shutter clicked, just as the motorhome, its engine straining at the grade and trailing a noxious black cloud of exhaust fumes, rumbled into view from the parking lot. At first it looked as if it would continue its way over the pass and down the other side. Instead it braked and quickly dove into the parking lot four spaces from the Porsche. The driver shut down its systems; the engine dieseled a few moments before finally dying, and the parking lot became still as the last remnants of exhaust wafted past the two men near the small silver sports car.

Jamie lowered the camera and grinned at his friend. "What a waste of film." Then he turned around.

Shit, thought Rod and tried to melt somehow into the background.

Jamie, camera still dangling around his neck like a tourist, walked around to the front of the car and took the remaining four cans of beer out of the Porsche by their plastic wrapper. He began to walk toward the motorhome.

The land yacht was at least thirty, maybe forty, feet long, the dual wheels in the rear signaling it as one of the larger models. It was white with a large brown stripe running the length down its side. A small red motorbike with a wire basket on the handlebars was bungeed across the front bumper like a dingy. An assortment of goods were strapped down on the roof, including lawn chairs, two bicycles, a chaise lounge, a folding table, a large folding umbrella, and a dog house. A spare tire was mounted on the rear, near the ladder to the roof. It had a white, faux leather cover over it. On the cover a mountain scene was depicted and painted in large red letters near the top was THE LELANDS–LANSING, MICHIGAN. The Lelands had pasted bumper stickers on either side of the license plate: IF YOU CAN READ THIS, YOU'RE TOO DAMN CLOSE and BUILT BY AN AMERICAN! BOUGHT BY AN AMERICAN!

As he walked across the parking lot, Jamie could see movement in the front seats through the tinted side windows. An older woman appeared to be in the passenger seat. She was yelling at and shoving the male driver. A small dog was yipping and scratching on the side door. The door's window was covered with decals of what looked to be every state in the union, with some national parks thrown in for good measure. Jamie recognized Old Faithful in the lower left corner.

The driver left his high back command seat and a moment later the door opened. A small black dog instantly raced across the asphalt toward Jamie puffing and barking as it circled him from a distance of two feet.

A small man with a pot belly who appeared to be in his early seventies stepped down painfully onto the asphalt, while clinging to the doorframe for support. It was a big step, and it took a moment for his foot to find solid ground. He was dressed in a lavender jumpsuit. The name *Bob* was embroidered in neat white script over his left chest pocket. The jumpsuit itself was open at the neck, and white chest hair was showing through the opening. He also wore a white, sea captain's hat with a black bill. It had an embroidered gold life ring and rope in the middle. He wore a pair of red, canvas deck shoes, with no socks. The older man was clearly ill at ease as he stepped down onto the parking lot and became even more so as he saw Jamie advancing toward him.

A woman suddenly appeared in the doorway behind her husband. She wore the same lavender jumpsuit and red canvas deck shoes. Above her pocket the name *Irene* was embroidered in the same spot as her husband's. Her head sprouted a profusion of hair rollers as big around as juice cans. Sparse, thin red hair was tightly wound around them, creating the illusion of bald spots between each. She was clearly agitated. When her husband turned halfway back toward her, looking for some sort of reprieve, she hit him on the shoulder and spun him around to face Jamie.

"Now, Robert, you give this hippie a piece of your mind. These two almost killed us back there." She crossed her arms over her ample bosom and glared at Jamie from the doorway.

The little black dog lost interest in Jamie and yipped over to the Porsche. It began to sniff at one of the rear tires.

Jamie continued toward the couple with a few large strides. He imagined the woman with a rolling pin in her folded arms; it would have completed the picture perfectly.

The husband turned back to Jamie, who had now stopped in front of him, towering over him a good foot, as he shrugged his shoulders and swallowed.

Rod watched from behind his car. Before the husband could say anything, Jamie offered the older man in the lavender jumpsuit his right hand. The man instinctively took it, and Jamie pumped away. "Sorry about that stupid truck driver back there a little while ago," Jamie said, as he continued to pump the other man's hand. "He should have moved over. But you handled that little emergency real well, I'd say. Sorry if it caused you any trouble. My name's Jim Anderson, but friends call me Jamie. Pleased to meet you, sir."

The husband started to open his mouth, but before he could do so, Jamie let go of his hand and then proceeded to pull the pop-top from one of the beer cans. The can opened with a rush of air at the high altitude, and some beer foamed out. Jamie held it delicately in front of him as it dribbled down the side of the can and onto the parking lot. He handed it to the bewildered husband and then rested a large hand on the man's shoulder. "Have a beer on me, Bob." Then, looking at the man's wife, he said, "Pleased to meet you, too."

Then he turned back to the husband and popped a beer for himself. Poking an elbow into the man's ribs, Jamie said, "All the way from Michigan with your lovely daughter here before she goes off to college I'll bet. Giving her a dose of America." He took a large swallow from his can and poked Bob Leland in the ribs again and laughed, "Or is she just a girlfriend, Bob? You sly dog."

Bob had clearly been expecting a confrontation and looked visibly relieved. "Why we're—"

Jamie clapped him on the back. "You sure picked a fine time to come out here with your girlfriend there, Bob. A great time to see Colorado: what with all the aspen changing and no crowds after Labor Day. Where're you headed?"

"Why, er, yes, we're headed to California to see the grandchildren…"

Jamie walked past Bob, toward the open door, and extended his hand to the woman. She frowned at him for a moment. This wasn't what she wanted at all.

"Let me help you down from there, Irene. Hey, that's a pretty name. You just have to see the view from over there, Irene." Jamie turned around. "Damn, Bob, where'd you pick up such a good-lookin' woman? Did you say *grandchildren*? Why, you must have had them by a different woman. This one is way too young." He turned back to Irene and, keeping his hand extended, took another swig from the beer can with the other.

Irene was completely taken aback by the tall, handsome stranger. She completely blushed at Jamie's words and, clutching one hand to her throat, extended the other, which Jamie took gently. She smiled at him, "I am his *wife*, you silly nut! We've been married for *forty-five years*, dear boy!"

Jamie held her hand as she took the big step down onto the asphalt with some difficulty. "You're jokin' with me, Irene. Forty-five years with this here fella. Why, you two don't look to be out of your forties." Irene regained her balance on the parking lot but didn't let go of Jamie's hand. Jamie gave her hand a squeeze and turned to Rod, who was still standing behind his car. "C'mon over here, Rodney, and meet Bob and Irene from Michigan," he said, as if they were his oldest friends in the world.

Then, still hanging on to Irene's hand, he draped a big arm around Bob's shoulder and began walking them over towards Rod and the Porsche. The little dog followed them, sniffing along the parking lot. His half-empty beer can dangled in front of Bob as he asked him, "That's a nice rig you have there, Bob. Must have set you back a pretty penny."

"About thirty-five thousand," answered Bob happily.

Jamie whistled. "That much, huh? She sure is a beauty though. All the way to California, huh? That's some trip."

As they neared the steps to the overlook, Jamie had an arm around each of them. He looked over his shoulder at Rod, who stood with his mouth open, and winked, then turned back to his newfound friends, pointing out the view as they neared the top of the steps.

Jamie called down to Rod, "C'mon up here. We'll have to get a picture of Bob and Irene next to the sign. After that we'll have to get a map out and show them some of the most scenic areas in the state." He turned back to the couple. "Want another beer, Bob?"

Jamie continued to talk to the Lelands for another twenty minutes, and after a picture-taking session with both parties' cameras—one of Rod and Jamie standing next to the Porsche, one of the Lelands and their motorhome—the older couple and their dog got back into the motorhome and waved good-bye like old friends as they roared past and started down the pass.

Rod, still shaking his head and smiling to himself, started the Porsche and backed out. As the two started down the pass, they could see the motorhome already two switchbacks ahead of them. Without taking his eyes from the road, Rod said, "You are one crazy person, you know that?"

Jamie took a last swig of his beer. "They seemed like nice people. I just didn't think we should cause them any more problems. After all, we did almost run them off the road."

"What do you mean, *we*?"

Jamie laughed and tossed the empty can over his shoulder. It hit the back window and landed between the packs. "Boy, you could tell that old lady was out for blood. I think she was going to make old Bob duke it out with me."

Rod took the first curve. "Yeah, I can just see her givin' old Bob the business for the last forty miles about us."

Both men laughed.

Rod steered carefully through the next two switchbacks, using the lower gears to let the engine brake the car as much as possible. This side of the pass was steep. There were no guardrails and, although the drop-off on the downhill side was not sheer, it was a very precipitous slope as the tundra tumbled away from the narrow shoulder.

Jamie finished his next beer in an almost-record three gulps and deposited this empty can under his legs on the front floorboard. He found another full can behind the seat and popped it open. "We're going to have to stop in Dillon and get some more beer, you know," he mentioned matter-of-factly.

"Yeah, sure," answered Rod, as he concentrated on the road, braking and downshifting into another corner.

They were just approaching the ski area, farther down the pass, when Jamie mentioned casually, "Oh yeah, damn, I almost forgot: I saw Phoebe the other night...mentioned I was coming out here, and she said to tell 'the lover boy' hello."

Rod crossed the centerline and stepped on the accelerator pedal by mistake at the mention of the woman's name. Then he tried to find the brake and had to wrench the wheel hard to the right to keep the car on the road. The Porsche fishtailed wildly as the tires fought hard to grab some little bit of traction in the gravel on the shoulder. Just inches from the edge, the tires spun, at last found some grip, and the silver car shot back onto the pavement just as Rod found the brake pedal. The Porsche stopped on the center line with two long, black tire marks trailing out behind, and the engine stalled.

Jamie, choking on his beer, held the now half-empty can out in front of him as the liquid ran down the sides and dribbled onto the floor mats. He leaned forward and tried to wipe some off the dashboard with his sleeve. The majority he could now feel had sloshed onto his lap. Jamie laughed, "Boy, I wish I had another beer." Then he poked Rod in the ribs with his index finger and said, "That little one-night stand of yours almost did us in, old buddy." Rod flinched as he tried to start the engine.

"What's the matter, I hit a nerve?"

Rod started the car. He squirmed in his seat, trying hard to pretend he didn't know what his friend was talking about. He let the clutch out and, after negotiating the last curve in silence, accelerated moderately down the now relatively straight highway.

He kept his eyes on the road and said quietly, "I was really, really hoping you wouldn't bring that subject up on this trip."

"C'mon, you had the time of your life—and all because of me."

Rod started to smile but caught himself. "I was practically raped. And at gunpoint no less. I should have called the police."

"Yeah, then you would have ended up on a Phil Donahue program about date rape. And anyway, that old shotgun wasn't loaded, and you knew it."

"I didn't know much of anything after a certain point," Rod said, as he reflected on their last reunion three years ago.

Rod had flown to Louisiana. It took six months to put the trip together and placate both his wife and his boss. But finally he had flown there, looking forward to getting away from the pressures of job and family. Boy, did he ever, as it turned out. He had written Jamie and carefully explained to him that he just wanted to visit and did not want to disrupt any of his friend's plans or upset his work schedule.

He needn't have worried.

The two men met at the New Orleans airport on a Sunday evening. After they picked up his luggage, they rode to the general aviation ramp where, to Rod's delight, sat a Bell Jet ranger, one of the smaller helicopters that Jamie flew out to the oil rigs in the Gulf of Mexico. Jamie then flew them back to his home base near the coast.

Rod spent the next week at Jamie's side, in the copilot's seat, flying hour after hour in several different types of helicopters. Jamie even supplied him with his own personal blue jumpsuit and hat. (Both still hung in his closet back in Denver.)

During the week he constantly marveled at the skill his friend displayed handling the complicated machines. The controls seemed an extension of his own body as he delicately set the choppers down onto the tiny landing pads on the oil rigs. After a while Jamie even let him do some of the radio work and fly a little, although the controls were bewildering compared to an airplane.

Often during the week, they ate some meals right on the rigs with the other workers, in the bowels of the immense steel structures. It was fun, with the jumpsuit and all, feeling a part of it, laughing and cussing with these rough men over huge sandwiches and piles of French fries: a whole heck of a lot different than munching on the tiny sandwich and apple his wife usually packed him, in a brown paper bag, to eat in the claustrophobic lunchroom back at good old Evergreen Mutual. He envied these men their rugged and dangerous jobs. It sure beat the hell out of the forty-second floor, where the most exciting thing was the gossip: who had been fired, who had been promoted, who was humping whom, who was getting the next divorce, who was having a kid, and on and on.

Those first five days were some of the most enjoyable of his life, but the adventure of being "on the job" was nothing compared to Jamie's first day off—the day before Rod was to fly home to Denver.

Jamie got off late in the evening on Friday, and the two friends simply went back to his apartment, took showers, had some beers, and then went out to a local restaurant. They went to bed early that night, as Jamie had promised a sightseeing trip the next day, followed by a real Cajun dinner that night.

Arriving home that Saturday afternoon, in Jamie's old, rusted Cadillac, they again showered, shaved, and changed clothes for the big night out. Rod had been looking forward to seeing some local color. That whole afternoon Jamie had been very secretive about their destination.

After leaving the apartment, they drove off in the old, noisy car. Rod was thankful the air conditioning both in the apartment and the Caddy worked. Although he had been getting used to it, the heat and humidity of the Gulf Coast in midsummer was unbearable for the most part.

A few blocks from the apartment, Jamie unexpectedly turned off the main road and, after driving a few blocks, pulled up in front of another apartment building. He let the motor run to keep the car cool and disappeared around the corner into the complex. He said nothing to his puzzled friend.

Rod relaxed, slumped in the worn cracked leather seat, looking forward to the evening, as the air conditioner blew cold on his chest. So far he had enjoyed every minute of his visit.

Laughter roused him out of his thoughts of one day flying a helicopter by himself. Looking out the side window, he saw Jamie walking across the parking lot with two women. He had an arm around each one, and they giggled at his small talk. He pointed to Rod in the car.

Rod slumped down even further in his seat. Both looked young— very young—to him. They both were dressed identically in tight fitting jeans and halter tops. One had blond hair; the other, red. Rod stared openmouthed from the Cadillac. He had begun to sweat as they approached the car, despite the air conditioner running full blast.

Jamie motioned for him to get out of the car, and Rod did. The redhead slid into the front seat, and the blonde, his date, Phoebe, slid into the back.

From then on, as the Cadillac roared off into the night, the rest of the evening was a blur to Rod. They arrived at a ramshackle roadhouse and bar an hour later. The meal was delicious, and the band loud. The women drank a lot. Rod drank a lot, after getting a lecture in the men's john from Jamie about loosening up.

Rod came to his senses the next afternoon just in time to catch the small commuter flight to New Orleans. He barfed in the men's room at the small terminal before boarding the small plane and again before boarding the larger airplane back to Denver. Then slowly on the flight home bits and pieces of the previous evening came back to him. He had never been unfaithful to his wife before, but he was pretty sure he had this time. It was a very unshaven, disheveled, guilty Rod Coleman who met his wife at the airport.

"I don't remember much about that night," Rod said. Then he added defensively, "I think I was raped."

"Sure, even the second or third time, too, I'll bet," Jamie said as he poked Rod one more time in the ribs.

Rod didn't say any more for a while as they descended farther and the mountains rose higher on either side of the road. He smiled to himself.

The air gradually warmed and Jamie rolled his window down as the Dillon reservoir came into view in the distance.

As they passed the Keystone ski resort, Rod finally broke the silence. "You know, that is the only time I've been unfaithful to Ann. In fact, that girl you set me up with down there is the only other woman besides my wife I've ever slept with." Then he added, "Not that I haven't had the chance."

"You don't have to be defensive with me, old buddy."

"Yeah, I know, but I just wanted you to know that. I felt guilty for months. And I'm sure Ann suspected something."

"Well, you never told me. How was it in comparison?"

"You're really a lowlife, you know that."

"Yeah, I know, you've told me that before. But how was it? I heard a lot of thumping and moaning going on."

"I don't remember much, to tell you the truth."

"Well, take it from me, Phoebe's pretty good pickings."

Rod let that fact sink in for a moment and then exclaimed, "You, too! Then who did she say—"

"I'll never tell you anything," Jamie interrupted. "I have to keep my pride. But she did say she liked your animal instincts."

The pair stopped for some more beer in the resort town of Dillon. They then joined the interstate once more for a few miles before leaving it and heading for the town of Leadville, on the other side of Fremont Pass. The sun had risen higher and the air, crisp and clear, was warming—a perfect October day.

They continued south from Leadville along the Arkansas River valley toward the small town of Buena Vista. To the west the impressive Collegiate Range of the Sawatch Mountains reared up in the dark blue sky, the lower slopes bathed in the brilliant gold of the changing aspen. Each peak, all fourteeners, was named after a famous Ivy League school: Mount Harvard, Mount Yale, Mount Columbia, and Mount Princeton. Rod stopped several times to take pictures while Jamie sipped another beer.

They passed through Buena Vista and, just south of the town, turned west on Colorado 654, a very narrow, twisting but paved road, which crawled up and over Philadelphia Pass before dropping down the other side into Elk Park, a long broad valley on the west side of the Collegiate Range. Topping the pass, Rod and Jamie could see the distant ridge of the White Elk Mountains thirty-five miles away, the western boundary of the park. In the clear air, they could easily make out the high point of the range, Mount Grant, near which lay their destination, Hourglass Lake. On the valley's floor, still ten miles away yet, the old white grain elevator of Crestridge stood out plainly amid the brown fields. Puffy, white cumulus clouds had formed over the valley in the afternoon, and their shadows blotted the park.

They arrived in Crestridge twenty minutes later. The town had seen better times in its 120-year history. At first there had been some mining interest in this part of the Rockies, and the little town was born as a small trading post. But prospectors had scoured this part of Colorado without much luck and any glory quickly faded in a few years. The town hadn't boomed like nearby Leadville and had remained over the years just a small ranching and farming community.

The town consisted of a main street, Colorado 654, about ten-blocks long, oriented east and west, with unpaved side streets running north and south for a few more blocks. The elevator on the west edge of town was now abandoned, some loose panels flapped in the wind, and grain was now trucked forty miles south to Gunnison. The old Rio Grande tracks had been taken up years ago. The old, weedy right-of-way could be seen snaking out of town. In the middle of the town stood a few stores, an old Grange Hall, a barber shop, a combination post office and town hall, and one grocery store and gas station run by an eighty year old woman who had never lived anywhere else. The old Crestridge School stood on the south edge of town where 654 turned to follow the railroad tracks. It was boarded up, and weeds grew in the schoolyard. The kids, like the grain, were shipped out every day to Gunnison.

Most of the houses in town were occupied by retired farmers and ranchers. In a somewhat new development, some people, retiring from Denver and cities back east, had built a few newer homes. Some of the houses in town were just plain falling-down abandoned or had FOR SALE signs rooted in front of them along the dusty streets.

There had been a mini-boom a few years ago at the announcement of a new ski area, financed by a group of Japanese businessmen, slated for development north of Philadelphia Pass. Speculators swooped down and bought up property quickly, expecting another Aspen, but plans were dropped, according to reports, when the Japanese were enticed to buy another ski area instead. Crestridge had lapsed back into its coma.

Rod entered the east edge of town and four blocks later pulled up near the gas pumps in front of the town's only store. A sign proclaimed CRESTRIDGE MERCANTILE, and underneath PROP. HILDEGARD PLATZ. The establishment was known locally as just "Hilda's store," and a stop here for gas had become a ritual over the years for the two men.

The building itself was a ramshackle, weathered clapboard affair that sat close to the main street, leaving barely room enough for the two faded red gas pumps, which were themselves relics of the 1950s: the old kind, with a glass window in the top filled with balls, which gas swirled through. A newer sign on one of the pumps read UNLEADED.

The store had a false front so that it appeared an important two stories tall in a town of one-story buildings. Behind the gas pumps was a roofed porch, which a long time ago used to be part of a boardwalk. The building had been converted into a general store and garage by Hilda's father in the 1920s from the original blacksmith's shop. The standard town bench sat under one of the windows adjacent to the front screen door. A battered metal and Plexiglas phone booth sat on the other side of the door.

The dark interior seemed to harbor every kind of commodity from nuts and bolts to chewing tobacco. Posters, some probably collectable artworks by now, plastered the interior walls. An old red Coke machine, the kind you reached down into, dipping your hand into the ice water on a hot day, grumbled against one wall.

On the west side of the store was an attached shed with heavily padlocked double doors that was also part of the original blacksmith's shop. It served now as a garage. In it, under a tarp, sat Hilda's 1941 Cadillac four-door convertible sedan on four flat tires. The woman, now in her eighties, hadn't been able to drive for years due to failing hearing and eyesight.

Hilda appeared at the door, in her customary print dress and soiled apron, and squinted through thick glasses at her customers, as Rod and Jamie climbed stiffly from the car. Her constant companion, an ancient German shepherd named Rolf, preceded her and gingerly lowered himself from the porch to check out the new arrivals.

Rod said loudly as the dog sniffed his leg, "Fill it up with regular." And then removed the gas cap.

The old woman stepped down to the pumps, unhooked the nozzle, and, after a little trouble, found the tank opening. On the last trip, they had tried to fill the tank themselves but had been scolded, so they knew better than to try and help.

Even though the sun was bright, it was late in the season, and the valley was at a lofty elevation. A cool breeze filtered around the buildings, prompting Jamie to roll down his sleeves. He buttoned them as he wandered over to the adjoining shed to stretch his legs and see if the vintage car was still parked there.

Rod walked to the rear of the Porsche, raised the hatch, and busied himself with checking the oil in the engine. Rolf, out of Rod's sight, began to casually sniff the front bumper and then leisurely lifted his leg on the right front wheel. Rod studied the dipstick: a quarter of a quart low. Without looking up he commented to the old woman, "Nice fall weather we're having, isn't it."

Hilda replied from the front of the car in a loud voice, "What!?"

He said more loudly, "Nice fall weather we're having!"

"Yes, it is," she replied, continuing nearly at a shout. "But I understand we're in for a change in a day or two. Just heard it on the radio. Can't ever predict Colorado weather once summer's over. Want your window cleaned?"

Rod looked up at the cloudless blue sky just as Jamie walked back over. He told Hilda, "Never mind about the window!" The woman nodded and withdrew the nozzle. She replaced it on the pump and squinted at the numbers.

Jamie poked Rod in the shoulder. "You don't have to talk so loud; I'm not deaf."

Rod gave him an exasperated look, shot the dipstick home, and lowered the hatch. In a normal voice, he asked, "Is the old car still there?"

"Yeah, along with some other antiques. How's the oil?"

"Just a little low."

"That'll be $13.19! Ten gallons! You boys need anything else!?"

"No, thanks!" Rod said, as both men followed her inside, where she took change for Jamie's twenty at the ancient, brass cash register.

Rod drove west on the main street, but instead of turning south on the paved road at the boarded-up school, he continued west on a county road. Where it turned to gravel two miles farther on, they passed a brown and yellow USFS sign, which read ELKMONT CAMPGROUND—22 MILES.

Jamie had become restless and began fiddling with the radio. He selected the AM band and ran the needle up and down the dial until he found KGUN in Gunnison. It came in weakly. A male voice was announcing the latest livestock prices. He looked at his watch. "Should be some news and weather in a few minutes."

Rod grimaced at the reception. "That's pretty bad. Why don't you wait until we get a little higher?"

"Yeah, you're right. I'm not interested in the price of pork anyway," Jamie said, as he clicked the radio off and leaned back in his seat. Then he added, "Why don't you replace this radio with one with a tape deck? I could use a little Nanci Griffith right now."

"This is the original radio, and I want to keep the car that way. And tapes are too expensive."

"You could always switch them back for crying out loud. You're the cheapest bastard I've ever known," Jamie said as he studied the approaching mountains. The road angled to the northwest now. He could clearly make out the three gorges that split the range and the deep cirque that held Hourglass Lake.

He never turned the radio back on.

In another mile they came to a three-way intersection. Another gravel road left the main one at a right angle and headed southwest. A sign next to this road proclaimed THE WHITE ELK RIVER RANCH—EST. 1882—PRIVATE PROPERTY—NO TRESPASSING. Both men read the sign as they passed through the intersection, and Rod slowed a bit.

Jamie pointed at the sign, "Should we drive on back there and try to get permission to cross that old asshole's land again. It'd cut probably four miles of rough hiking off the trip."

Rod speeded up and said uneasily, "No, what's the use. We've tried before, and all we get is politely and firmly turned around then followed back out the road."

"Assholes," Jamie repeated disgustedly, "Fuckin' rich people. I heard it's some old man who owns a bunch of hotels—or was it supermarkets? I don't know. Whatever, but what he's got what amounts to a private wilderness area that belongs to us taxpayers in his backyard but won't let anyone through. It's wilderness area. No timber cutting or anything like that to ruin his great view. Probably got some political pull somewhere. You'd think the Forest Service would make him give some kind of access through his land for poor folk like us."

"Look at it this way, if they did allow access and made it easier to get up into the White Elks, we'd be running into all kinds of people up there at the lake. This way it's harder, and we have the place to ourselves."

"Yeah, a real dilemma. But they could *just* let the two of us through, and no one else, couldn't they? Keep the Boy Scout troops and weekend yuppie hikers out."

"Are you forgetting you were once an Eagle Scout?"

"Naw, I'm not forgetting. And I'm *still* an Eagle Scout, pard. It's like being a Marine. Once a Marine, always a crazy-ass Marine. I'm just getting cranky in my old age, I guess." Jamie reflected and then continued, "You know, I don't know how old man Craigmore, our scoutmaster, stood all us little punks, when I think back on it. Guy must've been a real saint because we had to have been a real pain in the ass."

"Yeah, Craigmore and Mother Theresa."

"No, I mean it. No wonder he drank."

"I never knew that."

"Yeah, you could smell it on his breath at the meetings."

"Bullshit! You're making that up."

"No, I'm not." Jamie hooked his thumb over his shoulder as they drove on. "Anyway, even if that rich, old asshole let people hike through his land, no pack of little assholes could probably make the climb up to the lake. We'll probably always pretty much have it to ourselves."

"I sure do like that ranch house, though, with all those big logs. Sure would be a beautiful place to live."

"Probably owned by a bunch of Japs by now. They're buying up everything. Or worse some Arabs." Jamie pronounced it "A-rabs." He added, "I know one thing though; I'd sure like to fish that river below the ranch house someday. Looked like prime brown trout water. Maybe when I make my fortune, I'll get invited there for the weekend."

The road continued to the northwest across the wide valley, becoming more dirt than gravel. A few miles past the ranch road, it began to gain altitude as they reached the first foothills. The sagebrush gave way gradually to individual Ponderosa pines as the road climbed and became narrower and rockier.

Rod had to slow on the rough road because of his low ground clearance. The Forest Service graded it infrequently now. Budget cuts, they pleaded.

Rod worried about his car and fought the steering wheel as the tires caught in the ruts. "I'd sure hate to drive this in bad weather."

Jamie, gripping the dash, answered, "Not much more to go."

Suddenly there was a metallic clang as the low slung car bottomed out in a rut.

Jamie yelled, "That's a number five on the ass meter!"

Rod grimaced, "Shit, I wish I could have driven the old Olds!"

The road climbed higher now and started a set of gradual switchbacks. The Ponderosa pines closed ranks. At the top of the switchbacks, they entered a clearing. Other roads led back into the trees to camping pads. As they drove to the head of the campground, they spotted two other vehicles parked among the trees, their owners enjoying the fall weekend.

In another hundred yards, the road dead-ended in a small parking lot. Another car, a dusty blue Chevy wagon with fake wood on its sides, was parked alone in the lot.

A worn trail took off up the hill at the end of the lot. A faded brown and yellow USFS sign stood next to the trail. TAYLOR LAKE 4 MI. HOURGLASS LAKE 9 MI. A small, brown box with a hinged top was nailed to the post below the sign and was marked TRAIL REGISTER. A newer metal sign stood on its own two posts behind the older faded one. It was stainless steel with black letters etched into it and was supposed to last for just about forever. The first line, in larger letters than the rest, proclaimed WHITE ELK WILDERNESS AREA. Below this were a map and a large set of numbered rules.

Rod pulled in headfirst, leaving enough distance to the Chevy for a door twice as long as his to open, and turned off the ignition. He figured the Porsche hadn't suffered too badly in the last miles.

Jamie cracked his door. The wind whispered through the tops of the pines and carried a whiff of wood smoke with it.

CHAPTER 6

Miami, Florida

J uan Rivas awoke with a start and a bad headache in the darkened bedroom. Disoriented for a few moments, he rubbed his temples and then pulled his lean naked body up to a sitting position. Resting back against the dark, ornately carved mahogany headboard of the huge bed, he ran both hands through his jet-black hair and then reached over to the digital alarm clock on the matching bedside table. A simple gold chain and cross hung around his neck and swung to one side. Too vain for either glasses or contacts, he squinted at the glowing numbers. 12:55. A dot up in one corner and the little bit of light coming from under the shades were the only indicators that it was afternoon.

He turned on the heavy brass lamp on the table. The woman next to him stirred and shifted herself under the lavender sheet but did not wake.

He rubbed his eyes and laughed to himself as his memory came back. He reached for the pack of cigarettes and the gold lighter on the table. Next to them rested a gleaming gold Rolex Submariner, a dull black 9 mm Beretta auto with the safety off, and a leather wallet. No one could be too careful in Rivas's business.

It had been one hell of a party all right, amigo, he thought.

The freighter had made it into Norfolk untroubled, and even now fifty tons of the stuff was starting its trek to thousands of middle-class homes, businesses, and dorm rooms along the East Coast. It wasn't really his department anymore and so hadn't been a personal victory or anything, but that didn't stop him from celebrating all the same. If the bosses were happy, then he was happy; and just maybe they would let the incident last week slide if they found out, until he could make it up.

Rivas flicked the lighter and drew in a deep lungful of smoke. He let it out slowly and replaced the lighter next to the Beretta. No, he was in deep shit. No transgressions were overlooked in this business, however small, and the penalty never varied. You'd think it was the goddamned mafia, with all that *brotherhood* and *honor* shit. Maybe it *was* the damned mafia for all he knew.

He picked up the Rolex and clasped it around his left wrist.

No, it wasn't like the Catholic Church either that his mother had made him attend when he was little, where you simply said a confession to some old priest and you were cleared. No, if you broke a rule in this organization, you could literally be shark bait in hours. And he had seen it, too. Last year he had actually seen some poor slob trolled behind a boat. He had even been given a life jacket, so he wouldn't drown.

The legs had gone first.

Sort of like one of those executive training sessions at a big company like IBM or Exxon: an object lesson by the bosses for their underlings. He shuddered and took another drag on the cigarette.

It had just been a stupid little bet on a jai alai game: a supposed sure thing from an inside source. He had planned to make a little on the side that's all. Well, he did have a little time left until someone discovered the stuff was missing: time to make it up and to get even with his lousy inside source.

He pulled the sheet off and stood by the side of the bed stretching. His head pounded, and when he bent over to pick the black Speedo brief from the floor, he almost passed out. He slipped it on and then walked to the end of the bed where he picked up a black and gold silk robe. He tightened the sash on the robe and walked back to the table, where he picked up his wallet.

The woman had still not stirred. Well, she needs her rest after last night, he thought, as he peeled five one hundred dollar bills from the wallet and threw them on the bed. Then he put the wallet in one of the robe's pockets, picked up the Beretta and flicked on its safety, and left the room. He shut the door quietly after him.

The two Dobermans were waiting: Ricky and Alf, short for Ricardo and Alfonso. They yipped and cried, following him through the house. Specially trained for him, Rivas never had to question their loyalty. He walked across the large, sunken living room. Empty bottles and dirty ashtrays were scattered here and there on the expensive furniture. Some clothes were draped over the chairs. The cleaning crew would take care of things in a few hours.

He let himself into the study and lay the Beretta down on the desk. The dogs followed his every move with nervous eyes and, satisfied everything was fine for the moment, lay down on the rug at his feet, alternately panting and licking their chops. He pushed the playback button on the phone recorder next to the computer. No messages. Good, no one had called yet.

He walked over and drew the curtains back. Blinding tropical sunlight filled the room. The bulletproof glass gave it a slightly yellowish tint. Another hot fall day in Florida. He could see the heat shimmering off his red Mercedes 560 SEL in the drive and wondered if it had rained last night, because the top was down. The Mercedes, he had decided, was a piece of shit, despite the sixty grand he had paid for it. This was after one of his friends had called it an old rich woman's car. He had

had it four months and now decided he wanted a Ferrari. He wondered if they were expensive in Brazil, where he intended to run if either the government or his bosses came after him. He was a lot smarter than they thought.

Rivas could see part of the street, past the iron gates, and wondered what kind of truck or car the DEA had parked out there. They had been watching him for a few months now. They used everything from Lincoln Continentals to school buses.

He closed the curtains; the glass was bulletproof, but how bulletproof? He didn't want to find out. He sat down in the leather chair behind the desk and leaned back. Not bad, he thought, for a stupid spic in his early thirties who never got out of the eighth grade. He was the manager of a large corporate division, only the corporation wasn't listed in the Fortune 500. No, it was lots bigger than that. And they didn't just fire you for screwing up either.

Rivas had literally been carried across the ninety miles between Cuba and Florida by his mother when she fled Castro as a young girl with her sister. She gave birth to her son after the escape to Miami and then died soon after from complications, unable to afford a doctor or a proper hospital. Rivas was raised by his aunt.

His family had once been industrialists of some note in Cuba before the revolution: not rich, but very comfortable. His father had owned a large shoe and leather goods factory in Havana and had been cut down in a volley of machine gun fire by some teenagers in Castro's army.

Rivas and his aunt and some other surviving family members eventually left the Miami area and migrated to New York. Rivas grew up tough in Spanish Harlem. While kids in nice white neighborhoods concentrated on spelling bees, he learned to handle a knife by the age of eight. He had the ability of a natural athlete and was very quick. But there were no football teams in his neighborhood. That natural ability was used for self-defense.

By the time he was ten, he had cut three of his peers and had gained the respect of the older boys. At the age of eleven, he joined his first gang. A year later he killed an old man he and his friends had rolled for some Social Security money, and his reputation grew.

At seventeen he knifed two more people. In each case the police shrugged it off and pleaded lack of proof, but they knew him and his growing reputation. He had also begun dealing a little. He never used the drugs himself. He was too proud of his fine body for that.

At the age of eighteen, he became a little too ambitious and committed an almost fatal mistake by dealing in some other people's territory. As it turned out, these people had known of him and his reputation for quite a while. They had followed him much as a major league club watches a promising pitcher in the minor leagues. Rivas received an offer he couldn't refuse—not when the alternative was a ten-story drop.

That had been seven years ago. He had risen fast from just a street punk. His division did $250 million of business a year. He didn't sell cars or refrigerators or real estate. He dealt in cocaine—as much as he could import. The country was going bonkers over the white stuff.

Rivas never touched the stuff himself.

He leaned forward in his chair. The dogs' ears suddenly stood at attention. They followed his every move. He slid a notepad in front of him, picked up a pen, and began to organize the next few days, writing some notes to himself while waiting for the phone call.

He dropped his pen and leaned back. Shit, I'm in some trouble, he thought.

The newspapers, magazines, and high government officials had started labeling it a "drug war," and they weren't wrong. The government's sophistication was beginning to escalate in the past few years despite a tight budget. High tech was the order of the day in proposed federal budgets: radar balloons, E-2 AWAC spy planes, attack helicopters with night vision, and even an occasional F-16 or F-15: pressed into service for the "war," they were all being mentioned for the future as the politicians in Congress and the White House jumped on the bandwagon. Even now a law-abiding citizen had difficulty landing his Cessna at night at a county airstrip in Florida without being swarmed by a couple of helicopter loads of DEA agents armed to the teeth with M-16s. It was time to think about getting out. Drug-smuggling was fast becoming far less simple.

The organization had been losing airplanes fast, too. Old tactics just didn't work anymore. A few years ago, it was just a cat and mouse game with Customs. It had been easy to recruit out-of-work airline pilots or underpaid flight instructors to make a quick trip for some cash. But not anymore. Who wanted to mix it up with the air force? The odds weren't that good anymore.

But the level of sophistication had risen on his side, too, along with the price of doing business. Equipment to import the product, becoming more expensive, would pay in the long run.

The phone rang. Rivas picked up the receiver but said nothing at first. The voice on the other end sounded very distant and scratchy. Both men spoke in Spanish.

The other man simply said, "It is set. Monday morning, thirty-six hours."

Rivas glanced at the Rolex and did some quick mental calculations then gave the man a set of twelve numbers that had been passed down to him a few days ago. The other man broke the connection. Rivas replaced the phone on its cradle and then picked it up again, making sure he had the dial tone.

He punched in seven numbers and wondered just how secure this phone was. Supposedly it wasn't tapped; he had assurances from the organization, but still he didn't like to stay on long. He heard three rings and then the phone was picked up at the other end. A woman's voice answered, "Hello."

Rivas leaned back in the leather chair. "Hey, babe, how you doing? Busy packing?"

The woman replied slowly and coldly, "Where were you last night? I waited two hours and finally went home."

"Business, babe. It couldn't be helped. Honest."

"You could have at least called."

"I'll make it up to you, sweetheart."

There was no answer from the other end. Rivas added, "Promise… cross my heart."

The voice on the other end softened a bit. "Well, okay, but you do this all the time. You promise me something and then some kind of 'business' gets in the way."

"Hey, you know I love you. We're going to have that long weekend together aren't we? Just like I promised."

The woman softened up some more. "I'm almost ready. What time will you be by?"

Rivas looked at the Rolex. "Our flight leaves in a couple of hours. I'll be by in an hour or so. Plenty of time to get to the airport. Hey, I'm looking forward to seeing Colorado. Maybe even buy a cowboy hat, okay? You can teach me how to ride a horse, babe."

"Sure, a regular gaucho. I'll see you soon."

"Sure, good-bye."

Rivas hung up and thought about Debbie Forsyth. He had a nickname for her: the Debutante. Another rich bitch of many he had stumbled onto in Miami. But he had hit the jackpot with this one. And unlike the others, who had been too fat or too skinny, this one was a real piece of work.

He had been cruising the beach near the hotels looking for a little action. Maybe connect with a small sale here or there, you know. He had spotted her in front of the Miami Forsyth Hotel sunning herself and had watched from a distance for a while until he was sure she was smoking a little dope. Then, thinking he might sell her some heavier shit, he smoothly moved in for some conversation, checking out the long slim legs and shiny auburn hair tucked up in a ponytail. And he had struck pay dirt with the Anglo woman. After he had found out who she was, he wouldn't have minded had she weighed three hundred pounds and had a face full of acne.

She smiled and offered him a hit off the joint, but he refused. Then he smiled back, showing off a perfect set of teeth, and asked her to dinner.

He found her to be a very aggressive woman, something that did not quite fit into his Latin background. He knew the Anglos had a word for this, a *tomboy*. She seemed to compete in everything they did together from deep sea fishing to lovemaking. His machismo would normally not have permitted this, but he was after bigger goals.

He had his organization begin checking on her that first week. Then the big break came when her father died—an event that didn't seem to affect her much—and the brother took over the hotel chain. The fortune of the Forsyth hotel corporation began to crumble, and, through the sister, Rivas was able to penetrate it like a deadly virus.

From the sister he knew the brother was inept at management, and, more importantly, he found out he was also a user. Rivas dangled the bait, and Edwin took it, in the belief he could make additional millions safely and keep the corporation afloat. So far it had worked, and the last four years had been very profitable for everyone. The luxurious hotel chain provided endless rich customers and contacts. Rivas was heavily rewarded and promoted in the process. Although he had never been there, the remote Colorado ranch with its airstrip had proven to be an ideal spot to carry out most of the operation of importing cocaine and exporting money to be laundered. Not only was it very private and secluded, but also the area had minimum law enforcement. This hotel operation, and especially its Las Vegas connection, had become an important part of Rivas's growing operation—worth millions a year.

Thinking of Edwin, Rivas picked up the phone, cradled the receiver on his shoulder, and dialed the private number. He crushed out the cigarette in the ashtray as the phone on the other end rang and thought of his superior's decision to get rid of Edwin and replace him with the sister. Before he could weigh that operation in his mind, the other end was picked up.

"Good afternoon, Denver Forsyth Hotel, can I help you?"

"Please connect me with Mr. Forsyth's suite."

"I'm sorry, but he just left five minutes ago."

"Are you sure?"

"Yes, he left for the airport."

"Thank you."

Rivas replaced the receiver.

Well, he would just have to reach him at the ranch later, before they left Miami. He had to make sure Edwin had told his pilot when to leave Las Vegas. Edwin had not returned any calls. Rivas knew Edwin was becoming a scared man. The last time he had seen him, he acted depressed and looked like a prime candidate for a nervous breakdown. No guts. The brother was living in fear now of being caught. You could smell it. But he also desperately needed the money and the profit for Edwin Jr. on this weekend's deal was almost $2 million. Maybe they *should* get rid of him and let the clueless sister take over.

Rivas picked up the phone and dialed again.

"Las Vegas Forsyth Flagship, may I help you?"

"Yes, extension 717, please."

"One moment."

Rivas waited a few seconds and listened to the music piped over the phone. Another voice came on the line—this one heavily accented in

Spanish. "May I help you?" It was Don Ortiz, one of Rivas's lieutenants and the man in charge of distribution on the West Coast.

Rivas said in Spanish, "Don, it's me, Juan."

Ortiz spoke slowly. He was a cautious man. "Yes."

"Cut the shit. The stuff's going to be ready to go in thirty-six hours. It should land sometime early Monday morning. Timed to be at first light—just as we discussed. How is your end?"

Ortiz spoke in a lower voice, "You shouldn't be telling me this on this line. The feds…"

"Fuck the feds. I give the orders. Now what about it?"

Rivas could imagine the man on the other end wiping his neck with an ever-present handkerchief. The man seemed to sweat all the time. He was in his late-forties or early-fifties but looked ten years older. Heavy with deep jowls, his jet-black hair was becoming streaked with gray now but still glistened. He parted it in the middle. Ortiz would be wearing his customary starched shirt and dark narrow tie. The sleeves would be rolled up as he sat at his desk. If he wasn't swabbing his neck with the handkerchief, he would be rubbing and spinning his large emerald ring with his thumb as he talked—a nervous habit.

Ortiz was an old-timer in the organization. He had a wife and three kids, a comfortable home in a Los Angeles suburb. Rivas never thought he was all that smart. But he was loyal and ruthless in following orders.

Ortiz was also deathly afraid of flying, and this probably explained his nervousness on the phone with Rivas. The deal itself was no big deal to him. He wasn't afraid of the feds; he had done time. The hotel's small twin Cessna scared the shit out of him, but he would fly because he had been ordered.

"All the cash won't be here until Monday afternoon at the earliest. I still have some being driven up from LA."

"Not any earlier?"

"I don't think so. How much is coming?"

"One thousand kilos."

"No more?"

"The supply is tight."

"That will only last me two weeks at most."

"We're working on it. Another shipment soon. Like I said, things are getting tight, my friend."

"But we are excellent customers for the people in the south. They should trust us more. But still it will be late Monday before I have it all here."

"Okay, but we still expect the shipment from the south sometime Monday morning. They have been notified, and I don't think we can change that. Those people won't want it sitting on the ground that long."

"But it will only be a few hours at the most, and the location is very remote."

"See if you can hurry things along."

"I will do my best."

"Do you still have the correct number?"

"Yes."

"I will be leaving here in about three hours. After that you can reach me there later in the evening."

"Yes, I understand."

Rivas hung up and dialed again.

"Good afternoon, Air National, this is Cathy, can I help you?"

"*Si*, er, yes, please confirm a one-way ticket first class to Denver this afternoon for a Mr. Francisco Ortega." The hotel bitch could afford her own ticket. The name was one of three separate ID's Juan possessed. He knew the airlines rarely checked ID's of first class passengers.

"One moment, please."

Rivas could hear the reservation clerk tapping on the computer keys.

"Yes, Mr. Ortega, all confirmed: one-way, flight 783 departs at 5:20 from Miami International."

"Can you check on the car rental?"

"One moment."

More tapping of keys.

"Yes, sir, that is all confirmed. A Lincoln Continental—it will be ready when you arrive."

"Thank you."

"Have a nice day."

Rivas hung up and scratched two items from his list. He wished he had spoken to Edwin to make sure everything was okay before he had set things in motion. He would try him again before they departed Miami.

Rivas stood up, stretched, and then yawned. The deal was worth at least $30 million. They had waited almost three weeks for this shipment. Supply and demand—only demand far outstripped supply.

He lit another cigarette, picked up the Beretta after checking the safety again, walked back across the large living room and up to the bedroom. The two dogs followed closely. The woman was gone. He hadn't heard her leave, but the maid must have let her out the back. Too bad, he still had an hour to kill.

He lay down on the rumpled bed and wondered how close the feds were to him. They always got the people like him, never the real bosses. Then he wondered ironically just how close his own people were to finding him out, never mind the feds. He would leave the Mercedes in the driveway, leave through the back fence, and call a cab from a convenience store four blocks away.

Well, no matter, he thought, as he locked his arms behind his head. In another forty-eight hours, he would be way south of the border. Maybe not first class travel, from what he had heard, but that special airplane should be able to get him where he wanted to go for the right fare, and he would have plenty of cash to bribe the pilot.

CHAPTER 7

Colombia

George Vandenberg pulled the pipe from his mouth, spat into the oily puddle on the muddy path, and glanced up at the gray sky. A few random drops, bigger than the cold drizzle, patted his forehead and caused him to blink involuntarily. He replaced the pipe between his teeth and clamped down on it grimly. He pulled a handkerchief from his jacket pocket and surveyed the lush green valley while wiping his forehead. It was split for nearly two miles by the airstrip. The jungle tumbled down from both sides in a thick, wet, green mass. There was no hint of the immense, snowcapped peaks on either side, lost in the clouds somewhere two or three miles above. The airstrip was not level. No surveyors had helped lay this one out. It was lower in the middle than on both ends and curved a little to one side.

George's glasses had begun to fog the minute he had stepped out of the shack, but even with that he knew his vision wasn't what it used to be. Also, his arthritis was really acting up. That and the altitude had slowed him some today as he walked along the path and tried to convince himself that he wasn't going to die here. His unlaced boots squished in the mud, and a few bushes dragged wetly against his legs. Soon he would be seventy-five years old. Three quarters of a century, and he was finally feeling his age. George stopped to catch his breath, spit, and started walking again. Yep, he felt the altitude more now than two years ago when the operation had been forced to move away from the warmer coast.

Soon he came to a set of ramshackle, tin-roofed huts a quarter of the way along the strip.

There was no doubt about it, he thought, as he approached one of the huts; this was going to be his last job. He could feel it in his bones. Best-paying one, though. Not that there was any place to spend the money. And anyway, he was depositing most of it in a bank in Atlanta, for his grandchildren. Course, the children didn't know anything about it yet. It was getting to be a considerable sum. The folks that ran this hellhole paid real well, as long as you were a valuable commodity. And George was that. Just about the best damn airplane mechanic in the world when it came to old airplanes and big, oily radial engines. If he couldn't find the parts, he could make them in his little shop back at the end of the airstrip. Yes, his employer had been real generous. They could afford a few million a trip.

George pulled the hood on his rain parka over his head. He could see his breath in the cold mountain air, although ironically he was standing near the equator. The rainy season wouldn't be over for a few months. It rained mainly in the afternoons then cleared.

A coughing spasm overtook him as he neared the tin hut. He bent double over the path until it passed then straightened up, chest heaving. He pulled out the soiled handkerchief, wiped some spittle from the corner of his mouth while checking for blood, and remembered the other corners of the world he had served in besides this one.

The worst had been Greenland in the fifties he guessed. No doubt about that. But it was always the same in these remote places, no matter who you worked for. Half-assed accommodations, half-assed food, and half-assed weather. And always someone demanding that he keep them flying, no matter what. And he had kept them flying for over sixty years.

The first had been the owners of Northeast Airlines—then just a small line in New England, which had aspired to bigger things, but had eventually fallen by the wayside. That had been in the early thirties as a teenager.

Then he had migrated south to the New York area and had eventually hired on with the fledgling American Airlines, working on their new DC-2s and DC-3s. The DC-3, now that was an airplane, he thought for a moment. Still the best going. He could still take one apart blindfolded, and not many men could boast that today.

When the war broke out, he had enlisted in the Army Air Corps, as it was called in those days. He could have gotten a deferment because American needed him, but nothing was going to stop him from getting in the war. He already had over ten years' experience as a mechanic, and the army was glad to get him.

George was first shipped to North Africa and then later, England: from desert to rain and cold. He was in his element and kept B-17s patched up. He was by then a sergeant.

He even rode on three missions while in England. The first two were milk runs, but he had been suckered into the third, the ill-fated run on the ball bearing factories at Schweinfurt, Germany. His was one of the lucky ones. The Flying Fortress he rode in made it home on two engines with three wounded men aboard. After this George decided the old adage about never volunteering for anything in the military was probably correct.

After the war he stayed on with the newly named US Air Force and was stationed stateside for a while. He married during these years and became the father of two girls, Carol and Linda. Then in the late forties, George had been transferred back to Europe and had helped keep the planes flying for the Berlin airlift.

In the early fifties, he had been sent to the Philippines, this time with his family. He had worked on his first jets but never grew to like them as much as the big piston airplanes. They whined and reeked of kerosene. Soon he was caught up in the Korean conflict and left his family again. During the next two decades, he served at various airbases from North Dakota to Alaska, including the one tour in Greenland before shipping out to Vietnam.

Soon after he returned, he was told to retire as the Vietnam War wound down. He guessed himself surplus goods. One year later his wife died, and he was alone with no work: his daughters and grandchildren, whose best years he had missed, thousands of miles away.

He had moved to Atlanta to be closer to one of his daughters and her new husband, but this hadn't really worked out. But it was in Atlanta where he had learned about an outfit in Billings, Montana, which needed mechanics to work on their forest fire tankers. They flew surplus A26 Invaders with those big, familiar, oily radial engines, the same airplanes George had worked on in Korea and Vietnam. And it was at the airport in Billings, almost three years ago, where George had first met Tim McIntosh, poking around the small fleet of air tankers parked in a row behind the last row of hangars.

George drew the poncho up and stuffed the handkerchief back into his hip pocket. The rain began to increase, and the far end of the airstrip was lost in mist. The jungle became a single green mass as it faded into the rain and clouds. He began to hurry along the path as fast as his skinny old legs would carry him.

The valley widened a bit, and George came to the motley collection of buildings. There were two ramshackle huts constructed of plywood and tin. Both were covered with heavy, wet camouflage netting to blend into the jungle, as were the buildings George had just come from at the end of the airstrip. The rain increased more as George jogged up to the first hut. Water streamed from the roof and was caught along the base of the shack in deliberate ditches. The floor had been constructed a good foot above the dirt.

The second similar shack stood a few yards beyond the first—this was George's machine shop. Considering the location, it was superbly equipped. A small shed attached to it housed a diesel generator. Wires fanned out from its roof. As he neared George could hear the generator's muffled exhaust, and he remembered he had reminded himself to fill its tank.

Beyond these two smaller buildings, towering over them, stood two larger structures, also covered with camouflage netting. There were no walls, just large roofs supported by wooden poles and bracing. Two large aircraft, their tails inches from the roof, were parked underneath, protected from the weather and, more importantly, from observation. The dense foliage started immediately behind the airplanes and angled up the mountainside.

The aircraft were identical models, but the farther one was in need of repair. Skin panels were bare aluminum or different colors; inspection panels were missing. One engine had its cowling and propeller removed, exposing double rows of shiny, finned cylinders. A portable gantry stood nearby with its chain dangling.

The closer aircraft appeared to be in excellent condition, painted entirely in an evil-looking flat black with no markings except one. On the nose in 3-inch red letters were the words BAD BREATH.

On the far side of the structures housing these aircraft and outside in the weather were two more similar airplanes in bad states of repair. Also covered with camouflage netting, their tails disappeared into the trees.

George approached the first hut and peered in the window, being careful to stay away from the rain dripping from the roof overhang. His chest heaved, and he thought he might be in for another coughing fit, but the feeling subsided as he looked through the filthy window.

In the one, small, square room with a plywood floor, a dented kerosene heater stood, with a shiny metal pipe leading up through the ceiling. Next to the pipe on the stove sat a blackened coffee pot. Along the far wall rested two large footlockers. One was open, showing off its collection of crumpled clothes: an array of jockey shorts, socks, shirts, and pants. More crumpled clothes lay on top of the closed footlocker. Near the wall next to the door, a makeshift bookcase of old boards and concrete blocks stood crammed with dog-eared paperbacks. A discolored white coffee mug sat on the top shelf along with a thermos jug, a Sony Walkman AM-FM tape player, and a dark blue baseball cap with USAF embroidered on it. To George's left, along another wall, sat an old Baldwin upright piano.

George stood on his toes, directing his attention to the metal cot directly under the window and the man sleeping upon it. Tim McIntosh lay on his back like a mummy, his arms at his sides. The springs sagged under the thin mattress. A drab, old wool blanket covered his body.

George watched McIntosh for a moment. The sleeping man's body twitched erratically, and his head turned from side to side, telling George that the other man was probably dreaming. And dreaming badly. It could prove fatal to wake him as someone else almost found out a few months ago. George noticed the butt of McIntosh's Browning 9 mm peeking from the shoulder holster, which hung from the end of the cot. And on the floor next to a scruffy pair of boots and dirty wool socks lay an UZI 9 mm automatic.

He pulled back from the window and took the pipe from his mouth. It had gone out in the rain. George shrugged his shoulders and started to make for the other shack to check on the generator. It could wait until the other man woke up on his own. Meanwhile, he had work to do.

CHAPTER 8

The Dream

Tim McIntosh was one of those persons who slept with his eyes halfway open: one of those people whose eyelids never completely close but instead show the bottom half of the pupil and the white of the eye. He looked awake, but was in fact sleeping. Over the years all his military roommates, his girlfriends, and finally his wife found it disconcerting at first.

The dream was reoccurring more often now. It wasn't exactly a nightmare, no matter how horrible it got. Tim liked going back; he liked this dream. It had stumped some of the air force's best shrinks. While it was true he had shot someone when he had been awakened during the "Shoot the Gook" segment, what did they expect when you disturb someone in the middle of a dream? Besides, he had only wounded the stupid spic.

The dream always starts and ends in the same peculiar way. It always has three distinct parts. The "Shoot the Gook" part comes right before the Santa Claus ending. That is always the real puzzle: the ending.

The rain pounding on the tin roof doesn't wake him.

Captain Timothy McIntosh is back for yet another visit to Vietnam on Christmas Day 1969. The dream always starts toward the end of his 103rd mission, and he is at the controls of a very badly damaged F-105D.

A bright red dragon spewing flame from its mouth is painted down the side of the fuselage. Under the dragon are the words BAD BREATH. What has been ordered painted over at the tip of the flame is a man in black pajamas and a conical hat. This part, "The Bailout," usually happens fast. Really just a kaleidoscope of images and memories. There is the acrid smell of something burning. The control stick is jumping around in his hand as he tries to control the big, mottled, brown-and-green jet. The airplane shudders and trembles. The engine surges, losing power, and he is gradually descending toward the rugged green peaks.

Tim wonders where his wingman is as he descends through a thin cloud layer and sees the coast in the distance. He'll make it over the last ridge with little altitude. He wonders what happened to the aircraft. Did the gooks finally get lucky with their antiaircraft guns on that last pass over the burning village? Or was it his own bomb fragments? It doesn't matter. What matters at this point is the realization he isn't going to make the coast. The brass won't shed a tear over the loss. They had learned to hate his act. For example, how many times had he been told to paint over that artwork on the nose? Not good PR they had said.

Tim prepares to eject. He is getting low now and can even make out some people looking up at him near a rice paddy as he flashes over. A water buffalo stands nearby. The instrument panel is aglow with yellow and red warning lights. Before he pulls the ejection handle, he banks to the left and tries to aim the big fighter toward a distant village. Is it friendly or held by the Vietcong? Intelligence places an entire battalion in the area. Doesn't matter if it is or isn't, he thinks, as he pulls the handle. There is still one napalm bomb under the wing.

The ejection is too low, and suddenly he is lying in some unbelievably thick underbrush and vines, looking up at his parachute hanging from the dense canopy of trees. Still in his flight suit, the heat and humidity is unbearable. How long has he been out? He doesn't know, but he now realizes his ankle hurts.

Then he senses movement and sees the man in the black pajamas with the AK-47. The Vietcong soldier hasn't yet spotted the parachute or him. Tim carefully pulls the Smith and Wesson .38 caliber service revolver from its shoulder holster. The man in black comes closer. Tim uses both hands and lines the sights up on the man's head and pulls the trigger as the other man suddenly looks up at the parachute. The revolver kicks back, and the Vietnamese's head snaps sideways before he crumples to the ground. A feeling of pure elation fills Tim as he hops over to the dead man and relieves him of his automatic rifle. He forgets about any rescue attempt, as the hunted rapidly becomes the hunter.

Tim feels no fear as he makes his way through the jungle in search of the rest of the North Vietnamese patrol. He finds them and kills two more with short bursts from the AK-47. But, of course, the odds are always against him, and he is wounded twice, moments later, as he crouches in the tree line at the edge of the rice paddy. He turns and empties the clip blindly into the trees as he stumbles into the knee deep water. He notices the green shoots are just above the surface. The water at his feet begins to turn red from his own blood.

Tim drops the assault rifle and begins to pull out the revolver when another man in black appears in the trees and aims his rifle directly at him. Then another one appears. Then still another as Tim holds up his index finger in a final salute. His vision begins to blur. This is it.

But suddenly the jungle erupts. Two of the men in black are instantly cut in half. Trees are shredded as the roar of the turbine engine and the beat of the rotor blades fills his ears. Tim turns, and his world turns to black.

Now comes the puzzling part of the dream.

He thinks he becomes conscious for a moment and is staring up into the bright sky. His right arm is numb, and there is a fiery, white-hot pain in the small of his back. He is being dragged through the water, his feet making little red troughs. He tries to focus on the two men above him pulling on his arms.

They are both elves. Like the kind in Santa's workshop. Those kinds of elves. They are dressed in green and have little pointed elfin hats on their heads with bells on the tips. The green vests have diamond-shaped serrated hems. Around their waists are thick black belts with big brass buckles. They are also wearing light green leotards and little, pointed elf specials on their feet.

Tim glances over his shoulder at the Huey helicopter hovering inches above the water. It looks like standard army issue, except for the red nose and eyes below the cockpit. There are brown antlers sticking up and out of each side of the roof over the cockpit just below the rotor blades. The door gunner, another elf in elfin clothes, is crouched in place behind his machine gun.

The two elves manhandle him through the open door as the door gunner opens up. The noise is deafening. Bullets snap through the air. The helicopter takes a hit. He can feel the downdraft from the rotor blades. He is thrown quickly onto the floor as the chopper takes off and banks sharply from the trees. Just before he passes out again from the pain, the pilot turns around in his seat. Through watery, pain-filled eyes, Tim looks up from the floor. The pilot is Santa Claus, and he is grinning at him through his white beard. Tim takes a good look and blinks back the tears.

It is Santa Claus all right, with still another elf for a copilot. Santa has on his red suit trimmed with white fur. On his head is a red and white hat. The point trails over his shoulder and ends with a big white furry ball. His huge, padded stomach nudges the control stick and is held in by a big, wide, black belt. Big, black leather boots work the pedals. And Santa is also wearing a pair of Ray Ban aviator sunglasses—the ones with the mirrored lenses.

Before Santa turns back around, he looks at Tim and yells above the noise in the chopper, "Ho ho ho! Merry Christmas!"

Tim McIntosh woke up mean in the plywood hut. He cast the blanket off onto the floor and swung his legs to the plywood floor, sitting on the edge of the cot. The springs sagged under him and the metal edge of the frame dug into his legs. He wore a pair of worn, faded jungle fatigues, the kind with the big pockets down the side. He sat and rubbed his eyes with both hands trying to wake up fully. The strange dream was lingering.

Finally he stood up and stretched, placing both hands in the small of his back. The right side ached as usual. He tried to smooth out his rumpled red hair, noticing that it was now over the collar of his wool sweater. He felt the chill in the room, and the cold plywood on his bare feet. He shivered as he stepped over to the footlockers near the wall. He dug through the array of clothes and came up with a worn leather flight jacket. As he pulled it from the footlocker, he uncovered a five-by-seven, color photo of a woman in her early thirties, sitting on the steps of a porch, hugging a smiling, red-haired girl with a blue ribbon in her hair. The little girl is dressed in a blue, frilly party dress. The woman wears tan slacks and a green T-shirt. Someone had drawn a mustache on the woman with a black marking pen. Tim looked at the photo and hastily covered it up again.

He crossed the room as he slipped into the jacket and picked up a silver Zippo lighter and pack of Camels from the windowsill. Before he could light up, he spotted George Vanderberg walking stiffly up the path to the generator shack. Tim put the cigarettes and lighter back on the windowsill, took a couple of steps across the room, and opened the door.

It opened in the direction in which George was walking. Water ran in straight rivulets from the tin roof past the opening. He put two fingers in his mouth and whistled to get the older man's attention first, then yelled, "Hey, you old fart, where you going?"

George never turned or looked back. Instead he kept walking slowly up the muddy path and raised his right hand over his head, showing only his index finger.

Tim looked at the muddy ground. He really didn't want to put his boots on and run after George. He swore under his breath that he was going to get that son of a bitch someday. He yelled again, "C'mon, George, I'm sorry. I won't call you any names. C'mon back."

George turned around and began to walk slowly toward the shack.

Tim shut the door against the chill, went back to the window, and picked up the Camels and the Zippo. He withdrew a cigarette and flicked the lighter open. He automatically thumbed the flint wheel as he cupped the lighter to the cigarette. It sparked brightly but produced no flame. He tried again, holding it nearer. Sparks again, but no flame. Then he angrily threw the lighter across the room into a corner.

He took a few steps back to the cot, sat down, and fished a pair of wool socks from his boots. He wiggled his toes into the ends. They were stiff with sweat but would loosen up in a moment. He leaned over and groped around under the cot until his fingers closed around a half-full bottle of Jack Daniels. Unscrewing the cap, he took a swig and then leaned back against the wall. He remembered reading a Kurt Vonnegut book. "Breakfast of champions"—that's what the main character had called his morning martini, "breakfast of champions," taken from the front of a Wheaties box. He twisted the bottle around and looked at the label. He thought of another joke. What makes a Texas oilman happy? Answer: a glass of Jack, a handful of young tit, and a barrel roll in a Learjet.

The door swung open, and George stepped up into the shack. Water trailed from his coat onto the floor as he pulled the hood back. George turned around and carefully closed the door. Then he took the handkerchief from his pocket and began deliberately polishing each lens of his bifocals and holding them up for inspection in the light from the window across the room. Finally satisfied, he slowly put them back on his head.

Tim watched this deliberate exercise while setting the whiskey bottle on the floor next to the Uzi. He knew a lot about George after living here in this valley with him for the past two years. He now knew way too much about him to suit him. He knew George was from Maine, just outside Bangor. No one could hurry anybody from Bangor, least of all George. He was like one of those old guys you see on TV sitting around the cracker barrel in the general store, puffing on a pipe, speaking one-syllable words, and waiting patiently for the other guy to make the next move on the checkerboard. And Tim, the impatient redhead, knew that George knew that the slowness drove him nuts: a game the older man played because there was little else to do here in this godforsaken valley. The last trip north had been almost three weeks ago.

Finally Tim said with exasperation, "Goddamn you, you old asshole, you're dripping water on my floor! Now what's up?"

George took his pipe and tapped it hard against the wall behind him and studied the younger man sitting on the cot. Ashes and small, rocky tobacco cinders rained to the floor.

Tim picked up the Uzi and pulled back the bolt. He aimed it at George. "You old bastard! I ought to blow your head off for messing up the floor."

George still hadn't spoken a word as he calmly pulled his pouch from his shirt pocket and began tamping new tobacco into his pipe. He produced a wooden kitchen match and struck it along the wall. Putting it to the bowl, he inhaled deeply. The sweet aroma filled the room. He threw the match on the floor and stared back at Tim.

Finally he spoke, as he nodded toward the submachine gun, "Yep, you can do that all right, sonny. Put us both out of our misery. Me right away and you eventually, when they can't find someone else to take care of those museum pieces outside."

Tim knew this was true. He reluctantly flicked the Uzi's safety back on and laid it back on the floor. Then he stood up and picked a cigarette from the pack on the windowsill. Changing his voice to a friendlier tone, he asked, "How about a light, George? I'm outta lighter fluid."

The older man ignored his request and leaned against the door. He pulled a piece of paper from his pocket. "You've got a mission tomorrow, sonny. More nose candy headed up north."

"You're sure getting religion all of a sudden."

George flipped the piece of paper onto the cot. "They want you there at dawn on Monday. The cargo is coming in tomorrow by chopper if the weather's good."

Tim looked at the piece of paper. He studied it for a moment then grinned. "Looks like I'm headed for Colorado again. That fat guy's fancy-ass ranch near Gunnison. I'll sure be glad to get out of here. Maybe slip into town and buy some supplies real quick while I'm there. Going to be stretching the range a little bit. How's the weather been in the gulf and up north? Any hurricanes? The season should be just be about over."

George puffed on the pipe and blew some more smoke across the room. "How should I know about the weather, sonny? I'm sorry, but I didn't catch the Today Show this morning and good old Willard Scott. Far as I know, it could be good, but then again it could be bad."

"You're fucking brilliant, you know that, George. Anybody else ever tell you that?"

"Lots of times."

"How's the airplane? Is she ready to fly, or do you have to twiddle with some bullshit thing or another?"

"Yep, she's ready as far as I'm concerned, with just a little more checking. You know, sonny, I had to do some work on that right engine. I keep telling you not to overboost them so much."

"Sure, I'll baby them next time and end up in prison somewhere." Then, to torment the old man, he added, "I had them firewalled for nearly fifteen minutes on that last trip. You should've heard those babies howl." Tim got some satisfaction as George noticeably winced. He was a tough old bird, but you couldn't ever talk to him about abusing airplanes. It really upset him.

George became agitated and shook his finger at Tim. "I've told you to take it easy, sonny. You'll end up as shark bait for sure if you lose one of those engines with that load of fuel aboard."

"Well, now, it's not your ass flying that piece of shit is it? I'll do what I have to." Tim paused. "You know that invitation is always open to ride along and take care of your precious engines personally. See the homeland."

George sighed. Once an officer, always an officer. Fighter pilots were the cockiest sons of bitches in the world. George turned to leave. "She'll be ready to go tomorrow. Don't you worry yourself none, sonny."

"How about that match?" Tim said, as he held up his unlit cigarette.

The old man hesitated for a moment in the doorway, his back to the other man, as if considering the request. Then he stepped stiffly down, holding the doorjamb for support; his boots splashed in the mud, and he walked off toward his shop and the sleek airplane sitting behind it.

Tim looked at the empty doorway and threw the cigarette on the floor. Asshole, he thought. He stood up and walked over to the door. Before closing it, he yelled at George, who was now several yards up the path, "I was going to quit anyhow!" Then he slammed the door, walked over to the piano, and sat down. When the circumstances were just right, he had sworn to himself, he would be making one last flight for the organization. He hadn't come up with a plan yet, but when he did, just before that last takeoff, when old George was leaving the cockpit, he'd put a round from the Browning right into one ear and out the other.

Then he began playing some ragtime on the piano.

CHAPTER 9

The Trailhead

Jamie's boots crunched on the gravel as he walked from the car over to the trailhead. A sleek, gray-and-black Steller's jay hopped noisily from the top of one of the pines to a lower branch nearby. He cocked his head toward Jamie, looking for a tidbit.

The Forest Service had embedded old railroad ties into the bank for steps, and Jamie climbed these to the trail register box, which sat to one side of the trail entrance. He lifted the lid and looked inside. The Forest Service maintained a pencil on a string and a lined notebook divided into sections for the date, name, address, number in the party, destination, and comments. Jamie flipped through the dog-eared pages and located the last entry: Oct. 5, Troop 686, Montrose, CO, 6 Taylor Lake. Under "comments," someone had hastily written in a juvenile hand, "Ralph eats dorks."

Jamie laughed at the comment and remembered his scouting days. He could picture the whole motley crew of five boys being shepherded up to the lake for the weekend by a now battle-weary scout leader. He wondered if anyone in the troop had smuggled in a contraband six-pack for late at night, like he had done years ago. He shook his head. Or was it a couple of joints these days?

His thoughts ran to the equipment they had put up with in those days. Heavy canvas tents with no floors or mosquito netting. He had spent many a sweaty night buried in his fart sack choosing between the heat or the bugs. There were the heavy canvas backpacks with no frames, too. The straps dug deep, red furrows into everybody's shoulders. Crummy, wadded-up kapok sleeping bags with ducks or beavers or bears on the flannel lining. Cooking utensils turning terminally black over smoky campfires. The smoke always, always seemed to follow you no matter which side you stood on.

The space age had sure been good to camping equipment. Nowadays there were lightweight nylon tents, which weighed just a few pounds but could literally stand up to a hurricane. Small gas stoves: a twist of a knob and flick of a Bic, and you were in business. And freeze-dried foods that weighed ounces but provided a big meal with no fuss.

Jamie read through the pages of the register. Most of the names were from somewhere in Colorado. Some from Michigan. Two from California. One from Arizona. Most of the recent parties were from Gunnison, an hour away. All had taken the short hike up to Taylor Lake and had not listed Hourglass as their destination. He dug deeper into the register and found only a handful had attempted the hike into Hourglass during the entire summer. Even at that he felt a little jealous that someone else had visited "their" lake.

Under "comments," most had chastised the Forest Service for the condition of the road above the Elk River Ranch Road. One party from Colorado Springs had just written, "Fix the damn thing." Jamie picked up the stubby pencil inside the box and wrote the date, both his and Rod's names and addresses, the number in the party, and their destination, Hourglass Lake. Under "comments," he wrote, "Don't tell any Republicans about this place." He closed the lid and started back to the car. The sun felt warm on his face. He breathed deeply. The pines and the air at this altitude always smelled good, and he suddenly realized how much he had missed these mountains. It was always like that, he thought, when you were actively in a rut. A trip such as this one was always called for as a cure.

The jay became braver and flew down onto the path, hopping expectantly along behind him at a respectful distance. Another one swooped low over the parking lot, looked both men over, but was not as brave, landing instead in an old lodgepole pine twenty yards away.

When Jamie returned, Rod was sitting sideways in the passenger seat, putting the final touches on lacing up one of his boots. He looked up as Jamie approached, gave one final tug on the laces, and said, "Anybody ahead of us on the trail?"

"No, just some Boy Scouts going in to Taylor Lake for the weekend. As far as I can see, nobody's hiked into Hourglass since August. I signed both of us in the register." Then he asked, as an afterthought, "Do you remember Toadie Fruehauf?"

Rod tied the laces and looked up, "Yeah, the Fart King. What in heaven's name made you think of him?"

"I dunno; guess I was just thinking of those scouting days when I read the register."

Rod started lacing up the other boot. "Yeah, I saw him at the last reunion, the one you didn't show up for. That was four years ago. He's some kind of big-shot lawyer in Chicago. Married with three kids. Had a great-looking wife."

Jamie digested this information. "No shit. I wonder if they still call him Toadie anymore."

"Naw, it was Robert at the reunion. Not even Bob, but Robert. At least that's what the wife was calling him, so I played along."

"Jeez, whoever gave him the name Toadie anyhow?"

"How did anyone get their nickname? Remember Bird Williams?"

"Yeah, but he was skinny and looked like a stork. I can see that."

"He was at the reunion, too. He's a dentist in Nashville. Divorced twice. An easy two hundred fifty pounds."

"No shit."

"Yeah. How about Tank Williams?"

"He got his nickname from his size; that's obvious. Boy, I remember he was a hell of a tackle. Saved my ass in the backfield a few times. Whatever happened to him?"

"He dropped out of college and enlisted in the Marines, someone at the reunion said. Killed on his second tour of duty in Vietnam."

Jamie was silent for a moment and looked down at the gravel. Then he said quietly, "I didn't know that. That's too bad. A lot of good guys got it over there."

Rod stood up and walked around a little in the parking lot until he was satisfied his boots felt comfortable for the long hike. He looked at Jamie, feeling a little embarrassed the subject had come up between them. The war still hurt a lot of people.

He came back and leaned into the car to see if they had left anything. Then he picked up the Nikon from the driver's seat and laid it on the ground next to his pack. He leaned back into the car and asked Jamie, "Do you want this six-pack, or should I leave it on the floor?"

Jamie walked to the front of the car and pulled the climbing ropes out. "No, leave it out."

"You're not going to carry it all the way up there?"

"No, I got plans for it."

"Let's plan on going to the twenty-fifth."

"What?"

"You know, the twenty-fifth reunion."

"Yeah, sounds good to me," Jamie said as he closed the hood.

"Oh yeah, I almost forgot: Marsha Stephenson was at the last one, too, and asked about you."

Jamie reflected for a moment. Marsha Stephenson had been his flame for over two years: from the end of their sophomore year until graduation. She had been voted the head cheerleader both her junior and senior years, while he had been the captain of the football team. They had been voted "couple most likely to succeed" in the senior yearbook. They had parted during the fall after graduation. He to Colorado and the football scholarship; she to Indiana University in Bloomington. They had kept in touch for a while by letter and an occasional phone call. He had last seen her during Christmas vacation his sophomore year. After that, Vietnam had intervened, and just plain time after that.

Jamie said, "No kidding. How was she?"

"Same foxy Marsha. Same blue eyes. Same long blond hair, although there was a little gray this time. When I asked her about it, she joked and called the streaks 'highlights.' Happily married to some accountant, I think. Has a couple of kids. Teaches third grade in Indianapolis—or was it fourth? I dunno; she seemed happy. Her oldest daughter just got married awhile back and is pregnant. She is probably a grandma by now. You really ought to come to the next reunion."

"Oh, yeah, asked about me, huh?" For a moment Jamie thought maybe he should have stuck with it, but somehow he couldn't imagine himself bouncing a kid on each knee.

Rod readied his pack and joked, "Yeah, and there was a real sparkle in her eye when she asked about you, too."

Jamie shook his head. "Yeah, well…Jesus, a grandma, huh?"

Rod went and checked to see if they had left anything behind. Then he locked both doors. As he came back around the car, he asked, "Did you ever have sex with her?"

Jamie dropped his coil of rope and staggered back in mock astonishment, clutching his heart. "Why, Rodney, what a question! I'm surprised at you. How crude. You know I wouldn't ever compromise a lady."

"C'mon, there's nobody around but you and me. You two were a hot item for those years."

Jamie kept silent, went over to his pack, and began to secure the rope under the flap and along each side. "Maybe I'll tell you someday when we're old men rocking on the porch who can't get it up." He looked at Rod and furrowed his brow. "It's kind of personal, you know. Besides, it's been so long ago I forget."

Rod ran his pack's straps through their buckles and pulled them tight. Then he began tightening the straps that held the tent in place on the top and his sleeping bag on the bottom. Jamie carried the climbing equipment, and Rod the tent.

"Not likely you'd forget someone like Marsha. C'mon, you told me all about Nancy Thompson."

"Yeah, that was different. Everybody at that school got some from her."

"I didn't."

"Yeah, well, present company excluded. I remember trying to set you up though."

"I didn't have the time," Rod said defensively.

"Yeah, sure. Boy, was she wild. She gave Lester Schmidt a blowjob in shop during lunch hour one day, in front of everyone."

"No shit!" Rod exclaimed.

"Yeah, c'mon, you knew about that."

"I swear I never heard that until today."

Jamie laughed, "Look at us, we sound like a couple of teenagers."

"Or even worse—old men reminiscing."

"Yeah."

Rod hefted his pack up by its frame, raised his right knee, and rested it on his thigh for a second. Then he grunted and in one motion put his arm through one of the wide, padded straps, twisting his back so the heavy pack and silver aluminum frame fell upon it. He hurriedly reached behind him for the other strap and put his arm through it. The weight settled upon his shoulders. He grunted as he made some adjustments. "Darn, I forgot how heavy this thing is."

He took each end of the waist belt in his hand and made a little hop, quickly cinching the belt before the weight settled again, mostly against his hips. The tent in its green nylon bag strapped to an extension of the frame was three inches above his head. He walked a few steps around the parking lot, slightly bent over, trying out the sudden burden.

"How's it feel?" Jamie asked while standing his pack on end in preparation for lifting it upon his shoulders.

"Pretty good," he said, slightly out of breath, as he carefully bent down to pick up the camera. "Ask me in about four hours though. You know we ought to take one of your helicopters in to the lake and save some wear and tear on both of us."

"I've thought of that," Jamie said as he picked up his pack by the straps and slung it over his shoulders as easily as if he was putting on a coat. He shrugged his shoulders and fastened the waist belt. "But you know, it's against the law to land an aircraft in a designated wilderness area. Besides it would ruin the challenge, and there's no place to land up there. The only really level spot is that little bit of tundra by the outlet, where we put the tent, and it's way too small. Even for me. The rest is just too rocky."

"Yeah, I guess you're right."

Jamie asked, "Whatever happened to good old Nancy Thompson, anyway?"

"She married Lester four years after graduation when he got out of the Marines. He was an MP. They live in Muncie and have four kids. I understand he's been an Indiana State Trooper for the past thirteen years."

"Aw, true love."

"Yeah."

"I remember he had that hopped-up old '57 Olds with the flames running from behind the front wheels along each side: the car Mickey Ferguson set on fire during lunch hour. I'd be willing to bet he still lays a little rubber once in a while in his cruiser."

Rod agreed, "You're probably right. Once a greaser, always a greaser. It's probably in the genes."

Jamie stooped down and picked up the six-pack. "You ready, old buddy?"

"You bet. Let's do it," Rod replied.

Jamie turned and started for the trailhead, continuing to think about his high school days. Rod followed close behind. Their boots crunched in the gravel.

Jamie asked over his shoulder, "Is it true what I heard about Bruce Winkleman?"

"Yeah, he's doing time down in a federal pen in Atlanta for smuggling dope."

"Hell of a way for the class valedictorian to wind up."

"He always thought he was smarter than anyone else."

From the trail register, the well-beaten path continued steeply uphill. It was anything but a smooth thoroughfare. It had been ill maintained and badly eroded from rain and snowmelt as the water had run down the bare dirt instead of soaking into the soil. In a few spots, logs had been angled across the trail and braced on the downhill side by the forest service crews in an attempt to divert the excess runoff into the trees and preventing the trail from turning into one large ditch. But they had been put there years ago, and not much had been done since.

Jamie, his gray pack bouncing on his back and the six-pack dangling from one hand, jogged up the trail with enthusiasm some fifty yards, leaving Rod behind. He turned around breathlessly to wait for his friend, feeling his heart pounding in his chest after the short run. A chipmunk scurried across the path, stopped, blinked at him, and then ran into the underbrush with his tail up high. The two jays flew ahead chattering to each other, still waiting patiently for a discarded tidbit. Jamie watched Rod slowly walking toward him, thumbs hooked under his shoulder straps.

After the initial steep climb, the path leveled out somewhat but continued to gain elevation as it angled south across the forested foothills of the White Elk Range. Jamie stopped after another half mile. Rod finally caught up with him. Both men began to feel the altitude. Rod could feel his pulse pounding in his temples. The heavy pack seemed to be continuously pulling him off balance. He wiped the first pinpricks of sweat from his forehead as the breeze cooled him. He looked back toward the parking lot.

Jamie turned and began walking again. "Don't worry; it'll still be there when we get back," he said over his shoulder.

"What?"

"That damned car. Nobody's going to bother it way out here."

Rod turned to follow. Jamie's stride was longer than his, and it was hard to match. The sweat caused his glasses to slip down his nose. He pushed them up. His boots felt heavy and awkward. He quickened his pace a little and asked somewhat breathlessly, "Speaking of cars, do you still have the old Cadillac?"

"Naw, the transmission went out the year after you were down there, and I had to get some new wheels."

"New wheels, huh? You're showing some sense. What'd you buy?"

"An old Lincoln Continental: the kind with the suicide doors. It's a little rusty but runs like a dream."

Rod grimaced, "Why do you buy those old rust buckets? Those big pimpmobiles sound like the mufflers were worked over with an ice pick."

"Well, you can't take it with you." Jamie laughed. "Besides I like big cars. Plenty of room."

"Why not buy a new one."

"What and pay six grand for a cheap Jap econobox? No, sir, it'll be a cold day in hell before that happens, or I stumble on a few million in a paper bag."

"What about the energy crisis?"

"Fuck the energy crisis. Look at it this way: These cars were heading for the junkyard when I got hold of them. I'm doing my part by sort of recycling them. Besides I like the hood ornaments."

"I can't fault that logic."

The trail leveled out as it turned farther south along the contours of the foothills. The two jays gave up and headed back to the parking lot. In another mile, the trail began to slant downhill, and a distant roaring rose above the sound of the wind whispering through the tops of the spruce trees on either side. Now an occasional small stand of pure gold aspen burst upon the two men.

Suddenly the spruce trees gave way to a large grove of aspen, and the roaring grew louder. Another minute's walking brought them to the edge of the North Fork of the White Elk River. It rushed from pool to pool as it tumbled down the mountainside from Taylor Lake a few miles upstream. Gold aspen leaves were caught in eddies and circled round and round. Discolored marks on the boulders at the stream's edge indicated the much higher level during spring runoff when it would have been difficult, if not impossible, to cross.

The well-trodden trail to Taylor Lake made a right turn here and climbed westward along the stream's edge in a series of switchbacks to its source. A faint, narrower trail continued steeply down the stream bank. Jamie and Rod carefully followed this trail to the water's edge.

Upstream, the tip of a high rocky ridge soared above the trees in the distance. A few patches of last winter's snow still clung stubbornly to the granite in sheltered areas, contrasting with the deep blue sky. A small wispy cloud suddenly whisked across the edge of the treeless ridge, an indicator of the wind that must be even now sweeping across the peaks from the west. In a small cirque scooped out by a glacier, which had squatted on the White Elk Range thousands of years ago, lay Taylor Lake.

Downstream, the little river bounced and splashed its way eventually out of sight around a bend. Eastward in the distance under fluffy white cumulus clouds, the west flanks of the Collegiate Range spread out in a jagged dark outline on the horizon. Before them stretched the brown fields of White Elk Park.

Both hikers shed their packs for a short rest. Rod sat down on a boulder while Jamie hopped downstream from boulder to boulder with the six-pack in hand. He stopped on a suitable boulder and lay prone on the rock. Rolling up his sleeve, he jammed the beer into the lee of the boulder then worked his way back upstream to the other man. "There," Jamie announced when he arrived. "That should be plenty cold on the way out." He then rummaged in a side pocket of his pack and pulled a liter drinking bottle from it. He knelt in front of Rod, dipped the bottle into the cold clear water, and watched it fill up as bubbles streamed from its top. The bottle was filled in seconds, and he brought it up to his mouth, taking a long swallow. Then he filled it again before jamming it back into the pack's side pocket and zipping it shut. He exclaimed, "Man, that's so cold it hurts your teeth!" Then he nudged Rod. "Better fill up; last water until the middle fork."

Rod answered, "I filled mine up back in Denver. Besides, this is too low. I'm afraid of giardia."

"Well, you're going to have to drink some of this water in the next few days."

"I've got some purification tablets."

Jamie's shoulders sagged. "You worry about everything, you know that? I can't believe you'd ruin the taste of this great water with iodine."

Rod nodded upstream. "What if one of your Boy Scouts just pissed in the stream a few minutes ago?"

"You beat all," Jamie said, as he slipped his pack over his shoulders and cinched the waist belt.

Rod followed and both hikers jumped precariously from rock to rock until they stood on the far side catching their breath.

"I forgot about your trick of stashing the beer in the stream," Rod said.

"It'll be worth the effort on the way back," Jamie replied.

Then as they turned to follow the little-used trail up into the forest, Jamie added, "Well, old buddy, this is where we leave all the tourists behind."

Rod nodded in agreement as he followed Jamie up the far bank. He already had begun to favor his left leg. As he neared the top and walked into the trees, the old feeling of danger washed over him. He couldn't help it. It felt almost as strongly as a premonition at times like this. He felt maybe he should be home in the Lazy Boy watching the Broncos. Jamie had explained the feeling away in the past with a self-coined term: *rut-breaking*.

The sun continued to shine from a flawless blue sky.

In Los Angeles it had been raining hard all day.

CHAPTER 10

The Gorge

As the sun sank behind the high ridges, a long blue shadow spread coldly down the narrow gorge. Rod sat on a wide, flat rock with his feet dangling over the edge. The rock still radiated the heat of the day, in contrast with the sudden chill of the wind that swept down from the highest peak into White Elk Park. His boots were sitting wearily nearby; he reached down, pulled his sock around his heel, and massaged his left ankle. His hair was plastered to his forehead, and his T-shirt damp after the six-mile hike from the parking lot. He looked into the gorge between his feet and watched Jamie climb up from the river carrying a full water bottle in each hand. Behind Jamie the river made a slight turn and formed a large green pool before tumbling downstream toward the foothills. The sound of the water reverberated back and forth between rock walls. Another distinct roar could be heard upstream as the waters from Hourglass Lake plunged two hundred feet over the lip of the cirque onto the rocks below in three separate leaps.

Rod turned his attention from Jamie and looked downstream at the vista to his left. White Elk Park was still bathed in bright sunlight, as were the peaks of the Collegiate Range on its east side, although the blue shadow was racing in their direction. He wondered if another backpacker like himself might be sitting on one of the distant peaks watching the sunset. He could easily pick out the distinctive white grain elevator in the little town of Crestridge twenty miles away in the middle of the park. A road ran straight, along some distant fence line. Four miles from him but seemingly at the foot of his perch, he could plainly see the general outline of the White Elk Ranch. He picked up his pair of small binoculars. In the clear mountain air, he saw the green smudge, which would be the main house sitting in the middle of its carefully manicured lawn—this in contrast with the brown hay fields which surrounded it. He eyes followed the ranch's main road straight south for a mile or more before it turned east through the first set of hogbacks toward the county road and then into Crestridge. Farther south were a few outbuildings and barns. A dark line meandered just west of the road. Rod tracked it back north to the ranch house, following its serpentine course. He knew this would be the Elk River—the one Jamie had wanted to fish so badly all these years.

Now, as he watched, the shadow spread across the fields and finally to the ranch itself. Before Jamie had climbed up to the campsite, Rod turned and looked upstream. Hourglass Lake sat in a large, deep cirque carved out by a glacier thousands of years ago. The summit of Mt. Grant loomed just above the lake. He lowered the binoculars. The three waterfalls further upstream stood out in white contrast to the gray rock, which surrounded them now bathed in shadow. Because of the bend in the gorge below where Rod sat, this magnificent view was hidden from below. Few ever saw it, unless they were willing to hike the miles to this spot.

A sudden gust of wind pouring down the slopes caught him by surprise, and he shivered. He leaned over to pull his sweater from his pack. His legs felt like butter, and he wished he was in better shape for this. But the reward for the effort, he thought, was all around.

Jamie started up the last small pitch below the campground brushing aside the last, stunted, bush-like trees, which grew here at timberline.

It had been a long hike but they had made good time to reach this first campsite before sunset. Tomorrow would be more leisurely in that the lake was only a mile away. But tomorrow would also include the short rock climb up to the lake itself. All in all, hiking along the eastern flanks of the White Elks, they had gained over two thousand feet in elevation. The trail had been anything but level. It was poorly maintained. Many deadfalls lay across it, and they judged it had been at least a couple of years since the Forest Service had put a trail crew along it. The deadfalls had to be negotiated by finding a way around them, ducking under, or climbing over. Either way was a pain with a full pack. Rod had agreed with Jamie that walking downhill with a heavy pack was the hardest on the legs while uphill was the most tiring. They enjoyed a late lunch of Gouda cheese and Ritz crackers at the Middle Fork of the White Elk River. Then they refilled the water bottles and hiked the rest of the way to the south fork, making pretty good time for a couple of old farts. At the south fork, the trail petered out at the deep gorge. It did not continue on the other side. Supposedly a trail followed the river downstream to the ranch land. It was marked on Rod's USGS topo map, but they had never found it. It hadn't been used for decades. Hikers couldn't bother anyone at the ranch below.

At the south fork, they had begun working their way upstream on the north bank through the trees, along the barest vestige of a trail. The smooth rock walls rose steeper and steeper until finally they approached the timberline. The campsite lay on a tiny bench in the midst of some small, hardy trees, perpetually bent by the wind. Since the gorge curved slightly south at this point, it was the first time the outlet waterfalls from the lake were visible as they tumbled into the gorge below. Their campsite was several hundred feet below the elevation of the lake. Tomorrow they would slowly hike upstream the rest of the way to the base of the waterfalls and climb the rock wall alongside one of them to the lake above.

Rod carefully laid the binoculars on the rock as Jamie neared. He stood up with a groan and straightened slowly. In the few minutes he had been sitting on the rock, his legs and back had stiffened greatly. He pulled on the sweater and felt almost instant warmth from the wool. Next he reached into the pack and pulled out the nylon stuff sack containing the small gas stove. After this he reached in and found the red anodized fuel bottle. He set both of these on the rock at his feet and fished in a side pocket for the Bic lighter.

Jamie walked slowly up onto the little bench and said breathlessly, "Next time…it's your turn…asshole…to get the water." The way down to the crashing stream was steep, and they were at just over eleven thousand feet. He threw the opaque white water bottles at Rod, who caught one but missed the second. It rolled along the rock, and he barely caught it before it tumbled over the edge.

Rod set them next to the stove and fuel bottle and said sarcastically, "I thought you were in good shape. What's wrong, flatlander?"

"Spoken like a true Colorado resident. But you aren't wrong. It'll take me a few days to get used to this high altitude."

Rod removed two foil pouches from his pack as Jamie watched. Jamie asked, "What's for dinner, honey?"

Rod answered in his best attempt at a female voice, while placing his hands on his hips, "Nothing for you, big boy, until you get that tent set up for me."

Jamie picked up the tent bag and moaned, "God help me! Stuck way out here, and I've got to sleep in the same tent with a fag."

They both laughed.

Jamie unfastened the tent bag's drawstring and dumped the contents onto the ground. As he unrolled the tent with his foot, he looked up the gorge at the waterfalls and then downstream to the sunlit park. "Sure is something," he exclaimed.

"Yeah," Rod replied, as he stiffly sat back down onto the rock. "You forget over the years just how nice it is up here."

Jamie picked up the tent poles and started piecing them together, the shock corded pieces snapping together. "How come you never bring the family up to a place like this?"

Rod didn't answer right away but instead busied himself with assembling the stove and hooking up the fuel bottle. Then, after he thought about it a moment, he answered, "I don't know. Ann's just not the outdoorsy type or anything."

"You could just come up here with Rod Jr. when he gets older."

"Yeah, I know, but it would be a hassle. She's pretty protective of that kid."

"Even with his father, for Christ sake!"

"Yeah…but it's partly my fault. The only time I do something like this is when you push me. If you didn't drag me into doing things like this, I'd never go on my own. There seems to be always something to do at home on the weekends or else Rod Jr. is scheduled for some kind of activity by Ann, like his violin lessons on Saturday morning for instance."

"Is that why she's pissed this weekend and went out of town with the kid?"

"Yeah, I guess."

Jamie shook his head. "Man, you and little Junior, what a couple of pussy-whipped guys."

"Yeah," Rod sighed, as he twisted the knob on the side of the stove and gas began hissing out of the burner. He picked up the lighter, held it near the burner, and flicked the flint wheel. The gas ignited with a pop then settled down to a dull roar as he adjusted the flame.

Jamie got down on his knees and began to spread the tent out. "You know, I thought this might be the first trip where we brought Rod Jr.

along." Then he added sarcastically, "But heaven forbid if he learned some cuss words from his old godfather or heard his old man talk about women."

"You're right: she thinks you might be a bad influence."

"I don't know how you put up with that."

Rod was silent after this last statement for too long, so Jamie stopped setting the tent up and finally asked, "Are you two having problems?"

Rod leaned over and fished around in his pack for the stainless steel mess kit. His answer was difficult to come by, but he finally said, "Yeah, I guess we've been having some problems for a few years now. But show me a married couple who isn't. Probably my midlife crisis or something. I think we still love each other, but we're having a bad case of the blahs. We both feel trapped, I guess. She wants to go back to school, I think. And she's intent on recapturing her youth by Jazzercise classes at the health club."

"And what do you want to do?"

Rod stopped to look up at Jamie. "Huh?"

Jamie gave his friend an intense look. "Just what I said, dammit. What does Rodney Sr. want to do?"

Rod wilted under Jamie's glare. "I never gave it much thought."

"Bullshit!"

"Well..."

"C'mon, I know you better than that. Given a free choice, a free wish, what does Rodney Coleman want? Don't worry about anybody else. I want to know."

"No money problems?"

"No, let's say you've just won the lotto or found a million bucks in a shopping bag."

"Well," Rod said, as he unfastened the mess kit, took a pot from the nested set, and unfolded the wire handles. "It's no big deal."

"C'mon."

"Well, it's pretty simple. I'd really like to go back to school and get my doctorate. Then I'd like to teach English or literature."

"Do it."

"It's not that simple," Rod said defensively. "It's easy for you to say because you're single. There's nothing tying your butt down."

Jamie pointed a finger at Rod. "Look, don't end up an old man wishing about things. If you look at the problem, it's simple. Both you and Ann want to continue your educations. Probably for the same reasons. That's great. Have you ever talked about it with her?"

"No, not really."

Jamie became agitated. "Well, why not, for Christ sake?"

Rod thought a moment. "I guess we'd both probably feel selfish. Besides, where do we get the money? It's not free, you know. I'll bet tuition is two times what it was when you and I were in college. You single guys don't realize what it costs to run a family. Do you know how much braces cost for a kid? The bottom line is always money."

"Quit making excuses. Quit that stupid job of yours that you hate. Do it the way we did it. You've got equity in that split-level wonder back in Thornton. Sell it. Rent a shabby apartment like we did eighteen years ago. You've got to take a step back to take a step forward. It's not permanent, but you've got to make some sacrifices. Sell that stupid German car. You ought to be able to raise ten or twelve grand from it alone. All I'm saying is take a chance, before it's too late."

"Sell the house and car?"

"Sure, why not? For crying out loud, Rodney, get off your butt and do something instead of waiting for retirement. I wouldn't be surprised if that is exactly what Ann wants, too. Set sail."

Rod brightened up at the possibility but remained doubtful, "Jesus, I don't know. You might have something there."

"Look," Jamie said, "I have some money saved up over the years; I'll lend you what you need."

"There are a lot of 'ifs.' I still think money would be a problem."

"Just promise me you'll at least think about it, okay?" Jamie replied, as he stood up smiling and got back to the business of erecting the tent. He looked up and knew the wheels were starting to turn fast in Rod's head. Rod looked lost in thought as he bent over the stove. Jamie was pleased with himself, that he might have set something in motion. He had meant every word.

The blue, nylon tent fabric flapped in the rising downslope wind, and Jamie struggled with it. "Fuck, I can't remember how this thing goes up," he said as he tried to spread the tent and waterproof ground cloth out flat on the ground. "What's for dinner, anyway? I'm starved."

Rod was jolted out of his daydream and answered, "Beef stroganoff." Then he asked, "Do you really think Ann and I could pull it off?"

"I don't see why not. You sure won't know till you try." Then he added, "I hope you didn't pay attention to how many people it says one of those packages of freeze-dried food will feed. I almost starved last time."

"No, I got us each a package this time."

A gust of wind picked up a corner of the tent opposite where Jamie was kneeling, assembling the remaining tent wands, and folded back over itself. Jamie swore again, "Damn, you need six hands to set this up in any wind!"

"What if after all this sacrifice, I can't get a job."

"Worry about that when the time comes. I can just see it. Rodney Franklin Coleman, PhD. Hey, that has a good ring to it."

The wind picked up, and the little stove alternately roared and fell silent despite the windscreen. Rod peered into the pot. Tiny bubbles were forming quickly on the silver bottom. One by one they began escaping to the surface as the temperature rose to boiling. Now small wisps of steam began to rise off the surface. Rod reread the instructions on the foil pouches and waited for the water to come to a complete boil.

Rod kept his attention on the pot but was still thinking of his recent conversation with Jamie, the idea exciting him. He said to Jamie, "I'll give all this some thought and talk it over with Ann. You know, figure out some stuff like the cost and all. Maybe I'll drive up to Boulder and talk to some of my old profs." He looked at the pot. "Remember how we used to soap up the bottoms of our pots in Boy Scouts to keep the fire from turning them black?"

Jamie fumbled with the tent. It made a perfect sail in the wind as he tried to thread the shock corded poles through their fabric tunnels. "Yeah, I remember. Hey, how about giving me a hand over here. I forget how this son of a bitch goes together."

"Just a sec; let me start the food," Rod said as he took out his red Swiss Army knife and opened the big blade. He cut open both pouches of the freeze-dried stroganoff and carefully dumped their contents into the boiling pot. The dry hard pieces of beef and noodles splashed into the water and floated on the surface. Rod made sure both pouches were empty and then stirred up the mixture with his knife. Then he set the knife on the rock next to the stove, put the lid on, and looked at his watch. Finally he stood up and walked the few yards over to where Jamie was struggling with the tent.

Rod took one end of the nylon. "For one thing you have the rain fly and not the tent. Jeez, do I have to figure out everything for you?" he said good-naturedly. He was in a good mood. He helped Jamie lay the tent flat as the other man threaded the wands.

Jamie responded to his barb, "You know I have trouble with something this complicated."

"Shit, how do you fly a helicopter?"

"I'm not so good at that anymore either."

Rod passed Jamie the final wands. "What do you mean?"

"I think I have something wrong with my depth perception. I'm not sure, or if I'm imagining things."

"You're joking. Maybe you just are beginning to need reading glasses. We're almost there, you know. I'm starting to have a little difficulty focusing fast and reading my watch up close."

"No, well, maybe your right."

"Have you seen a doctor?"

"Are you kidding? And get grounded. Shit."

"How do you know you have a problem?"

"I've made a couple of dumb mistakes lately. Something I would never do. But yesterday, on my last flight, I miscalculated a landing on a rig, and we almost went over the side. Me and five other people."

Rod tried to offer an explanation. "Maybe it was just a mistake, or maybe a sudden gust of wind."

"I thought about that, tried to find some excuse, but a similar thing happened about four months ago. It's hard to explain. Suddenly things are further away than they look."

"What about your last FAA physical?"

"I passed no problem."

Rod tried to offer another excuse. "Maybe you were just tired or something."

"Maybe, but I don't think so. Remember today on the interstate, passing that motorhome."

"Yeah, that was pretty close."

"But it didn't seem like it at first. I thought I had plenty of room."

Both men bowed the poles and set them in place. Suddenly the small tent took its wind shedding shape and was up.

"Besides," Jamie added, "I think it might be time to hang up the wings."

Rod stopped fussing with the tent, pushed his glasses up, and looked at his friend. "What?"

"That's right, I'm tired of it. You're not the only one who's tired of his job."

"Yeah, but..."

"I know it seemed exciting to you when you came down that time, but to me it's become a real grind. Besides, if I do have some kind of vision problem, I'll be grounded anyway."

Rod threw Jamie the rain fly, and both men spread it out over the tent.

Then Rod said, "But you've been flying for almost twenty years. I can't imagine you doing anything else."

Jamie shrugged as they pulled the fly tight and began to anchor it with pegs at each corner. "That's the trouble: I don't want to do anything in particular. I just want to travel some and fish. I'd like to see some more of the world. Trout fish in New Zealand. Take a trek in Nepal. Maybe get into some kind of business."

"Well, why don't you just take some time off? You can always find a job later. Maybe that's what you need: a rest, like me. A change."

The tent was complete. The taut dome shape was already spilling the wind from its sides. Jamie unzipped the door and rolled back the flap while Rod walked over to check on the meal.

Rod knelt down and carefully removed the lid. Then he stirred the contents with his Swiss Army knife, checking to see if the freeze-dried food had sucked up most of the water. Jamie walked over and stood next to him, hands in pockets.

"I think I will have to ground myself after this trip and see a doctor. I can't jeopardize any more lives."

Rod was still stunned by the news and was just beginning to grasp the magnitude of it for Jamie. He said, as he stirred the stroganoff, "Yeah, you're probably right about that. But still it's hard to believe: you not flying."

Jamie walked over and sat down with his feet dangling over the edge of the rock.

Rod said cheerfully, "Almost ready. Hope you're hungry."

"You bet," Jamie replied and rubbed his stomach. "Look at us: a couple of middle-age has-beens."

Rod ignored the comment. "Reach over in my pack and give me the rest of the mess kit, and I'll serve you dinner."

Jamie leaned over and began fishing through the top compartment.

Rod frowned, "No, not the top, the bottom."

Jamie hesitated, "What's this doing in here."

"What?"

"This," Jamie said, as he pulled the large novel from the pack. It was a large, heavy hardbound copy of James Michener's *Space*.

"It's a book. What do you think it is?"

Jamie hefted the volume. "Must weigh two pounds or more." He indicated the waterfalls. "You think I'm going to hoist this up there, you're crazier than I thought. Why don't you just buy the paperback version?"

"Are you kidding? And pay almost four dollars? I got this from the library for free."

Jamie flipped to the back. "Jesus, it's six hundred twenty-two pages." Then he placed the book in the pack and withdrew the rest of the mess kit from the bottom compartment of Rod's pack. Rod began to spoon out the stroganoff.

Twilight was coming quickly now and the temperature was beginning to drop. The entire park was now completely in shadow. Only the very highest of the Collegiate peaks many miles to the east were still in sunlight. Jamie stood up, walked over to his pack, and dug deep into the bottom. He pulled out a brown wool sweater and quickly slipped it over his head. Then he leaned over and reached deeper still into the pack and pulled out two cans of beer. Carrying the beer, he walked back over to the rock and sat down. He pried one of the cans from its plastic holder and held it out to Rod.

Rod laughed and handed Jamie his meal in exchange for the can. "You asshole, criticize me for a book, and you're carrying in twenty-four ounces of beer!"

Jamie put the plate on his lap, popped the can open, and took a deep swallow before setting it on the rock. Then he hungrily attacked his food. With his mouth full, he said, "Necessities are necessities, old buddy. Hey, this shit's pretty good."

Rod sat down on the rock next to Jamie and also began to eat. He took a swallow from his can of beer and said, "You know, my mother is going to be doubly worried about you now."

"How so?"

"Well, she thinks you should be getting married. Now you're going to also be out of a job."

Jamie chuckled. "Yeah, I know. Every time I visit her she asks me if I'm seriously seeing anybody. Just like old Aunt Bee on the *Andy Griffith Show*."

Both men ate in silence for a moment. Finally Rod asked, "Why didn't you ever get married? Surely you've had the chance."

Jamie took another forkful and shrugged as he swallowed. "I don't know. I guess I'm just afraid of shag carpeting."

"What's that supposed to mean?"

"That's usually what they put in mobile homes. I'm afraid I'll end up in some crapped-out mobile home with worn-out shag carpeting with a big beer belly, a nagging wife, and a couple of screaming kids in diapers. Or worse yet, I'll end up just like my folks. Naw, marriage was never for me."

"It doesn't have to be that way. You just haven't met the right woman. My marriage is…" Rod stopped. It struck him in midsentence: maybe he wasn't so bad off after all.

Jamie continued, "Besides, she'd really have to be something special to keep up with me. What else were you going to say?"

"Oh nothing, just that marriage doesn't have to be the dead end you think it is."

"Maybe not, but I just don't think I could live with a woman for a long time." He laughed, "You know, not more'n three or four days anyway."

"Not with the right one? Your soul mate. You could live with her forever."

"You're starting to sound like your mom."

"Sorry."

"Besides I just don't think the right woman exists for me," Jamie said as he swallowed another mouthful and then tapped the side of his head. "At least the picture of her I have up here." Jamie sighed and finished the rest of his meal. He sat for a moment looking into the distance before he laid the plate on the rock. Suddenly he asked, "Where are the binoculars?"

"Should be in the top right pocket. Why?"

Jamie didn't answer but instead leaned back, unzipped the pocket, and removed the miniature glasses from their black case. He trained them on the flat valley at their feet.

Rod watched, puzzled at his friend's actions, then asked, "What about someone like old Phoebe?"

Jamie continued to scan the valley as he answered, "She's already married."

Rod was curious. "Oh, I didn't know that. When did that happen?"

"About four or five years ago. At least, she has a kid that old, so I'm guessing. Her old man works offshore on one of the rigs. One of the guys you ate lunch with when you were down there that time a couple of years ago. Great big burly guy: must weigh about two fifty or so. Looks like Paul Bunyan without the ax."

Rod paused with his fork in mid-flight between the plate and his mouth. "You mean—"

Jamie cut him off, "Yeah, Rodney, she was married that night we all went out to the roadhouse. Kind of adds some tang to the old memories, now doesn't it? You nailed a married woman."

"Jesus—"

Jamie cut him off again, "Funny, but it looks like there's an airplane taking off on the road near that ranch down there. Here, look for yourself." He handed Rod the binoculars.

CHAPTER 11

The Ranch

The sound of the engines and propellers increased to takeoff power and rattled the windows in their frames. Edwin Jr. sat on the long leather couch, pressing a phone to one ear and holding a finger in the other. He nodded twice and spoke with a louder than normal voice. As the twin Cessna accelerated down the road and away from the house, the noise diminished, and Edwin Jr. was able to lower his voice and remove the finger. He idly noticed the load of wax it had picked up and then wiped it on his pant leg. The propellers changed their pitch slightly and then faded to the southwest.

Edwin Jr. sighed, reached over to the knotty pine end table, and set the phone back on its cradle. He slouched and leaned his shoulders against the back cushion. The old leather squeaked, and the springs protested under his weight. He rested his hands on his ample stomach and began to twiddle his stubby thumbs nervously.

The couch sat midway across the large living room and faced the large wooden double doors and huge picture window, which faced the circular drive in front of the ranch house. In the grassy island created by the circular driveway sprouted a tall flagpole. The Stars and Stripes, the Colorado state flag, and the Forsyth pennant—in order from top to bottom—still flapped in the wind now pouring down from the White

Elk Mountains to the west. The sun had set moments before, and the room darkened in the twilight.

Mrs. Alison, the housekeeper, had remembered to raise the flags in the morning as was her custom but had left in a hurry when unexpectedly given the next three days off with pay after Edwin Jr. and Walt had arrived at the ranch in the twin Cessna just before lunch. She had been slightly miffed by the sudden change in her schedule; she didn't like surprises but decided to take advantage of Edwin Jr.'s generosity and visit her sister in Salida. She had left in her ancient Plymouth just a little after noon. Her first name was Pamela, but she had been known as Mrs. Alison for as long as Edwin Jr. had known her. He guessed she was somewhat over eighty years old now. Her sister was even more ancient. The family had simply inherited her with the ranch from the former owners over three decades ago. She was a prim, unrelenting, no-nonsense person who had ruled the house with an iron hand and kept it spotless. She had been on Edwin Jr.'s case most of his life, and he was relieved she wouldn't be around this weekend. Secretly he had always believed she was a fugitive Nazi storm trooper from an elite SS unit and wanted for war crimes, though he couldn't prove it. With her gone, he now had the place to himself.

The window frames threw a lattice of shadows across the polished wooden floors and the large braided rug in front of the couch. Small stained glass windows of various colors ran across the top and down the sides of the main front window. Just before the sun had sunk below the White Elk Mountains, the colors had danced around the room in elongated squares on the large stairway leading to the second floor, the dark grand piano, the gun cabinet along the rear wall, and the large moss rock fireplace on the northwest wall.

Edwin Jr. did some more serious thumb twiddling for another half hour and watched the orange glow slowly fade behind Mt. Grant. Then the western sky gradually turned to a deep purple, the mountains becoming a sharp black outline on the western horizon. The house was silent except for the regular ticktock of the grandfather clock, which stood next to the stairway.

When the Cessna had begun its takeoff roll, Edwin Jr. had been making final arrangements to set up a meeting next week to explore the possibilities of selling the hotel chain. He had decided to capitulate to one of his father's old rivals, John Rydell. Rydell wanted to buy controlling interest in the Forsyth chain to add to his chain of plush hotels in the Midwest and Northeast. Rydell was a crusty, old, white-haired innkeeper much like Edwin Jr.'s father. He had had similar beginnings, starting with a small eight-room motel near Buffalo, New York, following World War II. The only difference was he hadn't died like Edwin Sr. He had been after Edwin Jr. for some months now when he had learned of the Forsyth hotels' possible financial difficulties. Rydell had one hotel now in Atlantic City and wanted another one in Las Vegas. The Forsyth Flagship there would do just fine. The combination would make a formidable rival of even the biggest chains such as Hyatt or even Hilton.

The terms were good, although Edwin Jr. knew his father would turn over in his grave. Edwin Jr. would become a rich man and also a token member of the board, under Rydell. On paper it looked great except for one roadblock—that of course being the man his sister was currently shacked up with and, more importantly, the organization behind him. Even though Edwin Jr. had spoken with Rivas only an hour ago, he couldn't bring himself to tell him about Rydell's offer.

Edwin Jr. struggled to his feet with some effort. His bulk created enough momentum so that as he pitched forward, he almost stumbled on the edge of the rug into the magnificent wood and glass coffee table in front of the couch. He sighed and walked toward the front door. The wide pine floorboards cut from magnificent virgin timber over a hundred years ago squeaked under him. He opened one of the heavy front doors and stepped carefully down the three steps carved from native granite quarried near Gunnison. He walked across the driveway to the flagpole and stood for a moment surveying his surroundings. The night air was cold and had a sharp bite to it. The ropes slapped against the steel pole, and the flags above snapped in the wind. There was still a faint purple glow from the sun but already to the east and overhead were countless numbers of stars. Looking up Edwin Jr. thought he could already make out the silky path of the Milky Way. Guests at the ranch, especially those who had spent all their years in the city, were always exclaiming at the first sight of it. To the south he could see the few bluish mercury vapor lights guarding the various outbuildings and hay barns. The people who worked the ranch under lease and their hands all lived in Crestridge and wouldn't be back until Monday. Ted Murray, who dealt with much of the everyday work at the ranch and who kept the grounds, had also been given the week off.

Edwin Jr. unfastened the rope and unsnapped the three flags as he lowered them into his arms. Then he managed to free a hand to tie off the rope and walked to the dark log house holding the bundle to his chest. He knew the American flag should be folded into a neat triangular package, like he had been taught many years ago at school, but didn't care at this point. Yes, sir, when you're smuggling tons of dope into the country, why give the petty infractions in life any mind?

The large ranch house was really three distinct sections built at different times in the ranch's history. The three sections came together and formed a segmented U away from the driveway. The middle section, which faced southwest toward the White Elks and which contained the main doors, living room, dining room, and main stairway, was originally built over a century ago as a two-story log cabin, with the upper floors containing the sleeping quarters. Over the years first one wing then another had been added, and the original center section had been modified into one large area, exposing a beamed ceiling of huge pine rafters and eliminating the second floor entirely except for the rear part, which formed the landing at the top of the steps and which ran in both directions connecting the second floors of both wings. The main floor of the east wing connected with the dining room and contained the kitchen and storage areas, while the main floor of the north wing housed the big master bedroom and its huge fireplace. All the other bedrooms were on the second floors.

Edwin Jr. experienced some difficulty negotiating the stone steps in the dark but was finally successful in opening one of the front doors, and entered the dark living area. He unceremoniously dumped the flags on the couch with a grunt, found the switch to one of the brass lamps, and walked across the room to the large, wooden gun cabinet. Using the wall for support, he knelt down and ran his fingers along the bottom edge until he felt the key, hidden near one of the corners.

His father had been an avid gun collector and over the years had amassed a significant collection of both modern and antique firearms. Edwin Sr.'s passion included collecting guns that had played an important part in American and world history. Among those relevant to the history of the American West was a complete series of mint Winchester lever action rifles, a pair of early Colt 45 revolvers with pearl handles (in their original holsters), and a heavy Sharps buffalo gun. In addition to the collector guns, there were a variety of fine shotguns and sporting rifles.

Edwin Jr. fumbled with the key and unlocked the large glass doors. Unlike his sister, he knew very little about guns. His father had tried to teach him as young boy, but when the older Forsyth found his son feared them, he had given up.

The rifles and shotguns were standing upright and leaning against the rear of the cabinet in their individual racks. Dust had accumulated on most of the oiled metal parts. Cleaning guns was not one of Mrs. Alison's responsibilities, and they had not been touched since his father's death. This surprised Edwin: he thought a Nazi like her would surely go for one of the guns.

The pistols lay in front of the rifles and shotguns on a shelf lined with green velvet. Edwin looked them over. The automatic pistols seemed too complicated. He picked up two of the old Colt single action army revolvers instead. He seemed to remember that these antique guns had been a gift to his father by some business associate or another.

He juggled them in each hand. They felt heavier than he had first expected. He turned the pistols around and looked down the barrel of each one, wondering if they were loaded. He thought the chambers seemed empty, as he pointed the revolvers toward the floor. Now all he had to do was to figure out was how to load them and find some cartridges.

He gently laid the guns back in the cabinet on the velvet, bent over, and pulled open the first drawer in the bottom of the cabinet. Besides some gun cleaning kits, old magazines, and old rags, there were at least a couple dozen multicolored boxes of ammunition of all types and calibers. Edwin laboriously got down on his knees and began to go through each and every box, thinking that somewhere in the mess there had to be the correct ammo. He knew he was looking for smaller, fatter cartridges and soon eliminated the larger rifle and shotgun ammunition.

After a few more minutes of searching, he found a box of cartridges that seemed just about the right size. Printed in big letters on the end flap of the box was .45 COLT. He slid the box open and picked one of the cartridges out of the neatly stacked rows. He picked up one of the revolvers and wondered how he would load it. The cylinder didn't want to swing out like the modern revolvers he had seen on numerous cop shows. Finally he saw that a little door swung free on the rear of the cylinder on the left side. The cartridge in his other hand slipped in with precise feel, and he knew he had the right ammunition. He quickly loaded five more, filling the cylinder. Then he picked up the other Colt and loaded it, too, before struggling to his feet.

Edwin held both guns and pretended to aim them at the piano across the room. Like a little boy, he made noises and jerked the guns into the air as he pretended to fire them. Just like Clint Eastwood, he thought, although he gave no thought whatsoever to actually going outside and test firing them. He twirled one around his finger and began to marvel at the sense of power they were beginning to give him. He knew Juan probably carried a gun at all times. Feeling safer, Edwin tucked one of the heavy pistols tightly behind his belt and held the other one in his hand as he walked across the living room, through the dining room, and into the kitchen, flicking the lights on with his elbow as he entered.

The kitchen was larger than one would have expected even for a house this size and was obviously equipped to satisfy even the most difficult chef. It sparkled with cleanliness. There was a long wooden table, scarred with over a hundred years of use, in the middle of the tiled floor. It weighed several hundred pounds, judging from its thick hardwood top and elephant-like legs. Dozens of gleaming pots and pans of all varieties and shapes hung down on racks directly over the table within easy reach of whoever was doing the cooking. A long row of windows looked out toward the now darkened Elk Park and the mountains beyond. Running along the wall under the windows and between them were a couple of institutional size stoves, two ovens, and three sinks. Their stainless steel shone brightly in the overhead lights.

Edwin skirted the table and headed for the large refrigerator and freezer along the far wall. He pulled one of the handles on the refrigerator and swung the thick door open. First, he pulled out two of the Nestlé Crunch bars he had stashed there right after he and Walt had landed, and put them in his shirt pocket. He had seen a movie once where the spy hid a gun in the refrigerator, and now he laid one of the

Colts on the top shelf behind a pot roast Mrs. Alison had thawed for the coming week.

Satisfied, he closed the refrigerator door and retraced his steps to the living room, turning out the lights as he went. He stood near the window and unwrapped one of the candy bars. Holding it in one hand, he pulled the other Colt from his belt and twirled it on his finger while he took a bite of the rich chocolate. Then he laid the gun on the end table and settled into the couch.

This would be his last dealing with Rivas and his organization. He simply didn't need them anymore and would make them understand this fact of life. If not, then he would have to get tough. If he could just get through the next two days or so, he'd be home free.

Also, he was out of coke. Maybe Juan and his sister would bring some more with them. Then he would quit for good.

On both counts Edwin was a fool.

CHAPTER 12

The Climb

The nylon tent door flapped in the wind, and Rod awoke with a start. Disoriented, he lay still for a time and rubbed his eyes. He tried to remember where he was at the moment. Then his aching back reminded him he was still curled up on his side, snug in his down sleeping bag on top of a very inadequate foam pad, in a small, blue nylon tent perched on a ledge just above the timberline in the middle of the Colorado wilderness. He had been so uncomfortable for so many hours he was surprised he had dozed off for a while. He rolled over on his back, trying not to twist the sleeping bag around him. He stretched his legs out and groaned. They were stiff and sore from the hike yesterday. His head ached from the altitude, and his teeth felt furry. There had been no water to brush with after the meal, and he hadn't felt like hiking all the way down to the river to get some more. He rolled onto his other side and lifted the bag just enough to make a hole for his nose and one eye. It was just beginning to get light, which surprised him even more. He had slept more than he thought.

Rod threw the bag back enough to expose his head. He took a deep breath of the mountain air and coughed. The air certainly had a chill to it, and he could easily see his breath. Jamie's sleeping bag lay empty next to his. A small ray of sunshine came through the door and made a little patch of light on his friend's bag. He was outside somewhere, hopefully fetching some water. Rod pulled the sleeping bag back over his head and felt the warmth again. Another light gust shook the tent, and the door snapped again. He could hear the wind rustle the stunted bushes, which hung over the rear of the tent.

Rod wasn't one of those people who awoke instantly. He liked to lie awhile in bed, thinking about his day or just dozing off again. The trouble now was that he wasn't home in Thornton on the Beautyrest like he should have been on a weekend morning. And his bladder was giving definite signals to him from below.

The two men had sat up talking outside the tent until almost midnight, bullshitting about this and that. They both talked about the future. Jamie had told a few more war stories from Vietnam and the years afterwards. Rod especially liked to hear these. They had even talked about the days back in Boulder and even further back in Indiana. Finally, they had squeezed into the small tent one at a time and zipped themselves up in their sleeping bags. Rod had felt tired but just couldn't fall asleep, so after a while he had propped himself up against his pack and read the book he had brought along, with the aid of his small flashlight balanced delicately over his shoulder. The altitude was giving him a headache, and it would be a couple of days before he acclimatized completely, though he lived in Denver at its mile-high elevation. His heart pounded in his chest, trying to catch up, even as he lay quietly in his sleeping bag. Years ago this had caused him some concern until Jamie had deduced that if either of them had a bad heart, the hike in would certainly have killed them.

Jamie had fallen asleep almost instantly. Rod had forgotten what it was like to share a small tent with him. Jamie constantly moved around in his sleep. Rod could usually count on being hit over the head with an arm or awakened with Jamie's considerable bulk pressing him to one side on the uneven tent floor. The snoring was the absolute worst thing.

It came from deep down inside Jamie somewhere and worked its way up and out with his breath like some primeval beast growling. The snoring had plagued Rod for the years they had slept in the same room back in Indiana and then later in Boulder. The trick was to somehow keep Jamie off his back. If Rod could accomplish that, then he had ten to fifteen minutes to fall asleep in the very temporary silence. Rod usually gave him a good shove to roll him over. Jamie was such a sound sleeper that even this didn't wake him most of the time. Years ago Rod had become accustomed to the din in the middle of the night.

Rod lay still for a few more moments and then decided that he must roust himself out of the warm sleeping bag to relieve himself. It was inevitable. Might as well get it over with, he thought. He sat up stiffly and pushed the sleeping bag down around his waist. He rubbed some more sleep from his eyes and ran his fingers through his tousled hair. He had placed his boots along the tent wall next to him, and he reached into one and pulled out his glasses. He put them on, and the world came into focus. Then he withdrew his legs from the bottom half of the sleeping bag and shivered. He picked up his wadded-up pants and sweater and pitched them through the tent door. Each boot soon followed. The small tent, built for lightness and compactness, was no place to try and dress unless the weather was bad. Barely high enough to sit up in at one end, it sloped sharply toward the other, allowing just enough room for the sleeper's feet, in order to save space and weight. Even now as he sat up, Rod's head grazed the tent's roof.

He rolled over and came to his hands and knees then crawled out of the tent. The bright sunlight sparkled on the frost on the nearby bushes and grass. Rod stood up stiffly in his long underwear and quickly donned the rumpled pants and sweater. He looked around for Jamie. The sun was just above the Collegiate Range on the far eastern horizon. Patches of fog hung here and there below on the distant Elk River as it wound its way through the ranch below. He glanced up at the sheer wall far above him and then up and down the gorge. The sun was still low in the eastern sky and cast dark shadows. Rocks and vegetation stood out in stark relief. The river roared far below and was complemented by the distant waterfalls upstream. The sky directly above was marred by high gray clouds, and although the sun was shining now, he knew they would lose it by the afternoon. He shivered and hurriedly finished buttoning his shirt as a small gust of wind wrapped itself around him. Then he stepped back into the bushes and relieved himself, wondering at the same time where Jamie could be.

He walked over to the large, flat rock and sat down. He pulled on his wool socks after checking again for blisters. There were some sore spots that would bear watching later, but besides those his feet seemed in good condition. He discovered the water bottles were missing and so went to look far below at the rushing water. He spotted Jamie's clothes next to the large dark pool where the river made its bend eastward. He quickly eyed the rest of the area below but saw no other traces of his friend. Rod felt a surge of panic, which soon faded. Jamie always had a habit of wandering off for a while by himself. He usually went exploring after supper or in the early morning, to fish or do some solo climbing. In the past Rod had spent some anxious moments after dark waiting for him to return to the tent. But he always came back.

Just as he began to reach into his pack to retrieve his binoculars, he saw Jamie break the surface of the pool and begin to swim to the rocky bank against the swift current. Rod wondered how his friend could stand the icy water. He shrugged. But that was Jamie, he thought, as he turned and began to fix breakfast.

There wasn't that much he could do without the water bottles, but he set about retrieving the food, stove, and pots and pans from the two packs. He was just giving the red fuel bottle a shake to gauge how much fuel was left when Jamie came bounding up to the rock from below, dropped his small nylon daypack on the ground, and pulled the two water bottles out. He handed them to Rod. In his other hand, he held his spinning rod and reel. His blond hair, wet and dark, dripped onto his sweater. Rod took the bottles in both hands, yawned, and began to fix breakfast. Jamie leaned the fishing rod and reel against the tent and took two giant steps over to the flat rock. His bootlaces dangled from his untied boots.

Still recovering from the jog up the steep slope, he asked breathlessly, "What's for breakfast, old buddy?"

Rod poured some of the water into a pot and then lit the stove with a butane lighter he had fished out of one of the pockets of his pack. The stove lit with a *whump* and roared as he adjusted the knob. "Oatmeal!" he replied.

Jamie grimaced and wrinkled his nose, "I was afraid of that. But at least, did you bring some sugar this time?"

Rod set the pan of water on the small but powerful stove. Perturbed, he said, "Yes, I brought some sugar. Besides, this is that instant stuff, and it's laced with maple flavor and brown sugar anyway." He yawned again and pointed behind Jamie. "Why don't you start taking the tent down? Make yourself useful."

Jamie turned and said over his shoulder, "OK. Hey, I slept like a baby last night. How about you?"

"Not too good. Must be the altitude."

Jamie got down on his hands and knees and stuck his head into the tent. He began removing their gear and talking at the same time. "C'mon, you were sleeping like a baby when I got up. Snoring pretty loud, too."

Rod watched the aluminum pot and thought of the proverb. Tiny silver bubbles were forming on the bottom. The gas stove put out a lot of heat in a hurry, but you had to watch how much you used because their gas supply was limited and could be used up quickly. They had two bottles, enough to last them the entire trip. The trick was to catch the water just as it came to a rolling boil and then quickly shut the stove off. He answered Jamie, "I was up all night with a sinus headache because of the altitude and listening to your snoring again. I forgot how hard it is to sleep in the same tent with you. You move around all night like some kind of big, old bear in his den. I can understand why you have that king-sized bed back in Louisiana."

"C'mon, I have it from reliable sources that my snoring is worth putting up with. Some people actually find it a real treat to spend the night with me." Jamie cleared his throat. "If you know what I mean."

"Yeah, but I'm not one of them. I should have brought some earplugs."

The water began a rolling boil, and Rod added the oatmeal then turned the stove down. He stirred the mixture with a spoon. A moment later he announced, "Breakfast's almost ready."

Jamie had finished dismantling the tent and frame and was about to start to fold it up but instead turned and dug his mess kit from his pack. Then he joined Rod on the rock. Both men sat cross-legged with the steaming pot between them as Rod dished the oatmeal out.

"God, I hate this shit. Feels like glue going down," Jamie said as he slowly mouthed the hot oatmeal.

Rod pulled from his nearby pack a small bottle, which contained orange Tang crystals; he emptied half the bottle into the remaining water bottle. He screwed the top back on and shook the bottle hard while answering Jamie's complaint about the oatmeal. "You sure didn't complain back home when mom fixed it for breakfast."

"Well, that was different. I was being polite. I didn't want to hurt your mom's feelings, you know. Hey, you know they make great freeze-dried breakfasts now, too. Bacon and eggs, omelets, sausage."

Rod took a swig from the Tang bottle and grimaced. The icy mountain water was still so cold it hurt his teeth. He passed the bottle over to Jamie, who was already almost done with his first bowl of oatmeal and holding it out for seconds.

Rod dished him up some more and answered his friend's suggestion. "Those breakfasts are awfully expensive and really don't fill you up much."

Jamie swallowed half the bottle of Tang and then hungrily attacked the second helping of oatmeal.

Rod asked, "How do you stand swimming in that cold water?"

"Aw, there's nothing to it as long as you're only in a few minutes and keep moving. Besides I was getting a little ripe and having a hard time living with myself." He wrinkled his nose. "You ought to try it."

Rod took the hint. "Well, you're just going to have to live with it. I'm not going swimming and freeze my nuts off." He reached over and finished off the Tang, tipping the bottle up to be sure to get the last of the undissolved orange crystal sludge in the bottom. "I do wish you'd tell me where you're going. If something happened, I wouldn't have a clue where to look for you. This is no place to take chances."

"You worry too much, grandma. Nothing's going to happen."

Rod said defensively, "I know, but there could have been some undercurrents or something down there in that river. If you get hurt, don't think I'm going to haul your ass out of here. You just shouldn't take any chances."

Jamie finished his second bowl of oatmeal, saw there wasn't any more in the pot, and leaned back on his elbows. "That shit sinks right to the bottom of your gut, you know that? Good stuff. I'm glad I thought of bringing it along for breakfast." Then he patted his stomach. "Boy, I'm full." He continued, "You know, never see any fish below the lake. Must be some kind of barrier down below, and I guess they never stock it—just the lake. You'd think some fish would make it down, but I guess the falls are just too high." He looked upstream. "I wonder how they do stock it."

Rod answered, "I saw a show on channel 9 last winter. The game and fish department stocks these lakes every three or four years. Mostly by airplane. A single-engine Cessna with a fish hopper on the bottom; but for really rough spots, they use a helicopter."

Jamie looked upstream again. "They probably stock Hourglass by airplane. This is mighty high for a loaded chopper."

Rod began busying himself with cleaning up the dishes and asked, "How high can you fly a helicopter?"

"Depends on the model and weight. Probably thirteen or fourteen thousand feet for most. But the important question is: how high can one hover with a load? A turbocharged airplane could handle the job here easily, I'd guess, as long as there was room to maneuver."

Rod digested this fact and continued straightening up the area.

Jamie spoke suddenly, "Let's say there were three of us on a desert island, and one of us died, okay?"

Rod answered carefully, "Yeah?"

"Let's say the dead person was, uh, Madonna. Could you carve her up?"

"Madonna? What would we be doing on an island with Madonna? The Mother of Christ? How do you think these things up?"

"No, I meant that cute singer."

"What singer?"

"You've never heard of Madonna, the singer?"

"No."

"Rodney, you've got to get out more. I think she's going to be big." Then Jamie asked again, "Well, could you do it? Carve a filet from a leg, fry it up, and eat it?"

Rod replied quickly, "No, I'd never be able to do something like that."

Jamie laughed. "I'll bet you could if you were hungry enough. You'd be amazed at what you can do if you have to."

"You're crazy, you know that?"

Jamie returned to packing the tent and began good-naturedly criticizing his friend for not fixing enough breakfast, although he felt full. If he was still hungry now, how was he going to make it to lunch? Rod knew he was joking and went about meticulously stowing the stove, dishes, and various utensils back into his pack. Dishwashing would have to wait until later, when they were closer to water.

Their backpacking trips had long ago lapsed into a routine: who slept on what side of the tent, who carried what equipment, who erected the tent, who led the climbs, or who did the cooking, for instance. Jamie was fond of saying the last chore was evenly divided: Rod did the cooking, and he did the eating. Jamie constantly complained about not having enough to eat but always seemed to live nonetheless. Rod didn't mind this at all. He actually liked the planning, measuring, and food buying. He kept a running three- or four-day menu in his head. Jamie carried the lion's share of the climbing equipment and the trash, which they packed out in a plastic garbage bag. This division of duties and other routines had evolved over the years.

Once the camp was finally struck and everything was back in its place, they hefted the heavy packs once again and started out for their final destination, Hourglass Lake, a mile farther and a thousand feet higher up the gorge. A person might be able to walk three miles an hour on flat ground, but it would take them almost three times that just to reach the base of the waterfall pouring directly from the lake. The clear air made distances deceptive, seeming much closer than in reality they were. There wasn't really a trail to follow and they were burdened with heavy packs at an elevation of over eleven thousand feet.

They gained altitude rapidly, though, as they slowly made their way along the almost sheer north wall. Even at that the river gained more, and soon they were picking their way with difficulty over and around the garage-sized rocks along its bank.

They lost the sun and its comparative warmth an hour after starting out as a high, gray overcast drifted in from the west. The air rapidly cooled at the high altitude, and even with their exertions, they had to don their wool sweaters.

The roar of the three-tiered waterfall at the lake's outlet grew steadily louder as they approached. Finally three hours after leaving the first camp, they arrived where it tumbled the last sixty feet onto the rocks at its base.

A fine mist sent up by the crashing water penetrated the entire area. It coated the rocks, making them slippery and dark. The roar was deafening now as each man halted just out of range of the fine spray and icy wind. They automatically looked above them first for a moment and then simultaneously struggled out of their packs. They leaned both of them against the moss-covered rocks at the base of the wall they would have to climb.

Rod dug quickly into his pack and pulled out his blue Gore Tex parka, which he quickly donned. Then he found a rock and sat down stiffly. Although his legs were tired, they already felt stronger than they did the day before, and he found that he was able to catch his breath much more quickly now. As he sat, his eyes followed the river downstream as it tumbled whitely from rapid to rapid before turning the bend for its final descent through the gorge and into Elk Park. The ranch was no longer visible from his vantage point. Except for their equipment, the vista was timeless. There was no sight of anything man-made now. They were completely alone.

They now had to negotiate the three pitches up to the lake above them. Then they could relax and fish for the next four days. Rod was beginning to savor every moment. It had been too long for both of them.

Jamie stood back from the base of the cliff and surveyed the route upward. Actually, it was just beginner's stuff and straightforward, although requiring climbing equipment. The climb consisted of three pitches. The lead climber would work his way up using small ledges and cracks to place his feet and hands. He would be protected from falling by a nylon harness around his waist and crotch, attached to a safety rope, which he would loop through the various nuts and chocks he would place in the cracks. These were hexagon-shaped pieces of metal of various sizes, with a loop of stainless steel cable secured through a hole in one side. A climber picked the correct size nut and jammed it into a crack in the rock, the theory being that any downward pull on the nut would wedge it in even tighter. The safety rope was then run through a carabiner, a metal oval of one half inch aluminum with a spring loaded gate in one of its sides much like a safety pin, which in turn was also attached to the cable through the nut. As the lead climber went upward, the safety rope was belayed or held by his companion below. If the lead climber fell, the other man holding the safety rope could pull it tight and arrest his fall. The lead climber would then only fall twice the distance from his last protective nut.

Once the lead reached a good stopping point, the roles were reversed. The lead now held the safety rope and belayed his companion, as the other man climbed up to him. If the lower climber fell, he would not fall far before his companion would arrest his fall. The lower man also pulled the nuts out as he passed them. At no time was the rope used as a direct climbing aid unless absolutely necessary.

Between the top of the climb, which terminated at the lake's outlet, and the base of the waterfall were two wide ledges that made perfect stopping places. The water tumbled some sixty feet initially before hitting the first ledge. Over thousands of decades the action of the falling water had eroded a channel out on this ledge so that the water did not immediately spill over the ledge but instead flowed along it for some one hundred feet before tumbling to the next ledge another forty feet below. Here it did the same thing and flowed in the opposite direction of the upper ledge before making its final sixty-foot plunge to where the two men were now standing. So from a distance, the overall view was one of three separate falls and not one continuous one of almost two hundred feet. This feature probably had saved the entire area from being the major tourist attraction such a high waterfall would become. That and the fact that the area was far from the major highways that crisscrossed Colorado and the peaks were not as high and spectacular as others in the state.

Jamie looked up again and followed the route up the first pitch. It was the easiest of the three in that it was not quite vertical and contained an almost continuous supply of small cracks and ledges in the very solid granite that provided easy hand- and footholds. He began to unload the necessary climbing gear from his pack.

Rod also dug into his pack and brought out one of his empty water bottles and a small plastic case. From the case he extracted a folding toothbrush and a small tube of Crest. He tiptoed across a few slippery rocks and approached the base of the falls. The spray began to coat his glasses and dampen his hair. He leaned out and held the open bottle under the flow. The bottle was almost jerked from his hand as the pounding water caught it. Although he withdrew it almost immediately, it was almost half full as he did so. He balanced himself precariously on two rocks and took a long drink. His teeth ached from the frigid water. Then he retreated and began to methodically brush his teeth.

Jamie meanwhile had continued laying out the climbing equipment. He raised his voice over the pounding water. "I don't fucking believe it. Here we are in the middle of nowhere, or at least as close as you're going to get in the lower forty-eight, and you're worried about oral hygiene. I'll bet Kit Carson or the other mountain men didn't worry about it. I sure didn't see Robert Redford floss after every meal in *Jeremiah Johnson*."

Rod took the brush from his foaming mouth and yelled. "Yeah, but I'll bet those mountain men had plenty of gum disease and a big dentist's bill each."

Jamie laughed and shook his head. "Do you want to lead the first pitch or should I?"

"Go ahead, you do it."

"All right by me. How about something to eat? That fucking oatmeal has just about worn off by now."

"I had planned lunch at the top."

"You're always trying to starve me. I'll bet I've lost five pounds already," Jamie complained as he pinched his hard stomach.

Rod took a drink from his bottle, swished it around, and spit it out. He poured the remainder over his toothbrush, cleaning it off. He raised his voice again over the water, "Tough shit. If I let you have your way, you'd have eaten all the food for the entire trip by this morning. Just like a big, old dog who doesn't know any better."

Jamie persisted, "C'mon, just a granola bar or something."

Rod pointed to the top. "Up there or nothing at all. We should have just enough food. I've planned it all out."

Jamie countered, "We always catch our fill of fish; you know that."

"And what if we don't? We'd have to leave early."

Jamie knew it was futile to argue any longer. And, of course, Rod was right. He always had things planned out perfectly right down to the last snack on the hike out.

Jamie finally had the climbing equipment sorted out next to his pack. It was a simple climb, and the leader would carry all the climbing equipment to reach each ledge safely. He would then use the safety rope to haul the packs up to him before the second man started the climb.

Despite the temperature Jamie stripped off his sweater and T-shirt and then his pants. He stuffed the clothing into his pack and pulled out a pair of worn denim cutoffs. When the weather wasn't a problem, he preferred climbing in just a pair of shorts and boots. It gave him greater freedom of movement. He next picked up a black sling of tough webbed nylon, which he stepped into and brought up around his waist. This was the safety harness. He secured it in the front with a carabiner. Next he tied one end of the sheathed blue-and-red climbing rope to the carabiner and gave it a tug. Then he attached a series of climbing nuts and carabiners to the sling. These he could pull off as he needed them on the way up. The pieces of hardware jingled and jangled as he made some final adjustments to the sling.

Satisfied that he was ready, Jamie took one final look up the first pitch and then over to Rod, who was just fitting his toothbrush back into its holder. He shouted over the waterfall, "Ready, asshole?"

Rod hurried, "Give me a second, okay?" Then he placed the toothbrush and toothpaste back in their case and then into one of the small pockets alongside the main compartment of his pack. He then withdrew a pair of leather gloves, a nylon sling identical to the one around Jamie's waist, and a battered orange climbing helmet from the pack. He straightened up and put on the helmet, securing the chinstrap. Then he walked over to his friend and took hold of the climbing rope. He sat down in front of a rock outcropping and braced his legs on a boulder in front of him while at the same time running the rope around his back and under his arms. Suitably braced he could absorb the shock if Jamie slipped and arrest his fall. Rod scooted around a little making himself more comfortable. Then he yelled, "Okay, I'm ready. On belay!"

Jamie nodded in his direction and then faced the granite. He shouted over his shoulder, "Climbing!"

Jamie always enjoyed the start as well as the finish of the climb. Reaching up, he found a suitable crack and pulled himself up with one hand. Then he wedged his left foot in another small fissure, which supported him while he felt above him for a still higher hold with the other hand. He found it and straightened his leg, being careful not to lean into the wall and lose what little friction he had.

Rod slowly let the rope slip through his hands and around his body as Jamie made progress. But Jamie still wasn't high enough to insert a nut yet. Rod suddenly worried about the depth perception problem Jamie had alluded to yesterday. When Jamie was almost twenty feet up the wall, Rod yelled, "You'd better put in some protection!"

Jamie paid no attention, although Rod knew he must have heard him. Jamie was now approaching some forty feet above the starting point, and still he had put in no chocks to arrest him should he lose his footing. Rod was becoming more nervous by the foot as he tilted his head back to follow Jamie's progress. The height was fatal now. It was useless to yell over the roaring water. There was a nice, deep crack that ran the last twenty feet to the ledge, and Jamie quickly and deftly ascended this route to the top of the first pitch. He hauled himself onto the broad ledge and finally looked down at Rod some sixty feet below. Grinning, he indicated that everything was fine with a thumbs-up. It was Rod's turn as soon as the packs were hauled up by rope. Rod placed his leather gloves in his pack. It would now be Jamie's turn to belay him.

It only took a few minutes to secure the packs and haul them up to the first ledge. Both men indicated they were ready with hand signals. As he climbed Rod felt nervous and out of practice. His arms and legs felt weak. It had been quite a few years. Jamie should never have chanced the climb without a safety rope. But now, as the low man, if Rod should slip, he would only fall a few feet before Jamie caught him with the belay. As he climbed his breath became shorter, but his confidence grew. Soon he, too, was sitting on the ledge, catching his breath, as Jamie secured the rope. His arms and legs felt weak from the exertion.

They climbed the second pitch in rapid order. Jamie first—still with no protection—the packs second, and finally Rod last.

The third pitch was easy, and would bring them up to the lake quickly, but at this point, traditionally, they liked to sit on the second ledge, facing outward, to catch their breath, have a drink of water, and take in the view before the final climb. The feeling was much the same as waiting upstairs on Christmas morning until your parents woke up. And it was a pretty nice place to sit for a while. Both men were perched underneath an overhang, with their backs resting against the rock wall. Jamie dangled his legs over the edge, while Rod tucked his knees up against him. The view down the granite slabbed gorge was terrifying at this height as the river tumbled between its walls. At this location the base of the uppermost waterfall was some fifty feet to their right. Its clear, icy water tumbled onto their ledge and then abruptly made a right angle into a trough cut into the ledge. The water raced darkly through the trough toward the two men before making another abrupt turn just a few feet from them and tumbling downward.

Rod brought out his camera and took a picture of the scene then laid the camera next to his pack. Jamie offered him a half-full water bottle, and he took a long drink. Rod wiped his lips with his sleeve and set the bottle between them. Both men sat silently for a few moments as they gazed out at the panorama between their knees. The view was all the better because of the effort they had made to get there and the fact that they didn't have to share it with anyone. As Jamie had said earlier, this was not a place you just parked the car and skipped up the trail to see with all the other tourists.

Jamie said, "Sure is grand, isn't it."

Rod nodded at the understatement. No answer was necessary. Jamie picked up the water bottle and finished it. Rod picked up his camera again.

Rod said, "You know, this is my favorite place. I'd like to get a picture of the two of us here, but there just isn't room enough to set the camera anywhere and get a shot."

"There would be if you weren't so cheap and bought yourself a wide-angle lens. Besides, what do you want a picture for? I think it's better to rely on my memory."

"I don't know, just to have for posterity I guess. Someday we'll be too old to get up here. Do you ever think about that? I mean, getting old that is. I want to be able to sit in the nursing home with my pictures and rock back and forth."

Jamie just grunted, picked up a pebble, and threw it over the ledge.

Rod cleared his throat and continued, "You know, last night when you were talking about Vietnam, I remembered something that's been bothering me off and on for a long time."

Jamie turned to Rod. "Yeah, what's that, old buddy?"

"Well, it's just that it's been a long time ago, but I can't ever remember writing to you when you were over there. I remember keeping in touch when you were in basic training and then flight school—even Alaska, Germany, and Saudi Arabia. But not in Vietnam. I can't explain it. I guess it was the times. I'm really sorry."

Jamie turned and pitched another rock over the ledge. He knew this had probably been hard for Rod to say, and it had upset him at the time that he had never heard from his friend in the two years he had served there. "That was almost twenty years ago now, you know. It's hard to believe sometimes. Just don't worry about it anymore. But I do think I got a couple from you if it makes you feel any better."

Rod smiled. "It's just that I was caught up in all the protests and my schoolwork. I just can't believe I could have been that selfish not to have written more, now that I know all that you were going through over there. Anyway, I'm glad you guys finally got your memorial in Washington. You deserved it."

Jamie hadn't expected this and was at a temporary loss for words. He chucked another rock over the ledge. Then he said, "Thanks, Rodney, that meant something to me." Then he looked down. "A hell of a lot of guys needed that day in DC a few years ago. Did I tell you I went up there for it?"

"No, you didn't."

"Yeah, me and another ex-cav pilot I work with. Never met him in-country. Different tours. We couldn't commandeer a ship from the company, so we drove straight through from New Orleans to DC in my car."

Rod faked surprise. "You mean it made it?"

"Made it up and back. Don't be bad-mouthing my cars. Anyway, we arrived all decked out in our old flight suits with the medals pinned on and everything. Didn't have any idea what to expect."

"You still have your uniform?"

"Yeah, it was stashed away with some other souvenirs. But, anyway, we got there in time. Sure didn't expect all that happened." He hesitated for a moment and looked downstream into the gorge. "There were thousands of guys there. Most in some bits of uniform. God, it was great to see them!" Then he joked and laughed, "I'm sure glad I'm not getting old like the rest of them. Anyway, later I went up to the National Cathedral and listened to the roll call. I was too late for one of the guys who was killed on one of my ships. Guy by the name of Brown—a door gunner. Real funny guy from South Carolina. Got it just as we took off one day after dropping some grunts in the bush. Never knew what hit him. But I heard them read Chuckie Martinez's name. He was another crewmember who got shot on a rescue mission. Died later in the hospital." He paused. "Later I saw their names on the wall along with a couple of other pilots I knew over there." He paused once more and wiped a finger along the corner of one eye. "Goddamn, I can't believe how young we all were over there!"

Both men sat silent for a moment then Rod asked, "Would you do it again?"

Jamie kicked the back of his heels against the rock and answered, "I wouldn't trade the experience for anything, but I would never, never want to repeat it. No way, no how would I ever want anyone shooting at me again. I was extremely lucky, old buddy."

"But you're a good pilot."

Jamie looked slyly at his friend. "Yeah, I'll buy that, but looking back I can't believe how little I really knew or the shit some of us pulled over there. I was extremely lucky."

Rod looked at his friend. "Well, whether the war was right or wrong, I just wanted you to know that I think you did a good job, and I'm proud to be your friend and I was especially proud when you won the medal... that might sound a little corny but..."

"And in a costume." Jamie laughed and laid his hand on Rod's shoulder. "Thanks a lot for saying that; it means more to me than you might think." He hesitated. "Now let me tell you what happened at the end of that day at the wall dedication."

"Okay."

"Well, like I said before, there were thousands of people there: vets, moms, dads, wives, sons and daughters, and grandpas and grandmas. The damn US government even bought the beer. Park Service, I guess. Free hotdogs. Everybody's having a good time afterward. After a while I had to take a piss. Then I found out the people who organized the shindig forgot the portable toilets. There wasn't a one in sight. So I hotfooted it over to the Lincoln Memorial. Damn, you should have seen the line! So I had to finally jump down in some bushes near the Kennedy Center. Hero returns to Washington!"

Both men laughed.

Rod stood up stiffly and began to prepare for the final pitch to the lake above. The route was an easy one, following a crack that gradually became wider and less steep as it cut deeper and deeper into the rock wall.

Jamie stood up also and stretched.

Rod said, "I'll take the lead on the final pitch."

This surprised Jamie, but he said, "Okay, your turn, old buddy." Then he prepared to belay his friend.

When both men were ready, Rod began working his way up the face by jamming his hands and feet into the widening fissure. He set his first chock at ten feet above the ledge they had rested on and continued upwards. Although he had felt strong at the beginning of the day, the combination of exertion and altitude was beginning to wear on him. He could feel the energy drain from his arms and legs. Perhaps they should have eaten lunch or at least had a snack on the ledge below.

Jamie sat on the ledge, gradually letting the climbing rope slip through his hands as Rod climbed higher. In a few moments, Rod was out of sight above in the cool, dark crevice. They now had to depend on voice signals made more difficult by the roar of the nearby falls. Jamie could feel the other man's progress by the feel of the rope as he slowly let it pay out.

The crack widened as Rod slowly made his way up. He added another chock for protection. Some water seeped here and there, but miraculously none of the lake water could flow in this direction because it was blocked off apparently by a solid wall of granite. In the crevice now, the roar of the falls was muted. Little by little, the angle began to lessen until finally he was no longer climbing but instead scrambling easily up and around some large boulders that had lodged in the fissure. Rod looked upward twice but could only see the sky, now the color of pewter. The rope slowly trailed out behind him.

He paused once to wipe some sweat from his forehead. The air now definitely had taken on a chill. Suddenly, as he hoisted himself onto the last rock lodged in the fissure, he was at the level of the lake itself and could see his surroundings. He raised himself up onto the top of the boulder. His arms and legs were shaking from the exertion, and he almost lost his balance. Cupping his hands around his mouth, he yelled, "Off belay!" Then he gave the rope three sharp tugs.

Jamie knew now that Rod was at the top and attached the first pack to the rope. He gave Rod a sharp tug, and the other man began hauling up the first heavy pack. They repeated this for the second pack, and then it was Rod's turn to belay his friend up the final pitch. Rod sat on top of the boulder next to the packs with his feet firmly braced and slowly took in the slack as Jamie made the climb.

Jamie made good progress, and finally Rod could hear him just below, where the angle lessened. Jamie could easily scramble up the last few yards and yelled, "Off belay!" Rod stood and took in the rest of the rope. He coiled it around his forearm and then turned around, while waiting for Jamie to join him, and took in his surroundings. The very edge of the lake was close, perhaps twenty yards away and slightly below him over a rocky shoreline. The air was still now, and the glassy surface reflected the somber, gray granite walls and matching sky. Except for the water, Rod thought it resembled some earthly moonscape.

To his left some fifty yards, the outlet gurgled stream-like and shallow from the lake itself for those twenty yards in and around some well-worn boulders before suddenly disappearing over the edge. The sound of the falling water far below was hushed here. They would have to jump from boulder to boulder across the outlet stream to reach the campsite, the only flat, tundra-covered place around the entire rocky shoreline suitable for their tiny tent.

A rock careened down from far above, unseen in the distance, and the noise directed Rod's attention. He looked out across the lake into the long, narrow cirque which held it. More rocks fell as the first one dislodged others. Then it was silent once more.

The cirque had been literally scooped and ground out by its glacier thousands of years previous. The ice had melted, leaving this splendid basin and the lake.

The lake itself was about a half of a mile long, a few hundred yards wide at both ends, narrowing in the middle to perhaps fifty yards by its most prominent feature, two sheer cliffs guarding either side. These made travel to the upper end impossible. The shoreline of boulders disappeared on either side at the precipices, and the rock went sheer into the inky depths. The lake, seen from above a long time ago by perhaps the first miners in the area, was thought to resemble an hourglass in shape. The name stuck and had been printed on every map for the last one hundred years.

Except for the small rocky shoreline on either side of the sheer cliffs, which pinched the lake in the middle, tall vertical walls of granite enclosed the entire lake on both of its sides and upper end. The one and only break in the encircling walls was to Rod's right, at the lower end of the lake. Here the sheer walls had eroded and created a steep boulder-filled ramp up to the ridge on the north side of the cirque. With some difficulty a fit person could scramble up this rocky ramp and then follow the ridge to the summit of Mt. Grant overlooking the lake. The two men had made this climb on three different occasions.

Rod heard Jamie grunting just below and knew he would finish the climb soon. He turned and jumped lightly from rock to rock until he was standing at the water's edge. He remained still and peered down into the dark, clear water for a moment. Suddenly, three dark shapes appeared to his right, sleekly and effortlessly following the shoreline toward him. He remained absolutely still, and they slid by barely three feet from the toes of his boots. The big one in the middle was perhaps twenty inches long. The two flanking ones were a good fifteen inches. He could make out the individual spots on their backs quite easily— native cutthroat. The large one lazily fanned his wide tail and poked his nose above the surface, sucking in a microscopic insect and swirling the water. Rod held his breath. Suddenly, five more appeared behind the three leaders. Rod backed up slowly until he was out of their line of sight and then hopped back over the rocks to the edge of the precipice.

Jamie's head appeared just as Rod peered over the edge. Jamie quickly completed the climb and, somewhat breathlessly, stood with his hands on his hips and took in his surroundings just as Rod had done. He simply said, "Nice."

Rod answered, "Yeah, sure is. Better than any cathedral."

Then the two men secured their climbing equipment and hefted the packs for the final time. They jumped from rock to rock across the stream and walked up a little slope to their campsite.

CHAPTER 13

Family Reunion

The two men sat and worried over their respective secrets. The silence was broken only by the steady ticking of the antique grandfather clock in the corner, the wind occasionally rattling the window pane, and the infrequent, muted blast of the shotgun outside. Both men silently wished the next twenty-four hours would pass more quickly.

Juan Rivas sat at one end of the long, leather couch, trying his best to concentrate on an old edition of *Guns and Ammo* magazine he had found while inspecting the firearms cabinet. He held it open on one knee, mainly looking at the pictures. Reading was not one of his better skills. The large, old log house was cold, and he felt chilled to the bone dressed only in a white silk shirt open at the collar and a pair of tan, sailcloth pants tied off with a belt of the same fabric. He wore a large gold religious medallion around his neck on a gold chain. The table next to him held a quarter-glass of gin with the remainder in a bottle next to it. The alcohol had had little effect. He was still cold. His plan was now in motion, but he worried at all the variables: too many different possibilities, too many people involved, too many things that could go wrong.

Things had started out badly right from the start at Denver's impossible airport. The flight had been late, and Debbie had been forced to rent a small, four-door compact car herself instead of the Lincoln Continental as had been promised to Juan by another car rental company. He had offered the girl at that rental car counter first a hundred dollar bill, then two hundred dollars for a better car, but she had just shrugged her shoulders and said she was sorry, but there wasn't a big car available from any rental agency at the airport. They had driven the little car into downtown Denver, and, inexplicably, their reservation for one of the top-floor suites had been lost. The idiot manager had never met Debbie and didn't believe at first that she was really the sister of the owner. After repeated calls to the ranch, with no answer, they had been forced to accept a smaller room. Juan believed that the fat guy at the other end of the couch eating a candy bar was directly responsible for the reservation mix-up. He'd get even soon.

The next day Juan had begun to immediately hate Colorado and its mountains, as the underpowered car limped over one high pass after another. He longed for the straight, flat interstates of southern Florida and his powerful Mercedes. Debbie enjoyed the scenery and made him pull off numerous times to view it. Juan stayed in the little car with the heater running full blast. Finally, after a ridiculously long seven-hour drive, they pulled up in front of a large, Lincoln log house with the radiator steaming. The heater had quit back in Buena Vista. As far as Juan was concerned, Debbie could have this godforsaken state, its bumpkins—like the old hag and the dog at the gas station in the last town, where he had filled the tank—its ski areas, lakes, hunting lodges, trout streams, and snow-capped mountains. Debbie had sensed this, and they had driven in silence for the last hour, except when she had to give him instructions on where to turn. The red temperature light glared at them for the last twenty miles. And the oil light joined its little friend as they pulled into the driveway. And to top it all off, they had slept in separate bedrooms last night. Well, patience. He'd be rid of them all in twenty-four hours and off to a much warmer climate—for good.

He turned the page and looked at the pictures accompanying an article on a new everyman's 9 mm automatic with a fifteen-shot clip, for home defense. Impatient, he looked up from the magazine and out the large front windows. The mountains were now dull and gray under the overcast in the early evening light.

Ideally, one of the airplanes would have arrived this evening and the other tomorrow morning, and he would be on his way soon after the second one landed. Now even that was in jeopardy. He had spoken to Las Vegas just a short while ago and, because of a mechanical problem, the San Francisco connection was going to be hours late landing at the Las Vegas airport. The earliest it could arrive would be tomorrow morning. Juan had tried to suppress his anger at the foul-up, because it would have been out of character for him not to expect all the money. Besides, what were a few hours, more or less? Edwin had even dispatched his own airplane and pilot up to San Francisco almost cheerfully. This had been puzzling, and Juan was suspicious because it usually took a few threats to get the lazy slob to do something. Juan took another sip of gin and mentally tried to work out the new timetables for the airplanes. Today was Sunday, so one should arrive in the morning, and now the other one tomorrow afternoon. Their arrivals should have been almost simultaneous, if planned well, but he quickly thought of all the variables again. But a few hours apart would be just fine in the end.

He took another careful sip of gin. He had just a quarter of the bottle left. And to his amazement, he had found that this was all that was left in the house. What kind of rich people were these? No booze. And Edwin had said the nearest liquor store was almost sixty miles away!

He impulsively looked at his Rolex again. It dangled loosely on his wrist on its gold band. Then he looked out the window past the little rental car. God, how he hated this cold, windswept place. Nothing to do. Not even a damn TV to watch. You'd think these rich fucks would have installed one of those new satellite dishes by now. It was going to be a long twenty-four hours.

Edwin sat up at the other end of the couch and reached for another handful of Kleenex on the table next to him, simultaneously knocking over one of the empty Coke cans. He wished he could close his eyes and make everything disappear. He was dressed rustically but warmly in an old, red flannel shirt, a light blue wool cardigan, tan wool trousers, and old black field boots. Just the bottom button of the sweater was fastened over his huge stomach. It didn't reach his belt line far below, leaving six inches of shirt below it. He blew his red nose once more and added the tissues to the pile in the trashcan at his feet. It must be true about stress causing a cold, he thought.

Blam!

Another blast rattled the windows, and both men flinched. Edwin saw Juan instinctively start to reach for the black automatic tucked into his waistband and then relax.

Edwin blew his sore, red nose again and added the tissue to the pile again. He hated the man next to him. He had even thought of killing him since he had arrived with his sister. His death would solve a lot of problems. He had decided not to tell Juan and his sister about selling the hotel chain. He just wanted the deal completed and both of them gone forever. Edwin glanced over at the grandfather clock patiently keeping time in the corner. He did some quick mental calculations. Just another twenty-four hours, and he would be safe—and much richer.

Blam!

Another shot rattled the window again. Both men flinched again.

Damn her, Edwin thought. It's all my smart-ass little sister's fault I'm in this mess. What if the FBI or the DEA or whoever took care of drug smugglers were surrounding the house right now and getting ready to move in just as soon as the airplane touched down? Was there any guarantee this wouldn't happen? How long would someone like himself last in a prison? Not long, he knew. Some big muscle-bound prisoner's lover: that's how it would end up. And all the publicity after his arrest would certainly sour the deal for the hotel chain being worked out right now in Boston. The business would slip into bankruptcy in less than six months, and he would be left with nothing but a jail cell.

He glanced at the clock yet again. Less than a minute had passed. It was going to be the longest twenty-four hours of his life. To make matters worse, he was almost out of Cokes and candy bars.

Edwin looked at the Cuban. Juan looked back and smiled, displaying two perfect rows of white teeth.

Debbie Forsyth watched with satisfaction the clay pigeon disintegrate twenty-five yards in front of her. She lowered the over and under shotgun from her shoulder. She cradled it in the crook of her left arm and broke the gun open. Two smoking, red plastic and brass shotgun shells popped out and landed at her feet with the other spent ones.

Her long auburn hair was tied back in a girlish ponytail. She wore comfortable clothes: a time-softened green chamois shirt tucked into an equally time-softened pair of tan corduroy trousers she had dug out of one closets in her room at the ranch. They were clean yet smelled that certain musty scent of clothes packed away too long. She wore a dark green, quilted down vest over the shirt. Her arms were free to handle the shotgun. A pair of dusty Wellington boots, also found way back in a corner of the closet, adorned her feet. One pants leg was tucked into one of the boots while the other hung casually outside. Because it had become cloudy, her mirrored aviator-style sunglasses were stuck by their earpieces into her hair, well back on her head.

Her brother had been kind enough to point out the fact that there were more than a few gray hairs beginning to show when she and Juan had arrived last night. It had been pleasant of him to do so she had thought.

Still cradling the shotgun in her left arm, she reached into the right pocket of the vest and pulled out two more of the twelve gauge shells. She deftly placed each of them in the chambers and snapped the gun shut. Then she placed the safety on before she bent over, loaded the portable trap with two more clay pigeons with her free hand, and cocked it. The gun, a Browning presentation model, had been given to her father years ago by an Arabic sheik, who had stayed at the Las Vegas Forsyth and had enjoyed his stay, despite losing big at the craps table. As she straightened up, she ran her fingers over the exquisite engravings on each side of the silver-plated receiver. They depicted a hunter, gun at the ready, leaning forward behind his retriever, who was excitedly pointing at two fleeing pheasants.

A gust of wind whipped her ponytail over her shoulder as she remembered her father. He had loved this place as much as anything he had in the world, and it wasn't until she had come over the last hogback into the broad valley, which held the ranch, its meandering river, and the house, that she had realized just how much she had missed this place, and Colorado in general. She had felt a definite sadness as they had driven up in front of the impressive log home. It suddenly had seemed to her just a hollow shell without her father to bring it alive.

Debbie readied herself and stepped on the foot trigger. The two clay pigeons leaped toward the mountains beyond. One arched out straight from her. This one she easily pulverized with her first shot. The other one flew wildly to her right, and she deftly swung the barrel to follow it. In a split second, she had led it just right and hit it just at the gun's effective range. It also disappeared in a puff of dust, and the roar of the gun echoed down the broad valley.

Satisfied with her performance, she allowed herself a smile, broke the gun again, and ejected the spent shells. She reached into her vest pocket for two more shells, but found it empty. She had been keeping score with herself and now had used up two boxes of ammunition. She had missed three clay pigeons out of forty. She allowed herself another smile. Not bad. She still had it after almost seven years. There was no more ammunition in the house for the shotgun, and if she wanted more, it would be a long drive into Crestridge. Besides, most of the stores would be closed on Sunday evenings.

Debbie shrugged and decided that would be enough target practice for one day. She laid the shotgun over her shoulder and grasped the barrel with one hand under the wooden forestock. The shoulder portion of the stock hung down her back. She felt hungry, suddenly remembering she hadn't eaten since an early breakfast in her determination to be at her favorite spot on the river early. The place was a large deep pool in the midst of a jungle of willow bushes, where the river made a hairpin bend near the road a mile or so below the house. It was here, those years ago, where she had caught the huge brown trout hanging on the wall in her old bedroom at the ranch. The thrill of landing that big fish was still fresh in her memory. At first she thought she had snagged the bottom, until her line had amazingly and suddenly zoomed downstream and her reel had screamed as the trout pulled the backing from it. It took forty minutes of careful work to finally land him a quarter mile downstream. Nearly thirty inches long, it gashed her thumb with its teeth when she at last picked him up by the jaw. She proudly brought it back to the house to show her father, but he had just been leaving for a hurried business trip and had only glanced over his shoulder and waved as he boarded the airplane. Of course, her brother was jealous of the catch, and she had hidden the fish in one of the freezers and then begged the housekeeper to drive her all the way into Gunnison in order to take it to a taxidermist. He had mounted it in a curled fighting position with her fly still in its mouth. On the mounting board below were the date, place, and time of the catch, with an estimate of the weight, six and one half pounds.

To her delight upon returning home yesterday, she had found the big trout still on her bedroom wall. Her favorite fly rod was still faithfully leaning in one corner where she had left it. Mrs. Alison had cleaned the room of course but had left things exactly as they were.

This morning she had fished her favorite spot by the road for a few hours. Fog shrouded the willows and left big, round water droplets on the remaining leaves. She suddenly began reflecting on the direction her life had taken for the past years. She had been feeling tired and drawn out. Could age finally be catching up? No, it was more than that. Her thinking had begun to take a more responsible direction, too. Things in her life that had caused excitement suddenly seemed stupid and childish. Was this maturity at last? If so, it had taken a long time. Her attention was broken only by two small brown trout.

Now walking back to the house with the shotgun draped over her shoulder, her mind turned to the two men inside. She knew them now for the losers they were and realized just how much she hated each.

Her brother had been given every opportunity in life that she hadn't. He had bungled everything through stupidity and weakness. Why hadn't her father seen this? It was a puzzle. Maybe her father's generation viewed things differently when it came to women in powerful positions—a mindset that would be hard to break. She had some terrific ideas for the hotels. They just might turn things around. The business after all was partly hers.

She thought of the Cuban. Sure he acted in the macho manner that he thought was expected of him, but he was another weak man. She knew of the trouble he was in with his partners. He had been handed every opportunity that America was capable of and had turned to crime. She felt the weight of the shotgun on her shoulder and casually thought she could solve any problem with the Cuban quickly. Then she realized there was no more ammo for the gun and laughed to herself. He wasn't worth a prison sentence.

She stepped onto the wide circular driveway and hesitated. She looked at the house—the house where she had grown up. Yes, she had forgotten how much she loved this place, and yet she had turned her back on it for the past years. She felt an overwhelming desire to live here by herself without the complications of the two men inside. Somehow start over with a clean slate. Maybe actually try and run the place as a real working ranch once more. Then she remembered her hunger and continued toward the front steps.

CHAPTER 14

Storm Clouds

The low-pressure system intensified over California and then roared into Arizona before stalling momentarily against a high-pressure system over the central plains. But it wouldn't be stationary for long. As it sat over the desert, its counterclockwise rotation combined with the clockwise rotation of the high began pumping more moisture northward from the Pacific Ocean and Mexico, thus feeding itself. A tornado was reported in the Los Angeles area—a very rare occurrence. It began to rain hard in Las Vegas and later in the day in both Phoenix and Tucson. Rain didn't affect the activity in Las Vegas, but golf tournaments in the other two large desert cities had to be cancelled, along with a myriad of other outdoor activities. Flash flood warnings were posted. It began to snow at the Grand Canyon and other higher elevations.

Meanwhile, the first cold front of the season began to move rapidly out of Washington and Oregon into Montana. Helena reported six inches of new snow. Then Butte topped this with nine inches. By Sunday evening the front was south of Yellowstone National Park in Wyoming and headed for Colorado.

Also by Sunday evening, the high pressure over the plains, responsible for the nice fall weather in Denver, began to break down. This caused the low over Arizona to begin to move northeastward into New Mexico and the Four Corners area. The two weather systems would collide over the Colorado Rockies.

CHAPTER 15

Northbound

The cockpit smelled of old paint and cracked leather, of aviation oil and high-octane gasoline, of new plastic and simmering state-of-the-art microchips, and of the sweat of the hundreds of pilots and mechanics who had worked in its small confines during the last forty years.

George sat in the copilot's seat with his unlit pipe clamped hard between his teeth. He dared not smoke. He twirled a finger over his head and signaled the men outside in front of the airplane. They also rotated a finger and gave him a thumbs-up as he pushed the left engine's starter button. The propeller began to rotate slowly. George counted silently as each propeller blade rotated past the cockpit. Satisfied, he adjusted the mixture control slightly with his free hand. The engine coughed twice and belched some blue smoke from its exhaust stacks. He leaned forward a bit in his seat to make sure two of the men outside with the fire extinguishers were still in place. The top of the cockpit was made up of two green, tinted pieces of Plexiglas hinged in the middle. Their surfaces were streaked with water droplets even though the rain had ceased an hour ago. They were now propped open to the cool, night air as he continued to hold the starter button, while now simultaneously moving the left throttle a fraction of an inch. They were propped open for a good reason. They would provide an escape in case of fire. The wings and fuselage of the airplane were crammed with about thirty-two hundred gallons of high-octane aviation fuel. The left engine coughed twice more and suddenly caught with a roar. The propeller instantly was transformed into a spinning, silver disk, and flame shot from the exhaust stacks.

The old mechanic carefully checked the engine gauges. The oil pressure had risen nicely into the green arc on the gauge, and the oil temperature was starting to rise. Satisfied with this, he throttled the engine back into a loping idle. Then he motioned for the two men with the fire extinguishers to walk around to the right engine. As he watched them struggle around the nose of the black airplane with the heavy red bottles, he saw two other men in the shadows near the trees with automatic rifles, looking warily around the airstrip. Still two others sat in a jeep near the right wing. One was slumped in the driver's seat, and the other stood in the back with one arm draped over the heavy machine gun mounted in the rear. George diverted his attention back to the instrument panel. All the gauges glowed brightly now that the left engine's generator was on line.

Tim appeared in the cockpit and stowed some last-minute gear. Then he squeezed into the left seat just as George signaled the men outside that he would be starting the right engine. They gave him the standard thumbs-up sign again, and he hit the starter. It whined, and the big propeller started to turn slowly. He counted the blades passing by the cockpit. But unlike the other one, this engine caught quickly and roared into life. George idled it back, and now both engines were running smoothly with a loud rumble. The vibration could be felt all throughout the airplane. The sound and feel of the large radial engines brought joy to George's heart. There is not a sweeter sound, he thought. What had been hundreds of pieces of dead metal had been brought to life.

Now that both engines were alive, George would ride with Tim to the end of the airstrip. There they would allow the engines to warm up and test them at maximum power along with the other systems in the airplane. If both men were satisfied, Tim would be committed to the almost twelve-hour flight.

While the old man was starting and checking the right engine, Tim sat in the left seat and adjusted it. Then he began to unfold charts and put them on the clipboard resting on his lap. The evening was cool, even at this latitude, and would be downright frigid at the high altitude he would initially have to fly. He was dressed warmly in a pair of drab, insulated flying coveralls over a sweater, wool shirt, and surplus army fatigue pants. He also wore his old air force baseball hat and a grimy pair of brown cowboy boots with heavy socks. Tim was glad the past weeks of sitting around in this remote corner of the world were over and it was time for another flight. He was awake and alert and sober. At last, some action. The entire airframe seemed to tremble with the same anticipation, as the engines idled. He could hardly contain his enthusiasm and excitement as he readied himself for the long flight.

Tim and George had started inspecting the old airplane two hours ago. They had made sure everything was in order. Nothing had been overlooked. There were no suspicious leaks, and all the hydraulic fluid levels were full. The airplane was really in fine order. George had done an excellent job of restoring it to almost perfect condition. Previous trips had gone without a hitch. Then, after they had finished their inspections, the airplane had been laboriously fueled with the necessary high-octane gasoline hauled a long distance over the mountains by tank truck.

The cargo had been delivered earlier in the day by two heavily armed military-type helicopters, which sat to one side of the airstrip. Their uniformed crews were now spread out around the airstrip with their automatic weapons. These men had neither smiled nor talked to anyone.

The cargo consisted of five hundred carefully wrapped packages, each containing two kilos of some of the highest grade cocaine in the world. Properly cut, the value was close to $30 million on the street. Tim would make more money for this one trip than the most senior airline pilot in the United States would make in a year, or even two. The packages were properly secured directly behind the cockpit and forward of the first fuel tank.

After the cargo had been loaded, Tim had brought aboard his flight bag and the survival gear he insisted on carrying in the airplane. He had stowed these in the cockpit.

Now he sat in the left seat and slowly went over a personal checklist to ensure that all his equipment was in the aircraft. The Israeli-manufactured Uzi machine gun was in a scabbard behind his seat with four extra clips of ammunition. His Browning 9 mm automatic pistol was secured in a shoulder holster under his left arm with extra clips. These two items were the last ones on the checklist.

He folded the checklist over the top of the clipboard and began to program the navigational radios. The trip north no longer included any dead reckoning. The US government had helped out immensely on that account. Although the airframe was nearly forty years old, the communication and navigation radios and weather radar in the airplane's instrument panel were state-of-the-art. The latest TCAS collision-avoidance system was also installed, not so much to avoid a midair collision as to watch front and rear for other aircraft. This would be very important near the coastline of the United States and Mexico. In addition, the aircraft contained a very sophisticated autopilot. Most airline pilots would be envious of the instrument panel.

It was possible for Tim to use three types of navigation. First were the usual VHF communication and VOR radios that were mainly used to navigate in the United States. For this type of operation, these served mainly as backup. Second, was the latest LORAN receiver which could be used with accuracy within a few hundred miles of the coastline. The US Coast Guard maintained these transmitters throughout the country. LORAN had been a boon to smugglers after the electronic revolution had permitted the receivers to be scaled down to just a few pounds and usable in a small aircraft. But the best news yet was the third navigation system installed in the old A-26 bomber. This was the new GPS, or Global Positioning System, by satellite. Over the past few years the US military had launched a network of satellites. Thanks to the US government Tim's GPS set and backup one could home in on four of these at one time and accurately give his altitude, groundspeed, winds aloft, course and time to his next waypoint, and his position anywhere on Earth within a hundred feet. It was even more accurate for the military. Because of this, navigation for Tim was very easy. He could fly the very shortest route to his destination unerringly and thread a needle between two continents, while remaining over international waters and hopefully under any radar.

He doubled-checked each latitude and longitude for each waypoint and programmed them into the navigation radio. He punched various small buttons and watched the bright digital numbers on the radio's display swallow the numbers. Satisfied with his entries, Tim made one more visual sweep of the cockpit area ensuring all was in order. He fastened his seatbelt and shoulder harness and pulled both tight. Then he stowed the clipboard for the time being and put his left hand on the control wheel and his feet on the rudder pedals.

Reacting to the nervous excitement he always felt before a flight, going back to his military days, he punched George on the shoulder and gave him the thumbs-up signal. Normal conversation was impossible in the open cockpit. To be heard both men would have to yell. To save their voices, they used hand signals as much as possible. George rubbed his shoulder with one hand and motioned for Tim to take the throttles.

Tim gave one of the men outside the signal to remove the wooden chocks in front of and behind the nose wheel, placed his right hand on both throttles, and gently pushed them forward. The roar of the engines increased as the airplane came alive. The old Douglas bomber strained a little and then slowly began to inch forward on its long journey. George turned on the landing lights, and the twin white beams defined by the moisture in the air stabbed out suddenly into the darkness and the trees on the other side of the jungle airstrip.

There was a slight breeze in the valley, which favored the runway direction Tim intended to use, but really there was just one direction to take off as well as one direction to land. Steeply rising terrain at the end and sides of the long mountain valley that helped hide the runway and operation from air surveillance also made landing or taking off in any other direction suicide. No airplane could hope to outclimb these mountains in such a short distance. The takeoff would be toward the northeast.

Tim taxied onto the airstrip and carefully swung the heavy airplane to the right. He increased the power slightly on both engines because the mud and gravel airstrip rose slightly as they taxied toward the end where most of the men lived in their shacks. This grade would also favor his takeoff slightly. The large single tires on each landing gear dug into the soft surface of the strip under the weight of the airplane as he taxied. Tim reached the end of the airstrip a few minutes later and applied one of the main wheel's brake while simultaneously throttling back one engine and increasing the power on the other, which swung the bomber around neatly and pointed it down the runway.

George turned off the landing lights and plunged the area into darkness, but not before each man glimpsed one of the heavily armed jeeps on either side. One had led and one had followed the airplane down the runway. In addition, both helicopters were airborne now and hovering over the trees on each side of the narrow valley.

The two men started the final checklist before takeoff. George shouted the items, while Tim made sure the final tasks were done. Finally, both men were satisfied that all was ready for the long flight. Both engines were warm and running smoothly.

George stiffly pried himself from the right seat. He reached up and pulled both sides of the Plexiglas canopy shut and latched them. The cockpit became marginally quieter. There was a wide, convex rearview mirror attached to the canopy frame just above the windshield as well as one mounted on each engine nacelle facing rearward.

Tim took off his headset and shouted at the old man, "This hunk of junk sounds terrible! I'm flying a death machine!" In reality the engines were running smoothly.

George stood behind Tim and calmly drew out a kitchen match from his pocket. Then he removed his cold pipe from his mouth and held both in front of him. The smell of gasoline was present in the cockpit. Tim kept his eye on the match. George waved the match and the pipe in the air as he spoke. He leaned forward and looked at the engine gauges one last time. "She's running like a Swiss watch, and you know it. Better than when she came off the assembly line in forty-four. She'll get you there and back; don't worry. That is, if you're man enough to fly her, sonny."

"Look, I'm not your goddamned son!" Tim shouted then smiled and lowered his voice a little. "Why don't you just ride along, you old fart, and we'll see who's man enough."

George remembered the last flight he had been invited on in 1944. "No thanks, sonny. I'm too old to wind up in prison or get blown out of the sky."

"They only shoot if they catch you on the ground and you resist. Not supposed to fire on people in the air. Might be a doctor and his wife and kids coming back from the Bahamas and forgot to file a flight plan.

The US government can't be shooting up innocent people, the Congress says."

"Nope, not a chance I'll go. Besides you were in the military. Tell me they never screw up. Someday those boys in Customs are going to get pissed and scramble a couple of F-16s when they recognize this airplane and put a sidewinder missile up your ass, sonny. There's a lot of deep water between here and the Louisiana coast to cover things up."

"Not a chance. You know the military can't get mixed up in civilian law affairs." But Tim knew George was probably right.

"Sure, you keep thinking that," George said, as he turned and began to exit the cockpit, clamping his still unlit pipe between his teeth.

A small hatch door hung open just behind the cockpit and ahead of what used to be the bomb bay doors. Bombs however had been replaced by fuel tanks and high-octane aviation gas. He squatted down and turned around, surrounded by the neatly stacked packages of cocaine.

"You bring her back in one piece, sonny."

"Yeah, we'll go into the capital and celebrate."

George didn't hear Tim's reply as he dropped stiffly onto the ground between the loud engines. He closed the hatch and made sure it was secure then duck walked under the fuselage to the rear of the airplane. He gave the black underside a loving pat and then walked slowly to one side of the bomber, while hanging tightly onto his hat so it wouldn't blow away in the propeller's slipstream. He walked to one side of the makeshift runway to watch the takeoff.

Tim was suddenly alone. The adrenaline began to flow—a good feeling, just like the one he felt before a combat mission so long ago. He stared at the blackness before him. These takeoffs were never easy and always dangerous. But he knew the risks and variables he faced—as well as the rewards. So much depended on the flawless operation of the overloaded machine he controlled. Hundreds of parts had to run flawlessly for the next twenty-four hours. He took a deep breath and knew he took the risk not for himself.

Tim reached out and turned off the interior cockpit lights. The instrument lights bathed his face in an eerie glow from below. He gently turned a small rheostat, and the lights dimmed slightly. He turned the landing lights on and off twice and then left them on: the signal that he was ready. They cut two swaths of white light through the mist growing near the ground in patches. Magically, one by one, battery-powered, portable runway lights began to wink on as two men in a truck drove the airstrip deep in the Andes, making one last check, and placing the lamps near the edge of the runway. Tim saw the truck blink its headlights twice. The airstrip was clear. It was time to go.

He laid his right hand on both throttles and took one more look at the vital engine gauges. All seemed perfect as the engines idled on each side. He held the brakes and slowly inched the two levers forward. The needles rose on the manifold pressure gauges as the power built. The propeller RPM climbed and then stabilized as the governors hit their stops. The superchargers began to compress the thin mountain air into a more usable density. The airplane strained against the brakes just as Tim released them.

The old bomber, christened BAD BREATH on either side of the nose, began to slowly roll forward. At first, it gathered speed almost imperceptibly. The large tires crunched on the gravel and splashed through the puddles.

Without the benefit of a copilot, Tim had to alternately watch the airspeed indicator, the engine gauges for any sign of trouble, and the airstrip in front of him as he steered the grossly overweight airplane down the narrow, rough runway, knowing at the same time how vulnerable the nose wheel was on this model. An accident now, before becoming airborne, would surely result in an instant inferno.

The airspeed reached forty, and the needle came alive. Then sixty and the rudder became effective to help steer. He roared at seventy-five past his shack and the maintenance area and the other airplanes in various phases of restoration. Half of the airstrip had been used up now, and he was past the point where he could conceivably stop the bomber on the remaining wet and slick runway. He was committed to flight.

There were no nice FAA-approved lights indicating the end of the airstrip—just blackness ahead, where Tim knew some very tall trees stood. At eighty he could feel the airplane lighten on its landing gear as he began to test the elevator. At one hundred and ten he hauled back gingerly on the control wheel and felt the nose wheel leave the ground. The airplane continued to accelerate. The roar was tremendous. There wasn't much space left. The trees in the darkness at the end of the strip were rushing toward him. Blackness surrounded him now, and he was now flying solely by the instruments. The vertical speed indicator needle rose and showed him a positive rate of climb as the airspeed rose to one hundred and thirty miles per hour. The vibration from the main wheels ceased as they left the ground just as Tim reached down and threw the landing gear lever into the up position. A green light went out, and a red light came on as the wheels retracted slowly into their wells, and then the red light winked out. The airplane accelerated still faster suddenly without the landing gear drag, and he pulled the nose a little higher as he converted that energy to more lift and fought for additional altitude. He saw trees flash past just below him as he turned off the landing lights, which lessened his chance of becoming a target for a rival family. The navigation lights were also off. The only visible target now would be the dim red glow from the exhaust stacks. But there were some very sophisticated night scopes and heat-seeking weapons on the black market. Tim knew this and it didn't make him feel any more comfortable. At two hundred feet, he retracted the flaps and retrimmed the nose higher. The airspeed crept to one fifty. The controls began to lose their mushy feel, and the airplane felt more solid in his hands as the rush of air over them increased. The engines continued to roar at full takeoff power.

Tim concentrated on his precise heading down the narrow valley. He had sat around for over three weeks waiting for this flight, and his instrument scan felt rusty. The rate of climb increased again, but it was still nothing to shout about. If an engine failed or even hiccupped now, it would still be fatal. The airplane was so overloaded that one engine, even at full power, would not be sufficient to keep him from descending into the jungle.

He glanced at the big luminous dial on his Omega. Less than two minutes since the takeoff. He checked the GPS. It indicated he was on a precise course to the first waypoint between the high, snow-capped mountains on either side of him. When he reached the waypoint, he would have to make a thirty degree turn to the left toward another waypoint in order to continue flying this valley. If he forgot, even for thirty seconds, to make this turn at the precise spot, he would fly into the opposite wall. At another point further ahead, he would have to gain altitude in order to top a high mountain ridge and drop into a second valley. Then he would continue to the northeast toward the coast. His course to the north had been plotted as carefully as possible. The mountains would shield him from possible radar detection as long as possible.

Tim continued his instrument scan. The radar altimeter indicated five hundred feet above the terrain. The engines were still at takeoff power. He began to level the aircraft. At the same time he gently retarded the throttles and then the prop controls. The engine noise decreased and the prop sound changed pitch as the propellers quieted to a snarl.

Three miles back George heard this pitch change and knew Tim was on his way. He shuffled toward his shack and lit his pipe. The airplane may or may not return in a day and a half. Like England in 1944 or

Korea in 1950 or Vietnam in 1966. The president was correct on one thing: it was indeed a war.

Fifteen miles down the valley, Tim was too busy to make comparisons. He made his turn and concentrated on his new heading. The valley widened out somewhat here, but he would still be hugging one of the walls.

Once he had passed the midpoint of the airstrip on takeoff, he had been committed to the long and dangerous flight. At this point he would have never had sufficient runway left to stop. Once airborne there just wasn't sufficient room to safely turn the aircraft in the narrow valley and return to land. And a safe landing at the airplane's present weight would be doubtful. Many hundreds of gallons of fuel would have to be burned before he could safely land. He had no way of dumping any of it. A night landing was impossible.

As the old bomber continued to accelerate, the controls tightened. Tim slowly dove the airplane until the red needle on the radar altimeter read less than two hundred feet. Even so the standard altimeter ahead of him in the instrument panel indicated over five thousand feet above sea level.

He felt the powerful sleek airplane underneath him. The adrenaline was still flowing. He was involved in some action. He knew he was addicted to it and needed the danger and excitement.

Tim flew another thirty minutes, adjusted the engine power, and then began another climb. He would have to top the high mountains on his left somewhere in order to continue his northward flight. Soon he was at eight thousand feet and entering the cloud cover. He flew into the clear at ten thousand feet. Minutes later he had climbed to over eleven thousand feet, and he began his turn at the next waypoint.

Now that he was above the cloud layers, stars filled the canopy above his head. A thin layer of ice covered the windshield, too little for concern. The orange exhaust stacks flickered on either side as he shone his flashlight along the wing's leading edge. A thin, white coating reflected in its powerful beam but wasn't enough for concern yet. Here and there he could make out white patches of snow visible on the nearby towering peaks of the Andes in the starlight. The bomber was not pressurized, and he began to feel lightheaded in the rarified air; a slight ache began to pulse in his forehead: the first signs of hypoxia, the lack of sufficient oxygen to the brain.

The cockpit air was frigid now as he leveled out at over thirteen thousand feet, and he shivered despite his heavy clothing. He turned two knobs to bring some heat to the cockpit and waited. The airplane had been built as a fighting machine and not to pamper passengers. There was no insulation in the fuselage. The airplane droned on, and he waited but still no heat flowed from the vents. He fiddled with the knobs again. Then the realization came to him that somehow George had probably sabotaged the heating system. It wouldn't affect the flight much. He would just be at this high altitude for another thirty minutes. Most of the flight would take place over the warm Gulf of Mexico at sea level and then into the temperate fall weather in the States. But it was just enough to make him feel uncomfortable. The temperature inside the airplane was just below zero now as the GPS indicated he should begin a turn to the right, northward toward the coast. He would descend to warmer air in another twenty minutes and worry about getting even with George later.

The time passed quickly, and Tim knew from the GPS coordinates that he was now clear of the mountains. He had been at high altitude a very short time, but his head pounded at his temples, and he felt lightheaded. He reduced the power and lowered the nose. The altimeter began to unwind as he started down. The remainder of the flight to the United States would be within a few hundred feet of the surface. He first would be skirting the large coastal city of Barranquilla and needed to stay under the radar of its controllers and approach control.

As he continued his long and rapid descent, the lights of a few villages and towns began to dot the countryside below. The air in the cockpit grew warm and humid, then hot and sticky as he continued to lose altitude. He could smell the earth and the vegetation below as he neared sea level.

Finally, in the distance to his right, he began to see the glow of the larger city. He adjusted the engine power to the most economical setting and set the prop RPM at the lowest setting allowable, reducing their noise to an angry snarl. His radar altimeter again read less than two hundred feet as he hugged the earth. Far to his right, he could see the bright, white strobe lights of an airliner making its approach to the airport at Barranquilla, as he himself flew along with all his lights extinguished. Tim directed the weather radar downward slightly. A definite line indicated the coastline just ahead. A few minutes later, he crossed this line. The lights below suddenly disappeared and gave way to a depthless blackness. He smelled the sea. He was over the Gulf of Mexico and would not see land for almost seven hours. His course was north by northwest. It would take him through the Yucatan Channel and a safe distance from Cuba's MIGs.

He flew the old bomber within one hundred feet of the ocean on the radar altimeter and reset the standard altimeter. Then for the first time, he engaged the sophisticated automatic pilot. The airplane flew smoothly. He had been flying manually now for almost two hours since takeoff. He made a check of the instruments once more before unbuckling his lap belt and shoulder harness and then sliding the seat back. He then pried himself stiffly from the seat, trusting the black box to keep the airplane from diving into the dark sea below.

The cockpit was humid, and even at night he estimated the temperature to be in the high-eighties. He began to peel off all his now sweat-soaked clothing, boots, and shoulder holster as he stood bent over in the small space behind the seats, while at the same time keeping a wary eye on the instrument panel and controls.

Down to just his underwear, he folded the heavier clothing neatly next to his boots and pulled his battered duffel bag from behind his seat. The thought that he was standing practically naked in an airplane flying just one hundred feet above the waves at over two hundred miles per hour always struck him as funny somehow.

Tim pulled a simple gray T-shirt, an old tan pair of chinos, and a battered pair of Nike's from the bag along with a thermos, a Sony Walkman, three cassettes, a couple of sandwiches, and a battered paperback. These items he placed on the right seat before stowing the other clothing in the duffel bag. He pulled on the shirt, pants, running shoes, and shoulder holster and then placed his boots and heavier clothing in the duffel bag before slipping back into his seat. He sat sideways, with his back against the side of the airplane and his legs stretched out to one side of the control column. It was lunchtime.

He picked up the thermos, unscrewed the top, and poured himself a steaming cup of coffee while thinking to himself that the mountain-grown beans were indeed the world's richest, just as stated in the ad by Juan Valdez. Then he took one of the sandwiches and unwrapped it on his lap. He took a bite and washed it down with another gulp of coffee, realizing how hungry he really was.

He checked the instrument panel again. The airplane was dead on course for the next selected waypoint to the north according to the GPS, flying smoothly along just above the surface of the sea with an exact groundspeed of 190 knots while the radar altimeter's needle hovered right at one hundred feet. The autopilot was performing flawlessly. He thought for a moment about the scientific and military minds who had devised this satellite system of navigation. The weather radar was also clear for eighty miles but was beginning to show what looked to be precipitation at its extreme range. This could be the beginning of some big thunderstorms ahead. He searched the GPS's memory for another waypoint. The Louisiana coast was still over a thousand miles ahead. His fuel burn so far had been heavy due to the power the overweight airplane required, but that would decrease with the airplane's weight, and the speed would pick up. He looked over the instrument panel and the nose. Blackness—just his own reflection in the glass.

Satisfied that all was well, he reached for the worn paperback. It was Stephen King's recent novel *Cujo*. He was at the part where the woman and child are first cornered by the St. Bernard. He read for a paragraph and then checked on things again. He was flying illegally toward the most powerful country in the world—a country that he had sworn to defend. He would reach it at dawn. He thought for a moment. Maybe if he hadn't taken that shortcut when he was a kid and met the old man in the alley those many years ago, things would have been different. Then he took another bite of his sandwich and turned the page. You just never knew how things were going to turn out in the long run.

He was walking home from school slowly, daydreaming as usual, trying to put off as long as possible the liver and lima bean dinner he knew was waiting ahead at Aunt Eunice's house. She always had liver and lima beans on Wednesday. He also had to invent some kind of excuse as to why he had missed his piano lesson today. It had rained a few hours ago. He was trying to figure these things out while looking down at his feet splashing in the puddles when he missed his turn at Maple Street and instead found himself way down on Ash Street.

While his other classmates were off playing baseball or exploring the woods down by Sennott Pond most afternoons after school, Tim had to attend piano lessons three times a week for a solid hour: Monday, Wednesday, and Friday. Not that he didn't enjoy playing the piano—he did. And his teacher, Miss Poland, had told his aunt he definitely had talent, but rather most of the time he just wanted to be by himself. Miss

Poland gave out miniature busts of famous composers when a student attained a certain level of skill. Tim had eight of them, all on display on Aunt Eunice's mantelpiece, a record for a nine-year-old according to his teacher. She was a prim, proper person, who wore her hair in a tight bun and seemed to wear some article of black clothing at all times. Her house was dark and the furniture heavy and covered with doilies. The doilies were everywhere: on the tabletops, the backs of chairs, in the bathroom, on the shelves of the kitchen cabinets. Tim felt like he was suffocating most of the time he was there. His aunt was a similar person and, not surprisingly, the two women were close friends.

He thought of his aunt as he hurried down the alley off Ash Street. And he especially thought of her wooden spoon. And it was this thought, on this Wednesday afternoon, that made him take the shortcut through the alley.

As he scurried along, it was the smell of the glue and dope that made him first stop. He sniffed and was puzzled at the smell. He saw light coming from a crack in the door of a large, barn-like building to his left. The building was badly weathered, just as the house in front of it had also seen better times. There was hardly any paint left on the wood clapboards. Actually, in better days, it had been a carriage house for the large home facing Ash Street. Then with the advent of the automobile in Lincoln, Nebraska, it had been turned into a garage. Now it had an additional special purpose.

The boy shifted his music books to the other arm, stepped carefully up to the partially open door, and peeked inside. It was a wondrous sight! One he would never forget. Inside was a whole airplane! Aunt Eunice and her wooden spoon and liver and lima beans were instantly forgotten.

The old carriage house was mostly unlighted and dark except for an electric bulb hanging from the ceiling near one of the wings. There, an old man worked patiently with a brush, alternately dipping it into an old paint can and lovingly stroking the fabric covering the wing. The man wore an old pair of brown workpants splotched with many colors of paint and other stains. His gray shirt was in the same condition as was the denim shop apron tied around his waist. He sported a big white bushy mustache and sideburns, which matched the hair on his head.

On the workbench behind him sat a big, fat yellow cat licking a paw and paying no attention to anything in particular. As the boy's eyes adjusted to the dim interior of the old carriage house, he could see that the airplane was partially disassembled. It seemed ancient. Unlike the sleek metal airplanes he routinely saw out at the airport, this one seemed to be made mostly of wood and fabric and had two wings instead of just one. The wheels and tires were much like his bicycle's, just a simple rim and spokes. There was a big wooden propeller sitting high on the nose. It was a glorious sight all right!

The glue smell came from the clear liquid that the old man was painting on the wing. Now Tim could see an equally ancient fan on the workbench humming and swiveling back and forth. It wafted out the door and into the alley the strong smell that had attracted him. He stood quietly to one side of the sliding wooden door and watched the old man at work.

Suddenly, after a few minutes, the man, without looking up from his work, said casually, as he dipped the brush in the can of dope, "Look boy, are you just going to stand there and stare at me, or are you going to come on in and give me a hand with this here airplane?" He had a big voice. Then he stopped working, looked straight at Tim, and smiled through his gray whiskers.

The boy hesitated. He was embarrassed at being discovered. He backed away from the door and intended to run home.

"Well, what are you going to do, boy?"

But the airplane was a powerful magnet, and he edged his way into the old carriage house. He stood there shyly scuffing a toe on the packed dirt floor.

"What's yer name?" the old man asked in the big voice again after wiping his right hand on his apron and then extending it toward him.

The boy quietly stepped forward, shifted his books, shook hands, and then said solemnly, "My name's Timothy, sir...er, Tim." The man's huge hand had felt like old, dusty sandpaper.

"Well, mine's Russell...Russell Hardgrove. Don't be shy, son. And forget that 'sir' stuff. Here, meet Jenny."

Tim turned and eyed the cat on the workbench.

"No, no," the man laughed heartily in the big voice while holding onto his belt. "I meant the airplane. That's her name, Jenny. That old good-for-nothin' cat don't have a name."

Tim looked up in wonder again at the big wooden propeller in front of the shiny brass radiator. Jenny, he thought. What a beautiful name for an airplane. There was a Jennifer in his school class, but she was fat, and, anyway, the name fit the airplane much better. "You don't talk much do ya, son?" He handed Tim the brush. The wooden handle was sticky. "Might as well make yerself useful; here."

Tim set his music and schoolbooks on the floor, took the brush, and dabbed a little bit on the leading edge of the wing. His life would never be the same. The smell of dope and glue would forever bring his memory back to this very day, and he would know exactly when the passion had started.

"Timothy is a fine name, son. It was my father's name, God rest his soul." He guided the boy's hand for a moment. "There, now, take a little longer stroke."

Tim dipped the brush and tried again.

"There, that's just about perfect."

The boy smiled and then frowned again as he concentrated on the serious business of actually working on a real airplane. He stuck his tongue out and moved it around with the brush strokes.

The old man asked, "Where do ya live, son? I don't think I've ever seen you around these parts."

Tim could barely break his concentration to answer, "I live with my aunt over on Maple." Then he asked, "Are you building this airplane?"

The man laughed again. "No, sir, I'm not that smart. I'm only restoring her. She was built a long time ago, son. Probably a good forty years ago or more. I found her in a warehouse a few years ago collecting dust for the last twenty years. Been working to get her back in the air ever since." He paused. "You know, Lindbergh's first airplane was just like this one. He was around these parts for a while, learning how to fly back in the twenties. Maybe Jenny here was his airplane. They never have found that one, you know." He chuckled. "Wouldn't that be sumpthin—Lindbergh's first airplane?"

Tim dipped the brush again and paused. "Who's Lin...Lindbergh?" He had some difficulty with the pronunciation.

"Why, son, don't you know you Charles Lindbergh was—the Lone Eagle hisself?"

"No, sir, I've never heard of him before."

Russell grumbled, "Don't they teach you youngins anything in school about history? Why, he was the greatest flyer that ever was, son. Flew his little airplane, the *Spirit of St. Louis*, all the way from New York to Paris, France, all by hisself."

"Do you fly?" asked Tim.

"Why, who do you think is the second greatest flyer in the world?" He winked. "I even knew Orville and Wilbur personally."

"Who are they?" asked Tim.

"Well, I can see you need some real education in aviation matters," the old man said, as he rubbed his chin. "I'll tell you what; I need a helper here to help me finish up the old girl. Why don't you ask your aunt if you can come by after school and on Saturdays? But, mind you, you can't go shirking your schoolwork and music lessons."

Tim thought hard and sighed. "I don't think she'll let me."

Russell thought for a moment. "Maybe I can talk to her and make some sort of deal. What's your aunt's name, anyhow?"

"Eunice Baker."

"Eunice Baker, huh? Why, I think I know her. She's that old battle-ax, er, lady that runs the foster home over on Maple, isn't she? Is that where you live?"

Tim looked down and answered quietly, "Yes, sir."

"Let's see if I can't work out some sort of deal with your aunt. We wouldn't want to do anything behind her back, now would we?"

"No, I guess not."

Later, Russell walked Tim home. He was over an hour late. There they met a scowling Aunt Eunice at the front door. She tapped her foot impatiently while holding the dreaded wooden spoon in her folded arms.

Russell used a lot of charm and a trial deal was struck whereby Tim could help out with the airplane as long as he kept his grades up and attended his piano lessons. Secretly she was glad that Tim had found something to interest him, but she had no intention of ever letting him fly in that rickety, old machine. After a brief visit to the old carriage house and a look at Jenny and her pieces scattered around, she felt safe on this regard, doubting that the two would ever finish the project.

But work progressed slowly and surely. Russell and Tim worked together after school and sometimes on Saturdays. Piece by piece, bit by bit, the airplane was restored to its original condition. First the wings then the fuselage then the engine were returned to better than new shape. At the same time, Tim's grades in school soared into the mostly As with a sprinkling of Bs, and then all As. His music teacher awarded him three more busts of composers, and he began to win a few contests.

Finally, almost three years after Tim had stopped on that first day in the alley, the *Jenny* sat completed in the old carriage house. They opened the doors wide, and Russell and Tim—now twelve years old, an honor student, and accomplished musician—stood back, wiping their hands with old, red rags, and admired their work.

The *Jenny* sat on its new black tires and gleamed in the sun. The metalwork sparkled. The brass radiator looked like gold in the light. The shiny, heavily varnished propeller shone.

Russell made arrangements for the airplane to be trucked to a local airport a few miles away, a simple place with a grass runway and a few hangars.

Aunt Eunice was horrified and had certainly never counted on the airplane ever being airworthy. She again forbade Tim from ever flying in it. But a few days later, he slipped from the house early in the morning and rode his bike breathlessly to the little airport for the big event.

At first the old man was reluctant for the boy to go along on the very first flight. A lot could go wrong. He had found himself rusty when he had flown with an instructor friend the week before in another airplane. But the boy pleaded, and later that morning, both found themselves sitting in the old biplane with the engine ticking over slowly: Tim in the front cockpit and Russell in the rear. Both wore old leather flying helmets, goggles, and silk scarves. Russell had on his old, leather flying jacket despite the warmth of the beautiful, still Nebraska summer morning. The sun had just come up, not a cloud marred the deep blue sky, and the dew was still wet upon the tips of the grass blades.

Tim gripped both sides of the cockpit as Russell revved the engine and began to taxi to the end of the airstrip. Tim had read plenty about the exploits of the aces of WWI and WWII in the past three years, and now he was about to fly for the first time himself—and in an airplane he had helped rebuild! His excitement was almost overwhelming as he looked out through the wires at the wings he knew intimately on each side of him and then down at the fat, black rubber tires rolling through the grass. Along with Russell he knew every square inch of the *Jenny*. She was in perfect condition.

Russell turned the *Jenny* around and lined her up with the sides of the runway. He reached forward and tapped Tim on the shoulder. Tim turned around and Russell gave him a thumbs-up and then lowered his flying goggles. Tim returned the signal and lowered his goggles, too. They were ready.

Russell opened the throttle and the engine roared. Slowly the airplane began to roll down the runway and pick up speed. He pushed a little forward on the stick, and the tail came off the ground gently. Just a few seconds later, when Tim couldn't believe they would have enough airspeed built up, the *Jenny*'s wheels lifted from the grass, she skipped once gently, and then was airborne for the first time in decades. The people at the airport who had turned out to watch the first takeoff cheered in unison and waved madly as the *Jenny* flew by.

At two hundred feet, Russell banked her gently to the east and they climbed into the rising sun just as Aunt Eunice swerved her old maroon LaSalle into the gravel parking lot. She had discovered Tim's bed empty just barely fifteen minutes before.

Russell leveled off and flew over the city at an altitude of eight hundred feet. Tim looked down at the toy city and could hardly catch his breath. His scarf streamed out behind him and flapped in the slipstream. It was wonderful!

Then Russell wiggled the stick and tapped him on the head. It was the signal that the *Jenny* was all Tim's. He looked down at the quivering stick between his legs and hesitated for a moment. The *Jenny* started to nose down and drop a wing. Russell yelled over the engine and wind noise, "Take her, sonny!"

Tim grasped the stick and felt the airplane alive in his right hand. He gently pulled back and brought the nose up to the horizon. Then he put his feet up on the rudder pedals and started a turn to the left. The *Jenny* responded to his inputs. He was flying!

Russell died two weeks later. Tim walked down the alley, but the doors to the carriage house were padlocked. No one answered the door. He never found out what happened to the beautiful little biplane that he helped lovingly restored.

Tim had seen the thunderstorms first on the weather radar's extreme range. Then lightning flashes had brightened the night sky just over the horizon. Now a storm sat five miles ahead according to the radar and another to the left. On the radar screen they were brightly colored blobs of light: green on the irregular edges blending into yellow and finally red in the middle, where the rain was the most intense.

The air was still smooth as he adjusted the heading bug for the autopilot to follow. The line of storms was not solid, and he would run the gap between the two on the radar, being also careful not to lead himself into a blind alley. As he flew closer, rain began to rattle on the windshield. It formed rivulets that slowly worked their way back along the windshield and top canopy.

The airplane trembled a little in some turbulent air, and Tim commanded the autopilot to gain an additional hundred feet of altitude. Altitude was trouble in this business, he knew; the lower the better, but then again it wouldn't do anybody any good, especially him, if the turbulence from these storms suddenly pancaked him into the sea. He brought his feet over the power quadrant and rested them on the rudder pedals. Then he buckled himself in once more tightly with his seatbelt and shoulder harness.

A sudden blue flash of lightning bathed the cockpit in brilliant light. Tim squinted and studied the instruments and radar. This weather was probably just one of those small squalls that meander across the Caribbean, not really big enough to harm anyone, especially at his low altitude, but sizable enough to pay attention to and avoid.

As he cleared the one on his right, the rain stopped its rattle on the windshield, and Tim reached forward and changed the heading bug again on the directional gyro. The airplane banked automatically to the right and came back on course. His radar indicated another storm dead ahead about fifteen miles. And still another one to the left. When he flew nearer, he would skirt these to the right. The weather radar was indispensable at night.

Tim cupped his hands against the side window and peered outside, trying to glimpse who knows what. Maybe a light from a boat? Another flash of lightning from behind lit up the sea for a split second. There was nothing to see but the black, angry surface of the sea against the black sky.

He banked to the right to begin skirting what was hopefully the last storm in his path. He looked at the luminous dial of his Omega. It had been more than three hours since his takeoff. He should be more than two hundred miles north of the South American coast now. It was almost time to switch the fuel tanks in order to keep the airplane in balance, and attend to Mother Nature himself.

After his first, early-morning ride in the biplane with Russell, Tim didn't fly again for almost six years. The ride home that morning with Aunt Eunice in the LaSalle had been an icy one. He had received a stern lecture on following rules and keeping his word. The incident had then been forgotten by her.

But Tim didn't forget his first airplane ride as easily. He had tasted flight, even if it was for such a short duration, and was determined to become a pilot. But flying was an expensive proposition. When he considered the airplane rental and instruction, there was no way to manage it on his meager allowance.

On some days he would ride his bicycle down to the little airport and just sit and watch the few airplanes take off and land. He even rode a few times all the way out to the larger Lincoln Municipal Airport, where there was more traffic to watch come and go.

But rebuilding the old *Jenny* with Russell had taught him patience. He now knew that any worthwhile goal usually did not come easy. And to reach the goal he now had in mind, he would have to put his plan together piece by piece.

At the age of twelve, he decided he would be admitted either to the Air Force Academy or the Naval Academy—a lofty goal indeed. The goal of becoming a jet fighter pilot became insignificant to all else. And he set about gaining his goal with unstoppable determination.

All through high school he strove to fit the exact mold of the perfect candidate for these two service academies, without ever mentioning his ambition to anyone. Until his senior year, everyone assumed he would aspire to the University of Nebraska. And to Aunt Eunice's delight and pride, Tim spent hour after hour studying to maintain his 4.00 average. He also continued to perfect his music, spent time in various clubs at school, and excelled on the wrestling team in the fall and the baseball team in the spring. During his senior year he was elected class president and finally graduated the following spring as the class valedictorian. He made a stirring speech about attaining life's goals. It was a fitting one in that he had indeed been appointed to attend the new Air Force Academy in Colorado Springs the following fall.

Aunt Eunice smiled at the thought that at last her strict upbringing had turned out a winner. She never suspected for a moment that a twenty-minute airplane ride would have such an overwhelming effect on him.

In the fall he packed his two suitcases, kissed a wet-eyed Aunt Eunice good-bye, and boarded the train for Denver. Two days later, he was at the academy, where the first day he immediately began to ask when he could start flying and met his roommate for the next grueling four years, Harvey Brown.

Harvey had come from Texas. He spoke with a very slow drawl, which only served to mask an incredible mind and quick wit. Their backgrounds and personalities were very different. Harvey had come from a big farm family of four boys and three girls, whereas Tim had been abandoned at an early age. Harvey played the trumpet and was six inches taller than his roommate and forty pounds heavier. He had quick reflexes and had been a star quarterback at his high school in southern Texas—no small feat where football reigned supreme. The academy coach had sought him out that very first day. Both had an intense desire to fly and become fighter pilots above all else. Their friendship and rivalry began almost immediately.

The four years at the academy were a mixture of heaven and hell for the two cadets. The standards were the highest. The training was intense. Tim competed on the wrestling team and became a first-class shortstop on the baseball team. In his last three years, Harvey became the star quarterback for the Fighting Falcons. The team had three winning seasons and invitations to two bowl games. The pros were definitely interested in him. Together they played handball in fierce competition but never resolved who was better. And both men played in a popular cadet band formed for various social events.

They got their chance to fly in their second year, when they entered a program intended to screen potential Air Force pilots. Both were natural pilots and scored very high with their instructors. And both soloed the academy's little Cessna trainers on the same day during their second year. Blind luck permitted Tim to accomplish this feat before Harvey, and he would never let the other cadet forget that he had soloed first. It was the moment both men had waited for, and for Tim that day when he finally flew by himself ranked right up there with that first ride with Russell in the *Jenny*. He thought sadly of the old man when he climbed out of the Cessna. What would Russell have thought? Would he be proud? Sure he would!

During his final year at the academy, Tim met Karen. Harvey had been dating a local girl from the Springs (as the city of Colorado Springs was known to all the locals). Susan had been impressed by Harvey's new, red Corvette convertible. Tim had not really dated anyone during his previous three years at the academy or even previously in high school, instead devoting most of his time and energy to graduating as an Air Force pilot. Harvey thought it was high time he met someone. After all, they would be finished in a few months. Both men had been accepted into flight training after graduation, and it was time to start celebrating. Karen was Susan's best friend, and soon Tim found himself on a very awkward double date.

Tim wasn't impressed with Karen at first and vice versa. Both were people who kept to themselves, and conversation was difficult. She was two inches taller than him. The evening went badly. Harvey and Susan, two outgoing people if ever there were some, tried with difficulty to shore things up over dinner. The two couples then went to a movie. It was the Frank Sinatra film *Von Ryan's Express*. Afterwards, Tim, trying to vainly make small talk, mentioned that he had liked the flying sequences, particularly the old German fighter planes. Karen quietly corrected him, stating that the airplanes were in fact a small liaison model used during the war and painted to look like fighters. Tim disagreed, but Karen held firm. The argument escalated good-naturedly. The only solution was to turn around and see the movie again, leaving Harvey and Susan standing on the sidewalk grinning at each other outside the movie theater.

Two hours later Tim conceded that his date had been correct. Later, over coffee at a nearby restaurant, he found out his quiet date had a United Airlines pilot for a father, had soloed at the age of sixteen, and had had a pilot's license for over six years. In fact, she was a flight instructor at the nearby Black Forest glider port and had her sights set on becoming one of the first women airline pilots in the United States. She impressed him the next day with an exhilarating ride in a high-performance sailplane, taking him over Pike's Peak.

Harvey only smiled when Tim related this to him back in their dorm room. He and Susan had known it all along.

Graduation was a happy occasion for everyone, ending in the traditional uniform hats in the air. Aunt Eunice had made the trip to Colorado Springs by train and was proud. She gave Tim an expensive Omega chronograph as a graduation present. He even managed to give her a big hug afterward, something he had never done before. Both girlfriends also attended.

The next day Karen and Tim drove Aunt Eunice to the airport and, despite her protests, gave her a first airplane ride in a pretty blue-and-white Cessna. To her great surprise, she found herself enjoying the experience and did not find any unpleasant sensations while they circled over the academy and downtown. Later, she cancelled her train tickets and flew back to Lincoln on United Airlines. She insisted on meeting the pilot personally as she boarded.

Soon after graduation, Tim and Harvey were assigned to Vance AFB in Oklahoma for flight training. A year later, after graduating top in their class, they married Karen and Susan in a double ceremony.

The honeymoons were short. Soon after, both men found themselves assigned to the same squadron in Thailand, flying mission after mission over North Vietnam. The fun was suddenly over. His best friend, Harvey, was killed in action six months later by a North Vietnamese SAM missile.

It had been nearly four hours since leaving the coast, six hours since takeoff, and Tim was cautiously approaching the narrow Yucatan channel. Only one hundred fifty miles wide, between Mexico and Cuba, the GPS indicated he was some eighty miles from the Cuban coast and Castro's MIGs. There was a rumor that Cuba had shot down two suspect aircraft in the past few months. The United States government had lodged no protests. The radar altimeter still indicated a steady one hundred feet above the Gulf of Mexico. The aircraft had burned over two tons of fuel at this point but still felt dangerously heavy.

Tim peered forward through the windscreen. Nothing ahead. Blackness. He leaned forward and picked up the clipboard he used to keep track of the fuel burn. It was an intricate process, and the airplane had to be kept in balance.

As he straightened up he saw the starboard navigation lights first, then the huge funnel, the triple masts, and the white superstructure. There was no time to react. The funnel was black and white with a large, red W in the middle. It was belching black smoke that was trailing to one side. The ship flashed underneath him in less time than it took to take a breath. A man was standing at the rail smoking a cigarette and raised his head. Tim could smell the diesel fumes from the ship's engines as he roared overhead. His right wingtip just cleared the large forward mast.

There had been no time at all to disconnect the autopilot or even command it to climb. He had missed both the funnel and the mast by just feet. If he had just grazed either one, the resulting explosion and plunge into the sea would have been spectacular and fatal. Thirty feet lower, with the tons of aviation fuel he was still carrying, the ship and the men aboard her would not have had a chance.

He tried to look back through his side window. Blackness. It had been very close indeed.

Tim continued into the moonless night. He doubted whether the ship would report the near miss to anyone, if indeed he had even been seen. Although if indeed he had been seen, they would surely guess his mission and maybe report the incident to US Customs. He would be hundreds of miles away by then. He yawned. The radar indicated no weather on the horizon. Dawn was just hours away.

Tim adjusted the autopilot to track a more northwesterly course. He noticed the right cylinder head temperatures were slightly higher than the left engine. He tapped the gauge, but it did not move. It was still well within tolerances, but it would bear watching further.

He yawned again and tried to stretch within the confines of his seat. The hours just before dawn were always the worst. His body ached for sleep. He pried himself up, tended to the fuel tank switching, and then climbed back into his seat, where he made another note on his clipboard. He had finished the paperback and had no more to divert his attention. Instead he picked his Walkman off the top of the instrument panel and started a well-worn cassette tape. His back ached. An old, scratchy Fleetwood Mac song pounded his ears, and he turned down the volume. The Louisiana coast lay four hours straight ahead.

Tim was evacuated unconscious to a nearby field hospital by the helicopter crew who had miraculously rescued him under heavy enemy fire after he had ejected into the rice paddy. His serious wounds were treated as well as could be expected under the conditions, and he was flown again a short time later to Saigon, where he was transferred to an awaiting medevac jet with other wounded, and flown to Clark AFB in the Philippines. All this took barely eighteen hours. Listed in critical condition and not expected to live—or if he did, to suffer possible brain damage due to an immense loss of blood—he regained consciousness four days later. A few weeks later, his condition was downgraded to serious, and he was airlifted once more, this time back to the States and a military hospital in San Francisco.

The bullet, which had torn through his body, had finally lodged near his spine but not before causing nerve and muscle damage to his shoulder, nicking a lung, missing his heart by millimeters, and inflicting still more damage to a kidney, before it stopped. His right arm was numb, but doctors were confident that given physical therapy he would regain most of the use of it. The damaged kidney was removed a week later. More importantly, he seemed to still possess all his mental faculties.

Captain Timothy McIntosh's flying career with the US Air Force was over. Shortly after this the Santa Claus dream became a recurring nightmare.

Tim's stay in the VA hospital lasted some six months, and Karen moved to San Francisco. Eventually the physical wounds healed. The doctors should have begun to worry more about the mental wounds, but their patient loads were tremendous at this time. Soon after his release, Karen became pregnant. Tim was honorably discharged from the air force three months later and given a disability pension.

The couple was at odds as to what to do with their lives after his discharge. He had planned to stay in the air force until retirement. They both returned to Colorado Springs and found a place to live. She resumed her flight instructing, while he restlessly sat around the small apartment. Although not qualified any more to fly for the military, he had recovered sufficiently to easily pass an FAA medical exam for civilian flying with no limitations. A month after their daughter Shannon was born, Tim was hired by a small regional airline in Florida. They packed up and moved to Miami a few days later.

Compared to his air force days, the airline job was dull, unrewarding, low paying, and hard on family life. He was stuck behind the seniority wall that all airline pilots face. It governed all advancement, and he would find himself flying as a copilot for years. But he had a family to support now, and the job was better than no flying job at all.

Three years later Tim was furloughed by the airline during a period of cutbacks. The marriage began to encounter some problems at the same time. Karen suggested that they both try to enter a more stable career. After all, he did have a Bachelor of Science degree from the Air Force Academy and was a decorated veteran. There should be plenty of doors open for him. Instead, he found a job flight instructing at one of the numerous flight schools in the Miami area.

The regional airline furlough lasted over two years. When he returned, he was still a copilot, and the airline job was still hard on the family life and low paying. A year later, Tim had an argument with one of his captains on a flight and was fired two days later for displaying a bad attitude. A month after the firing, Karen packed her bags and took Shannon with her on the first flight back to Colorado Springs, leaving Tim with a month's paid rent and an old Pinto hatchback with a bad muffler.

The dream began occurring more regularly.

A few months later, while playing the piano at a bar in Miami, Tim met Juan Rivas for the first time.

The eastern sky had gradually become lighter, and the stars over the old bomber's Plexiglas canopy had begun to fade. Tim rearranged the charts on his clipboard and checked the navigational radios. He had now been flying for over ten hours. His eyes felt scratchy and tired. He had finished the last of the coffee and sandwiches.

As the eastern sky continued to turn from deep purple to deep blue and an orange glow seeped above the horizon, he at last began to see the surface of the sea rushing by just below the airplane. The air in the cockpit had become increasing cooler as he had flown north, causing him to don his old sweater and curse the inoperative heater once more. He was less than an hour's flight from the Louisiana coast, and it was time to become alert. This was the riskiest part of the entire flight, as he prepared to fly illegally into the United States.

Tim had entered US airspace on over a dozen trips so far, bringing perhaps a few hundreds of millions of dollars' worth of cocaine into the country single-handedly in past years. He had encountered trouble only once. The last trip had been up the Atlantic coast, and on the way back, hundreds of miles offshore, a pair of F-16s, probably on some type of training mission, had flown close to him. They had looked him over and then quickly left. He had surmised they were unarmed and low on fuel. And, besides, he was headed south, the wrong direction.

He preferred to fly ashore in Louisiana in the early morning hours just after sunrise because he had another trick up his sleeve. The government was slowly attempting to close the net on its southern shores with tethered radar balloons. But there were still few of those, and it was still a huge area to cover. And Tim's airplane had its own special radar aboard, the same system developed for airliners in response to Congress's knee-jerk legislation mandating collision-avoidance devices. So day or night didn't mean all that much to the really sophisticated smugglers. Actually, daytime was a little better in that Tim could also visually check if he was being pursued.

Most smugglers' aircraft were slow, civilian models with limited range, even with extra fuel tanks fitted in the cabin. They mostly island-hopped their way north, landing in little, dangerous, out-of-the-way airstrips where gasoline was fifty bucks a gallon. Tim's airplane could stay aloft for over thirty hours and could exceed three hundred miles per hour. He could fly nonstop as far north as Maine or to a rendezvous far inland, as he was doing on this trip.

The sun's fiery ball edged over the horizon. For the first time on the flight, Tim could see a definite horizon. The sea was flat and calm.

He switched off the autopilot. The airplane had now burned some four and a half tons of fuel. As he retook control of the plane, after many hours, the controls responded better—more crisp and tight. It was time to begin to slow down. He reached out with his right hand and slowly brought both throttles back. The engine noise changed pitch. The airspeed began to decrease, and he retrimmed the airplane. As the airplane continued to slow, he lowered the flaps and retrimmed again. At the correct speed, he lowered the landing gear. The green light indicating it was down and locked winked on. He reset the power until the old bomber was stabilized at one hundred forty miles per hour. The controls felt mushy in his hands at this slow speed.

The coastline of the United States was heavily defended, in theory, but the defense department would not pay much attention to a single, slow target if detected, although Customs and the DEA certainly would when alerted. It simply wasn't smart to fly toward the United States at three or four hundred miles per hour and arouse the interest of another party with big guns.

And he had another trick up his sleeve. One hundred forty miles per hour was approximately the cruising speed of a jet-powered helicopter, the type used to service the numerous offshore oil rigs.

The sun was now well above the horizon. Tim's body was waking up as its natural rhythms took over, and he was feeling better. Two white birds flew across his nose close to the waves. He was close to the coast now, perhaps fifty miles if he wanted to check. It promised to be a fine fall day. He studied the GPS, then leaned forward and squinted into the distance. What he was looking for should be just a few miles ahead, and visibility was good this morning. He had carefully calculated its location and used it many times.

Finally, he saw it on the horizon about ten miles ahead. At first, it appeared to be an out-of-place skyscraper as the huge drilling platform rose hundreds of feet above the Gulf and cast a long shadow in the sunrise. Tim reached behind him and pulled his sunglass case out of his duffel bag. He pulled them out with his free hand, hooked them behind his ears, and snapped the case shut. The drilling rig grew larger, and its features were more distinct. The platform stood on four huge cylindrical legs a hundred feet above the waves, which broke white against them. The derrick rose another two hundred feet above its platform. A large sign attached to one of the steel girders proclaimed *TEXAS #27*. Another towered in the distance, to the right of the first one, then another, their derricks also rising high above the waves.

As he neared the platform, Tim reached over and turned on the radar transponder to its standby setting for the first time. The transponder had four small windows on its front panel, which displayed a number in each of them. The number 1200, the radar code for civilian aircraft flying on their own under visual flight rules, was selected.

He flew closer and now could make out tiny figures on the platform's deck. A helicopter, its blades idling, stood on the minuscule helipad, which jutted out on the west side of the gigantic structure. Tim now was level with the deck roughly a few hundred yards to the west and flying through the platform's long shadow.

A man appeared at an open door built like a hatch on a ship in the first level just below the deck. He wore a white apron and hat and carried a large garbage can, which he tipped over the side. As the garbage cascaded into the Gulf of Mexico, he looked up at the sound of the old bomber's engines. He had seen this black airplane once before and had guessed its probable mission. Why else would anyone fly such a big airplane so low to the water headed north? The man in the apron and hat was a cook's helper on the drilling rig. He waved at Tim as he flew by and then raised his clenched fist in a salute. Tim returned the wave casually and rocked the wings slowly. The helper was still a little high from some cocaine himself the night before. He had burned most of that morning's toast and had been threatened for the third time with losing his job if he didn't shape up. He watched the black airplane disappear into the distance toward rig number 35.

After Tim rocked the wings, he turned for the next drilling platform. He switched the transponder on. There was a lot of helicopter traffic in the morning servicing these rigs, and he hoped he would be mistaken for one of them, if indeed he was being watched by anyone. For the next forty minutes, he flew a random pattern back and forth among the steel giants. He saw two more helicopters landing on helipads, looking like dragonflies alighting on a bush. It was a waste of precious fuel but worth the effort if anyone was really tracking him. Finally, he brought up the coordinates for St. Jacques, Louisiana, on the GPS and turned north.

The town was the home for dozens of the helicopters that serviced the oil rigs out in the Gulf, and any potential trackers would just see a chopper returning home.

Thirty minutes later he skimmed over the beach and tidal marshes at fifty feet—the first land in almost two thousand miles. Flying low over the flat bayous, Tim retracted the landing gear and added power. The old bomber accelerated as he brought up the flaps. When the airplane was clean, he pushed the throttles farther forward. Lighter by almost eleven hours' worth of fuel, soon the airplane was flying at over three hundred miles per hour and still accelerating. The land below flashed by in a blur at this low altitude as Tim gently began to apply back pressure to the control wheel and climb in a tight spiral. As the climb and turn grew steeper, Tim began to feel the g-forces push him into the seat. He checked both mirrors on either engine and the one mounted just above his head on the forward edge of the canopy. Soon he was more than a mile above the ground. He saw nothing in his mirrors after he started the abrupt maneuver. If a Customs or DEA airplane had been following he hoped that he would have caught a glimpse of it in the surprise maneuver. The government boys were fond of tucking in just behind and below the airplane they were following, in the suspect pilot's blind spot. Also the TCAS hadn't given him any alert as it would have given the airliner it was designed for if another aircraft was in close proximity. Still turning steeply to the left, he could detect nothing but the empty sky and swampland bisected by an occasional reddish dirt road.

He banked suddenly to the right and watched the mirrors. Still nothing. If, indeed, he had detected an interdicting airplane at this point, Tim would have just simply turned south and headed back to South America the way he had come. He could still outrange any airplane at this point. The pilots that were eventually caught were the ones flying stolen airplanes, who had to land before running out of fuel. Tim didn't have this limitation. Much money had been invested in *Bad Breath,* and, so far, the effort had paid off handsomely. The return was hundreds of millions now, he estimated. And soon a second and third identical A-26 would be in service. Any following airplane would eventually have to turn back, and he doubted if anyone could coordinate to intercept him hundreds of miles out in the Caribbean on his way back to the mountain base or any of the other dozen airstrips he had knowledge of. The stakes were huge with this much pure cocaine. It would be better to be patient and try another day. He had plenty of fuel. Silently he wished for the weapon systems and radar in his F-105 that he had flown so long ago in Vietnam. Although outdated now, he knew it would do the job on any following government airplane. Indeed, George was presently looking for a similar, more modern system through the connections their organization had in Third World countries desperate for cash.

Tim was confident that he had not been detected and leveled out at ten thousand feet on a northwesterly heading toward his Colorado destination. He readjusted the throttles, propeller controls, and fuel mixtures to their most economical settings then switched the autopilot on again. At this altitude he would use much less fuel than he had skimming the Gulf of Mexico. Picking up the clipboard, he checked on his fuel burn and did some more switching of the elaborate fuel system to keep the airplane in balance. He still had an ample reserve to return to South America. Tim checked the GPS once more and fine-tuned the heading for the autopilot.

It looked like another successful penetration. He leaned back in his seat and watched the Louisiana countryside slide under his nose. He hummed to himself and tapped the black control wheel. He was back home again.

In fact, a US. Customs aircraft, a converted business jet, had flown toward this section of the Louisiana coast on what would have been an almost collision course with Tim and the A-26 some forty minutes before he had passed the first drilling rig. However, the frustrated government crew had to return prematurely to Houston when the aircraft had developed an electrical problem. As Tim crossed into Oklahoma, it now sat idle on a concrete ramp while its crew, complaining about the bureaucracy they were saddled with, finished their shift with a hotly contested game of gin rummy. New parts were expected in two weeks after the correct government procurement forms were filled out in triplicate on Monday morning.

When first propositioned by the Cuban in the bar, Tim had flatly refused. But Juan was persistent, and a week later Tim again received an offer. This time he took the bait. It would prove to be so easy. For three thousand dollars, he would fly a single-engine Cessna with extra fuel tanks to a small island southeast of Puerto Rico and land at dusk on a small, rough, unlighted dirt airstrip. He would take on the cargo and return to Florida just before daybreak. There, he would land at a predetermined spot on a mostly deserted county highway some fifty miles northwest of Miami and abandon the airplane.

The flight went smoothly, and he encountered no problems. He left the airplane, almost out of fuel, sitting in the breakdown lane. A patrolling deputy found it later in the morning, not an uncommon occurrence for this officer in this part of Florida. The airplane had been stolen the week before in Lansing, Michigan, and belonged to a prominent heart surgeon. It hadn't been reported stolen for almost three days. By that time the thief had flown it south and sold it for ten thousand dollars cash, a tenth of its true value. Tim's first cargo of cocaine had a street value of close to $5 million—a small load by most smugglers' standards.

Tim had entered a new world. He found he enjoyed the risk, the excitement, and the adrenaline rush as he approached the coast. The almost identical feelings he had felt in Vietnam long ago were being rekindled, and he felt somehow he was getting even with a society that had dumped him on the street after he put his life on the line for it. And it put some sorely needed cash in his pocket.

A month later he repeated the same flight, only this time in a larger, twin-engine airplane filled to the ceiling with two tons of marijuana. He boarded first and then the airplane was loaded, including even the aisle. There would be no escape out the rear door in the event of a crash. He accepted the risk and was paid nearly ten thousand dollars in tens, twenties, and fifties.

Tim made four more trips over the next two months, hauling cocaine, and pocketed another twenty thousand dollars. But he was puzzled with his Cuban contact and the organization behind him. For all the millions of dollars realized by the smuggling flights, it seemed to Tim a complicated and hazardous process to get the drugs from South America to Florida as it involved many men and what turned out to be mostly disposable aircraft. Large amounts of cash also had to be flown south.

On his seventh trip Tim's luck ran out as he landed once more near dusk in a stolen airplane on a tiny dirt airstrip along the beach of a small island. The men came from nowhere, and he was severely beaten and left for dead under the tail of his airplane. The four men left quickly in a boat with almost a million dollars in cash. The incident dispelled any idea Tim had that there might be honor among thieves. He regained consciousness the next day under the hot sun and was able to fly back to Florida in much pain.

Juan shrugged off the incident as the cost of doing business. Secretly he knew he could buy another pilot. Tim didn't think the "loss" was all that acceptable because it had been his ass on that island. Juan figured Tim would simply walk off and quit. In that case he would know too much and have to be dealt with severely. But to his surprise, Tim said he could propose a new, safer method of smuggling drugs in and cash out if only he could talk to the head of the organization. He had an idea. They would have to invest some money, but it would pay off handsomely.

Two weeks later he was in a first class seat on an airliner flying to New York. He rented a car and drove to a prearranged spot at a shopping mall on Long Island. There he was picked up by four men in a limo and driven around randomly, while blindfolded, for almost an hour. They stopped once at a McDonald's for lunch. Tim had a Big Mac while the other men joked in the car. When they removed the blindfold, he found himself with two men in a shadowy library stacked high with bookshelves in what he took to be a very large house. He could hear the ocean outside but had no other clue as to his whereabouts. He guessed somewhere on Long Island. The two men in the shadows were obviously very intelligent and businesslike. One spoke with a Latin accent, and the other man did not. They were older, probably in their late-fifties or early-sixties. One of them had snow-white hair. They seemed to be on equal terms. Tim felt he was in the presence of two CEOs from Fortune 500 companies. From their conversation Tim surmised that the real power lay in South America and that Juan Rivas's segment was rather small and disorganized, even though the Cuban was responsible for importing millions of dollars of illegal drugs a month. Tim wondered how much the really heavy hitters imported.

Both men listened very intently and politely to Tim's proposal and were impressed by his knowledge of aircraft and logistics. They talked of competition, growth, cost-benefit ratios, and loses, which had risen in the past year.

Some hours later he was again blindfolded and driven back to his rental car in a roundabout fashion. The two men had accepted his proposal and given him what amounted to a blank check.

The next week he had flown to Billings, Montana, to inspect four old, tired forest fire bombers—exactly what he was looking for to implement his plan. The four airplanes were for sale at almost salvage prices and sat in the weeds on the west side of the airport covered with streaks of oil and forest fire retardant. There were a few dozen of these models left in the United States out of the thousands that had been built during World War II. Some sat forlorn like the ones he was inspecting, waiting for the scrap yard; some were in museums; a few were still pulling duty in other parts of the world; and a few lucky ones were in the hands of rich collectors, restored to almost-new condition.

As Tim ran his hand along the filthy side of the first bomber in line, he met George, who had driven out to see what the trespasser wanted. The meeting turned out to be an important bonus to the organization. Nobody knew more about the A-26 than the old mechanic.

The four airplanes had been manufactured over three decades previously and had done yeoman duties as forest fire bombers the past twenty years. They had been replaced by newer, more powerful turbine-powered airplanes. All had been built by the Douglas Aircraft Company in early 1945 as very fast, highly maneuverable, medium-attack bombers, requiring no escorting fighters. All four had never left the United States; they were declared surplus after World War II and stored in the desert. Two had been put into service during the Korean War and then mothballed again. The other two had been sold surplus to civilian companies in the mid-fifties and converted into fast, comfortable executive transports before Bill Lear and others invented the business jet. They were doomed when this happened in the 1960s, simply parked and forgotten. All four were eventually bought by the outfit in Billings and converted to forest fire bombers. The rugged airplanes, stripped of their armament and extra crewmembers, were capable of carrying a huge load of forest fire retardant. What had made them first perfect for the air force, then as an executive transport, and finally as a forest fire bomber, made them ideal for smuggling. Like the fast, rum-running boats during Prohibition, they were ideally suited to their next assignment.

The owner of the flying service in Billings was paid in cash the next week, and a few weeks after that, the four airplanes disappeared south.

The airplane bucked and trembled in the turbulence and then flew out of the rain shower. Tiny beads of water, left quivering on the windshield, were swept back over the tail into the slipstream. In the cold cockpit, Tim now wore his blue, insulated coveralls over his long underwear, wool shirt, army fatigue pants, and ragged wool sweater. As he neared his destination in Colorado, he also wore his shoulder holster with the 9 mm Browning tucked under his left armpit. Visibility between the rain showers was excellent in the clear western air, at least one hundred miles. Pikes Peak, towering over the city of Colorado Springs, was easily visible fifty miles ahead, its summit now obscured in gray clouds. The weather was clearly deteriorating, and all the radio stations up and down the Front Range were predicting the first snowstorm of the season.

Tim felt a sense of urgency after receiving the latest weather report. Conditions usually became worse in the mountains first. But it didn't look that bad just yet, as he scanned the horizon. Except for the occasional shower, the ceiling seemed high enough to fly the mountain passes to the ranch airstrip. First though, he wanted to make a slight detour just north of Colorado Springs.

Although the right engine's cylinder head temperature had risen another needle's width since crossing the Louisiana coast four hours ago, it was still well within safety margins and was running smoothly. *Bad Breath's* controls felt tauter, and the speed had increased considerably now that bomber had burned almost five tons of fuel in the last sixteen hours.

Twenty minutes later he turned and paralleled the interstate running north out of Colorado Springs then turned his radar transponder off. The rugged Rampart Range, where he had done survival training, towered to his left. It had begun raining again, and the drops lightly streaked the windshield. Below, half the traffic had turned its headlights on, and the southbound cars' lights reflected on the wet asphalt. Just ahead and to his right, nestled against the dark, pine-covered foothills, he saw the first of the square, modern buildings of the Air Force Academy. Moments later he banked to the left and looked down past his wingtip at the silver, peaked academy chapel, surrounded by the familiar classroom buildings. He continued to make wide, lazy circles in the sky. It was prohibited airspace to civilian aircraft, and the controllers at the Colorado Springs airport were probably having a shit-fit right now, if they had noticed his target. There was the football stadium where Harvey had played so well. And there was the academy airport, pivoting under his wings, where he had soloed so long ago. Also the first dorm and the mess hall where he had to sit ramrod straight and eat his meals.

He noticed a familiar shape parked on the expanse of concrete near the chapel as he circled. It was a camouflaged green, tan, and gray F-105D Thunderchief. The same fighter he had flown in Vietnam over two decades ago. It was completely out of service now with the air force and had been so for many years. Harvey had been blown to bits in one of those, he remembered. Most had been scrapped, and only a few had been saved for memorials, such as this one, or museums. It was just an antique or curiosity now, much like he was, its engines stilled forever.

He continued to circle and thought of his four years down there and the promising air force career that never was. They were the best years of his life, he knew, and he again thought of the good friend he had lost in that senseless war.

As he was about to depart, he noticed four cadets in their blue uniforms and slickers hurriedly crossing the concrete near the F-105 in the rain. They stopped and looked up at the sound of his engines.

Tim flew north for a few minutes and then made a turn back to the south toward the academy. He increased the power while simultaneously losing altitude until he was just at treetop level. He crested one small, forested ridge and then flew lower still. The buildings grew larger in the windshield. He cleared the first row by fifty feet, his engines rattling the windows in their frames. He flew lower still, just to the left of and level with the chapel. The four cadets turned once more at the sound of his engines and then dove onto the wet concrete at his approach. Directly over the memorial F-105, he hauled back on the control column while banking hard, resulting in a tight, steep, climbing turn over the old fighter. Then throttling back, he wagged his wings in a salute before turning south but not before smiling to himself as he watched the four cadets pick themselves up and begin to brush off their once immaculate uniforms.

Tim followed the interstate southward over the city of Colorado Springs and worried he was now being tracked on radar if his primary target had been noticed by anyone at the Colorado Springs airport to the east. Surely, frantic phone calls were being made presently from the academy. The control tower at the little airstrip there would have seen him. It had been a stupid stunt alright, but by the time anything could be done, he would be headed into the mountains and lost completely on any radar screen.

Even in the light rain, visibility was good. The huge granite massif of Pikes Peak reared up, over eight thousand feet above him to his right, the top lost in gray clouds. Tim scanned the sprawling city to his left and wondered where his daughter was at the moment. All the letters had been returned by his ex-wife, and the money, too. But from friends he maintained contact with over the years, he knew Shannon was now in her sophomore year in high school down there. He checked his watch. She would probably be in class right now, with the goal of med school sometime in the future. He had been told she was as ruthlessly ambitious about that as he had been about the academy. He smiled and knew she was a chip off the old block for sure. Good for her. Karen had remarried years ago and was still teaching students how to fly those wonderful sailplanes. Her present husband was some big-shot insurance salesman. Tim wished he could just land and visit his daughter, but of course that was impossible. The restored bomber was too obvious and had no registration number.

A lump formed in his throat. He tried to remove it by directing his attention back to the highway below, which led the way south, just past Cheyenne Mountain, the granite home of NORAD.

Still flying low at one exit on the highway ahead, he hungrily spotted a McDonald's and a Burger King, and his thoughts were diverted. How long had it been since he had eaten some good old American fast food? Or even a decent meal? He felt like a citizen of a foreign country. Or even worse—a citizen of no country. It had been almost three years since he had spent any great amount of time—more than a few hours— in the United States. His stomach growled and reminded him that it had been hours since he had finished off that last stale sandwich and thermos of coffee.

As the city finally passed behind him, he took one last look over his shoulder and wondered again what his daughter was doing right at this moment. He was so close—a thousand feet of air and a few miles. Then he turned in his seat and tried to drive it from his mind. But still, how astonished would she be when she received the money on her birthday in a few months? More than enough to comfortably carry her through medical school and then some. Maybe she would think differently of her old man then.

A moment later, just as he was banking over the foothills beyond the NORAD site, he caught some motion out of the corner of his eye. He quickly turned and was surprised and horrified to see a mottled green-and-brown F-4 Phantom a half mile to his left and closing the gap rapidly as the sleek fighter decelerated to match his speed.

Soon the jet was barely fifty yards off his wing tip and moving in closer like a big watchdog on the prowl. Tim could see the pilot and radar operator clearly in their drab flight suits and white helmets. Their sun visors were down, and their oxygen masks hung limply in front of them.

Tim held his course and watched. He waited for their next move.

The large, twin-engine fighter was as large as the old WWII attack bomber and a thousand times more deadly. A white skull and crossbones on its large black tail made the airplane look even more sinister. The skull was locked in an evil grin. Below the tail Tim saw written NORTH DAKOTA AIR NATIONAL GUARD. Tim continued to hold steady as the Phantom moved in still closer. It now assumed a nose up attitude and lowered its flaps to keep in pace with the older, slower airplane. The two airplanes were now so close their wingtips almost touched.

Tim waved at the other two men, smiled, and weighed the possibilities and options. Had they been following him all along? He knew the international signal for landing was to lower the landing gear, but the military pilots hadn't done that yet. He continued to wait for the other pilot to make a move. Tim had vowed to himself never to be captured. He would ram the other airplane before that. He tightened his grip on the control wheel.

Now the other pilot seemed to be talking to the radar operator in the rear seat and gesturing. Twice he pointed at Tim. Then the jet pilot smiled and gave Tim the traditional thumbs-up sign followed by an okay sign. He then saluted. As Tim returned the salute, the military pilot suddenly banked and turned back toward the city, which was now twenty miles to the northeast.

Tim watched puzzled as the fighter, trailing black smoke, disappeared over his shoulder.

The jet pilot and the younger radar operator had been returning from a military practice area south of Colorado Springs when they had spotted the old attack bomber just before they were going to contact the Colorado Springs radar approach controller with the intent to land back at Peterson AFB. Unbeknownst to them the controller was frantically trying to contact them after tracking the old bomber's target from the vicinity of the Air Force Academy after dozens of complaints. The pilot and radar operator were on a weeklong training mission from their base in Fargo, North Dakota, and enjoying themselves immensely. The radar operator had a girlfriend in Colorado Springs, one of many. The pilot, now retired from active military duty, owned a successful Pontiac dealership in Fargo and had, in fact, flown B-26K Invaders in Vietnam similar to the one Tim was flying. He had spotted the familiar shape while flying back from the practice area. Thinking the black airplane was a restored warbird in private hands, he had flown formation with it while excitedly telling his much younger, and bored, radar operator some war stories. But they were running low on fuel and had finally had to break formation. It wasn't until the pilot had indeed contacted the radar controller at the airport that he had learned everyone was looking for Tim's airplane. The jet pilot, protesting he was very low on fuel, had turned around, but by that time the black airplane had disappeared into the foothills and off the radar screens.

Forty miles south of Colorado Springs, Tim now flew at low level, westward along US Route 50 past Canon City and the Royal Gorge Bridge, losing himself in the mountains. He continued to follow the highway past Salida and then over his last hurdle, Philadelphia Pass. He encountered some more snow showers, the weather rapidly deteriorating across the high peaks, but had no real weather problems as he lost altitude after the pass and flew toward Crestridge and the ranch airstrip beyond.

As Tim flew westward for the final fifty miles, the weather worsened. Visibility and ceiling were dropping rapidly, and he had to fly lower still to follow the state highway into Crestridge. A mixture of rain and wet snow beat on the windshield. He estimated the visibility at barely two miles. He checked his watch. Ten minutes had passed since the pass. The fifty miles should take roughly twenty minutes. He retarded the throttles even more and slowed the airplane. It would be tricky just finding the ranch now; his previous trips had usually been in good weather, but to turn around and fly the thousands of miles back, so close to the destination, was unthinkable.

Twenty minutes had passed, and he strained to see out the windshield. He should be close now. Suddenly, almost before he realized he was there, he flew over the town and its white grain elevator, at barely five hundred feet. The town disappeared behind him as he banked sharply to the right and followed the gravel road to the northwest. There was no other way to find the ranch now except by sheer pilotage. To fly too far would put him right up against the foothills and then the high mountains themselves, which lay west of the ranch. Visibility was barely a mile now as he followed the gravel highway looking for the ranch road and that first hogback. The airstrip was right behind it. Tim slowed further and lowered the flaps to their first setting.

There, just below, was the ranch road. He banked sharply over the red-and-white sign. Now, near the foothills, the visibility dropped further as he flew through big, heavy snowflakes. He would have just one chance at the landing. He had little idea which way the winds were blowing, but the straight portion of the road behind the hogback, leading up to the ranch house, was at least a mile and a half long, he knew.

Suddenly the hogback moved under him, and the road turned north along the river valley. He had cleared it by barely a hundred feet. He had been here before, but in better weather conditions, and he tried to visualize the terrain. He had to keep the road in sight.

Tim selected the next flap setting and then lowered the landing gear. He glimpsed the outbuildings and roared over them at barely one hundred feet. The road straightened. This was it. He had to land.

There was not enough visibility or ceiling to try and circle for another approach.

He selected the final flap setting and slowly eased off the power. The black airplane sunk closer to the road. Tim sensed his groundspeed was too high and knew he must have a tailwind. Visibility was barely a quarter of a mile now as large snowflakes streaked by the cockpit windows. The road ahead of him disappeared as if into a gray wall.

Just a few more feet and he pulled the power back to idle. The airplane sagged toward the road as he eased the control wheel back. Almost imperceptibly the main landing gear kissed the wet asphalt with a squeak, and he was on the ground. He gently lowered the nose wheel and began to brake lightly on the slick road. The airplane had slowed to a crawl as he made out the vague outline of the ranch house ahead, and a plain, four-door compact sedan parked in front of the house materialized out of the snow falling at the end of the drive.

CHAPTER 16

Slush

By Monday afternoon the spiraling low-pressure system had intensified. It had moved out of New Mexico and swung northeasterly from the Four Corners area into southeast Colorado, pulling warmer, moister air up from the south in its wake. By Monday afternoon the cold front had swept down across Colorado, joining the low, and then had stalled in Colorado near the Kansas border. By late evening the counterclockwise flow around the stalled system was causing upslope conditions over the entire state.

The "chain law" was put into effect by the Colorado State Patrol on most of the mountain passes for the first time since early the previous spring. Denver's Stapleton Airport was experiencing limited visibility and low ceilings, causing long delays for departures and arrivals. Passengers squirmed in uncomfortable chairs and grumbled to one another. The airport bars and bookstores were doing epic business.

Denver's streets turned to slush, and roads began to freeze on the overpasses in Denver's first snowstorm of the season. At the old Mousetrap interchange, a semi failed to stop and rear-ended a four-door Plymouth driven by a couple from Orlando who were inexperienced in driving in the snow. The truck, owned by a large office supply company, careened off the Plymouth, ran up the guardrail, and then turned on its side, causing a shower of sparks. The trailer then ruptured and disgorged its load of ink, typewriters, filing cabinets, office chairs, and half a million ballpoint pens across I-70 and down onto I-25. The two major highways had to be closed for hours.

CHAPTER 17

The Night Shift

Mindy Jackson was curled up in her robe in the red, velour swivel rocker with her feet tucked under her, watching the TV. Her mind was not currently on what was on the picture tube. Johnny Carson's face was being beamed into her living room late at night in a rerun with Rodney Dangerfield as his guest, but she was thinking of another type of screen at the present moment.

The two targets merged on the luminescent screen and were one. Three hundred people. She held her breath. Ten agonizing seconds later, the radar display updated itself, and there were again two blips.

Mindy reached absentmindedly for the familiar red-and-gold can of Diet Coke near the lamp on the table then fished for the bent straw with her lips. She sucked some of the room-temperature liquid out and replaced the can on the table near the open bag of Fritos. Near the Fritos lay a partially eaten Sara Lee cheesecake still in its aluminum foil pan. A fork rested on the bottom of the used portion of the pan. Next to the chair on the floor lay a portable hair dryer and a Danielle Steel paperback. There was a small clock on top of the TV. Mindy looked up and noticed it was 11:20 p.m. She had to be at work in forty minutes.

The targets merged…

Mindy ran her fingers through her Dorothy Hamill–style, dark brown hair and decided it was almost dry. She looked again at the clock and sighed. It was time to get dressed. A shiver ran through her body at the mere thought of returning to that awful place. She pulled the pink bathrobe tighter around herself then reached over and picked up the fork from the Sara Lee pan and stabbed another piece of cheesecake, while experiencing more waves of guilt at the probable caloric intake in that one bite. She had been pigging out since four o'clock, which was the end of her day shift, had missed her aerobics class down at the Beautiful Gal Spa, and had probably gained five pounds by now. It had been a terrible day. She had almost single-handedly killed over three hundred people. It was more than one person could stand.

The targets merged...

Mindy uncurled herself from the chair. She slowly walked over and turned off the television set. Johnny Carson's face faded. She felt drained, all used up. She looked again at the clock. Maybe she should call in sick. Yeah, then that asshole sexist supervisor would accuse her of using PMS as an excuse again. Don't give him any ammunition. She was in enough trouble as it was. Besides she didn't have any sick leave left.

Mindy started down the hall to the bedroom to get dressed. She wanted desperately to go to bed and sleep, not work all night. Who came up with these terrible schedules anyway? She had already worked a full day shift. Now after eight hours off, she had to report back for her final shift of the week at midnight. Two evening shifts, two day shifts, and then a final night shift. It was hard for the body to take. The older, hardcore guys liked the schedule though, and it stuck. They said it gave them four days off, but the irony was you used one whole day just to recuperate from that final night shift.

The targets merged...Three hundred people...

Ten minutes later Mindy stared in the mirror and made the final adjustments to her hair. She wore a pair of dark blue slacks, which suddenly felt too tight, a light blue gingham blouse, and a yellow sweater. Satisfied with her looks, she turned from the mirror and slipped on a neon-yellow and chartreuse nylon ski parka. A couple of tattered ski lift tickets from last season still fluttered from the zipper when she pulled it up. She wrinkled her nose at the caloric disaster next to her chair as she turned off the light. Then she stepped into the hallway and secured the deadbolt to her apartment with a click.

Mindy walked down the short hallway to the outside door, which led to the parking lot. Surprisingly, the door offered some resistance, and she had to shove it with her shoulder. She was even further surprised by the five inches of new, wet snow that blanketed the walk and the parking lot. It had been snowing as she had driven home eight hours ago, but it hadn't been sticking and the streets had just been wet. Preoccupied with the day's events, she hadn't bothered to look outside since returning to her apartment.

It was still snowing lightly, and the bright lights in town were reflecting off the low cloud bottoms as she took her first tentative steps toward the parking lot. Snowflakes sparkled as they drifted down past the streetlights. The apartment manager obviously hadn't yet bothered to shovel the walks or start in on the parking lot. At this hour there was no traffic moving on the street. A single set of tire tracks curved through the parking lot. It was still fairly warm, just below freezing, and her feet squished in the near slush as she walked toward her car. Mindy thought briefly of retreating to the apartment and putting on a pair of boots, but she was already running late. She continued to walk in the wet snow and almost instantly felt the cold water begin to seep into her shoes.

The targets merged...

Her old, baby blue VW diesel rabbit was nothing more than a white lump as she tiptoed to the door and brushed some snow from the keyhole. Unlocking the door, she slowly and carefully opened it, but the snow caked on the door and window slid off in a minor avalanche and fell in a pile on her now soaked shoes. And, as she opened the door still farther, a portion of the wet snow perched above the door on the roof cascaded down and landed on the front seat, the door sill, and the floor.

Mindy threw her purse over onto the passenger's seat and then reached into her ski parka's pockets but realized too late that she had left her gloves on the kitchen counter. Leaning into the VW, she unlatched the front seatback, bringing it forward, and began to search in the dark for the combination snowbrush and ice scraper. The interior of the Rabbit was in disarray. A plastic litterbag hung heavily from the knob of the glove compartment door. It overflowed with used, lipstick-stained tissues. Five or six of these lay on the floor in front of the passenger seat. The driver's side floor mat was missing. A Kleenex box was stuffed between the seats above the handbrake. A yellow, magnetic Smiling Face was stuck above the radio next to a sign which read THANK YOU FOR NOT SMOKING. A Michael Bolton tape protruded from the cassette deck.

The targets merged...

Mindy struggled to find the scraper in the back seat, brushing aside the flotsam there. More used Kleenex, an empty Wrigley's Spearmint gum wrapper, three empty Diet Coke cans, and a dead Barry Manilow tape, which had spewed about ten feet of its shiny brown guts out on the floorboard. But no ice scraper.

Mindy sighed and pushed the driver's seat back into place. Then she brushed off the seat as well as possible with her sleeve and sat down. The seat instantly felt cold and wet. She fished her keys out of her purse and stuck the ignition key into the lock. The battery was low, but the diesel finally caught and rattled to life. After shoving the heater control to defrost and setting the fan on high, she flicked on the windshield wipers. The little electric wiper motor groaned, and the blades quivered at their base as they valiantly tried to throw off the inches of wet snow.

She tried turning them off and on quickly, but they failed to budge. There was a faint odor of ozone in the air as the wiper motor overloaded. She cursed softly and fished through her purse for her gold-and-blue Visa card. Finding it, she climbed back out of the car into the slushy parking lot.

Pulling her hand as far as possible into her sleeve, she began to bulldoze the snow from the windshield. Then she took the card and began to scrape the layer of ice that had formed under the snow. She took stabs at the ice. Her hands were raw and sore by the time she had chiseled out a four-inch hole on the driver's side. Then the credit card snapped in two. She fished one broken half from the snow on the hood.

Mindy angrily opened the driver's door and threw both pieces of the Visa card as hard as she could into the car. She then sat down on the soaked seat and swung her wet feet inside. She slammed the door with a thump. She was running late for her shift now and couldn't afford to. Not after today.

Mindy tried the wipers again, but they were still frozen as tight as a ship caught in Arctic ice. The four-inch hole she had hacked out with the plastic would have to do until the defroster could do its thing. Large, wet snowflakes were already filling up the hole she had made.

She crunched the transmission into reverse and let out the clutch. The Rabbit started backward, humped itself a couple of times in the deep snow, and then spun itself down onto the layer of ice underneath. She tried again, but the car just started to sling sideways, dangerously close to the car next to her. She spun the wheels again, but it was futile.

Mindy left the Rabbit sitting in its spot with the door open. The dome light would gradually run her battery down during the night. She trudged back across the parking lot to her apartment to call a taxi. There was no way she would make it to work on time tonight. She wondered what else could go wrong.

Walt James stood next to the pay phone with the receiver hard against his right ear. The index finger of his left hand was firmly jammed in the other ear. The engines of the business jet fifty yards away screamed at idle. Its two red anti-collision beacons reflected in the puddles on the general aviation ramp at the Las Vegas airport. The whine of the jet's engines increased as the pilot began to taxi down the ramp under the orange glow of the sodium vapor lights. Walt removed the finger from his ear as the noise diminished, but it was too late. All he had was the dial tone. He looked at the receiver in his hand briefly and then angrily hung up.

The brisk wind caught at Walt's unbuttoned topcoat as he walked down the ramp at McCarran Field in Las Vegas, and it flapped behind him. He grabbed at it and attempted to button it as he walked toward the airplane. He realized then that he was wearing the same clothes he wore on Friday: the same shirt, same tie (now loosened), pants, shoes, socks, underwear—everything. He finished buttoning the coat and ran his hand over his chin and felt the two-day stubble. The wind was cold, and he jammed his hands into his pockets. His eyelids felt heavy and scratchy. He desperately needed a shower and a warm bed. He felt like shit and was in no mood to fly, especially in this weather.

Since Saturday morning Walt figured he had had a grand total of four hours of sleep. When he had returned to Las Vegas, he and his girlfriend, Rita, had cavorted until almost four in the morning. It had been a big mistake, for he had then to fly Don Ortiz to San Francisco. He had hoped for a quick turnaround and back to Vegas, but no such luck. He had been forced to catnap all night and most of the next day. They had just arrived back in Vegas a couple of hours ago.

Now he was preparing to fly to Colorado. No one understood that there was no way to find the ranch airstrip in the dark in the storm that was pummeling the mountains of Colorado. The Gunnison airport was below minimums, and Denver airport was close to it.

He had just tried to tell them exactly that on the pay phone a few minutes ago. Why not wait for morning? he had reasoned. Or tomorrow afternoon, when the weather was predicted to clear? Fly or be fired, he had been told. What was the hurry? But Walt knew the answer to that question.

The hotel chain he had so loyally worked for all these years was a sinking ship. He knew that. And why not just hand Don Ortiz the keys to the airplane and let them find someone else? He knew the answer to that question, too. He knew too much. Quit now and his body would be feeding coyotes out in the desert before dawn. No, they would force him to fly. These people were tough and meant business. And he knew all about their precious cargo. Yes, Walt knew too much about the past few years and his boss's dealings. As he approached the twin Cessna, he thought maybe he could jump ship in Denver. At least fly that far and make a run for it. Empty the savings account and disappear.

When he was closer to the Cessna, he saw that Don Ortiz had ordered one of the large, white Cadillac limos from the hotel to be driven out on the ramp and parked on the other side of the airplane. Its engine idled smoothly as its exhaust rose up and was whipped around the car by the wind across the ramp. The trunk was open. Don was removing one last large, heavy brown suitcase from the car. Then he silently closed the trunk lid. Three more identical suitcases, already unloaded from the car, stood next to the airstair door. Walt knew there were more similar suitcases from San Francisco already inside the overloaded Cessna. A cigarette suddenly glowed from inside the limo, its dim light indicating at least two other men in the front seat, silently watching the operation.

As Walt walked around the tail of the Cessna, the limo quietly purred back across the ramp and parked just beyond the security fence next to a sinister-looking black Mercedes. Don Ortiz hefted the four suitcases into the interior of the Cessna, boarded, and then began sliding them down the aisle on the carpeting.

Walt waited at the bottom of the steps as Don secured the last suitcase and then sat down in the rear passenger seat and buckled his seatbelt. Walt climbed the steps, turned, and pulled the airstair door shut, checking to see that it was secure. He began making his way up the aisle to the cockpit. Don Ortiz grunted and moved to one side as Walt brushed past. Walt noticed reflected in the glare of the ramp lights a slight sheen of perspiration on the other man's forehead just below the jet-black hairline. There were also small beads of sweat on the other man's upper lip just above the pencil-thin mustache. He was nervously fidgeting with the large emerald ring on his right hand, sliding it around and around as he always did before takeoff. As Walt made his way to the cockpit, Ortiz pulled out a white handkerchief from his jacket pocket and began dabbing his forehead, revealing the large automatic pistol he always carried in a shoulder holster on his left side. The perspiration wasn't from the effort of loading the suitcases. Don Ortiz was very afraid of flying. But, thought Walt, you had to admire him. Somehow he always toughed it out back there with no complaints. This man was a good soldier and always carried out his orders. Walt knew the man sat through most of the flights with his eyes closed. Well, tonight's flight, given the weather, should really be something for him to endure.

As Walt squeezed past the suitcases, Don asked politely with a Spanish accent, "How's the weather tonight?"

Walt wondered whether he should tell him about the advisories the weather service had issued for turbulence and icing in the clouds, about the fact that the Gunnison airport was below minimums for landing and Denver not much better, about how it would be impossible to find a tiny airstrip at a remote ranch in this kind of weather, and about how badly this airplane had been maintained, but not wanting to upset the man, he answered, "No sweat—a little snow in Denver, that's all. We should land at the ranch in about two and a half hours. Make sure your seatbelt is tight though. Could be a little bumpy until we gain some altitude."

Don Ortiz paled, swallowed, and pulled the seatbelt even tighter. It made a significant indentation across his ample stomach.

Walt finally squeezed past all the suitcases and levered himself into the left seat in the cockpit. He began making his before-starting checks. The fuel gauges indicated completely full tanks. Although this dangerously and illegally overloaded the airplane when added to his and Don's weight and the weight of the heavy suitcases, they had enough fuel to fly to Denver and back to Las Vegas or even north to Casper, where the storm had already passed and the conditions were improving.

When he had finished all his checks, Walt turned on the master switch for battery power, set the left engine's throttle, prop, and mixture controls, and pushed the starter button for the left engine. The starter spun the propeller as Walt jockeyed the controls. The left engine had been hard to start recently, he knew, but it finally caught and roared to life. The right engine caught immediately and also roared to life before settling into a loping idle.

Walt turned on the radios and let them warm up for a moment out of habit. It was unnecessary. They were solid-state electronics now and available for instant use. Then he turned on the navigation lights and red anti-collision beacons on the belly and the tail.

Walt tuned in the ground control frequency and reached for the microphone hanging in its holder under his side window. He made sure no other pilot was using the frequency and then requested taxi instructions and his clearance to Gunnison.

The controller read the clearance back rapidly and issued taxi instructions to the active runway. Walt jotted down the clearance and acknowledged the controller's instructions.

Walt replaced the microphone in its clip and advanced the throttles. The Cessna began to move, and he flipped on his landing lights. Two white beams shot out and illuminated the wet ramp as he advanced to the active runway. He stopped just short of the runway and conducted his pretakeoff checks. Both engines seemed in order and were now idling smoothly. All pressures and temperatures were normal, and the needles were in the green arcs on their gauges.

He dialed the tower frequency into the number one communication radio and pressed the microphone button. "McCarran tower, twin Cessna 837 Foxtrot Hotel's ready to depart instruments to Gunnison."

The tower issued its curt reply. "837 Fox Hotel, cleared for takeoff, fly runway heading, and have a nice trip tonight."

Walt draped the microphone over his left knee, switched the radar transponder to on, and added power. The Cessna swung onto the runway, and he applied takeoff power. As the airplane accelerated down the runway, he glanced at this watch. 11:22 p.m. It seemed to take a little longer to gain takeoff speed to Walt. Perhaps it was the extra weight. But the engines seemed to be producing the correct amount of power as he monitored the gauges. At 95 knots Walt brought the nose up, and by 100 knots the Cessna lifted off the runway.

Walt quickly brought the landing gear up and turned off the landing lights. Darkness surrounded the Cessna, punctuated only by the red rotating beacons.

The same metallic voice came from the speaker in the ceiling of the cockpit, "Twin Cessna 37 Fox Hotel, climb on course, contact departure control one one nine point seven, goodnight."

Walt picked up the microphone, "Roger, on course, departure one nineteen seven, goodnight."

He banked to a more northeasterly heading and brought the power back to climb settings. Some light turbulence shook the airplane as it entered the cloud cover. Walt reached back and drew the curtain closed between the cockpit and the cabin.

Don Ortiz crossed himself at the change in pitch of the engines and propellers then dabbed his forehead once again with his sodden white handkerchief.

One of the en route air traffic control centers of the Federal Aviation Administration sits in the middle of roughly six acres of government land in the northwest portion of Longmont, Colorado, just off Seventeenth Avenue. It was constructed in the 1960s and originally sat all by itself well out of town. But the city grew by leaps and bounds in the '70s and '80s, and now the fortress-like building is situated right in the middle of suburbia. There is a large Safeway store just to the west of the government's high-security fence, which runs around the perimeter.

The control center itself is a large, three-story, windowless building bristling with antennas on its roof. There is a two-story administration wing attached on the west. This wing has windows and houses the various offices, training rooms, and a cafeteria. Farther to the west of this wing is a large parking lot for the government employees and various visitors.

Seventeenth Avenue runs east and west along the northern perimeter, and there is a security gate and checkpoint about midpoint along this edge. The main drive runs south for half a block to the complex past the guard shack at the entrance.

Although this air traffic control facility is located in Longmont, some thirty miles north of Denver, it is officially known to all pilots in contact with it as Denver Center. There are twenty of these air traffic control centers located around the United States. They were all located purposely some distance from the metropolitan areas from which they derive their names in the belief that they would be less vulnerable in case of nuclear attacks. Of course, this was before the days of multiple nuclear warheads with almost pinpoint accuracy.

Each center is responsible for air traffic control for the vast amount of airspace between metropolitan areas. Denver Center's airspace extends from the middle of Kansas in the east to as far west as the Grand Canyon.

While the occasional air traveler might glimpse the glass-enclosed control towers at the various airports around the country as they look out the windows along the airport concourses, they never see the en route control centers, which employ thousands of air traffic controllers and have none of the glamour of the towers. They are sometimes likened to big, dimly lit factories where no controller sees the light of day for his or her entire shift.

Jack Houseman leaned precariously back in his chair and recrossed his feet on the desk in front of him. The midnight shift of controllers had come and gone to their assigned positions, and he could relax now. He turned the *Hustler* magazine sideways to get a better view of the model and then took another small swig from the silver flask. A man needed some kind of fortification from the cold, he thought. He smacked his lips and belched. Yep, he needed to warm himself up a little this time of night. Government rules dictated that all government thermostats had to be locked at this temperature or that. All those Washington folks had it all figured out, he thought, as he took another swig and ogled the model on the next page. Trouble was, all those fool lawmakers didn't have to spend the entire eight-hour shift in a little glass-windowed shack with the door opening and shutting all the time. The thermostat was locked under a nice secure plastic cover. No tampering allowed. The place never did warm up all night. Damn government.

Jack leaned forward and picked up the remainder of an egg salad sandwich from his beat-up, black lunch pail. He automatically took a bite and turned the page again. Where did they get these women, he thought? And how did he get so darn old so fast? He took a second bite and recrossed his legs.

Jack Houseman was the first and only line of defense in the security of the entire complex tonight. The other guard, Bernie, had called in sick, and no one could find a replacement. Just himself and his old Smith and Wesson .38—all six bullets.

Jack had been a Denver cop for twenty-six years before retirement two years ago. His wife just couldn't put up with him full time and had died nine months later. He was alone now. Yes, he did have a daughter in Anaheim and two grandchildren, but he usually only saw them at Christmas. He had been hired by an outfit who had won the security contract put out by the FAA. The lowest bidder. The FAA decided to save some money and hire rent-a-cops, who came much cheaper than full-time government employees, with their retirement and benefits. So Jack was going to become a double-dipper in a few years when he became eligible for social security on top of his police retirement. And the seven bucks an hour the guard outfit paid him came in handy. He was almost sure no terrorists would ever drive a big truckload of explosives through this gate past his guard shack. There were plenty of better, well-known targets around.

Jack yawned and flipped through another page. He checked his watch. Jesus, it was only a little after midnight. Seven and a half hours to go. How in the world would he keep awake? Then he noticed a car coming west. It slowed and flashed its turn signal in his direction. The cab pulled up adjacent to the brightly lit guardhouse and splashed to a halt in the slush. Its windshield wipers, weighted down by ice, swished tiredly back and forth out of sync.

Mindy opened the rear door and walked around to the driver's side. She fished a five dollar bill from her purse and handed it to the driver. She didn't expect any change. The driver put the worn-out car in gear, backed out onto Seventeenth, and started back into town. Mindy walked over to the guardhouse door.

Jack had seen her climb out of the cab and recognized her. He quickly put his feet on the floor and stashed the *Hustler* in an empty drawer. The slim flask went discretely behind the thermos in his lunch pail lid. He donned his hat, opened the door, and stepped out into the dreary night. He turned up his collar as a gust of cold air blew past the guardhouse and rattled the chain-link fence on either side.

Mindy stepped up onto the curb and noticed the clock inside. It read 12:22. She began fishing in her purse for her ID. Jack raised both hands and, realizing he was swaying a little, dropped them quickly. He smiled at Mindy, who was still concentrating on the inside of her purse. "That won't be necessary, Miss Jackson. I know who you are. Just go on in." Well, Jack, he thought, you really ought to see the ID, but she's a cute little thing, and you might score some points here. He faked some more concern by asking, "What's wrong with the VW?" Jack always remembered people's cars—an old habit from the Denver PD.

Mindy reshuffled her purse and answered, "Thanks a lot. I don't know what's wrong with the car. I think the battery is shot." She was embarrassed. She couldn't remember the old fart's name. Jim or Steve or something.

Jack belched once and brought his hand to his mouth, but it was too late. He leaned as far forward as possible and leered. "Well, that's too bad. We could go back to my place and you could let me jumpstart you. I'm an expert, and my battery's all charged up."

Mindy understood the guard's innuendo and for a moment thought of reporting him for sexual harassment. She had smelled the liquor on his breath, too. Maybe throw in an alcohol violation, too. But, instead, she just sighed, turned, and walked toward the main entrance some fifty yards away. Let someone else do the complaining.

Jack Houseman watched her walk away. He swayed and caught the door for balance.

Mindy walked ten yards and turned. She touched the side of her mouth with her hand and said, "You've got some egg salad on you." Then she purposely giggled like a teenager. "Better wipe it off." Then she turned around again and walked toward the front entrance.

Jack took a swipe at his mouth and came off with a big glob of egg salad from his sandwich. He wobbled back into the guard shack and shut the door. Bitch, he thought. Then he looked at the thermostat under its plastic security cover. Goddamned government, he thought for the hundredth time that night.

Mindy arrived at the main door on the north side. Normally, she would have entered the west door off the parking lot. Each door had a security system and a code. There was a small protected box to the right of the door with a standard ten number keypad. To gain access, an employee had to enter the proper four-digit code. It had been changed two days ago, and Mindy tried to remember it. It was changed roughly every week. There seemed to be endless memos on new codes. Mindy remembered tonight's code: 6969. Everybody's favorite.

Mindy punched in the correct numbers, heard a click, and pulled open the heavy glass door. She walked into the lobby and stomped the slush off her shoes. The warm air felt good. Her feet would dry out in a few hours.

The lobby was darkened this time of night. It was the standard, government issue lobby with its vinyl chairs from the sixties, a few sick-looking potted plants, and a receptionist's desk to the right. The required framed pictures on the opposite wall—the President, Ronald Reagan, the secretary of transportation, and the director of the FAA—smiled down on all who passed through the main doors. In recent weeks, since the pay raise for government employees had been pushed back to April, someone had taken to periodically drawing mustaches on all the pictures with a magic marker. Rumors had been flying throughout the facility about the identity of the culprit. Memo after memo had been sent out from the facility chief's office with dire warnings to the guilty party. The vandal hadn't struck for almost a week now, but still Mindy glanced at the pictures out of habit. All the men were still clean-shaven today at this hour.

The hall to the right led past the receptionist's desk, empty at this time of night, to the various offices, including the facility chief's, the man who held this hellhole together. This hallway then turned left back toward the cafeteria and a break room in the rear, or south side, of the center. Just past the receptionist's desk in the hall was a large display of two-inch pictures of everyone who worked at the Denver Center, with their names on small plaques underneath. This display was in a constant state of flux and never up to date, as new hires came in, people transferred to what they thought were greener pastures, and other people did indeed retire to these greener pastures at last. Mindy's picture had just been added, and she had been working at the center over eight weeks after returning from her initial training in Oklahoma City. There were still the pictures of two controllers who had suffered heart attacks last winter. One had died at home, and the other had recovered but was still fighting the FAA for a disability retirement, trying to prove the stress of the job had caused his attack. Both men were in their early fifties. There was a picture of another who had had a mild stroke while working the afternoon traffic into Denver from the east in bad weather by himself. All of forty-eight years old, he had become a legend, slurred speech and all. He, too, was battling the FAA's lawyers. The FAA's stance was simple: there was simply no stress on the job. This made things easy. If stress didn't officially exist, then the FAA didn't officially have to deal with it when it made people sick.

Mindy turned to the left in the lobby and opened a fire door, which led into a stairwell. She ascended a short flight of steps and entered the ready room, which contained a locker for each controller and some worn-out vinyl couches, chairs, and tables.

The room was empty. The shift had just started. It would gradually fill up as controllers doubled up on positions later in order to let other controllers catch some sleep. Half a dozen at a time would be sprawled out on the broken-down lounge chairs and couches. The room was a real pit. One enterprising controller kept an air mattress and pillow in his locker. It was against policy to sleep, but no one enforced this rule. The real artists could catch just about four hours of sleep on an eight-hour shift. Mindy walked over, dialed in the correct numbers on the combination lock, and opened her locker. She hung up her coat. She then shut the door and, after extracting her ID badge from her purse, walked back across the room. She clipped the badge to her blouse as she reentered the stairwell.

A heavy security door on her right led into the main control room. A sign on the door warned in bold black and red letters: SECURITY AREA: ID BADGES MUST BE WORN AT ALL TIMES BY FEDERAL PERSONNEL. No one scrutinized the badges really. One controller had substituted a picture of *Mad Magazine*'s Alfred E. Newman for his own picture for months until someone important had caught it. The real security was in everyone on the shift being familiar with everyone else. Strangers stood out like a sore thumb. Mindy punched in the correct code on the electronic lock and entered the control room.

The main control room was the heart of the entire complex. It was large and had roughly the same dimensions as a high school basketball gymnasium. It had a distinct electronics-and-stale-cigarette smell, much like a busy video arcade at a mall. There was always a distant hum from overworked fans. The stairwell door entered the room about three-quarters of the way along the west wall placing most of the room to Mindy's left. To her right was a hallway leading back toward the cafeteria and the training area containing the radar simulators. Ahead of her and extending to the right clear across the room were the various supervisors' desks. The remainder of the room to her left was the dimly lit, carpeted core of the facility.

Four rows of radar screens and consoles divided the room and stretched to the north wall. Two of the rows were back to back in the middle of the room. Their high consoles effectively divided the room in half. Each row had ten radar positions.

To the first time visitor, it was very impressive. To a controller who worked there day after day, it was a sweat pit the likes of which hadn't been seen on the planet Earth since the days of the Black Hole of Calcutta. The radar displays and the computers that backed them up were outdated the day they were installed. They could fail at any moment and did so with regularity.

The room purposely had a high ceiling. The FAA had installed a glass enclosed walkway across one end, so taxpayers could look down on the whole operation and be suitably impressed. This walkway seemed to be the only reason the room had been designed to be almost two stories high.

To the casual observer, the room seemed orderly and professional. Whereas during a day shift there might be one hundred fifty people working at one time on the floor of the control room, and in bad weather it could be bedlam, during the nightshift when traffic was light there might be twenty at any given time.

As Mindy walked across the room to her sector, she spotted Luther Young ahead, sitting at his desk. Young was the assistant chief in charge of the nightshift. His desk blocked Mindy's way to the second row of radar screens and her position. She was training on the airways sector to the west and southwest of Denver, encompassing the entire southern half of the state of Colorado.

Young was kicked back in his chair as far as possible, seemingly defying gravity, with his feet up on his desk: *max lean*, as most controllers called it. He was absorbed in a phone call, the receiver pressed hard to his ear. A product of the Marine Corps, he was a short, stocky man with a pink face and a military haircut. He was no doubt abusing the federal telephone system, talking to some other buddy in another facility. Most controllers and supervisors thought the free long distance was a perk worth hundreds of dollars a year. Mindy thought of the incident that afternoon: her *deal*, as controllers called it. It was looking more and more like she could just sneak on past Young.

As she continued across the room, Mindy's eyes left Luther Young for a moment to see who was going to be working with her tonight. She silently wished her trainer, Jimmy Clark, the one she had had the deal with, had called in sick tonight. Clark was a product of thirty years in front of radar screens at various facilities all over the country. If most average burnout cases were compared to, say, a lightly browned piece of toast, then Clark's burnout was molten titanium, and he was an asshole to boot.

Mindy looked back at Young and wondered if he had found out about the deal yet or not. He was still yakking on the phone. She decided to make her break. Her blood pressure shot up twenty points. Did he know about the incident that afternoon or not? Mindy clutched her purse and hurriedly strode across the room to her position. She drew even with Luther's desk. So far, so good. She turned the corner around the middle radar displays, and there was Jimmy. He sat at the third radar screen from the end. He had a headset on his fat, little, liver-spotted head and was leaning back in his chair with his hands behind his head. A cigarette dangled from his mouth with an ash at least a half-inch long. Traffic must be light, Mindy thought. She also thought the letch must have all kinds of fantasies about her. Jimmy had twenty-two years in. A long time in the trenches. Three more until retirement.

With twenty feet to go, Luther hung up and yelled across the thirty feet to her, "Mindy, step over here. I want to talk to you."

Mindy felt trapped. He must know about that afternoon. How could he not know? She stopped, put a smile on her face, and turned back.

Luther stood up and grasped the handle of his favorite putter, which had been leaning against a filing cabinet near his desk. As she approached him, she saw the practice putting hole twenty feet or so across the carpeting near another vacant desk. It was one of those kinds which automatically returned the ball. Luther pulled a golf ball from his pants pocket and gently placed it on the floor at his feet. Lining up the shot carefully, he complained, "You're late again, Mindy. This is the third—no—the fourth time in the last three months. I hope you have a good excuse, and it better not be one of those female problems again." Then he stroked the ball.

Mindy watched it roll slowly into the hole and then get spit back out. Well, this pig of a man should know this "course" pretty well, he's been playing it for years, she thought. Mindy said, "I'm sorry, my car wouldn't start. I had to wait and take a cab."

The ball rolled back to Luther's feet, and he trapped it with the putter head. He began to line up another shot. Like a pro he kept his head down as he stroked the ball again and asked the floor, "How's the training going? Any more problems?"

The truth was that the training was going horribly, and he knew it. The "problem" he was referring to was Mindy's former trainer until two weeks ago. Mindy was still thinking of filing sexual harassment charges against him if they came any closer to washing her out of the program. Luther knew this. It was a standoff. Jimmy had been assigned as the new trainer in order to deliver the coup de grace. Mindy replied, "It's been going real well. I'm finally getting the hang of it, I think."

Luther stroked the ball again. "Well, that's good. Remember, if you have any more troubles, just come to me and we'll try to handle them informally first. I just don't know of anything that can't be solved with some good old-fashioned talk." The ball broke a little left and hit the mark again.

Mindy knew what "informally" meant. Sure, you bet. Informally meant no paperwork, no union, and no proof in the future. Luther Young would like that. Mindy answered, "Sure, okay."

The golf ball came rolling slowly back to Luther's feet. "Well, you'd better get to work. It should be an easy night. Not much traffic in this weather."

Mindy had been dismissed. Without saying a word, she turned around and headed for her sector. As she approached her radar position, Jimmy took his hands from the back of his head and rocked forward in his chair. His practiced hand rolled the slue ball in the middle of the console just below the large radar display. By rolling the ball, the controller moved a cursor around the radar screen enabling the computer to see which target the controller wanted to work with. As Mindy watched, Jimmy put the cursor over a target and then tapped some numbers and letters on his keyboard and waited. The target and its data tag began to flash, indicating he was handing control of the aircraft over to the next controller's sector. He looked intently at the radar and grimaced as cigarette smoke drifted up into his face. The target stopped flashing, indicating that the next controller had acknowledged the handoff and the aircraft could be sent into his sector.

Jimmy keyed the push-to-talk switch connected to his headset and spoke to the pilot hundreds of miles west of the center. "Delta 471, contact Salt Lake Center, one two seven point three five."

He waited silently as the airliner replied and then said, "Yes, Delta, I've got your icing report, moderate-to-severe rime ice from one four thousand to flight level two one zero."

He waited a few seconds more and then was satisfied that the airliner had indeed contacted the other controller in Salt Lake City. Then Mindy heard him mutter something under his breath. Jimmy always did that.

He had been at war with most pilots for over two decades. They were overpaid prima donnas in his book. Mindy had heard all the adjectives in the past two weeks, especially during the morning and evening rushes. After the handoff, Jimmy leaned back in his chair once again and clasped his hands behind his head.

Each sector had two positions, the radar controller and the manual controller. The manual controller sat next to the radar controller and helped keep track of the airplanes under his control, with paper flight strips in plastic holders. The manual controller's job was crucial in case the radar failed. Mindy was training for the manual controller's position but also worked as a radar controller under supervision, with both positions combined when traffic was light such as tonight.

As Mindy walked behind Jimmy to her chair, she noticed her former trainer, Greg Wallace, with whom she had had the trouble in previous weeks, working two radar screens down. An open pizza delivery box lay on his console along with a can of Pepsi, testifying to the fact that he was not getting a break tonight and eating right at his position. Someone must have called in sick tonight, and he is manning the sector solo for the entire eight hours, thought Mindy, as she glanced his way. He felt her stare and looked over at her. Then he took a cold slice from the box and jammed it into his mouth, chewing with his mouth open while continuing to look in her direction. What a nice display of immaturity, thought Mindy. And a great John Belushi imitation, too. Greg and Jimmy were the only controllers working on this row of positions tonight, and Mindy would have to sit between them.

She set her purse on the console, and Jimmy looked up, noticing her for the first time. She sat down in the chair next to him. There were only four flight strips in the rack in front of her, meaning Jimmy was only working four aircraft at the moment. So far he hadn't said a word to her.

She looked at the radar display in front of her and wondered what had come about since that afternoon. There were four targets moving across the hundreds of miles of airspace encompassed by the radar display: two Deltas, an American, and a private jet. As she looked, the computer updated the display, and the targets jumped a fraction of an inch forward.

Finally, he decided to acknowledge her presence and turned toward her, still leaning back with his hands behind his head. He said sarcastically and loudly, "Well, it's about time you got here. Where ya been? Out bangin' yer boyfriend? A lot of help you've been." Then he looked down at Wallace and winked. Clearly he was trying to get her goat.

"My car wouldn't start." It didn't sound convincing at all.

Jimmy asked her, "Where's your headset?"

"I guess I left it in my locker. I'll go back and get it."

In her rush to get past Luther, she had forgotten it.

"Yeah, how do you expect to talk to anybody without it?"

Mindy stood up and walked behind him. Jimmy gave a discreet thumbs-up to Wallace and rocked forward in his chair. His cigarette ash, now longer than any law of physics said was possible, fell on his shirt, and he brushed it off. He tapped on his keyboard again, waited, and then keyed his mike. "Delta 486, contact Salt Lake Center, one two zero point three five."

He listened for the acknowledgment then muttered under his breath, "Yeah, goodnight to you, too, buddy."

The ready room was dimly lit now as Mindy entered it for the second time. The lights had been extinguished for the night. The only illumination came from the stairwell lamp shining through the five inch square window in the heavy security door. She stumbled twice before her eyes became accustomed to the dark and she could find her locker. As she grabbed her vinyl headset pouch and shut the door, she could already make out two comatose forms slouched in a couch and a chair. The night shift had begun, and, given the weather, it was going to be another long night with Jimmy.

His navigation radio indicated he was over Hanksville, Utah, and Walt leaned forward and twisted a small knob, which rotated the heading bug clockwise. The autopilot obeyed and changed the aircraft's course to a more easterly heading. He yawned and stretched as much as his seatbelt allowed then glanced at his watch. 12:42. He rubbed his scratchy eyes with both hands and tried to shake the sleepiness from his head. The two engines droned loudly on either side. That sound was enough to put you to sleep, he thought. He looked over at the left engine. The rotating beacon on the tip of the tail briefly outlined it and the propeller disk in red every few seconds. He had climbed through some heavy overcast leaving Las Vegas and had picked up a little ice, but now they were in the clear. Bright stars shone overhead in the black sky. The dim, white cloud tops were several thousand feet below him, and the air was smooth.

The radio speaker above his head suddenly came alive with the controller's voice, "Twin Cessna 7 Foxtrot Hotel, contact Denver Center on one two two point six five, goodnight."

Walt picked up the microphone and acknowledged the controller's instructions, "Okay, Denver on one two two six five." Then he tuned the radio to the correct frequency and pressed the mike button. Simultaneously, the airplane entered the dense billowing storm clouds that rose up in front of it.

Jimmy and Mindy had traded places fifteen minutes ago. They were barely an hour into the shift. She now sat directly in front of the radar display, and he slouched in the other chair to the right. Both sat in silence. Mindy was lost in her thoughts. There was little traffic. Two targets inched across their sector. One was a Learjet on its way to Kansas City, according to its flight strip, and the other was an American flight bound for Chicago. Another target inched its way from the west and would be handed off to them by the Salt Lake Center controller soon. Jimmy was officially training her now. A new controller was allotted so many hours to check out on each position, and he was determined to burn up as many hours as possible even during the periods of light traffic. Mindy had decided Jimmy's cigarette breath was even worse than it had been that afternoon.

Further to their right, Wallace sat slumped forward in his chair with his head resting on his arms. He had no traffic right now in his sector. The empty pizza box lay on the floor along with the Pepsi can.

Jimmy fished in his shirt pocket for his last pack of Camels. He pulled the final cigarette from the pack, crumpled it, and then threw it on the console, where it landed next to the almost full ashtray. He lit the new one with the old one. The radar position was enshrouded with blue smoke. Mindy tried to fan the smoke away with little success thinking all the while how much her clothes reeked every day when she came home, not to mention the damage it must be causing to her lungs. The FAA was very nervous about not permitting smoking while on duty since the majority of controllers had to smoke while under stress.

Jimmy tapped the thick glass covering the radar display and pointed out the target inching its way toward the boundary of their combined sectors. The flight strip indicated a twin Cessna with the call sign N837FH. Its destination was Gunnison. The electronic data tag following the radar target also confirmed it was N837FH, presently at seventeen thousand feet with a groundspeed of 160 knots. He said to Mindy, "I think you have a customer."

Mindy focused on the radar display through the blue haze. A small letter *h* in the data tag was flashing, indicating the controller in Salt Lake City now talking to N837FH wanted to hand the aircraft off to her. Mindy punched the airplane's computer number into the keyboard and pushed the enter key. The letter *h* turned to an *o*, and the flashing stopped, indicating that the automatic handoff had been made.

Thirty seconds later the twin Cessna pilot's voice came in loud and clear over her headset. "Denver Center, twin Cessna 7 Fox Hotel is with you level at one seven thousand."

Mindy answered, "7 Fox Hotel, Denver Center, roger, radar contact."

Jimmy hissed, "Don't forget to use the aircraft's full call sign on the initial contact, and you don't have to say 'radar contact' because he is going from one radar facility to another and was never out of it. I told you that yesterday. You only say 'radar contact' on the initial contact or when it has been lost and then regained. I'm going to have to write that up."

"Sorry, I forgot."

"Well…" Jimmy took a puff and blew out some more smoke.

Meanwhile Walt asked, "Denver Center, this is 7 Fox Hotel. Do you have the latest Gunnison weather?"

Mindy replied, "7 Fox Hotel, standby, sir."

Jimmy offered some more advice. "You really never have to call any pilot *sir*."

Mindy busied herself in calling up the latest Gunnison weather on another video screen near the radar display. "I was just being polite."

"Yeah, well…"

She punched in the correct identifier for the Gunnison airport, and the information appeared on the screen in code.

Jimmy said, "Chances are that asshole pilot will want the Denver weather, too."

Mindy entered the correct code, and the Denver weather appeared with the Gunnison weather.

She keyed her mike. "7 Foxtrot Hotel, Denver Center. Are you ready to copy the latest weather?"

Walt answered, "Go ahead, Center."

"Roger, it just came out. At 0650 Zulu, Gunnison is reporting an indefinite ceiling one hundred feet, sky obscured, visibility one sixteenth of a mile in blowing snow, temperature minus six degrees, dew point minus ten, wind three two zero at two five gusts thirty, altimeter two nine eight nine."

The minimum visibility needed to land at Gunnison was one half of a mile.

"Roger, 7 Fox Hotel has that. Thank you. I'll keep heading in that direction, but when I get a little closer, if it's not any better, I'll more than likely go on to Denver."

"Roger, the Denver weather's much better at ceiling five hundred and visibility at three miles in light blowing snow."

"Roger."

Mindy wondered why anyone would fly in such terrible weather, but she knew that pilots in private airplanes were not as restricted by weather rules as the airlines. Both she and Jimmy had forgotten the icing report given by the airline pilot just as Mindy had reported to work.

Jimmy stubbed his last cigarette out in the overflowing ashtray. He had gone through a pack since the midnight shift had begun. In purely reflex action, he patted his left shirt pocket and remembered that was his last pack. He looked at the flight strips. Traffic would be light enough for him to leave the position for a few minutes and head for the cigarette machine in the cafeteria. He had two departures from Denver in thirty minutes, and there was the twin Cessna to the west. The only other two airplanes he was working would be handed off soon to Kansas City Center to the east. He patted his pocket again. He needed another cigarette and wanted to take a piss. Jimmy made his decision and stood up. He asked Mindy, "Do you think you can handle it for a few minutes?"

Mindy thought of that afternoon. Was it possible no one else had caught the error that had occurred while she was unsupervised? But she suffered no illusions. He had no confidence in her at all. Nicotine was making the decision at present. She answered in a small voice, "I think so."

To say otherwise and not show even the smallest bit of self-confidence would knock her down a peg again. She did not want to be left alone but was caught in a dilemma. On the other hand, she would like to get rid of him for even a few minutes. Besides, what could happen in ten minutes? It was the middle of the night. There were only a couple of airplanes under her control, and none even needed any separation. She would have to make a couple of handoffs. That's all. She should know enough about this business by now to handle that.

Jimmy stood there and gave her a little briefing. "Okay, the traffic is light. There's no separating. Just let them go on their merry way. I'll be back in a few minutes. I'm just going down the hall and get some more butts."

Mindy nodded.

Jimmy walked behind her and hesitated. He fished in his pants pocket for some change and pulled out a quarter, which he threw on the console in front of Mindy. "There," he said, "don't let any of those assholes get any closer than the width of that quarter." It was the standard joke for trainee controllers as they learned to estimate the standard five-mile separation on the radar screen.

As Jimmy walked by the assistant chief's desk, he stopped and spoke to Young. Young leaned his putter against the desk and then joined Jimmy as he headed for the cafeteria. They had both walked ten feet when Young made a dash back for his desk and the putter. He had almost forgotten it. If he left it alone, someone would surely sabotage it in his absence.

Mindy looked at the radar screen. In a few minutes she would have to hand off the Learjet to another Denver Center controller whose sector tonight encompassed the east side of Denver clear to the Kansas border. He was somewhere in the same room but way over on the other side. Mindy didn't know him or hadn't even probably met him, even though they were now working fifty feet apart. The airline flight would also have to be handed off, but Jimmy should be back by then.

The voice of the pilot in the twin Cessna came clearly over her headset again. "Denver Center, 7 Fox Hotel. Any change in that weather at Gunnison?"

Mindy answered, "Uh, 7 Fox Hotel, standby, sir." Her voice seemed higher with Jimmy gone. She told herself it was all routine. No separating. No heavy traffic. She checked the weather. It was still the same. She keyed her mike again. "Uh, 7 Fox Hotel, the Gunnison weather is still the same. Visibility is one sixteenth of a mile in blowing snow."

"Okay, how about the Denver weather?"

"Standby, sir."

"Roger."

Mindy obtained the Denver weather. It had improved a little in the last thirty minutes. "Denver Stapleton is presently reporting six hundred overcast, visibility two miles in light snow, wind zero seven zero at eight, and the altimeter two niner, niner niner."

"Okay, Gunnison looks like a no-go; I'd like clearance on to Denver. Can you give me a vector direct?"

Mindy thought for a moment. She knew she had done this before but with a trainer always backing her up. And she knew how to make the proper entries into the keyboard. She'd have to coordinate this eventually with Denver's approach control, but Jimmy would be back by then. But the big question was where the heck was Denver in relation to this airplane, she thought. She looked at the compass rose around the radar screen, at the airways depicted on the radar screen converging toward Denver, and at the twin Cessna's target. There were some rules for this, she knew. She started to ask herself why the pilot just didn't navigate on his own, but decided that sounded too much like Jimmy. Well, if she was wrong, he'd sure correct her in a few minutes.

Just as she was about to issue the pilot a heading his voice came back over her headset. "Denver, this is 7 Fox Hotel. Did you get my request for a vector to Denver?"

"Uh, roger, 7 Fox Hotel." Mindy put one finger on the target and another finger over near Denver. She estimated the angle and looked at the compass rose around the radar screen again. "Fly heading zero seven zero, vector for Denver."

"7 Fox Hotel, okay, heading zero seven zero, thanks."

"You're welcome, sir."

The target on her screen changed course slightly. It was now on a heading for the highest terrain in the state of Colorado.

Walt snapped the microphone back into its clip. He twisted his heading bug to the heading the female controller had given him, and the autopilot obeyed by banking the airplane slightly to the left. He leaned back in his seat and rubbed his eyes. Then he stared at the engine gauges, but they refused to come into focus. He was tired. Denver was over an hour and a half away, and he would have to fly a somewhat tight approach in there. He tried to focus on the altimeter, with little success, too. He leaned back again. His head nodded, and he forced it up. The engine on either side droned on. The air was smooth. He nodded off again, and this time his head rested gently on the left side window. Walt began snoring. In a few minutes, the windshield began to turn opaque as the ice started to slowly build up on every surface of the airplane. It was not hindered in the slightest by any deicing equipment on the airplane, because it was all turned off. The ice began to build rapidly on the wings' leading edges, the rudder, the horizontal stabilizer, and the propellers. The ice slowly began to disrupt the smooth flow of air over all of them. The airplane's weight became greater and greater. The autopilot compensated at first by pitching the nose up to hold altitude. The weight of the airplane increased rapidly. Both engines began to work harder. Walt snored louder.

Jimmy and Luther walked to the cafeteria together. Luther told a bad joke, and Jimmy laughed anyway. He was not above brownnosing the assistant chief, although he had not liked or respected the man for the last twelve years.

In the cafeteria Jimmy bought a cup of coffee and complained to the sleepy cashier about having to pay two cents extra for the lid in order to carry the coffee back to the control room. The cashier had heard him bitching for the last seven years and ignored him. She handed him his change and went back to her *Cosmopolitan* magazine.

Jimmy removed the lid and took a sip and complained to himself that it was too hot. Then he found a discarded copy of the *Denver Post* and folded it under his arm. Next he went to the cigarette machine and bought another pack of Camel regulars. He headed back to the control room after saying good-bye to the assistant chief, who had ordered a cheeseburger and fries.

Midway down the hall leading back to the control room, Jimmy turned to make sure he was now out of the assistant chief's line of sight and then ducked into the men's restroom. He walked across the tile floor and selected his favorite middle stall. After checking to ensure that there was an ample supply of the rough, government issue toilet paper, he undid his pants and sat down. Gently placing the coffee cup on the floor, he pulled the fresh pack of Camels from his shirt pocket and lit up. He inhaled deeply, savoring every tiny molecule of the tobacco smoke. Then he unrolled the newspaper and began reading the sports page. The Denver Broncos were doing badly as usual.

He looked at his watch and decided he could afford a few more minutes. The girl could handle it until then he figured. He took a Maalox tablet from his pocket and began chewing on it between drags on the cigarette and sips of the coffee. Then he grunted and farted.

Mindy didn't think Jimmy would be gone so long. She looked at the radar display. He had been right: there really wasn't much to do, but still she was nervous. Relax, she told herself.

She reached over and picked up her purse. She began picking through it until she located her nail file. Then she began reshaping a little here and a little there on her left hand. She felt a little calmer than eleven hours ago. The incident had begun to fade. Maybe no one did know. Maybe, just maybe, she should postpone her decision to quit and return to her old PE job at Monroe High School in Des Moines.

Eleven hours earlier she and Jimmy had been working a high-altitude sector in the relatively remote northwestern portion of center airspace. At the time it had been fairly easy for her for the past hour—just numerous over flights, mostly headed east or west. Jimmy was kicking back and smoking butt after butt.

But the controllers manning the low-altitude sectors in and out of Denver were sweating bullets as the weather worsened. Jimmy's help had been needed to help sort things out at the next console as the two controllers there slowly went down the tube. Airplanes were being shunted into holding patterns all the way to Kansas as the weather dipped periodically below minimums at the Denver airport.

The rush hours in bad weather had never failed to hold Mindy in awe, and she believed she might never be good enough to work it someday. She had never even attempted to work those sectors yet in her training. An airplane took off or landed every thirty seconds at that airport. When the weather got bad, everything bottlenecked—hundreds of flights during the dayshift. The FAA honchos liked to use the term *flow control* as a PR tool when dealing with the public, but in reality everything sort of went bananas.

Jimmy had been helping the other two controllers next to them while trying to keep an eye on her and his own position. Eventually he forgot about his trainee for almost ten minutes.

Mindy handled things well for the most part. Then came the big mistake.

One airliner had been eastbound at 35,000 feet and another southwest bound at 31,000 feet. The pilot of the one at 35,000 was getting a bumpy ride and had requested 29,000 feet as a cruising altitude. At the time they both seemed so far apart to her that it didn't seem to be a problem. She had looked over, but Jimmy seemed to be very busy. Her mistake had been issuing orders for the pilot of the higher airliner to "descend at his discretion." He had for some reason started down late, and she had become a little too busy with a handoff to notice. When she had noticed, they were only a few miles apart and closing at over eleven hundred miles an hour, each oblivious to the other.

Mindy stopped her nail filing as she thought again about the incident. She began to feel the nervous perspiration again prick her neck.

She had had plenty of time to react to the situation and her error. But she had frozen in place, staring at the impending collision, and had done absolutely nothing. This was the part that bothered her. How could she be expected to do this job if, at the first sign of an emergency, she froze in place? Hundreds of people headed for their doom, and all she had to do was press the mike button in her hand and talk.

The fiery doom had been avoided. Jimmy had taken over again just minutes after the incident. It was just a matter of hours ago, although it seemed like an eternity. If found out her career was probably doomed. Jimmy would get some time off, and remedial training at best.

Mindy glanced at her watch. Jimmy still hadn't returned from the cafeteria. She rolled the slue ball until the cursor rested on the Learjet's target and prepared to hand him off. He was fast approaching her eastern boundary. She hit the proper keys, and the next controller took the handoff.

She keyed the mike. "Lear two four alpha, contact Denver Center on one two two point seven five. Goodnight."

The pilot replied, "Okay, Denver, on one two two point seven five. Goodnight, honey."

Mindy grimaced at the word *honey*. She was starting to believe that pilots were indeed assholes just like Jimmy said. She went back to studying her nails and failed to notice that twin Cessna 7 Foxtrot Hotel's groundspeed indication had dropped almost thirty knots in the last few minutes.

The hard, clear ice slowly encased the airplane as Walt slept. It had built up solidly on the windshield, wings, tail, and propellers. The autopilot fought hard now to hold altitude. It pitched the airplane's nose up higher and higher. The ice reshaped the wings' contour, decreasing lift and increasing the airplane's weight. Despite still being at cruise power, the airplane slowed and was now approaching its much higher stall speed, the speed at which the wings would lose their lift altogether. Walt continued to snore in a dreamless sleep.

The ice on the propellers grew heavier and heavier and then began to fling off big chunks that bombarded the side of the airplane. Walt heard the ice banging on the fuselage but couldn't quite piece together the sound and the fact that he was fast asleep. He began dreaming. He was back at his girlfriend's apartment, and the noise was instead someone knocking on the door. But why would someone knock on the door in the middle of the night while he was sleeping? His unconsciousness eased a little bit more, and he heard the roar of the engines. This troubled him even more. Why did he hear airplane noises in the apartment? The airplane began to tremble as it entered its first buffeting just above the much increased stall speed. Suddenly, he remembered that he was in an airplane high above the Rockies and not a warm, snug apartment, and he came awake with a start.

The buffeting increased. The stall warning horn began to wail. The situation was a dangerous one, and instinct from thousands of hours in the air took over automatically. Walt shook the sleep from his head and pushed both throttles forward followed by the prop controls. The engines roared, and the propellers howled with the sudden increase in power, and the airplane surged forward.

But the airspeed continued to decrease, and the airplane was still approaching a full stall. Walt quickly disconnected the autopilot and pushed the yoke forward to lower the nose and gain some airspeed back. The buffeting decreased, but the altimeter began to unwind. Ice continued to pummel the sides of the airplane. Walt began to sort out his priorities and to think of the granite peaks just a few thousand feet below.

The airplane buffeted again, even with the increased airspeed, and he knew he could never regain any lost altitude. The altimeter continued to unwind. He had to get rid of the ice by activating the deice boots and switching on the propeller anti-ice heat.

Walt next fumbled for the microphone. He depressed the mike button and in a calm voice said, "Uh, Denver Center, 7 Fox Hotel, I'm picking up ice. I can't maintain my altitude. I'm declaring an emergency and request vectors to the nearest suitable airport. I need a lower altitude."

Mindy stopped filing her nails. Had she heard right?

Her mind began to reel and then go blank. Suddenly, she couldn't remember the lowest possible altitude in her sector and other pertinent information—all things she had committed to memory and taken a test on. She looked up at the illuminated map above the console but couldn't put it in her mind with the location of the pilot in distress. It was no help. She had cleared the pilot off the airways direct to Denver. What ice was he talking about? Then she remembered the airline pilot reporting ice to Jimmy when she had arrived at work. She had let this pilot fly right into it with no warning. Perspiration popped out on her forehead.

She had to make a decision.

She summoned up her courage to yell over to Greg a mere fifteen feet away, but Walt's voice distracted her. "Center, 7 Fox Hotel is outta sixteen thousand now and can't hold altitude! I need vectors to the nearest airport! Do you read 7 Fox Hotel, Center?"

Mindy froze as if her jaw were wired shut. The target had disappeared from the radar display.

Walt put the mike back in its clip and wondered why the center didn't answer. He had drifted down to almost fifteen thousand feet now and knew the highest peaks were just above fourteen thousand feet. He had activated all the deice devices. The propellers were heating up and not flinging as much ice as before. The black rubber boots on the leading edge had inflated and helped shed a lot of the load, but the wing itself behind the boots was still carrying a huge load of the stuff on the top and bottom, and he could see that the ice was steadily building up again on the rubber boots. But the altimeter and the rate of climb indicator indicated a descent, despite the fact that both engines still roared at full power. Walt set his radar transponder to 7700, the emergency code.

He had never fallen asleep in an airplane before now. He had heard other corporate pilots talk about it. He knew entire three-man airline crews had dozed off on long trips. But never him.

The altimeter had now stopped its unwinding and indicated just above fifteen thousand feet, and Walt felt things were finally getting under control. What had seemed like hours since he had awakened had in reality only been minutes.

He picked up the mike again.

The left engine had been flown over four hundred hours beyond the manufacturer's recommended time between overhauls. It was under full power and straining to keep the airplane aloft. An exhaust valve in the number two cylinder suddenly cracked at its lower end, causing the cylinder to lose compression. The cracked valve then separated into two pieces. As the cylinder's red-hot piston came to the top of its travel, it collided with the broken valve, which punched a jagged hole in its top and then continued downward along with the pieces of the piston top. The debris was devoured instantly by the crankshaft spinning in its bearings. In a matter of seconds, the entire engine was completely destroyed.

Hot, black oil under pressure began squirting from the engine as if someone had cut its throat. The left engine lost power and began to shake violently on its now loosened engine mounts as the remaining cylinders continued to ingest and burn high-octane aviation fuel.

Walt noticed the roughness first, which was followed quickly by a wild yawing to the left. He quickly countered with hard-right rudder pressure. His eyes went to the engines gauges. They told the story. The left engine's oil pressure was dropping rapidly. He cursed under his breath. He had no choice. He must shut down the engine and feather the propeller. He did this as calmly and quickly as his thousands of hours permitted. The yaw to the left diminished as the propeller blades aligned themselves with the slipstream. Still he added more rudder trim.

The right engine was still running at maximum power. Walt thought quickly, wondering how long that one would last. His eyes went to the altimeter. He had already lost three hundred feet in the last minute! He pitched the nose up, but the airplane trembled again on the verge of a stall. There was no way he could now hold altitude with this load of ice on the one engine.

Walt picked the mike up and tried to keep the urgency from his voice. For the first time in his career, he had to declare an emergency.

"Denver Center, 7 Fox Hotel. Mayday—repeat—mayday! I am declaring an emergency—repeat—emergency! I've lost power in the left engine. Unable to maintain my altitude. Request vectors to the nearest available airport!"

It had been barely two minutes since he had awakened. He unkeyed the mike and waited.

Silence.

Mindy stared at the radar display. Had she heard the pilot's last transmission correctly once more? She began to panic and breathe rapidly. The twin Cessna data tag was jumping around the screen, trying to tie into a target. She had no idea where the airplane was now. Words wouldn't come from her mouth. She tried to press the transmit button on her mike, but her thumb wouldn't work. Her nail file dropped to the floor, and her purse slid from her lap, emptying its contents under her chair.

Walt pleaded on the radio, a sense of urgency now in his voice, "Denver Center, repeat—mayday! Emergency! I'm going down! Do you read!?"

Another voice, a deeper one, suddenly came on the frequency, showing concern and a questioning tone. It was the captain of the westbound airliner Mindy was to hand off soon to Salt Lake Center. The pilots had been listening to Walt and were incredulous that no one had answered him yet.

"Denver, this is American 418. Are you receiving 7 Foxtrot Hotel? He is declaring an emergency—repeat—emergency. We can relay for you, Center."

Mindy didn't answer the American flight either. Her upper lip began to quiver.

The airline captain began to speak to Walt directly, "7 Fox Hotel, American 418 has received all your transmissions, but we can't get through to the center either. What's your position and altitude? We'll attempt to relay."

Walt was thankful for the airline crew's attempt to help and answered, "American, thanks a lot. I'm somewhere east of Gunnison. I'll attempt to get a radial and distance to you. I'm just going through fourteen thousand five hundred. If nothing else, I'll try to—"

The airplane began to buffet badly again as though approaching stall speed once more. Walt dropped the microphone before finishing what was to be his last crucial transmission. It slid out of his immediate reach under the seat. Then the airplane began to yaw worse in newly found turbulence. He sensed correctly that he was near the high peaks somewhere, the turbulence being created as the winds howled over the mountain tops. The microphone didn't matter anymore. He was too busy just keeping the crippled airplane flying. His last transmission was incorrect in that he was due north of Gunnison many, many miles and not to the east as he thought.

The American flight tried once more. "7 Fox Hotel, how do you read American 418?"

There was no reply. Both pilots in the Boeing 767 looked at each other. The captain raised his eyebrows, set down his coffee cup, and tuned the number two radio to the emergency frequency. He waited to hear the squeal of the other airplane's emergency locator beacon indicating a crash.

The airline captain tried Denver center once more. "Uh, Denver, this is American 418. Where in the hell are you guys!?"

Silence.

Mindy continued to stare at the radar display. He still had not come back into radar coverage. The computer was programmed to think in these situations. Even though there was no more radar contact with the airplane itself or its transponder, it did have stored in its memory banks Walt's last known heading and groundspeed. With this information the computer continued to present a data tag on the screen moving along his projected track. The computer had gone into its coast mode with the symbol CST appearing in the data tag to indicate to the controller that he wasn't watching a real target.

Walt continued to ride the airplane down. He would keep it flying right to the end. He presently had no idea what his position was and hadn't the time to figure it out. The altimeter now read just above fourteen thousand feet.

Mindy fainted, and her head drooped onto the console.

The American captain was still puzzled at Denver Center's lack of response and decided to broadcast into the blind himself on the emergency frequency.

"Any FAA facility, American 418. Emergency—repeat—emergency!"

Greg Wallace woke with a start. He knocked the empty pizza box onto the floor next to the discarded Pepsi can. He wondered at first if he had been dreaming. He tried to clear his head.

The American captain broadcast again on the emergency frequency and began to circle his 767 in a shallow turn to the south in an attempt to remain in radio contact with the stricken airplane should Walt broadcast again.

Jimmy, meanwhile, with cigarette dangling from the corner of his mouth and the *Denver Post* tucked up in his armpit, rounded the row of radar consoles and spotted Mindy with her head resting near the keyboard. For a moment, he was doubly delighted. First of all, he had beaten Luther Young back from his break with no problem, and now he could write up Mindy for sleeping at her position. She would be one step closer to washing out of the program and being thrown out the front door forever. As he approached her, he began to think up some smart-assed comment to make when he woke her up. He moved in for the kill.

But Jimmy was in deep trouble and didn't know it.

The American flight had been at 35,000 feet when the pilot had broadcast on the emergency frequency. A good portion of the controllers at Denver Center, Denver Stapleton control tower and approach control, the Colorado Springs tower, and the Denver flight service station had also heard the call. Now every controller was trying to answer him, even though most were too far away. Confusion reigned for a moment. Greg Wallace was trying to kick-start his brain into motion. Then everyone remained quiet.

The American pilot answered the confusion. "Denver Center—repeat—Denver Center only. American 418, we have a mayday from another aircraft. How do you read us?" The pilot unkeyed his mike and then questioned the legitimacy of every controller's birth to his first officer.

Greg Wallace keyed his mike and answered the American flight just as Jimmy walked up smirking. "American 418, Denver Center, loud and clear. Go ahead."

"Denver, 7 Fox Hotel—I believe a twin Cessna—is icing up and just lost an engine. Did you read him at all? We can't raise him anymore. Do you have him on radar? We were talking to some gal down there on another frequency when all this happened."

"American 418, standby."

Greg looked over at the next position at Jimmy and Mindy. American 418 was still in their sector, and she was the only female controller on duty that night. Jimmy was shoving Mindy on the shoulder in an effort to wake her up. Greg Wallace unplugged his headset and hurried over to the pair. He tried to explain quickly what was happening to Jimmy.

Jimmy turned white as he looked at the radar display. He tried to size up the situation. The data tag of the twin Cessna was definitely in the coast mode. The time lapse since the computer had seen the airplane's target was such that the data tag was now jumping around the screen vainly trying to lock on to a target.

Jimmy roughly shoved Mindy to one side and pushed his chair in position. His career was passing before his eyes, and there was quite a bit of salvage work to do. He sat down, plugged in his headset, and placed it on his head. The wires tangled, and he cursed. The bitch is going to tube me after all, he thought. The fucking female trainee had lost one and had ruined his career. He began to think of all the explaining ahead of him. The FAA had a big wooden cross down in the basement for just such incidents, and the facility chief had a hammer and a bucket of rusty nails. He would be the scapegoat for good old Uncle Sugar himself. Then there would be the inquiries of the NTSB, the National Transportation Safety Board, and their squinty-eyed investigators. Those people really went for the jugular. He had seen it happen plenty of times to other controllers in his twenty-odd years on the job. But it had never happened to him. Not until now in all those years. He thought he had developed plenty of experience in covering his ass until tonight. The champ was definitely going to take the count tonight. He sneered at Mindy's unconscious form and entertained thoughts about kicking the chair out from under her when Luther Young walked around the corner, putter in hand, twirling it like a big baton.

Jimmy, ass-coverer extraordinary, thought he had better make it look good anyhow. The airplane was probably spread across some mountainside anyway. No one survived a crash in these mountains. Yep, he'd better quickly cover some tracks at least. And he'd better put his voice on the radio transmission tapes somewhere.

He keyed his mike and remembered to put some concern in his voice. "Seven alpha fox, er…7 Fox Hotel, Denver Center. How do you hear?"

Jimmy waited and expected to hear no one. The data tag had given up and disappeared. The plane and passengers were probably crow bait by now. The trick was to get a little frantic for the people investigating the crash. They liked to hear a little bit of that on the tapes. He tried again, "7 Fox Hotel, Denver Center. How do you copy!?"

Still no answer from the pilot of the twin Cessna.

All kinds of excuses ran through Jimmy's head. How long had he been in the can anyway? Just a few minutes at most. He had just read the sports page and had only smoked one cigarette. How long would that take, for Christ sakes!

Jimmy saw the target of American 418 now. The pilot was making a wide circle over in the western part of the state. Just as the captain of that flight was about to call the center, Jimmy keyed his mike first. "American 418, do you have a problem?"

The pilot of American 418 answered, "No, Denver, we don't, but it might seem that you have a big one."

Walt had heard Jimmy's voice breaking up and trying to call him but was just too busy to fumble around to find the handheld microphone. Despite his efforts, the crippled airplane continued to descend. He made a final decision and carefully made a shallow 180-degree turn to the southwest.

Seconds before, he had vainly tried to find his position, with no success. The decision to turn around was a real gamble. He had had no time to find the map or any navigation frequencies. He had only memorized the Gunnison frequency over the years. He had tuned it in and had gotten the slightest quiver of the course indication as it tried to center on the radio's display to indicate the proper course to the station. It was intermittent but had indicated that he was somewhere northeast of Gunnison and closer to that city instead of Denver. He had been correct. Walt had been slowly descending between the towering Front Range west of Denver and the Collegiate Range southwest of Leadville. Both ranges had sharp, rocky peaks over fourteen thousand feet, which were now above his altitude.

Walt heard Jimmy's voice once more but ignored him. There was nothing the air traffic control center could do now anyway. It was up to him to get himself and his passenger out of this mess anyway. At their weight the airplane couldn't hold altitude on one engine even with that engine at full power. He would have to come down somewhere eventually. He would try for an emergency landing somewhere in Elk Park if he couldn't somehow make it to the airport at Gunnison. If he was lucky, he would be able to set the airplane down in a big, wide wheat field. If he wasn't lucky, well, then that was it. Right now he just wanted to walk away from the wreckage.

He was still applying much rudder pressure, and his leg began to ache. The altimeter continued to slowly unwind as he held his course to the southwest. The navigation radio was still intermittent and still unable to give him a distance from Gunnison. He knew the only explanation was either he was too low and far away to receive the station adequately, or the big peaks were blocking the signal. He held on and tried not to think of the latter.

In reality, the latter was indeed true. Walt was just east of the Collegiate Range and descending toward the broad-shouldered Mt. Yale, a mountain with a summit of just over fourteen thousand feet. Walt was now four hundred feet below the summit and headed directly for its rocky crest.

The turbulence increased. Walt's leg ached more, and he was drenched in sweat. The collision was seconds away in the swirling snow and wind.

Then Walt let up on the rudder pedal and reached down to rub the calf of his leg. The twin Cessna yawed wildly to the left, throwing it off its deadly course. It passed just to the left of the jagged summit, missing it by barely a hundred yards and flew into Elk Park.

As he flew from behind the shadow of the high peaks, Walt's navigation radio came alive. It indicated a steady course toward Gunnison. Walt miraculously knew his position to be over that wide expanse of sagebrush and wheat fields. The rate of descent was slowing, although they were still going downhill. If Gunnison wasn't feasible due to its distance, just maybe a crash-landing near the ranch was possible. He'd try for that now.

For the last time, scratchy and distant, he heard Jimmy's voice arguing with the American flight that had tried to help. Walt set the course indicator for the ranch's airstrip. Another five minutes and he would turn south before reaching the White Elk Mountains on the other side of the park and begin spiraling down over that fix. He had completely forgotten about his passenger.

To Don Ortiz the flight had been at first like every other normal one he had had to endure, one of stark terror. Since they had iced up and lost the engine fifteen minutes ago, it had passed somehow beyond that threshold.

Ortiz had not moved so much as an inch in those past fifteen minutes as he held the armrests in a death grip and stared out at the oil streaking down the sides of the ruined engine. His silk shirt was dark with sweat. Huge stains radiated out from under each arm and grew wider until they disappeared under his belt. His starched white handkerchief was little more than a sodden rag on his lap. Sweat covered his head and stung his eyes then dripped from his shiny, black hair onto his shirt collar. The smell of fear and sweat filled the tiny cabin. But now a new panic was creeping up into his throat, and he felt he had to get out of this airplane.

His hand went down to the seatbelt buckle. He had to tell the pilot to land this airplane as soon as possible. He wanted this airplane on the ground now! He wanted that little door behind him open, and he wanted to step out on something firm.

Ortiz flipped the seatbelt buckle open. His hand went to the big, nickel-plated Colt .45 automatic under his arm. He unclipped it from the sweat-stained holster.

The airplane trembled slightly and smoothed out. Snow still swirled past the windows. Then the twin Cessna took a vicious drop. Ortiz grabbed onto the armrest with his free hand. White knuckles were no joke in this airplane. The air smoothed out again. He looked down the aisle, but the curtain was blocking his view of the cockpit.

The flight hadn't been very bad until twenty minutes ago. Then the ice started banging on the sides of the fuselage like gunshots. And then the engines had surged before the one on the left had cut out. He had seen the oil streaking down the sides even in the dark. They were going down. He was sure of it. Panic had begun rising in his throat.

He had begun to feel the overwhelming desire to breathe fresh air and step onto the ground once more.

Ortiz released his death grip on the armrest and drew back the slide on the Colt while looking to see if a round had entered the chamber. The hammer was cocked and ready for business. He flipped the safety off and slowly, carefully rose from his seat.

He bent over and made his way to the cockpit around the suitcases jammed between the seats. If the pilot didn't follow his order, he knew he would simply kill him and land the airplane himself, not realizing in his panic how irrational that thought seemed to be. As he reached for the curtain dividing the cabin and the cockpit, the trigger felt greasy with sweat.

The air had smoothed considerably and the right engine still seemed content. Walt eased his grip on the control wheel and realized just how hard he had been holding it. He reached up and loosened his shirt collar and tie.

The altimeter still slowly unwound. They were just above 12,500 feet now.

He had tried to level the airplane, but each time it had buffeted and threatened to stall. He had to lower the nose each time to remain flying. If only I could shake that damn ice off, he had thought more than once. This particular airplane should have been able to fly on one engine easily above 15,000 feet at a normal weight. But not tonight. You could throw out the manual tonight. Walt knew the airplane had been grossly overloaded at takeoff in Las Vegas but still manageable on two engines and maybe one. But the ice had changed all that. Walt wondered just what the airplane's ceiling was at present. Seven thousand feet? Maybe nine thousand feet? Well, that was anybody's guess now, as also was the stall speed of the airplane.

The elevation of the Gunnison airport was roughly eight thousand feet, and most of the terrain of Elk Park, including the ranch, was a little higher than that. If he could hold ten thousand feet on one engine, he just might make it all the way to the airport and make a difficult approach. We just might make it after all, he thought.

Walt looked at the course indicator. He was nearing the area of the ranch. As soon as he was sure of his position and terrain, he would turn south toward Gunnison. He'd head over the broad, flat valley if he had the altitude, and if not, then he would attempt a landing in what were probably near blizzard conditions in White Elk Park and hope for the best.

He checked the altimeter again. Still just above twelve thousand feet. The needle slowly ticked counterclockwise from one white mark to another, each one twenty feet.

No more stupid mistakes now.

Walt began to get optimistic and form other plans. He had plenty of fuel even at the rate the right engine was gobbling it up. Maybe he could try for Grand Junction if Gunnison didn't work out. He could try and follow the Gunnison River valley downstream. In a few moments, he would try to raise someone on the radio.

Walt changed hands on the control wheel and felt beside his left thigh for the clipboard. He would need the charts for all this information. He caught the movement of the curtain from the corner of his eye.

There was a loud crack, and his attention was diverted. A large, dinner plate sized piece of ice flew off the windshield into the slipstream.

Another smooth, dirty yellow piece broke off the left wing next to him and was pulverized instantly against the side of the airplane.

Walt stopped fumbling for the clipboard and looked out the clear section of the windshield. He saw the rotating beacon reflecting off the moisture in the clouds at each sweep. The ice seemed to be melting and falling from the airplane. Quickly, he looked at his course indication. It was now a few needle-widths from the center. A few more moments and he would turn toward safety. He groped for the microphone cord and pulled it toward him until he had the microphone in hand. He would try and report his position. He dialed in the emergency frequency and pressed the mike to his lips.

The curtain dividing the cabin from the cockpit was swept back suddenly.

Walt twisted in his seat and became aware of the gun first. He froze. The hammer on the Colt automatic was cocked back. There was a finger on the trigger. He looked back at the instruments and then further over his shoulder at Ortiz. The man was wide-eyed and dripping sweat as his eyes darted around the cockpit. Walt had had a German shepherd as a kid. One day it had been hit by a car and had dragged itself into the garage. The dog had sat in the corner with the same look in his eyes—a look that said panic, fear, and mistrust.

Walt could also now smell the fear of the other man as he leaned into the cockpit. He held his breath, not noticing the course needle had centered. They were directly over the ranch.

Ortiz hesitated for a moment as his eyes darted around the unfamiliar cockpit, and then in a release of panic, he lunged forward at the controls. He grabbed the throttles first. The right one was far forward against the stop, and he yanked it back. The right engine lost power. It backfired loudly at the sudden change. The airplane wallowed and began to mush. The stall warning horn blared loudly. The airplane passed directly over the ranch house and continued toward the mountains, which towered beyond to the west.

Walt yelled and released his grip on the control wheel. He grabbed the other man's wrist with both hands and tried to pry Ortiz's hand from the throttle. "Let go! Let go! You're crazy; we have to have power!"

Ortiz was strong, and Walt couldn't break his grip.

The stall warning sounded again, and the airplane shook, causing Ortiz to release his grip in order to grab onto something to gain his balance. Walt took advantage and rammed the throttle forward. The engine surged, backfired again, and then caught. It roared into life. But the airplane was still buffeting badly. Walt pushed the control wheel forward. The shaking stopped, but they had lost more altitude. They were at twelve thousand feet. The stall warning was silenced.

The twin Cessna had now flown into the steep gorge of the south fork of the White Elk River. It was now trapped on both sides with high, jagged rock walls hundreds of feet tall. There was no room to maneuver or turn back.

Some more ice flew from the windshield.

Walt looked at the course indicator and was horrified to see they had overflown the ranch. He had to start his turn now. He started a turn to the left, praying with all his might that he had time.

The airplane banked to the left just at the point where the gorge itself turned to the left. They had missed the right wall by feet and were still following the gorge into the cirque almost perfectly.

Meanwhile, Ortiz had gained his balance and now lunged for the copilot's control wheel on the right side of the cockpit instead. The airplane came out of its bank and flew level, and Walt once again fought for control, clawing at the other man's arms.

More ice flew from the windshield into the slipstream.

In the struggle for control, Walt sensed the gun at the side of his head a fraction of a second before Ortiz pulled the trigger. He shoved the other man's hand away, but it was too late.

The explosion in the tiny confines of the cockpit was deafening. The bullet literally parted the top of Walt's skull and exited just above the top of the window, taking some of his hair and brains with it. The bullet hole began to whistle as the airplane began to depressurize.

Walt was still alive for a few more moments. He stared unbelieving at the instrument panel, knowing he had been wounded. In his final seconds, he was only dimly aware of his surroundings. There was the decaying airspeed, the stall warning horn, and the buffeting as Ortiz yanked back on the control wheel. His arms wouldn't move. He was powerless now to counter the other man. As he sank lower into the black void, he thought he saw a waterfall for just the smallest increment of time. Then the queerest of things...He thought he saw a mirror. The entire airplane was reflected in a mirror as the strobe lights flashed against it. Time slowed down, and the airplane in the mirror got closer.

Walt died just before the impact.

The twin Cessna lightly kissed the water and skipped like a flat stone. It was airborne again for a hundred yards, staggering through the air, trailing icy water from its wings and right propeller. Then, almost with relief, it mushed into the lake and caught the right wingtip this time. It cartwheeled twice in a violent motion before miraculously slamming down again on its belly. The right wing and engine buckled upward at a crazy angle upon the final impact. It expended its final energy and mushed slowly toward the shoreline, like the last motions of a drowning swimmer. The bow wave it created broke on the nearby rocks and dislodged the paper-thin layer of ice, which had patiently formed along the shore that afternoon. The airplane finally stopped barely seventy-five feet from the shore and then began to settle tail first into the frigid, black water. The right engine finally sputtered and died.

Don Ortiz still had a death grip on the control wheel upon the first impact. He stared numbly through the windshield. As the airplane became airborne again, he squeezed the trigger of the Colt twice more. The bullets destroyed Walt's instrument panel.

On the second impact, Ortiz was thrown headfirst into the middle of the instrument panel, crushing it and his skull simultaneously. Then as the airplane cartwheeled, he was thrown unconscious wildly back down the aisle over the now jumble of brown suitcases and bodily into the rear bulkhead, which buckled under his impact.

He was still alive as the airplane finally came to a rest tail low, and the water from the lake began to seep into the cabin. The water quickly covered his legs and lower torso, and he began to float until his head and chest came up against one of the rear seats pinning him. The water continued to rise, submerging him completely except for the arm still gripping the Colt tightly, which lay above the water on the opposite seat. The airplane settled onto the lake's rocky bottom with a muffled scraping sound, and the water stopped rising in the cabin when it was barely two inches above his forehead. Bubbles gushed from his nose and mouth, and Don Ortiz convulsed and twisted as he drowned.

One of the suitcases had come unlatched at the impact. Packets of money floated in the cabin like toy boats. One two-inch bundle of one hundred dollar bills bobbed against Ortiz's caved-in forehead and then circled around behind his left ear.

The battery shorted out, and the interior plunged into blackness. Large, wet snowflakes fell lightly and began covering the portion of the slanted fuselage still above the surface.

CHAPTER 18

Overhead

Tim snubbed his cigarette out on the flagpole in the middle of the circular drive. It was almost 1 AM and the big log house behind him was dark and quiet. No one has lowered the flags or the pennant and they hung limply above him in the cold, still air. He had been restless, unable to sleep, and had decided to take a walk. The snowstorm had abated in the last hour leaving two inches of wet snow on the drive and on the wings and tail of his large black airplane. Although visibility had increased in the past hour the clouds still hung low and wet overhead.

He had been on the ground too long for this type of operation and this worried him. Although the brother had insisted that with the gate locked no one could enter Tim knew he was vulnerable.

He began to light another cigarette when he heard the faintest sound of the airplane coming from the east. He paused as its sound became more audible. Then, in a few minutes as it seemed the airplane was directly in the clouds overhead, its engine noise diminished suddenly before roaring back to life seconds later. It continued to fly to the west toward the jagged White Elks.

Tim turned to follow the sound. He lit his cigarette, inhaled, and thought, shit.

CHAPTER 19

Ripples

Rod lay on his back wide awake in a blue, nylon cocoon of goose down sometime after one in the morning. He could see his breath in the tiny flashlight's bright beam, which was precariously balanced on the pack behind his head. He had his knees bent, and the open book rested against his thighs. It was a tedious process to read in a tent when the temperature was below freezing, he thought, as he removed one arm from his warm sleeping bag and turned the page while carefully positioning the rock again that held the book open. He quickly placed his arm back inside the bag. The hood of his sleeping bag was drawn around his head. Still, he wore a knitted hat on his head. He did indeed resemble a mummy after which his type of sleeping bag had been named. Rod was up to the part in Michener's book that described in detail the Gemini program: two brave astronauts crammed into a tiny capsule.

Next to him, so close that their sleeping bags touched, Jamie stirred and rolled over on his side. At the present moment, Rod could relate very well to those astronauts far from home. There was even some Tang left in their packs.

Both men had finally retreated to their small tent about four that afternoon because of the weather. They had been tent-bound ever since.

They had laboriously prepared and eaten their dinner in the tent as well. Big, wet snowflakes, the first snow of the year in the high country, had fallen and piled up quickly on the rocks and small patches of tundra around them. The main entree had been freeze-dried sweet and sour pork followed by small, lunchbox-sized cans of vanilla pudding.

Rod removed his arm and turned a page again. He put the rock back in place and buried his arm in the sleeping bag again. He had dozed off earlier only to reawaken again a few hours later. Not able to fall asleep again, he had decided to read a little.

He was uncomfortable. They had been in the tent for over nine hours now, and Rod apparently had an eight-hour bladder. He had been trying to ignore this fact of life for the past forty minutes because Jamie's bulk blocked the door to his right. Rod sighed, read, removed the rock, and turned another page.

He would have to make a decision soon about getting out of the tent. He hated to leave the snugness of his sleeping bag. Everything was damp. The sides of the tent sagged inward with the weight of the wet, new snow which had collected on the rain fly. Rod reminded himself to punch the sides of the tent again in an effort to bounce some more snow off.

Rod had one of their large, green, plastic garbage bags pulled up over the lower end of his sleeping bag. This kept half of him off the wet floor. His foam sleeping pad supported the other half. The uneven ground under the tent left folds and depressions in the floor where tiny puddles of icy water pooled. The down fill of his sleeping bag would act like a huge sponge should it come into contact with any water.

Outside the night was black and still. The wind and snow showers had ceased earlier, leaving an icy fog covering the lake through which large, wet snowflakes drifted down.

Earlier they had argued good-naturedly whether or not it should be called fog or were they just wrapped up inside a big cloud that had settled onto the mountainside and cirque. Rod had argued vehemently that fog and cloud were one and the same. Jamie had countered with the opinion that there had to be clear air between it and the ground to make a cloud; anything else was fog. Nothing had been settled. Afterward they had played two games of chess on Rod's tiny, magnetic board. Jamie had scored a surprise victory in the first game, and Rod had tied the series one all with the second. They had decided to play the tiebreaker in the morning if the weather was still bad. After the last game, Jamie had dozed off. Rod had fallen asleep later only to awaken again and start reading the Michener book.

Jamie now slept soundly on his side with his back to Rod. He had been sleeping on his back until a few minutes ago and snoring very loudly. But a couple of punches to his shoulder had caused him to turn over, and the solitude had returned. Jamie was a deep sleeper and hardly anything would wake him up. Rod could now hear the gurgle of the lake's outlet stream fifty yards away.

Rod turned another page and tried to concentrate on the thick book in front of him, but his full bladder intervened again, and he couldn't concentrate. He had to make a break and get it over with quickly. If he had just done it ten minutes ago, he'd be comfortably back in the sack. This caused him to reflect on how difficult even the simplest of tasks became in situations like this. He had read books by men who had climbed Everest. They had written how it could take hours just to put on their gear and boots or melt a pint of water. Although he and Jamie were not on the side of Mt. Everest, still he would have to climb out of his snug sleeping bag, climb over Jamie, unzip the tent, somehow drag his boots with him and put them on, and then step out into the cold in his long underwear. Then he would have to repeat the entire process to reenter the tent and his sleeping bag.

He was trying to concentrate on the book again when he first heard the airplane. At first it was distant, and he thought it must be someone overflying the mountain range. Maybe the pilot was headed for Aspen. During their stays at Hourglass, they would occasionally hear an airplane overfly the lake although it was certainly off the airways. But it wasn't unusual.

Rod read another paragraph and blanked the sound from his mind for a moment. Then he noticed the sound of the airplane growing louder. He stopped reading and listened. It was becoming a lot louder in a hurry. It seemed to Rod that the sound was coming at him from the east, behind his head, and not from overhead. The engine and propeller noise didn't have that laid back cruising note. This airplane was really straining. Rod lay still and listened.

The sound of the airplane increased more. It seemed to be coming right at the tent. The sound increased further and became a loud roar.

Rod instinctively hunkered down as far as possible in his sleeping bag.

Suddenly a bright, white, pulsing light illuminated the fog. The noise was deafening as the airplane flew over and missed their tent by barely fifty feet.

The noise then began to fade. The engine sound was interrupted twice a few seconds later, revved loudly once more, and then disappeared completely.

The night was still once more except for the outlet stream gurgling over the rocks a short distance away. It was as if it had not happened.

Rod sat straight up, unbelieving. He swallowed once and pushed his glasses up on his nose. His tight bladder was all but forgotten for the moment. The event had happened so fast it led him to wonder if he had been dreaming. He thought hard about it. No, of course not, he was sure he had been wide awake.

Rod also knew that no airplane could out climb the high cliffs at the other end of the lake even on a clear day, much less when it was dark and foggy. The rock walls rose almost sheer for over five hundred feet from the boulder-strewn shoreline barely a half mile away.

A moment of déjà vu flooded over him. When he had been ten years old, his family had rented a cabin on a lake in Michigan. Jamie had come along, too. One foggy night the whole family had been sitting on the porch swatting mosquitoes when everyone had heard a fast boat crossing the lake. Then the motor had revved before everything had become still again. The next morning a fisherman had discovered the demolished Chris Craft splintered on the far shore along with three dead teenagers and some empty whiskey bottles. Rod was sure then there had been an accident—just as now.

Jamie hadn't moved an inch through all the noise and light. He was still sleeping soundly just a foot away. Rod reached over and gently pushed his shoulder a few times. He whispered, "Hey, c'mon, wake up. There's something weird going on."

No dice. Jamie began to snore softly.

Rod raised his voice a little more. "C'mon, Jamie, wake up!"

The other man rolled over on his back and began to snore even louder.

Rod turned and carefully kneeled on his foam pad. His back brushed the roof of the tent. He placed a hand on either of his friend's shoulders and began to shake him. "C'mon, Jamie, wake up for Christ sake!"

Jamie snorted and began to snore again.

Rod resorted to the old standby and pinched Jamie's nose and covered his mouth. Soon the other man was coughing. Rod released his hands.

Jamie snorted and smacked his lips. He rubbed his face and tried to sit up.

"Whatso, huh? Whosit? How so?" he mumbled.

Jamie opened his eyes. He propped himself up on one elbow facing Rod. With the other hand, he continued to rub his eyes.

Rod knew from experience it would take a few minutes for his friend to wake up completely. Meanwhile, he pivoted on his knees, felt around with one hand while holding his flashlight, and began searching for his boots.

The light shone in Jamie's face for a moment, and he complained grumpily, "Hey, c'mon, get that light out of my face!" He looked around the tent to get his bearings. "Jesus, it must still be the middle of the night. What's going on? Why did you wake me up?"

Rod asked, "Didn't you hear it a minute ago?"

"Hear what?"

"The airplane that just went over. It barely missed the tent. I think it crashed into the lake."

Jamie rolled over on his other side so that he was facing away from Rod. He pulled the sleeping bag up around his head. His voice was slightly muffled. "C'mon, Rodney, give me a break. What airplane? You were fucking dreaming, pal."

Rod found his boots. "No, I wasn't. Look, I'm not kidding; it flew over just a couple of minutes ago. It barely missed the tent. It couldn't have been higher than fifty feet. I can't believe you didn't hear it."

"I'm going back to sleep. You were dreaming, old buddy. Nobody flies around here in weather like this."

Rod reached over Jamie and began to unzip the door.

Jamie muttered as Rod bumped him, "There is something seriously wrong with you, old buddy."

Rod ignored him and rolled the door back. He secured it in its clip and strap. Then he placed both boots outside on the snow-covered tundra and widened their openings by pulling their tongues forward, so he could just step into them.

As he prepared the boots, he told Jamie, "I'm going out and do some looking around."

Jamie muttered, "You're fucking crazy, you know that? Jeez, you wake me up in the middle of the night with a nightmare. You beat all, pal."

Rod crouched in the tent and prepared to launch himself outside and into his boots.

"I remember once you thought a flying saucer had landed in the back yard."

"I was only ten then."

"Yeah, well…"

Rod stepped out into the night. Both feet landed in their respective boots. He straightened up and looked around. The fog was thick. The tiny beam of his AA flashlight was useless, disappearing four feet from his hand. He switched the light off and listened. The night was pitch black and still. The only sound was still the stream gurgling over its rocks a few yards away.

Rod stepped forward a few feet, trailing his bootlaces. He stopped. There was not the slightest breeze now. He switched the flashlight back on. It seemed to have stopped snowing but for an occasional flake drifting down in the weak beam of his flashlight. There was about four inches of wet snow packed around the rocks. The hike out was going to be difficult.

He listened again. What did he expect anyhow? Screams for help?

Rod turned when he heard Jamie moving around behind him and muttering obscenities. The other man placed his boots just outside the door also and prepared to leave the tiny nylon tent. Then Jamie made his move. One foot landed in a boot but the other slipped off and landed in the wet snow. He hopped and cursed as he quickly picked it up and inserted it in the boot.

Rod moved to the edge of the lake. Jamie made his way up behind him a moment later. Both men peered into the gloom and listened. Finally, Jamie said, "I don't hear a thing. You were dreaming, old buddy." Jamie was still only dressed in his fishnet long underwear. So was Rod but in addition he had a sweater on, so he was warmer. Jamie wrapped his arms around himself and muttered, "Damn, it's cold out here, must be the moisture in the air with this ice fog."

"We're inside a cloud."

"It's fog."

"Hey, c'mon, be quiet for a second, okay?"

"Sure, but I still think you were just dreaming. It was just a dream, Rodney."

"Shh!"

Both men stood and listened for another few minutes.

Finally Jamie broke the silence again. "Look, as much as I'd like to stand here in the *fog* and meditate with you in the middle of the night, I'm getting cold. I'm going to take a piss and climb back into the sack, and I don't want you climbing back over the top of me trying to cop a feel on your way into the tent. Besides, I doubt if there is anything we can do about it until daylight. C'mon, it's too cold to be standing around out here in our skivvies."

"Okay, but I'm sure of what I saw and heard. There might be people out there that need our help."

"Sure there are, Rodney. Hell, I'll bet if you had a wet dream about Farah Fucking Fawcett we'd be searching around the rocks looking for her, too." Jamie paused then added, "Like I said, there's nothing to be done about it tonight anyway." He turned and walked back toward the tent.

Rod suddenly remembered his stressed bladder and reluctantly followed Jamie, trying to light the way. The flashlight was growing dim.

After both men had turned their backs, small ripples began to inch along the shoreline, disturbing the glasslike surface and the thin layer of ice that had begun to form in the tiny nooks and crannies. The waves lapped the shoreline, but both men were already out of earshot.

CHAPTER 20

Bad news

The phone downstairs had rung eight times in the darkened house before Edwin sleepily appeared on top of the broad wooden steps leading down to the living room. He had thrown his robe on and now tied the sash around his ample middle as he stumbled down the steps wondering who would call at this hour of the morning. His eyes began adjusting to the dark, but not before he collided with the end table next to the couch. Snow covered the lawn and reflected some outside light into the large room. He instinctively knew it couldn't be good news. Good news didn't come on the phone in the early morning hours before dawn. The phone had rung a dozen times as he turned on the lamp and picked up the receiver in mid-ring.

He growled into the phone, "Hello, who is this? Do you realize what time it is?"

The man on the other end answered politely, "Hello, I hate to bother you at this time of night, but I'm looking for a Mr. Edwin Forsyth."

Annoyed that his unlisted number at the ranch had been given out by someone, Edwin answered icily, "I'm Mr. Forsyth."

"Mr. Forsyth, this is Henry Kincaid at the Federal Aviation Administration's regional office in Denver. I hate to wake you, but I'm afraid I have some potentially bad news."

Edwin felt his heartbeat increase as he lowered his bulk onto the couch. There could only be one reason for this middle-of-the-night call from any government agency with aviation in the title.

"Yes, go on."

"Well, Mr. Forsyth, I'm sorry to say that your company airplane, November 837 Foxtrot Hotel, has been missing for several hours on a flight from Las Vegas to Denver. We think there were two men aboard. Your pilot of course, a Mr. James, and another unidentified man. As you probably know, the weather has been extremely bad this evening. Your pilot reported icing problems and then engine trouble. He disappeared off our radar screens approximately two and a half hours ago."

Edwin couldn't get his breath. He sat there for a moment dumbly holding the receiver to his ear.

"Mr. Forsyth, are you still there?" Henry Kincaid asked.

Edwin hesitated and then put the receiver back in front of his mouth. He cleared his throat. "Yes, of course, where?"

"I beg your pardon."

"Where did it happen? What about the two men?" And, Edwin thought, more importantly, what about the close to $30 million in illegal cash aboard?

Henry Kincaid answered, "Er, that's the funny thing. We don't know exactly where the plane went down. We, of course, know exactly where it disappeared from the radar screens, at what altitude, speed, and direction. Even its rate of descent. But radar coverage over the mountains is mainly at higher altitudes. The airplane disappeared off the radar screens at a very high altitude and, er, not exactly where it might have crashed. It looks like the airplane ran into trouble over in the Leadville area, and that's where the search will be concentrated as soon as the weather permits. It could be down somewhere in the Front Range area between Leadville and Denver. So far no one has detected an emergency locator beacon signal, or simply the ELT, as we know it."

"And the two men?"

Kincaid answered seriously, "Mr. Forsyth, we always assume that the occupants of the airplane have survived. The Civil Air Patrol and ground units from the various sheriffs' departments will begin searching as soon as weather permits."

"Yes, of course. Is there anything I can do?"

"We thought that you should notify the families of your two employees. That hasn't been done as of yet."

"Yes, of course, I will see to it. Anything else?"

The FAA man answered, "Pray to God we'll find them alive and just a little bit cold. We find survivors all the time. Rest assured we'll do our very best here in the regional office."

Edwin's mind was racing a mile a minute. His concerns were far from the lives of Ortiz and James. "Yes, I will. Thank you for calling. Good-bye."

"Goodnight."

There was an audible click as Kincaid hung his phone up and the line went dead. Edwin held the receiver in front of him for a moment looking blankly at it. Then he replaced it on its cradle. Little beads of sweat popped out on his lower lip and forehead. He prayed to God, too. He prayed to God that both men were dead and the airplane would never be found.

In his office at the FAA's regional office in Denver, Henry Kincaid hung up the phone and leaned back in his gray government issue chair. He put his feet up on his gray government issue desk with its black rubber top and then clasped his hands behind his head. It was almost four in the morning, and he was still angry that he had been awakened in the middle of the night. His gray government issue Ford Tempo had been hard to start in the cold as usual, and the roads into Denver had been a mess.

His stomach growled, and, now that he had tracked down Forsyth and made the call, he toyed with the idea of sending his assistant in the next office out for some Dunkin Donuts and real coffee, not the government issue kind.

Kincaid, a GS-13 step 9, yelled to his GS-9 step 2 assistant in the next room, "Hey, Jim, come over here!"

The other man yelled back, "Just a sec!" He then quickly appeared in the doorway with two cups of coffee. "Did you get hold of that hotel honcho?"

"Yeah, just hung up on him a moment ago."

The assistant walked into the office and placed the Styrofoam cup in front of Kincaid. "What did you say to him?"

Kincaid leaned forward and picked up the cup.

He swallowed. "You know, I gave him the standard-issue FAA bullshit." He chuckled. "Hell, those two guys in that airplane haven't a snowball's chance in hell in this weather. They're probably smeared over a couple of hundred yards of mountainside right along with their airplane." He paused and yawned. "Jesus, I hate getting up in the middle of the night." He took another sip. "This coffee's a little too hot. By the way do you know where that Dunkin Donut shop is around the corner on Evans?"

CHAPTER 21

The morning news

T*he Denver Post*
Tuesday, October 9, 1984
Weather Hampers Search for Downed Plane
By Caroline Martinez
Denver Post Staff Writer

Bad weather conditions prevailed again today over the mountainous Front Range west of Denver, hampering the initial search for a twin-engine airplane carrying two men. The airplane disappeared from radar screens last night on a flight from Las Vegas to Denver. The pilot who had reported icing problems to the air traffic control center in Longmont later declared an emergency when he developed engine trouble, says FAA spokesman Henry Kincaid. Kincaid also said that despite the best efforts of the controllers at the Longmont center, voice and radar contact was lost over the rugged terrain west of Denver. Kincaid also said the pilot was warned about icing conditions by the controllers. The radar tapes are being analyzed closely, and the FAA will be able to precisely pinpoint the crash site soon, he said.

The FAA spokesman also said no emergency locator transmitter signals have been picked up in the area either by overflying aircraft or the Russian COSPAS satellite, which was successful in locating two downed aircraft in the Canadian wilderness three months ago.

A Civil Air Patrol spokesman said their organization has aircraft on standby and will be airborne as soon as weather permits.

The downed aircraft was on a routine business flight and is owned by the Forsyth Hotel chain. The manager of the Denver Forsyth declined comment other than to say that the pilot was "very experienced."

The names of the two men are being withheld by authorities, pending notification of their families.

CHAPTER 22

The Far End of Hourglass Lake

A gust wrapped itself around Rod. It caught his parka's hood and whipped it around his ears before flattening itself on the boulders directly behind him. He shivered as he watched Jamie begin his rappel down the last sheer pitch toward the upper section of the lake and its narrow, boulder-strewn shoreline directly below them. Their tent was just a tiny smear of green in the distance at the outlet end of the cirque. He tightened his tension a little on the safety rope as it slid through his gloved hands. Their quarry lay silent almost at Rod's feet some twenty or so yards out in the icy, steel-gray water.

The ice fog and snow had finally lifted some hours ago after dawn, but visibility had remained low for quite a while after they had eaten breakfast until the wind had begun to pick up. Then it had improved sufficiently to see to the other end of the lake from their campsite. But even now, as Rod glanced up, the higher rock walls and jagged peaks were enveloped in gray, swirling clouds and frozen mist.

Rod watched Jamie's progress for a few moments, but then his attention was drawn once more to the downed airplane. It was almost submerged. Its nose was cocked upwards at a ridiculous angle, and its tail was almost completely submerged under deeper, blacker water indicating the tail was probably resting on a shallow ledge of some sort. The left wing and engine were partially submerged, while the right wing and engine were canted up at a crazy angle like some modern sculpture. As Rod watched a light chop broke along the fuselage just above the very rear windows. The waves danced along the airplane's flanks and then reformed to break moments later along the rocks, peppering them with an icy spray. Neither man had detected any movement within the airplane.

That morning Jamie, as usual, had been the first to awaken. Rod had slept soundly after they had crawled back into the tent and was surprised to find the gray light of late morning filtering into the tent when he had awakened. Rod had had a feeling of some type of expectation, which he couldn't identify, when he had awakened, much like a child on Christmas morning, until he had remembered the airplane flying over in the middle of the night. When he had remembered he had sat up quickly, fumbled for his glasses, and pulled the tent flap back only to be disappointed. The visibility was barely one hundred yards. The cirque was still shrouded in an icy fog. He had stumbled from the tent only to spot Jamie all bundled up in his red down parka and gloves fishing near the lake's outlet stream.

Later, over another breakfast of instant oatmeal and brown sugar, they had argued over Rod's "dream." They were still sitting there a half hour later when the fog had lifted. Rod had his back to the lake, so Jamie had been the first to spot it. He hurriedly swallowed a mouthful of oatmeal and excitedly asked for Rod's binoculars.

Rod had turned quickly and saw it also. If he had had any doubts before, Jamie quickly had lost them as he sat near the tent and steadied the miniature binoculars with his elbows on his knees. Through the glasses it had been easy to make out the partially submerged airplane, with the right wing and engine protruding above the lake's surface at a crazy angle.

Jamie's first words were "Jesus Christ, you were right all along."

A moment later, Jamie—a man of immediate action—had forgotten all about his breakfast and set about quickly organizing a rescue effort. He quickly assembled food, water, clothes, and climbing equipment. Then he stuffed everything into their larger packs. Much to Rod's dislike, the dishes and utensils from breakfast and the stove had just been placed inside the tent without being cleaned. Jamie allowed him no time to even floss and brush as he and Rod planned a route to the airplane.

It was impossible to simply skirt the shoreline around to the airplane because of the two towering granite walls which narrowed the lake at its middle and lent it its shape and name. The base of both of the walls on either side dropped sheer into the water, and there was absolutely no shoreline to walk on for a few hundred feet on either side. Instead, they would have to scramble up to the steep, windswept ridge on the north side of the lake and hike along it through the boulder field just under the summit of Mt. Grant. Then they would have to climb down the steep and dangerous west face of the cirque to near where the airplane lay in the icy water. Although they had been to the summit of Mt. Grant many years ago, it had been during the summer in excellent weather. Neither man had even been to the upper end of the lake in the past.

The airplane would be out of view during the climb, and one final check with the binoculars had still not revealed any movement within or around the airplane before they set out.

The scramble up to the ridge had been made difficult by the amount of snow on and between the huge boulders, which had tumbled down the steep slope since the last glacier had withdrawn. Most of the ridge was free of snow except near the summit boulder field, where it had drifted. Here, the first snow of the year was hip deep and it had taken them almost an hour to negotiate a few hundred yards.

They had expected the worst at the upper end of the lake but, surprisingly, had made their way down quite easily. They had only to use the safety rope mainly as a precaution on two pitches because the rocks had been slick with wet snow. In warmer weather it wouldn't have been necessary. The only difficulty was the final sheer wall down to the rock-strewn shoreline. This they would have to rappel. The climb up this wall from the lake later promised to be moderately easy as there seemed to be plenty of small cracks and ledges. But both men had serious misgivings about what to do if indeed they found any injured people in the airplane. Jamie thought this particular model could hold up to eight passengers.

Rod let the smaller multicolored safety line slip through both hands and across his back and watched Jamie bound easily down the last ten feet to the rocky shoreline at the west end of the cirque. Jamie's small daypack bounced up and down each time his feet touched the sheer rock wall. The heavier climbing rope whipped around in circles below his feet.

Jamie finally landed at the base of the wall, and he unsnapped his brake bar and carabiner from the climbing rope. He undid the safety rope and then looked up at Rod and grinned.

He cupped his hands around his mouth and yelled, "Your turn! It's a piece of cake!"

Rod waved back and smiled weakly.

Rappelling was a fast, easy way to descend once you were on your way, but Rod had always hated that first step over the edge at the beginning. He had never gotten used to it.

But before he attempted it, they had to lower their packs with the lighter safety line. After this was accomplished, Rod prepared for the descent. Satisfied that everything was in place, that both ropes were secure, he stepped over the ledge. Once you were started, it was a piece of cake. Using one hand to help brake the rope, Rod easily descended to Jamie's side in a few moments.

Jamie let go of the safety rope and hopped across a couple of large boulders to the edge of the water. Rod scrambled over the rocks and joined him. Jamie nodded toward the wreck. "I don't think there is anyone alive in there. If anyone did survive the wreck and didn't get out right away, they probably were unconscious and drowned. That airplane has to be almost half full of water." He pointed at his feet. "And nobody lasts more than a few minutes in water this cold."

Rod nodded in agreement. He didn't think anyone had survived either, and he was uncomfortable. He had no experience with dead people.

Rod sat down on a rock next to Jamie and struggled to get the straps of his daypack over his bulky, down-filled parka. Succeeding, he placed the pack between them. The airplane seemed much bigger now that it was right in front of them, separated by a dozen or so yards of water. The streamlined nose, almost shark-like, pitched up in front of them. The tip of the tail was just showing above the water.

Rod asked, "What do you think we ought to do about this? I'm sure someone is looking for it. We gotta hike out and notify the authorities."

Jamie wiggled out of his pack, placed it next to Rod's, and looked up at the sky. It was still gray and overcast. Low clouds still swirled around the higher peaks. He said, "I don't think there will be much searching in this weather." He then proceeded to untie his boots.

Rod sat in silence for a moment. He watched Jamie remove his boots and then his socks. He thought his friend might be tending to a blister at first. But when Jamie pulled off his parka and then stripped off his wool sweater over his head, it finally sunk in.

Rod asked, "Hey, you're not doing what I think you're doing?"

Jamie unbuttoned his wool shirt. "There's only one way to find out about the people in that airplane, old buddy, unless you can come up with a boat in about two minutes."

Rod was suddenly worried and pleaded, "Hey, c'mon, Jamie, don't go out there. That water's like ice, and this wind will make it worse. Let's just head out. Go back to the tent and pack things up. Let's cut the trip short a few days. The weather's shitty anyhow. We'd get to the car tomorrow sometime and then notify the authorities. They have to be looking for it."

Jamie had stripped down to only his pants and was unbuckling his belt, "You're forgetting one thing, old buddy."

"What's that?"

Jamie's voice took on a hard edge. "What if someone is still alive in that airplane? What then? What if it was you out there?" Then his voice softened. "Look, we just can't leave without finding out, can we? What would I tell people? I'm sorry; I just couldn't swim that lousy sixty feet to look in a window. Besides, I'm in shape and can handle this. We'll tie the safety line around me so if something happens you can reel me in like a big old bass."

Rod knew Jamie was right but couldn't shake the feeling of not wanting to become involved. And why hadn't he himself volunteered to swim out there? He knew now that Jamie had been thinking of this the entire time. But the thought of swimming out there hadn't even crossed his mind until now. There were people like Jamie in this world, and then there were people like himself. People who didn't want to become involved in anybody else's problems. The nervous feeling of wanting to be anywhere else but standing on this rock began to creep into Rod's panic center. What if someone was alive out there? What if there were dead people in that airplane? He imagined mutilated bodies floating to the surface like some horror movie. Rod had never seen a real, fresh dead person—or any dead person, except his father at his funeral. That hadn't been real bad. He had looked like he was asleep. But these were real dead people. Freshly dead. There had to be a difference. Jamie, on the other hand, was used to this stuff. In Vietnam he had carried bodies stacked like cordwood in his helicopter. He had said that sometimes there were more parts of people than people. Then he had had to land the helicopter on a shallow river sandbank afterward and wash the blood out of his chopper with buckets of water. Sure, thought Rod nervously, this was no big deal to him. Rod stood up and felt faint. He began to shiver even in his down parka. He leaned back and took a deep breath. He wished he was somewhere else: back home in his Lazy Boy recliner, reading a magazine, might be nice.

Jamie had stripped off his pants and wool shirt and was beginning to remove his long underwear. He looked over at Rod as he pulled the underwear over his head. "You don't look so good; what's wrong?"

Rod looked down at his boots and then over at Jamie, "I...I don't know. This is all getting to me." He pointed to the airplane. "I don't think we should be messing around with this. I have a bad feeling about all this. I think we ought to leave right now and just report this to the authorities. Let them take care of it. I don't think you ought to be swimming around in that cold lake or go near that airplane."

"C'mon, Rodney, don't back out on me now. Where's your curiosity?" Jamie said, as he stripped the remainder of his clothes and stood naked on the rock. He lightly punched Rod's arm and laughed. "Besides, what are we going to tell people when they ask all about the gory details? And I need a good man on the other end of the safety rope."

Rod said slowly, "Well, I guess you're right." He thought to himself that it was useless to argue. Once Jamie was in motion it was impossible to stop him.

Jamie laughed again as he picked up the end of the safety rope and began to tie it around his waist. "Hey, I've got an idea: why don't you join me for a swim?"

Rod took one end of the rope and sat down on the rock. He was still shivering in his down parka and there Jamie was, standing naked about to plunge into the lake. He couldn't shake off the feeling of doom. Rod forced a laugh and attempted to make light of the matter. He shook his head. "I'm not going in there and freeze my nuts off, asshole."

Jamie replied lightheartedly, "Well, screw you, too."

Jamie was standing on the rock stark naked making his last minute preparations. Rod could see the gooseflesh all over the other man's body. If anything, the wind had increased. The waves still brushed the shore but now resembled miniature ocean breakers as they neared the rocks. They curled over on top and splashed just below Rod's feet. His friend was a tough cookie Rod thought.

Jamie sat on the edge of the rock he had been standing upon and gingerly dipped one foot into the lake. He exclaimed, "Oh, that's cold!" But clearly to Rod he was enjoying himself. Then he lowered his other foot and ankle into the lake. With a splash he lowered himself the rest of the way and pushed off. The crystal clear water was a lot deeper then it looked, and it splashed at his chest. Jamie took a stroke as he began his swim toward the airplane and simultaneously let out a stream of profanities. "Fuck! It about took my breath away when it got up to my nuts!" He then turned on his back and took a few strokes just as if he was taking a morning swim in a backyard pool and not a frigid lake at twelve thousand feet above sea level.

Rod remained sitting on his rock, huddled in his down parka. Jamie was strong and swam easily up to the nose in a few moments. The water was still shallow enough for him to stand on the rocky bottom. He dogpaddled around and under the right wing. Rod lost sight of him and stood up in order to see behind the airplane better, but Jamie was still out of sight.

Jamie swam along the right side of the tilted, white fuselage. He stopped for a few seconds at one of the side windows. He was in suddenly deeper water now and had to tread water and grab the airplane. He peered inside. He had been in the water just a couple of minutes but even at that he could begin to feel his extremities start to numb, one of the first signs of hypothermia. He knew his time was limited to just a few more minutes. He swam around the submerged tail and reappeared on the left side. Rod was relieved to see him and sat down again. He slowly let the safety line slip through his hands.

Still treading water, Jamie tried the door at the rear of the fuselage. The handle had apparently jammed during the crash and failed to work. He swam forward, grabbed the trailing edge, and pulled himself up onto the left wing. Dripping icy water, he crawled forward on the slanted wing to the cockpit and then knelt next to the pilot's window.

Rod watched Jamie study the interior of the cockpit intently. He yelled over the wind, "Hey, what's going on out there? What'd you find something?"

Jamie didn't answer but instead moved back and studied the cabin area through the first window. Untying the safety rope, which had run its length, he crawled to the leading edge of the wing and let himself down into the lake between the forward fuselage and one of the propeller blades. He swam quickly toward shore and pulled himself up onto the rock next to Rod a few moments later. While Rod began pulling in the safety rope, Jamie dug into his pack and began to towel himself off with a spare shirt he had brought along.

Rod hauled in the safety rope which slipped smoothly around the airplane and back to shore.

Jamie was a bundle of blue gooseflesh as he tried to dry himself as quickly as possible. He exclaimed, "Jesus, that water's cold! I don't think I could have taken another five minutes!"

The sun suddenly shone through a break in the clouds raising the air temperature a quick fifteen degrees as Jamie dove into his clothes and down parka.

Rod coiled the rope and laid it on the rock. "So, what did you see out there?" he asked as his curiosity mounted.

Jamie sat down on the rock next to Rod's and tried to soak up what little warmth the sun offered. He swept his wet, darkened hair back with one hand. Water glistened on three-day-old beard. He looked over at Rod for a moment and hesitated. Then he spoke in a low voice, "Rodney, old buddy, you're not going to fucking believe it. I mean, I guarantee you're not going to fucking believe it!"

Rod shrugged and asked, "What am I not going to believe? How many people are in that airplane?"

Jamie held up his hand and grinned. "In due time, old buddy, in due time. First, I have to find myself a sharp, flat rock about the size of a book."

"A rock? What for?"

"I'm going back out there and try to get inside."

Rod wasn't ready for this and asked again. "What for? They're all dead aren't they?"

Jamie wrapped his arms around himself and tried to warm up for the second swim. "Yeah, they're dead. As near as I could see, there's two guys in there. The pilot up front and some other guy half floating in the back. I couldn't see the cabin very well, kind of dark." He winked and grinned at Rod. "I want to get in and look around a little."

Rod knew that grin and wink. He said nervously, "C'mon, Jamie, let's get out of here and report this. It's a long hike out, and we gotta get packed up. I don't like this one bit. You're not telling me everything."

Jamie looked around the shoreline. "C'mon, hurry up and find me a rock. I'm freezing my nuts off. I don't know what's the matter with you. There's nobody around within twenty miles, and I guarantee there aren't any ghosts in that airplane."

Rod reluctantly stood up and hopped down off the rock. He began picking in and around the larger boulders that dominated the shoreline.

Finally, he came up with a square, block like rock about the size of a softball. He climbed back up next to Jamie and handed him the rock.

Jamie hefted the rock and passed judgment. "Yeah, this ought to do."

Rod tried to explain, "I guess I'm just spooked by this whole deal." Then his curiosity overcame him. "What are you going to do with that rock anyhow? And what are you going to check out in the airplane?"

Jamie removed his clothes once more and slipped from the rock back into the lake. This time the water felt warmer than the air. He turned and picked up the block-like rock. "In due time, old buddy. You'll see what I'm talking about. In due time."

Jamie then tucked the rock at his side like a quarterback carrying a football through the line. He pushed off and began side-stroking toward the wrecked airplane.

Rod cupped his hands around his mouth, raised his voice, and asked again as Jamie swam toward the wreck, "What are you checking out?"

Jamie turned on his back and held the rock on his stomach much like a sea otter. "Well, for one thing there's a bullet hole over the pilot's window, and it looks like the top of his head has been blown away!"

Rod puzzled this as Jamie reached the airplane again. He placed the rock on the left wing and then climbed up again onto the leading edge. He got to his knees, steadied himself on the slick, tilted wing, and picked the rock up with one hand. He had decided the pilot's side window was his best bet. It was the largest and probably would be much easier to break out than the thicker front windows. The oval cabin windows along the side of the aircraft were just too tiny to squeeze through.

He transferred the rock to his right hand and placed his hand against the top of the window frame to steady himself. He brought the rock over his head and then came down hard against the Plexiglas window. There was a sharp crack, but the rock merely bounced off the window causing him to lose his balance and nearly slide off the trailing edge of the wing. He managed to hold onto the rock and regain his balance.

Rod saw Jamie fall and quickly stood up. He was relieved when he saw his friend climb back to his knees.

Jamie saw that his first blow had had an effect. He had chipped the window, and there were now cracks radiating out from the corners. The wind picked up and flattened the water surrounding the airplane. He was beginning to shake uncontrollably from the cold, and he knew all too well about hypothermia and its effects. He braced himself with one hand on the smooth, white skin of the airplane and drew back the other arm. He brought the rock down harder this time. The window shattered. The pieces caved inwardly. Several large sections landed on the dead pilot's back.

Jamie pried the rest of the broken window pieces from its molding. He then quickly made sure there were no jagged edges to drag himself over. It was going to be a tight squeeze as it was. He flipped the rock into the water in front of the nose where it landed in the water with a *thunk*.

Jamie had to fit his large shoulders with his arms in front of him through the opening diagonally, which allowed for the greater distance. His flesh rubbed on the window frame. Soon he had most of his torso through the window while now standing on the wing. He looked around the cockpit for supports as he leaned over the dead pilot's body. Water sloshed between the seats in the cockpit. Despite the effort he smiled at the thought he was probably mooning Rodney and the peaks surrounding the lake.

Concentrating once more, he reached over and grabbed the armrests for the copilot's seat and turned sideways to facilitate bringing his hips through the window opening. His legs scraped on the frame and then the dead man's back as he brought himself inside. He did not want to exit this way and reminded himself to try to open the main cabin door in the rear from the inside.

Jamie twisted and pulled himself upright. He stood bent over between the two pilots' seats and surveyed the cockpit. Although still cold, he was somewhat warmer now that he was out of the driving wind. The curtain separating the cockpit from the cabin lay draped on his shoulders like a cape. Water sloshed around his ankles. The smell of gasoline was strong. He could see Rodney standing on the rock beyond shading his eyes. Jamie waved through the windshield indicating he was still fine. Rod waved back weakly.

The pilot was dead—that was plain to see. The back of his head was missing as he slumped wide-eyed over the control wheel. Dried blood had matted his hair around the opening from which shredded gray tissue welled up.

The instrument panel had been all but destroyed. Loose multicolored wires hung here and there. The radios spilled out their solid-state guts of transistors and circuit boards. The throttle, propeller, and fuel mixture control levers were splayed at odd angles as if something heavy has crushed them. Papers and charts bobbed at his feet. A thermos bottle floated near the copilot's rudder pedals. He saw another neat, round bullet hole in the middle of the altimeter.

Jamie brushed the curtain aside as he turned toward the cabin. He saw the money and caught his breath. It was much more than he had seen from the outside through the tinted windows. It was everywhere. Single-banded packets floated by themselves. Whole armadas of packets were jammed into the corners of the cabin.

Jamie looked down the aisle. The water deepened quickly. A large, open suitcase floated in between the seats in front of him. Seven more, still secure, bobbed between the seats to the right. At least five more floated on their sides near the rear of the cabin by the body of the dead man.

Jamie shuffled forward, the water quickly coming up to his thighs. He bent over and scooped up a packet of money much like dipping a net into a tank for a goldfish. He steadied himself by placing the other hand flat against the ceiling. The bills, all hundreds, were heavy and soggy. He dropped this packet and stirred through ten more that were bunched up against the seat on his left before he picked up another. He whistled softly. This packet was at least three inches thick and also contained all one hundred dollar bills. Jamie laid this one on the seatback to his right and stirred through more packets until he scooped up another thick one again containing all one hundred dollar bills. He carefully placed this one next to the first one. Then he began cautiously making his way down the steeply canted aisle toward the dead man. At the rear bulkhead the water quickly rose to his stomach leaving a few feet of airspace between the water level and the ceiling.

He pushed two of the heavy suitcases out of the way as he grasped one of the man's arms. He began to pull him from behind the last seat while admiring the large emerald ring on one of the man's fingers. The body came free suddenly, and Jamie tugged it into the aisle.

Rod stood on the rock and shaded his eyes, worrying about Jamie. He had been able to see him standing in the cockpit, but now he had disappeared into the cabin, and he had lost sight of him completely. He shifted the weight on his feet and worried. The safety rope was coiled on the rock next to him. Should he get ready himself to rescue Jamie? That would be a switch, he thought, after all these years together. And that water looked very cold. Finally, he knelt down and opened his pack. He rummaged through it until he came up with the small black leather case for his binoculars. He unsnapped it, withdrew them, and dropped the empty case at his feet.

Where he stood, he knew he didn't have enough angle to see clearly into the side windows of the airplane, so he began to scramble down the shoreline, hopping from rock to rock. Finally, he thought he had enough of an angle and jumped down from the last rock into a tiny, sandy cove. He braced himself against one of the waist-high boulders and trained the binoculars on the airplane.

Starting at the cockpit, he slowly scanned the entire fuselage from front to rear. The registration number for the airplane was submerged, and he hoped Jamie had seen it so that they could report it to the authorities. Most of the tail was also submerged, but he could still see some of the hotel's logo, although he didn't really know what the lettering meant at the moment. Canted at an angle, the left half of the orange crown was still visible, and the very tops of the stylized green *F* and *H* were above the waterline. The waves lapped at the middle of the *F* and at the top of the *H*. Rod knew he had seen that logo somewhere but just couldn't place it at the moment. He scanned back along the windows and thought he caught some movement in the cabin through the dark, polarized windows, but just then the sun disappeared behind a cloud, making it more difficult to see inside. He muttered a few curses under his breath and wished Jamie would hurry. Rod still had bad feelings about this whole mess.

He lowered the binoculars for a moment and looked at the sky. The clouds still swirled around the peaks surrounding the lake and, if anything, looked heavier, as if it would certainly snow again.

Rod brought the binoculars back up and this time trained them on their camp at the opposite end of the lake. The little tent was still intact. Its rain fly flapped and rippled in the wind. Without taking the binoculars from his eyes, Rod swiveled and refocused on the wreckage. This time he thought he saw some movement inside one of the cabin windows. He's been in there too long, Rod thought. He continued to scan the airplane and wondered again about the registration number. He absentmindedly trained the binoculars on the tail and the crown logo. Where had he seen that before? He thought about the logo for a moment. He looked again at the orange crown. There was something peculiar about it—something different this time.

Then he knew, and a wave of panic flooded through him. A minute before, the water level had been just above the crossbar in the *F*, and now it was at the very top. The *H* had disappeared. Rod squinted harder into the binoculars, trying hard not to see what he knew to be true. Now the *F* was almost gone.

The airplane was sinking, slowly sliding into deeper water.

Rod began yelling and waving his arms to get Jamie's attention. He cupped his hands around his mouth and screamed at the top of his lungs. "Jamie, get out! It's sinking! Get out!" It was no good. The words were just pushed back by the wind. He began to panic and frantically looked around at his feet. He picked up a baseball-sized rock and flung it as hard as he could toward the wreck. It landed twenty feet short with a small splash.

The very tip of the tail was all that now showed above the water. The left engine was almost completely submerged. The lake lapped just below the broken cockpit window.

Rod scrambled from rock to rock yelling at the top of his lungs. As he vaulted onto the rock where their packs and Jamie's clothes lay, he scooped up another rock. He stood at the very edge of the boulder and flung the rock as hard as he could. Now that he was closer, this one landed with a *thunk* on top the fuselage and glanced off into the lake with a splash. He yelled some more and listened. The wind ruffled his parka. The waves broke noisily at his feet.

Inside, Jamie had realized the airplane was sinking at the same time he had heard Rod begin shouting. He felt the floor begin to tilt. Then scraping sounds came from below him as the tortured metal began to slide along the rocky bottom. He realized too late his sudden weight at the rear of the cabin must have been just enough to offset the precarious balance. Trying to keep his cool, he first leaned over to the rear cabin door and tried the handle. It was jammed. The handle wouldn't budge. He would have to climb out through the cockpit window again.

The airplane suddenly lurched to a steeper angle, and he froze halfway up the aisle. Then it pivoted to one side. The noises stopped for the time being. Jamie resumed pulling himself delicately up the steep aisle toward the front. A rock bounced off the top of the cabin. He gained the cockpit and was about to literally dive through the broken window when he felt the nose pitch down slightly. His weight was acting on the airplane like a playground seesaw, and it seemed stable to him for the moment. With someone standing in the cockpit, its weight must be balanced precariously on the rocks under its belly for the time being. But the water beyond was over one hundred feet deep. The airplane, he knew, would now be a deathtrap for anyone who tried to climb inside. And it still might slide away into the deep water as soon as he climbed out. Not wanting to test this theory any further, there was no question he had to get out quickly.

But before he lunged headfirst over the dead pilot and headfirst through the shattered window, Jamie reached quickly behind the curtain into the cabin. The airplane groaned once, and this time Jamie didn't hesitate. He lunged for the shattered window and landed clumsily on the now nearly submerged wing. Then he quickly dove toward shore while looking over his shoulder to see if the airplane was still there as he swam.

Rod was greatly relieved to at last see Jamie's head and then shoulders finally come through the window. He, too, knew the airplane might sink at any moment. Rod waved and then watched Jamie swim toward him. He was making awkward strokes and seemed to be holding something in his hand. Rod turned and began to pick up some of Jamie's clothing. He would be ready for him when he emerged from the icy water. Rod's mood lightened somewhat. The worst seemed to be over, and they could start back.

Jamie hoisted himself up onto the rock, and Rod handed him his long underwear. He took the underwear and in exchange handed Rod the two packets of soggy money.

Rod stared dumbfounded at the money. He held a packet in each hand as he stood there with his mouth open. Each was thick and heavy.

He turned them over and looked at them carefully. A one hundred dollar bill showed on each side, back and front. He looked up at his friend, puzzled.

Jamie exclaimed as he dried himself, "Holy Christ, I thought I was a goner when that sucker started to sink! I don't think I would have had time to get out the window if it had gone under. I don't know about you, but I've had enough swimming for the day!"

Rod still stood there dumfounded. Jamie dried his stomach and started on his legs. Goosebumps stood out over his entire body and, his lips were blue.

Rod found his voice and held out the money. "What's this?"

Jamie began to dry his hair. "What does it look like, old buddy? Lettuce?" Then he laughed, enjoying himself immensely for a moment at Rod's expense.

Rod turned the packets over again and exclaimed, "Jesus, there must be at least fifty thousand dollars here!"

Jamie dried his back and answered in a matter-of-fact voice, as if he was always finding vast quantities of cash, "I figure closer to a hundred thousand myself. Hey, throw me my other clothes will ya. Damn! I'm still freezing my nuts off!"

Rod held the money in one hand and stooped over to pick up Jamie's clothes. He pitched them over to him. Jamie began to dress.

Rod shook his head and asked, "I don't understand. What's going on?"

Jamie pulled his sweater over his head. His hair was still slick and wet from the lake. "Your guess is as good as mine. There are two dead guys out there: the pilot, who was shot in the head, and another big, fat guy in the back." He pointed to the money Rod held. "The cabin is just littered with money like that. You've got just a tiny part. I mean it's everywhere. And that is just from one of the suitcases that came open. There's at least a dozen or more that didn't come unlatched." He took the money from Rod and held it in front of him. "There must be millions in there, old buddy. And probably more in the wing lockers." Jamie turned and stared out at the wreck. Then he casually tossed the two packets back to Rod. Rod fumbled with the packets and then clutched them to his stomach.

Jamie sat on the rock and drew his feet toward him. He began putting on his thick wool hiking socks. He turned and smiled up at Rod. "And we"—he pointed at himself and then at Rod—"us two, have got to figure a way to get it out of there, old buddy."

Rod recoiled, "What! What are you talking about? Are you crazy?" He held out the packets again. "We can't steal this money."

Jamie stood up and stepped into his boots but didn't lace them. He put on his down parka. He had dismissed Rod's questions as trivial. He rubbed his chin and looked back at the airplane. Although lower in the water, it seemed to have stabilized for the moment. "I just have to figure out a way. We're going to have to give it some thought." Then he turned to Rod and asked, "You got any ideas?"

Rod exclaimed, "Ideas! You're nuts." He held out a packet. "This isn't our money. Somebody's got to be looking for it right now. We've got to report this as soon as we get back to a phone."

Jamie edged over and put a large hand on Rod's shoulder. Rod looked at it and up at Jamie. "Now look, let's not get too hasty about what we're going to do. There is such a thing as salvage rights."

"Salvage rights? I will repeat that you are crazy. Salvage rights only apply to ships at sea that are unmanned and adrift. We're talking about a plane crash in a lake in a wilderness area for crying out loud."

Jamie pushed up his parka's left sleeve and slipped the watch from his wrist. Rod looked puzzled. It was the first time he had noticed in all the excitement that Jamie had another watch on besides the big Seiko flight chronograph he normally wore. Then Jamie pulled a large ring from his left index finger that Rod also had overlooked in all the excitement with the money. Jamie held out the watch and the ring in both hands and said, "We can always split the money. Here, take your pick."

Rod starred at the watch and ring. They were both exquisite. The ring consisted of a very large emerald in a simple but elegant gold setting. Rod had never seen an emerald in his life, much less one this size. He was positive though it was surely the real thing and not a fake—the green, deep and clear. The stone alone was probably worth thousands if not tens of thousands of dollars. But the watch was one of the most beautiful he had ever seen also. And one of the thinnest. The face was dark gray, almost black. Elegantly simple, the only markings were at the twelve, three, six, and nine o'clock positions—each a small diamond. The band was black grained leather; the case pure gold. The diamonds sparkled in the sunlight and drew Rod's hand toward it. Jamie handed it to him, and Rod instinctively looked at his Timex. Although an hour behind, the expensive watch seemed to be still keeping perfect time. He examined it closer. The small name PIAGET was hidden behind the hands. Somehow he knew this was no Kmart special.

Jamie slipped the ring back on his finger and held out his hand to admire it. He joked, "Well, that's a relief; I thought for sure you'd go for the ring." He pointed at Rod's wrist. "Why don't you pitch that cheapo watch in the lake?"

Rod looked up, the spell broken. "We can't keep this money and stuff. It belongs to someone else."

Jamie sighed and said, "Haven't you gotten it yet? Finders keepers. All this cash in suitcases? Isn't that suspicious to you? It's got to be illegal somehow. Got to be. People just don't fly around with millions in cash like this in airplanes. Legal money is transferred by check or bank-to-bank by computer."

Rod thought it over. Jamie was probably correct. Still expressing his doubts, he said, "What if it isn't? What if it is legitimate money?

I don't want to end up in prison or something." He looked down at the watch. "You just can't strip dead people of their jewelry like this. Besides, someone is going to be looking for this airplane." Rod nodded toward the wreck. "They're probably homing in on the emergency locator beacon right now with a satellite or something."

Jamie turned and looked at the airplane and then back at Rod. "Don't worry about the federal pen. Look, we're just Joe Schmoe citizen. The most we'd get would be a couple of years at a minimum security prison with tennis and shuffleboard. More than likely just probation."

Rod couldn't believe his ears. Jamie actually was thinking about the possibility of prison. He looked down at his boots and said simply, "I can't go to prison."

"You still don't get it, do you? This is our one chance. Sure there are going to be some risks. We've got to go for it, old buddy."

Rod protested, "You don't understand. I've got a wife and kid. A house with a mortgage. My family and the bank are depending on me."

Jamie ignored him. He rubbed his chin. "As to the ELT...don't think that's a factor. The antenna is mounted on the rear of the fuselage just forward of the vertical stabilizer. It's been under a couple of feet of water since the crash." He looked out at the wreck again. "Shit, I should have broken it off when I was out there. I wasn't thinking. I'll get it on the next trip."

Rod didn't like the look in his friend's eyes. He couldn't believe he was still planning on recovering the money despite his protests to the contrary.

Rod asked, "What next trip?"

Jamie put his hand on Rod's shoulder. Rod looked at the hand and back at Jamie. Yep, he thought, there's that look he knew so well. There's a lot of danger in that look, he knew.

Jamie said, "You and I are going to be millionaires, old buddy. We're probably the only people on the face of this Earth right now who know exactly where this airplane is sitting." He hesitated, as if to let this fact sink in on Rod, then pointed and continued, "That airplane is balanced somehow like a seesaw. When I got back up to the cockpit, things sort of stabilized. Now look, you're a lot lighter than me. We'll both swim out there. I'll get in first through the window, and then you'll climb in after me. With both of us up front, it's not going anywhere. And I'll stay up front to balance things while you go into the back and get the money."

Rod broke his friend's grip on his shoulder and angrily turned around. He stared up at the precipice. Their climbing rope still dangled in the wind.

Jamie protested, "Hey, what's wrong with you anyhow?"

Rod turned and pointed a finger at him. His neck was red, Jamie noticed. He had never seen this look before. Rod held up the index finger he had been pointing. "You're crazy, you know that? Number one, that wreck is a deathtrap. We'd both get caught in there, and the next thing we'd be under one hundred feet of water. There just isn't a safe way to do this, and I have a family to think about." He let his middle finger join the index. "Number two, what you want to do is illegal, and I don't want any part of it. I don't intend to become a common criminal. Someway, somehow, someone will find out about it. You said you think it was crooked money. What if the crooks find out about us? Do you think they will politely ask for their million dollars back? No way. We'll end up with concrete overshoes on." He held up his ring finger also. "Number three, I don't know how to swim. Remember that? Here!" Rod took the watch off and thrust it and the money at Jamie's stomach then turned around. He folded his arms.

Jamie took the two items. "Are you done ranting and raving?"

"Yeah."

"Good!" Jamie scratched the bottom of his chin as if lost in thought. "Hmm, there's got to be a safe way to do this. The only argument I'm buying right now is your not knowing how to swim."

Rod turned around.

Jamie grinned. "I still say you should have taken those lessons down at the Y when you had the chance. It wasn't so tough swimming in the nude, when you got used to it."

Rod smiled at the memory.

Jamie continued, "And you're probably right about it sinking. It's balanced just right." He looked up at the climbing rope. "We could try and tie it off, maybe around one of the props, but I don't think we have enough rope to do it properly. And that airplane has got to weigh a couple of tons or more full of water. We just don't have enough to do the job properly—"

Rod cut his friend off. "You just don't listen to me, do you? I said I don't want any part of this."

Jamie tried to soothe things. "Now don't be too hasty about all this. Absolutely no one knows we're up here except your wife."

"What about the trail register? We signed in there."

"That's simple; we'll just tear the page out when we get there"

"What if some ranger has already collected it—what then?"

"Jesus, what if...what if. What a worrier. Shit, I keep telling you to loosen up a bit. You gotta remember this is a once-in-a-lifetime deal. No more pushing pencils at the insurance company. Did you ever think of it that way?"

Rod hesitated, "Well..."

With the mention of Rod's job and his reaction, Jamie knew he might eventually have him. A wedge to be driven. He held out the expensive watch. "Here, take this."

Rod shoved Jamie's hand back and shook his head. "No, I still don't want any part of this. Now let's get out of here. Back to the tent and pack up." He looked at his Timex. "We could be at the car sometime late tonight." Then he bent over and started to organize his pack.

Jamie shrugged and put the watch and money in the bottom of his pack. He also began to prepare his gear for the climb.

As the two men readied themselves in silence, above them a sudden snow shower began working its way around the summit of Mt. Grant. In a few minutes, it had settled upon the lake. Large, wet snowflakes swirled between them.

Jamie pulled on his stocking cap. Rod continued to arrange his gear in silence. Jamie watched Rod. He cleared his throat. "Uh, you know you're probably right about all this."

Rod was instantly wary at Jamie's change of mind. He knew some sort of deal was about to be elaborated. If Jamie used his full name he would know for sure. His earlier anger had subsided. He said defensively, "Well, you know, I was just trying to do the right thing. Keep us out of trouble."

"Sure you were, Rodney Coleman. I just sort of got carried away. We just can't go around stealing money. Besides, they'll be looking for this airplane as soon as the weather clears. But just think of the story you'll be able to tell around the water cooler for the next twenty-five years at your boring job. About how you found an airplane with millions of dollars aboard but did the right thing."

Rod answered slowly, "I'll have to give someone a call when we get down to a pay phone in Crestridge: the sheriff's department, the FAA, someone."

The large snowflakes swirled between them.

"Yeah, you're going to have to do that, but do me one favor."

Rod sighed, "What's that?"

"If I think of some way to get at this wreck safely between now and then, just promise me you'll keep quiet and at least give *me* a chance at the money."

"Don't you ever quit?"

Jamie shrugged, "Look, I won't involve you. You can stay out of it, although I will probably need your help. You're the only one I can completely trust on this. But there has got to be a way to pull this off. Just let me think on it for a while."

The sudden snow shower lessened. It moved across the lake, completely obscuring the far end and their tent.

"What do mean by 'not involving me'? That's impossible. I'm here right now with you, just a few feet from that airplane and two dead guys. They're probably from some drug cartel or mafia or something. All kinds of people will know we took this trip together. I *am* involved, no matter what you say or do."

Jamie slung his pack over his shoulders and hopped off the rock. Rod turned and watched Jamie begin working his way over to the base of the cliff from which their climbing rope still hung.

While Jamie busied himself with the gear and prepared to start climbing, he turned and called over his shoulder to Rod. "That's right; you're involved in this, Rodney, whether you want to be or not, so why worry? Now, do you want to lead or should I? Now that we really can't do anything, I'm anxious to be out of here."

Another snow shower swirled onto the lake from above.

Rod reluctantly followed Jamie to the base of the cliff. Why worry? He knew the answer to that question because he had known Jamie Anderson all of his life. As Jamie readied his climbing harness and the safety rope, Rod thought he heard him mumble something about scuba gear. "What did you say?"

"Nothing. Just thinking to myself."

As he donned his helmet, Rod turned and faced the crash. The airplane had disappeared in the snow, but he knew it was still there, yards away, no matter how much he wanted it to vanish. The weekend had started out as a simple backpacking trip and reunion. All that had changed now. He felt as if he was being swept into an ever-narrowing whirlpool somehow by events out of his control.

CHAPTER 23

Morning at the Ranch

Gray morning light illuminated the living room. The house was quiet. In the distance the Elk Mountains were invisible in cloud and snow. No one had awakened. Edwin sat on the sofa and worried. He had been rooted to the same spot since receiving the news from the nice FAA man hours ago. Kincaid had not called back since the initial call with the bad news. Edwin glanced absentmindedly at his watch. Hopefully, no one had found anything or ever would. That would be best. Colorado was a large, mostly mountainous state, and there were thousands of ravines and canyons where a tiny airplane could be lost forever. The others should be stirring soon, and he would have to give them the news.

Everyone had stayed up until midnight drinking what alcohol was to be found in the house. Mostly they listened to the pilot play the grand piano. Edwin had to give the man credit; he could sure play.

Although the mountains were still obscured, the valley's weather had improved considerably over the previous night when the first storm of the year had struck. A brisk north wind still rattled the windows, but the sun was beginning to occasionally poke through fast breaks in the clouds, bathing the house in intermittent bright sunlight. The shrubs outside the window trembled and shook off clumps of melting snow. The fields beyond the wet driveway lay under almost two inches of fresh snow. Now centered in eastern Kansas, it had been a typical, fast-moving, early-fall storm. Most of the snow would be gone by late afternoon.

Edwin just sat and watched the scene outside, a man resigned to his doom. His legs were crossed, and the upper one bounced nervously under his bathrobe. He wondered when the local sheriff with a couple of his deputies would pay a visit to the ranch after learning about the missing airplane and putting two and two together. The man was nearly seventy and a sharp cookie. He was a tall, thin, leathery old coot who didn't miss a thing and had run the county for over thirty years. The sheriff and Edwin's father had been good friends. They had hunted and fished together. But the sheriff had never been back to the ranch since paying a visit to give his condolences after Edwin Sr. had died.

The local press would have surely learned of the missing airplane. They would be trailing the sheriff out here also.

Edwin bounced his foot some more and thought of the surprise they would get when they drove around the sleek, black, drug-running airplane outside stuffed full of cocaine and then actually got to meet a genuine drug smuggler and a genuine drug dealer, who also just happened to be his sister's boyfriend.

These were Edwin Jr.'s thoughts when Juan made his sleepy appearance at the top of the stairs. He stumbled down the steps behind Edwin Jr. while rubbing his eyes and then brushing his hair back with his fingers. He was still dressed in the flimsy, tropical clothing he had worn out from Miami the day before. The ever present automatic pistol was stuck in his waistband. He crossed the room to the large windows in front of Edwin Jr. and took a moment to look at the snow. He said over his shoulder, "Jesus Christ, will you look at that, man! I haven't seen snow in over ten years!" He shivered and stuffed his hands in his pants pocket. "Sweet Mary, mother of Jesus! Man, it's fucking cold in here. Don't you have a furnace or nothing?"

He crossed the room again past Edwin Jr. As he walked toward the dining room, he hugged himself and asked, "Hey, man, what did you hear from the other airplane? Did they call? The weather looks like she is getting better. Are they still in Vegas or something? I sure wish they would get here, man. Hey, did you notice it's cold in here." He walked back to Edwin Jr. and snorted, "Hey, man, nice robe. My grandfather had a robe like that." Then he headed back toward the dining room and ultimately the kitchen.

Edwin Jr. had let Juan do all the talking and hadn't said a word. He leaned over, opened the single drawer in the end table, and withdrew his father's ancient Colt revolver.

Juan, still muttering to himself, and having looked through the refrigerator and most of the cabinets unsuccessfully for something to eat, returned through the dining room. He leaned against the doorway to the living room, folded his arms, and complained to Edwin Jr., "Hey, man, don't you have nothing to eat in this house, man? I mean like Cheerios or anything?"

Edwin turned and aimed the old Colt directly at Juan's chest.

If Juan was surprised, he didn't show it. He casually unfolded his arms then asked smoothly, "Hey, what's this shit all about?" He pointed to the Colt with his left hand and slowly slid his right toward the Beretta.

Edwin Jr. pointed the barrel of the big revolver at the automatic tucked into Juan's waistband. His hand was shaking as much from the weight of the old Colt as his nervousness. "Don't even touch it. I don't want to shoot you. I just want you and my sister and that asshole pilot to leave." Then he shouted, "Just leave, that's all!" Edwin Jr. raised the Colt and aimed it right between the Cuban's eyes.

The bore of the gun looked huge to Juan. He shrugged. "Hey, man, why all the melodramatics? What's this all about?" He did not move his hand any farther from the Beretta.

Edwin Jr. stood up heavily, the Colt still leveled on the other man with one hand, the other on the sofa's arm for support. When he had gained his balance, he said, "The other airplane is not late. It crashed somewhere in the mountains last night during the storm. The federal authorities called me. They're going to be searching for it as soon as the weather gets better."

As if on cue, the sun broke through a gap in the clouds, and bright light streamed through the front windows. Juan suddenly forgot the gun. He took a step toward Edwin Jr. "Jesus, man, we got to get out of here! How long ago did they call? Jesus, lower that fucking gun, man, and let's wake the others! There must have been thirty million in that airplane!"

Edwin Jr. kept the gun leveled at the other man's midsection. He said as calmly as possible, "The FAA called about four hours ago, I'd guess. Now, I want you to take your gun out slowly with two fingers and drop it on the floor. Then you can leave with the others. I just want you, your friends, and your organization to leave me alone. And take that asshole sister of mine with you." Edwin Jr. again pointed to the automatic pistol in the other man's waistband. "C'mon, please put the gun on the floor," he stammered.

Juan could see the other man's hands shaking. He thought it might be fear or anger. He couldn't tell. He took a step closer.

Edwin repeated, "I'm warning you—no, no closer! I don't want to hurt you. I just want you to leave." He readjusted his finger on the trigger and swallowed.

Juan took two more steps toward Edwin Jr. The fat man backed up a step and thrust the gun forward. The Cuban smiled and casually walked the remaining distance between them. He grabbed the Colt's barrel. Edwin Jr. closed his eyes and pulled the trigger. Nothing happened.

Juan jerked the gun from Edwin Jr.'s hand and then pulled his Beretta out. He casually thumbed off the safety.

Edwin Jr., a look of fear and puzzlement in his eyes, began to back up slowly. He bumped into the end table. The heavy lamp crashed to the floor.

Juan examined the old revolver and admired its lines. He turned it over in his hand and then aimed it squarely at Edwin Jr. and pulled the trigger. Edwin Jr. flinched and tried to cover his face. Again nothing happened. Edwin Jr. slowly lowered his hands.

Juan looked at the old Colt again. Then he aimed it at the ceiling, but this time he cocked back the hammer himself. He pulled the trigger. The gun discharged with a roar and recoiled mightily in his hand. The bullet splintered the side of a wooden support beam in the vaulted ceiling before lodging itself in a larger one just below the roof. The acrid, black powder smoke filled the room.

Juan opened the small hatch just behind the cylinder with one hand and began pushing out the remaining five cartridges one by one, letting them drop to the floor. He kept the Beretta pointed at Edwin Jr.

When the Colt was empty, he said casually, "You know, man, you really are a dumbshit. You shouldn't go around pointing loaded guns at people unless you know how to use them. You almost had me fooled, you fat shit." He hefted the old revolver. "This is an old gun. It's what gun nuts call *single action*. Do you know what that means? No? Well, it means that you have to pull back on the hammer yourself before you pull the trigger." Juan cocked the Colt with a metallic click. "See?" Then he aimed the revolver at Edwin Jr.

Edwin Jr. winced and threw up his hands again. Juan pulled the trigger, and the hammer snapped against an empty chamber. Juan laughed and threw the Colt onto the sofa. Then he thrust the Beretta at Edwin Jr. until the barrel just grazed his forehead. With suddenly fury, he screamed at Edwin Jr., "I ought to kill you right now, motherfucker!"

Edwin Jr. backed up against the sofa and then stumbled backward. Off balance, he sat down heavily, vainly trying to get at least one arm behind him for support.

Juan followed him down, gun still against his forehead. He leaned over him, "Give me one good reason not to pull the trigger, you fat chicken-shit." He gestured with his free arm, pulling it toward his chest. "C'mon, man, just one reason."

Another voice came from across the room. "I'll give you a good reason, you little Cuban spic."

Juan kept the gun trained on Edwin Jr.'s forehead and turned slowly. He looked over his shoulder at the other man.

Tim McIntosh stood in the doorway to the other wing. He held his Browning Hi-Power automatic in both hands, police-style. He had it aimed directly at Juan's back. Juan could see this man was no amateur. Although not necessary to fire the weapon, the hammer was pulled back. Just a light touch on the trigger would discharge the 9 mm pistol.

Tim motioned with the barrel. "Now, why don't you just ease that gun down onto the couch there?"

Juan did as he was told. He raised his hands and turned around.

Edwin Jr. slumped down against the cushions.

Tim continued to sight along the barrel directly at Juan. "Now, why don't you tell me what's going on here? What was that shot all about?"

Juan licked his lips. He was angry at himself for letting the pilot enter the room unnoticed. "Hey, man, I don't have no quarrel with you." He tried to relax his voice. "Hey, man, the other airplane crashed, man. This asshole here has known about it for hours and didn't tell us. We got to get out of here."

Tim looked at Edwin. "What's he talking about? What's he mean the other airplane crashed? Who told you?"

Edwin Jr. sat and sweated on the couch. He blubbered, "The FAA called. It crashed sometime in the night. In the mountains. About one hundred miles east of here as near as they can tell, toward Denver."

Tim's eyes widened. "You mean it was on a flight plan? How stupid can you people be? They'll be looking for it!"

Edwin Jr. cleared his throat and said defensively, "I guess so. I don't know anything about flying. It was the hotel's airplane and pilot. We've always used him."

Tim looked at the Cuban and then back at Edwin Jr. "You dumbshits! You dumb assholes! You mean you fly around all the time on fucking flight plans in this business? Jesus Christ, I can't believe it!"

Juan looked around nervously and said, "Hey, man, no arguments, we've got to get out of here. Someone will eventually come here. We've got a shitload of cocaine parked right outside the door."

Edwin Jr. added, "He's right; my father was good friends with the local sheriff. He's probably on the way out here from town right now."

Tim moved to the other side of the room near the windows. He kept the gun trained on both men. Although the higher peaks were still shrouded in clouds, the visibility in the valley had improved considerably since the storm. The darker, lower, forested foothills west of the ranch could be seen plainly. He would have enough ceiling to takeoff safely and make his way south.

Juan repeated in a squeaky voice, "Hey, man, we've got to leave pronto. I'm on your side, man. I can't do any more time."

Tim answered angrily, "Nobody's on my side, asshole, but me. Don't give me any bullshit. You're both going to help me clean the snow off the airplane. If you two do a good job, then I just might let you live, which is more than the people who run this show will probably do. Understand?" Tim needed their help, but he had every intention of shooting the Cuban.

He walked toward the two men, keeping the gun trained on them and rubbing his temples with his free hand. He wished he had gotten more sleep. It was a long flight back south. He could feel the start of one of those special headaches. He had been on the ground too long. He was a sitting duck now that the storm had moved out. The tension was building in his forehead.

He told Edwin Jr., "We need a couple of brooms and a stepladder. Now get going. And no funny business." He motioned Edwin Jr. away from the couch, but Edwin was still frozen in place. He was unaccustomed to being ordered to do anything. Tim motioned again with his gun hand and barked, "Now get off your fat ass and get going! I'm losing patience with you assholes."

Debbie Forsyth quietly appeared at the top of the steps. She carried her father's shotgun she had used the previous afternoon. Sizing up the situation, she descended the steps. She held the gun to her shoulder. She countered Tim's threat to her brother. "And I'm losing my patience, too, Mr. McIntosh."

Tim started to turn, but Debbie warned him. "Uh-uh, not so fast, or it'll be the last move you make. You know I can use this thing. Now you drop the gun."

Tim dropped the Browning to the floor and grinned to himself. With any other woman, he might have chanced the shot, but he knew she was different and did indeed know how to use the expensive over and under shotgun. This was getting to be like a Marx Brothers film, he thought. Everybody was getting the drop on everybody else. Who was next, he wondered. The Lone Ranger?

Debbie said, "That's better." She motioned to Juan to pick up the pilot's gun.

But Juan was already in motion and quickly scooped up all three guns, including his own and the antique Colt.

Edwin Jr. settled heavily back onto the couch.

The Cuban walked over to Debbie's side. He also pointed his Beretta at Tim and said, "Hey, nice going, baby." She still had the shotgun trained on the pilot, and he could see her trigger finger twitching. This caused some concern to Juan. He looked at Debbie. "Hey, don't shoot him, honey. I figure we're going to need him to get out of here."

Debbie pulled the trigger twice in succession. There were two clicks.

Tim remained calm and moved toward the two.

Juan raised the Beretta. "Hey, not so fast."

Tim stopped as Debbie replied, "Sometimes it's just a game of bluff."

Tim smiled and thought he could maybe like this woman. She had a certain fearless style about her—a toughness. Then he turned to Juan and asked, "What do you mean, you need me?"

Juan said, "You, my friend, are going to fly us out of this country in your airplane."

Tim replied, "I'm not your friend, and I'm not flying either you or your girlfriend there anywhere."

Juan waved the Beretta. "No, be reasonable, man. I have it all set up. We will both live to be old and rich men, especially with all that nice, white cargo still aboard your airplane."

"You fool; I'm flying all that back to South America."

"You're the fool, man. What about the money you were supposed to bring back, eh?"

Tim shrugged, "Not my fault. I'll explain it. You know as well as I that they've had losses before. What was on that plane? Twenty or thirty million? Peanuts to the people who really run this show. You try to double-cross them, though, and you'll be dead in five minutes."

Juan laughed nervously, "You're the fool, man. You'll be the dead one five minutes after you land. They are very unforgiving. Maybe they will think the airplane that crashed is some kind of double-cross. Some kind of setup to take advantage of the bad weather, eh? Your only proof would be if the authorities actually find the lost airplane. And I don't think old Edwin here wants that to happen, do you Edwin?"

Edwin just shrugged.

Tim said, "I think they trust me, and, besides, I have nowhere else to go. They know my loyalties, which is more than I can say for you. I'll take my chances."

Juan laughed nervously, "So you know about my little transgression. I was going to pay them back."

This time it was Tim's turn to laugh, "Sure you were. I know that they probably want you dead."

Juan waved the gun again. "Well, all this doesn't mean much as long as I have this, eh? You're taking me where I want to go."

Tim laughed again, "Fuck you. But I'm just curious. Where do you want to go?"

Juan noted the sarcasm. "Eventually, Libya, where I have some friends."

"I have barely enough fuel on board to get back to South America. We'd never make it to Africa. I hope you know how to swim and have plenty of shark repellent with you."

Juan flushed with anger. "Don't take me for a stupid man. I've worked it all out. We have gas waiting for us in the Caribbean through my contacts. My only regret is not having all that lovely cash from the other airplane along like I had planned, but what you have aboard will do nicely, eh?"

Debbie asked, "You were going to hijack everything from the beginning? You are a fool, like he says. They'll hunt you down and kill you."

"I think they already want to do that over a lousy couple of kilos." He asked the pilot, "Isn't that right? Weren't you ordered to kill me?"

Tim answered, "That's right, asshole."

Juan turned to Debbie and shrugged. "See, I'm already a marked man. I have everything to gain and nothing to lose." He turned back to Tim. "Now, let's get going and get that airplane ready to go. We've already wasted too much time, man."

Tim asked, "And if I won't fly you anywhere…what then, asshole?"

"Oh, I think you will, man. You know I won't hesitate to shoot you if you don't. Like I said, I have nothing to lose. You and I are survivors, man. You'll be thinking of a way to get me eventually. I'm a challenge to you, man. Am I right?"

"Okay, you win. Let's get going. Like I told the fat man, I need a ladder and a broom."

Juan handed Tim's Browning to Debbie butt-first and asked, "Do you know how to use this?"

She took the gun casually, pulled back the slide a fraction of an inch to see if a round was in the chamber, and then let it slap shut. She said with heavy sarcasm, "I think I can figure it out. What happens to my brother?"

Juan looked at Edwin Jr. with disgust, "He gets to stay and answer to the authorities when they find his company airplane full of drug money. And when they do, he'll not only go to prison, but the bad publicity will sour his deal with that other rich asshole."

Edwin Jr. looked up. He was surprised, and Juan spoke again. "Yes, man, the organization knows all about it. You did not do well to underestimate us. Do you think they would let you sell off all your hotels that are so lucrative to us? They would kill you first, so your sister inherits everything." Then he ordered Debbie, "Cover the pilot while he prepares the airplane. Stay a good distance from him. He's tricky, man. And don't let him into the airplane at all. I will be the first to enter and check things out. He's probably got another gun or two in there." Juan snapped his fingers. "Now let's get going!"

361

Debbie motioned to Tim to start moving and said, "Go on through the dining room. The broom and stepladder are in the kitchen in a big closet near the back door."

Tim turned around and disappeared through the dining room doorway with Debbie following at a safe distance. They both returned soon with Tim carrying a folding ladder under one arm and a well-worn straw broom in the other. With Debbie still covering him with the gun, the pair left through one of the heavy front doors. They disappeared to the left along the driveway toward the airplane.

When he was sure they were both outside with no problems, Juan clicked the safety on and stuck the automatic back in his waistband. He turned and started for the stairs.

Edwin Jr. asked as Juan left, "Where are you going?"

Juan stopped on the second step and turned. "Now, where do you think I'm going? I'm going upstairs to get my things together, man." The Cuban plainly was not worried about the fat brother. Whatever resistance he had was now gone. He seemed firmly rooted to the sofa.

Edwin Jr. blubbered, "But what about me? What's going to happen to me? My business? I'll be ruined when all this comes out!"

Juan turned and began to climb the steps slowly. He turned again. "I don't give a shit what happens to you, man. You're on your own in about fifteen minutes. You'll have plenty of time to sit there on your fat ass and try to figure things out."

Edwin pleaded, "But what if they find the hotel's airplane with the money? How will I explain it to the authorities?"

Juan snickered, "If I were you, brother, I'd start worrying about the other side."

"What?"

"My bosses, eh? Those people will be plenty pissed to lose the money. They will think you've fucked it up, man. They'll come and take it out of your fat hide."

Edwin Jr. pleaded again, "Please, take me with you."

Juan turned around again at the top of the stairs. "Hey, man, your sister and I just don't want you around. And besides, there is not room for your fat ass in that airplane. There is only one seat, man. You'd make it overweight." Juan laughed again. "Get it? There is only a seat for me and the pilot." He disappeared down the second-floor hallway.

Debbie escorted the pilot to his black airplane. He carefully placed the ladder next to the right engine and made sure the braces were in place before beginning to climb onto the wing. He held the broom in one hand and balanced himself with the other. The clouds were breaking up. They swept overhead. The breaks between them bathed the driveway in bright sunshine melting the snow in earnest on the dark metal skin of the old bomber. Water dripped onto the asphalt.

Debbie was amazed how big the airplane seemed when you stood right against it. It was huge. The single main landing gearwheel and tire was almost to her waist. The engine and propeller seemed to tower over her. She looked up and watched Tim's progress.

Even though the stepladder was a tall one, it was still about three feet short of being adequate. Although Tim stood on the top rung, the leading edge of the wing was still above his waist. He leaned against the wing for balance and pitched the broom onto the top of it. It landed softly in the wet snow. He then boosted himself onto the wing on his stomach, came to a kneeling position, and stood up. The job would not be a difficult one. The air temperature was in the mid-thirties now, and the black skin was absorbing the heat from the direct sunlight at present. He bent over, picked up the broom, and began pushing the snow toward the trailing edge of the wing, where it cascaded over the flaps and ailerons onto the ground and left the wing wet and smooth. He couldn't chance the fact that the snow might slide off on takeoff. Tim was aware of accidents where other pilots thought the very same thing, but the snow had stuck, disturbing the airflow and destroying lift.

He worked his way along the wing toward the fuselage with Debbie following him along on the ground. He had not forgotten the small submachine gun tucked in its scabbard behind the pilot's seat, but the Plexiglas canopy halves were latched from the inside. There was no way to duck inside except to climb down and go in the belly hatch, which hung open.

When he finished with the right wing, Tim carefully stepped over the fuselage and onto the left wing. A slip could mean a fall of ten feet. Somehow he must get inside the airplane. He knew the Cuban would never let him go first. So it must be the sister.

He stopped sweeping for a moment and looked down the road for vehicles. He looked down and told the woman, "I'll be finished here in a minute, and then I'll do the tail surfaces. I really should check the oil in each engine, too. I've got some heavy, five-gallon cans of oil in the airplane." This was untrue. Although he did indeed have some oil in cans inside the airplanes, George had modified the engines with oil tanks of extra capacity for the long flights. The large, air-cooled radial engines did consume a lot of oil, and he did want to check the level, but there should be plenty left.

Debbie had walked around the nose. She looked up and shielded her eyes against the bright sky. "What'd you say? I couldn't hear what you just said because of the wind."

Tim raised his voice as he brushed more wet snow onto the driveway. "I said I need to check the oil in each engine, too. There's some extra inside the airplane."

"So?"

"So, I need to get inside the airplane."

"You know I can't let you do that. You might have another gun in there. You might even be able to start up this thing and leave."

"We won't get very far without oil."

"Nothin' doin', mister."

Tim resumed his sweeping. It was mostly water, now that the sun was out so strongly. "Pardon the cliché, but how did a nice girl like you get mixed up in this business with a scumbag like that Cuban?"

Debbie followed along on the ground. "I might have said the same thing of you."

"Touché."

Debbie continued though, "I loved my father. Worshipped him, I guess, when you come right down to it. I hate to see my brother run the business he built and his memory into the ground." She shrugged her shoulders. "I thought it would help things somehow. As it turns out, I guess it didn't."

"I take it you don't have any say in the business at all?"

"None of it. My father left it all to Edwin except for an allowance. He was an old-fashioned person about women being in management. I had plenty of ideas at first, but my brother ignored me."

Tim changed the subject. "Why are you going away with that scumbag?"

"I don't love him if that's what you think. I think he's a lowlife. Basically, right now, I have nothing else to do."

Tim shoved the last clump from the left wing and leaned on the broom handle. He looked at Debbie. "That's a shame. You're a smart woman." Then he said, "Please go over and get the ladder."

"No, I'm not letting you from my sight. You'll have to climb back over to the other side."

Tim laughed, "Yes, smart." He nervously looked down the road as he climbed over the top of the fuselage. "You know all these people are just using you. Right from the very start." He pointed at the house and looked at Debbie. "That Cuban has no intention of taking you anywhere. He won't need you any more than he'll need me when we get to where he wants to go. And there are only two seats in this airplane, and he knows that also." He looked back up at the house. "He's stringing you along, so you'll cover me out here, while he packs. Don't be stupid. Let me have the gun."

As Tim climbed onto the right wing, Debbie walked around the nose and stood by the right engine. "I'm not a stupid woman, Mr. McIntosh. And as far as being used, I knew what I was doing from the start. If I thought he was going to leave me with my brother, as you say, I'd kill him."

Tim threw the broom to the ground, and then knelt on the wing. He gingerly began to let himself down, feeling for the top step of the ladder with his toe. "That's mighty big talk. Have you ever killed anyone?"

Debbie didn't answer immediately. She thought about how hard it had been to pull the trigger on that first elk all those years ago. But the second one had been much easier. "No, of course I've never killed anyone."

Tim shook his head as he climbed down the ladder but didn't comment on her answer. Debbie, keeping her distance, retreated to the nose of the airplane. She read the words painted below the window. "What's this mean, anyway? Why is this painted on here?"

Tim looked at her and frowned. "It's none of your business. It's kind of a cross between a joke and a good luck charm. I had something like this painted on another airplane halfway around the world and a long time ago, that's all." He changed the subject. "C'mon, hurry up; we've got to do the tail next." He picked up the ladder and broom and turned.

The pair walked to the tail of the airplane. Debbie still covered him carefully with the pistol. The horizontal stabilizer was much smaller than the wing but also sat a few feet higher. Still, Tim quickly cleared each side by standing on the top rung and just blindly sweeping the broom back and forth. He almost lost his balance twice in a strong wind gust. What snow was left slid off quickly and fell to the ground. He felt he had cleared most of it. He could still make a quick check by opening one of the canopy halves and standing on his seat.

Tim folded the ladder and laid it in the snow-covered grass next to the broom. The snow covering the asphalt had melted quickly in the sun, leaving the driveway wet. The takeoff should be no problem now if the engines would start. He brushed some snow off his coveralls and, instead of walking toward the house, went in the opposite direction, hoping to buy a little more time and persuade the sister.

Puzzled, Debbie followed him. "What are you doing? We have to get back to the house."

Tim walked to the left wingtip and then strolled under the wing, pretending to inspect it. He stopped at the left landing gear and peered up into the wheel well. "I'm just preflighting her, making sure there aren't any suspicious leaks—that sort of thing." Which was true. He wiped a finger across the shiny, tubular gear strut and then straightened to walk around the front of the left engine while making a show of standing on his toes and inspecting it. He eyed the open belly hatch. Then he turned to Debbie and said, "Look, I'll give it to you straight again. That Cuban boyfriend of yours is not going to take you anywhere. If you're lucky, he won't kill you and your brother when we leave. I have no quarrel with you. Hell, I don't even know you. If you don't want to stay here, I'll give you a lift to South America. You'd probably like it down there." He extended his hand. "Just give me the gun and I'll take care of things in the house."

Debbie thought about this for a moment. She motioned for Tim to start walking back to the house. "Let's get back inside. As long as I have this, I still control the whole situation."

Tim turned and began to walk around the nose of the airplane along the driveway. Debbie followed him onto the front steps. Before he opened the door, he looked over his shoulder and said, "Last chance."

Debbie frowned and answered, "Open the door and be sure you walk straight into the middle of the room."

Tim complied with her instructions and pushed open one of the heavy doors. She followed him into the house as the door swung shut. She held the automatic in front of her and was glad to be out of the cold wind.

The Browning was yanked from her hand so fast she only had time to let out a startled yelp.

Juan stepped from behind the door. He quickly put the pilot's Browning in his waistband and motioned for her to join her almost catatonic brother on the sofa. Edwin Jr. sat and stared at the opposite wall. As she sat down, she glanced at the pilot. She saw his knowing look in his eyes. He had been correct.

Startled, Debbie turned. "What did you do that for? I—"

Juan cut her off. "I was hoping you'd use that door. Now walk quietly over to the sofa and sit down next to your brother." Juan giggled. "You know, man, I think you Forsyth kids should really get to know each other better."

Debbie walked over to the sofa but defiantly refused to sit next to her brother. She looked down at Edwin Jr., but he turned his head in order to avoid the fury in her intense glare. Then she turned and faced the Cuban.

Juan walked casually over to where she stood and smiled at her. She tensed as he studied her for a moment. Then he struck her hard against the side of her face with the back of his hand. The blow came as a surprise, and she staggered to one side as he ordered her again to sit on the couch with her brother. As she retreated to the couch, she glared at him and rubbed her jaw. "You bastard, I thought you could hit harder than that."

Tim smiled at her brass.

Juan raised his hand as if to strike her again but saw the pilot move in the corner of his vision. He spun around quickly and leveled the automatic at the pilot's chest. Tim froze.

Juan's anger seemed to fade quickly as he walked over to the doors and picked up a small case. He motioned with the gun for the pilot to move toward the door as he ordered him verbally to do the same. "Move quickly and do not try anything foolish. I will not hesitate now to kill anyone in this room—even you—to make my escape. Do as I say, and you will be a rich man."

Debbie sat next to her brother and threatened Juan in a low, menacing voice. "You bastard, I should have known not to trust a lousy lay like you. You're nothing but bottom slime."

Juan laughed, "I'm still in a good mood, bitch. But don't push me, man. You know my temper. I have decided to leave you two alive. Be thankful." He hesitated for a moment. "Hey, man, think about all the good times we had. I'm really sorry that the airplane has only two seats." Then he laughed again.

Debbie looked quickly at the gun cabinet and just as quickly realized her mistake.

Juan snickered as he opened the door for the pilot. "You're maybe thinking of killing me? Not very nice. But the guns are all unloaded. I made sure of that a few minutes ago. Here, see for yourself." Juan backed up to the gun cabinet. He selected one of the expensive hunting rifles. Pulling it from its rack, he hefted it with one hand. "A nice weapon. But useless, I am afraid." He threw the rifle across the room where it landed with a clatter at Debbie's and Edwin Jr.'s feet. "Go ahead, pick it up."

Debbie remained seated next to her brother.

Juan clicked his tongue. "Not going to do it, huh? That's too bad; I wanted to see the disappointment on your face when you found the firing pin was also broken, man. You should eventually be able to get it fixed. I am sorry; it is a very beautiful gun. Probably one of your father's favorites, I would think, man. But I just couldn't take the chance you'd find some more ammunition in the house somewhere." He laughed again as he put his small suitcase down. He stood to one side of the gun case and, still covering the pilot with one hand, toppled the heavy cabinet with the other. It crashed heavily to the floor.

Juan motioned Tim to the door. "Now we go, friend. Please keep your hands where I can see them." Indicating the small suitcase, which he had just picked up, Juan told him, "I have all the necessary charts and positions for your navigational radios. Once we get to the point where your fuel doesn't permit a return to South America, I think you will see it my way."

Tim grunted as he pulled the door open then walked onto the porch and down the steps. Juan followed him, leaving the brother and sister sitting on the couch. All his instincts told him to kill them both. He hesitated even now, as he followed the pilot along the drive. But instead he merely shrugged, as he heard the heavy front door shut with a final thud.

The instant the door shut, Debbie sprang from the couch, disbelieving her and her brother's good luck that the Cuban had not shot them both. She quickly crossed the room and ran up the stairs taking two at a time. Bewildered, her brother stood up and called after her, but either she didn't hear him or chose to ignore him for the moment.

She gained the top of the stairs and ran down the hall. She knew two things for certain about the elderly housekeeper who had worked for the family for decades: the old woman always tended to keep things properly in their place, and she had always had an aversion to guns of any type.

Debbie turned left and threw the door to her childhood bedroom open. She ran past the neatly made bed and breathlessly reached the large closet at the far end of the room. She fumbled with the latch. It should still be where Debbie had left it years ago, before she had moved out for the last time. Her heart pounded, and she told herself to calm down. The latch clicked, and she threw both doors open. She pushed aside old bedding and clothes that had been neatly stacked and sorted.

The closet had a musty, mothball smell to it. She worked her way back to the far left corner. It was still there.

She grasped the oiled walnut stock and pulled the Winchester hunting rifle from the closet. A presentation grade model 70 in .308 caliber. She cradled the rifle in one arm and opened the bolt. The leather carrying strap dangled below her waist. The bolt rotated easily and slid backward with a precise, slick, machined feel. Her father had given her the rifle over twenty years ago, when she had been a teenager. She had preferred to keep it secure in her closet instead of the gun case along with her father's guns. It was one of her most prized personal possessions. Its weight and feel were at once familiar.

But there was no ammunition. The magazine was empty.

Debbie laid the rifle on the bed and began pawing blindly along the shelf above the clothes rack, hoping one of the yellow boxes was still there. Her hand gripped a rectangular carton, and she withdrew it. She was grateful to hear the cartridges pinging against each other. The box felt half full—maybe ten rounds.

Debbie opened the ammunition box one-handed and flipped the box over, grabbing two of the long, brass shells while letting the remainder drop to the floor along with the empty box. They scattered around the room.

Her hands shaking and trying to remain calm, she awkwardly loaded the two shells into the rifle's magazine from the top, pressing down with her thumb. She then slid the bolt, shut causing one of the cartridges to be loaded directly into the chamber. She checked to make sure the safety was off while walking over to the window in her room. She looked out, but the view was blocked by the slanting roof at the end of the house. She could only see the tail of the black airplane jutting over the lawn. She would have to go to the other side of the house into one of the spare rooms across the hall at the end of this wing.

Debbie left her bedroom, hurriedly crossed the hall, and flung the door open to the spare bedroom directly across from hers. The large and multipaned windows were in dormers. They were hinged on each side and latched in the middle. She undid the latch on the side away from the airplane, so her view would not be blocked by the window itself, and was thankful that the screens had been efficiently removed for the winter but that the storm windows had not been put in place. They were probably too heavy for the old housekeeper to handle by herself. Not wanting any movement to attract attention, she stood to one side behind the curtain and slowly opened the window until it rested back along the dormer. She sunk to her knees, removed the covers on each end of the telescopic sight, and rested the rifle on the window sill. The front two-thirds of the airplane was in full view about forty yards from the east end of the house.

Debbie could hear the voices of the two men seemingly raised in some sort of argument. She swung the rifle back and forth. The airplane seemed huge in the sight. She was really too close for a telescopic sight and muttered under her breath, hoping it was still in adjustment after all these years. It had last been sighted in at a distance of two hundred yards for hunting elk. That adjustment would have to be taken into account. At that distance even a powerful rifle bullet would drop some inches due to the constant pull of gravity. At the shorter range the bullet would go high. She would aim a little lower. The telescopic sight had a limited field of view, and Debbie took her eye from it. The two men were standing along the side of the fuselage behind the right engine. They hadn't seen her, but she did not have a clear shot. She looked back into the sight and moved the crosshairs up until they rested squarely in the middle of the right cockpit window. The window sill provided a very stable platform for the rifle. Debbie waited.

The voices of the two men were raised again. Most of it came from Juan. Debbie leaned her head to one side, and she saw both men walking forward now to the nose of the airplane. They stopped just in front of the right propeller. Juan still held his gun on the pilot. Then the pilot positioned his shoulder against one of the propeller blades and began to move it. As he did so, he looked up. Debbie couldn't be sure if he had seen her in the window. If he had, he didn't show it. The Cuban now stood in full view with his back to the house.

Debbie quickly pivoted the rifle on the sill. The crosshairs centered about eight inches below Juan's left shoulder.

She told herself not to think about it, held her breath, and gently squeezed the trigger as she had been taught.

The Winchester kicked hard against her shoulder. The shot echoed out across the fields as a small hole simultaneously appeared in the Cuban's back, and he was pushed forward violently. He staggered and twisted. The bullet passed completely through him but not before mushrooming as it splintered two ribs, collapsed a lung, and then ripped out the lower portion of his heart completely. It tore a silver dollar–sized hole in his chest as it exited. The bullet then narrowly missed the nosewheel tire as it ricocheted off the pavement and whined into the distance. Before he died, Juan looked toward the house with pain and bewilderment, seeing Debbie at the open window. He then looked down at the bloody hole in his chest and fell facedown to the wet pavement. A circle of blood began to ooze from beneath his body.

Tim jerked at the sound of the shot. He dove to the ground and watched the other man fall. After a moment, he too looked up at the open window and watched Debbie eject the spent shell casing and slide the bolt home again putting a fresh cartridge into the firing chamber. He was caught in the open and knew the crosshairs were now on him.

Tim got to one knee, cupped his hands, and yelled, "Nice shot. You saved me the trouble." Then he got to his feet and walked the few feet to Juan's body. He kicked the other man a couple of times then began to bend and reach for the Beretta automatic near the Cuban.

Debbie shouted, "Stay where you are. I don't want to make this a double, Mr. McIntosh."

Tim straightened and raised his hands. He turned to the house. The rifle was trained on him. He smiled.

Debbie continued, "I know what you're thinking and maybe you could move fast enough to duck behind the landing gear. Or maybe I'll miss. To tell you the truth, I have only one round left in this rifle, and I wouldn't want to waste a bullet on you. No, I think I'd try for a nice stable target like one of your tires. But I don't think you want to be marooned here, do you?"

She was right. His one goal now was to get the hell out of here. Tim nodded his head as she went on. "Like you said, we have no quarrel between us, and I do want your airplane and that body out of here. They're cluttering the driveway. I'll have to let you go. Take that dead Cuban with you and maybe that'll put you in good graces with your bosses. Proof of your good intentions or something."

Tim yelled back, "That's all?"

Debbie raised her voice again, "That's it. Now, if I were you, I'd get moving. And don't forget where this rifle is aimed in case you get some funny ideas about that machine gun behind your seat."

"You knew it was there all the time?"

"That's right; I took a tour of the cockpit yesterday. You might want to put the full clip back in it. You'll find it under the right seat."

Tim bent over the body and picked up the dead man's automatic. He then turned Juan over and pulled his own Browning from the man's waist. He checked the safeties on each weapon, unzipped his coveralls, and tucked both guns under his belt. He then walked around the other man, grabbed each arm, and began to pull him toward the belly hatch. The body left a smear of fresh blood along the asphalt as it was pulled forward.

The belly of the aircraft was some four feet above the ground, and Tim had to lift Juan up into the airplane. He avoided the blood. It didn't take much effort. The Cuban only weighed about one twenty. He pushed the body to one side and then hoisted himself into the hatch. He pulled it shut with a clang and secured the latch from inside. Juan's body lay in a fetal position and stared up at the pilot as he made his way forward to his seat. Tim chuckled to himself as he stepped around the body. "Remember, no smoking and fasten your seatbelt, fella." He would dump the body out over the Gulf of Mexico.

Tim squeezed into his seat, unlatched one of the canopy halves, and pushed it open. He hurriedly began to run down the prestart checklist, hoping the cold engines would start with little trouble.

Debbie saw the pilot enter the cockpit and took a deep breath. She relaxed more when the propeller on the left engine began to turn slowly. The engine belched out two small puffs of smoke, and she thought she heard it backfire once. Then she realized the sound had come from behind her inside the house.

After Debbie had run upstairs, Edwin Jr. had shakily stood up, walked through the dining room, and then into the kitchen. He had slowly opened the freezer door, pushed aside the roast, and pulled out the matching Colt .45 revolver of his father's. Thanks to Juan's impromptu lesson, he had the knowledge this time to pull the hammer back fully before sticking the barrel into his mouth. The old pistol worked with perfection and most of the rear portion of Edwin Jr.'s head was instantly splattered throughout Mrs. Alison's gleaming kitchen.

Tim started both radial engines with some difficulty because of the cold. He secured the canopy. He tightened his seatbelt and shoulder harness and began to taxi immediately. The wind was from the north, so he would have to taxi all the way to the south end of the long, straight access road to the ranch on which he had landed less than twenty-four hours ago, which seemed ages now. He would have preferred to let the engines warm up a little more, but he was in a hurry, and the time it took him to taxi and do an abbreviated run up at the end of the road would have to suffice.

In a few minutes, he reached the point where the road turned east through the ranch's outbuildings and over the hogback to Crestridge. He turned the large airplane around carefully and faced north. He ran down the checklist quickly. The engines were running smoothly. The cylinder head and oil temperature needles were just coming alive. Satisfied, he ran the engines up to full power and released the brakes. With almost half the original fuel supply gone, the airplane accelerated strongly into the wind. Tim was airborne less than half the distance down the road. He retracted the landing gear quickly as he banked slightly to fly directly over the beautiful log house and the circular driveway. He dipped a wingtip and touched his forehead in a salute as he roared overhead. She shielded her eyes from the bright sun to look up but didn't wave as he swept over her.

Tim climbed out to the north following the valley and gaining altitude. He brought the power and propeller RPM back to their climb settings. The airplane bucked in some mild turbulence as he knifed up through the puffy white clouds a few thousand feet above the range land. Above the clouds the airplane was climbing solidly now in smooth air as he retracted the flaps. The sky overhead was the deepest blue. The sunshine was brilliant. His spirits soared as they usually did on a day like this. He reached for his sunglasses. From horizon to horizon, jagged peaks, brilliantly white with the first snow of the winter season, jutted above the clouds. To his immediate left the White Elks reared up. Partly out of habit, because most turns are made to the pilot's side for visibility, and one other reason, Tim banked to the left, which was out of his way slightly, and took in the view as he climbed up and over this mountain range, which overlooked the ranch below. The old bomber was climbing strongly as he neared the highest peak in the range. The mountaintop pivoted below his wing as he came around to a southeasterly heading.

Something caught his eye as he began to level the wings. Perhaps just a reflection on the lake below. He looked down. The wind ruffled the lake's surface and reflected the dappled sky. There it was. The tiny, white airplane was right under him near the west shore of the hourglass-shaped lake. It looked like a tiny crucifix in the water.

He banked more steeply and circled the hole in the cloud cover. It had to be the hotel's airplane. Maybe the pilot had tried for the ranch's airstrip after all. But the authorities were searching farther to the east.

Tim throttled back and continued to circle. The airplane looked to be just a short distance from the ranch, but the rugged terrain surely made the site very remote.

The clouds closed in as Tim grinned broadly. The lake and airplane were suddenly gone beneath a white blanket. There was an easy way into the lake after all, he suddenly realized, as he leveled the wings, steadied his course, and flew south.

There was no way he could have seen the two tiny figures near the waterfall at the other end of the lake. And the two men could not hear his engines because of the thundering water.

CHAPTER 24

Back at the Trailhead

Rod bent forward under the pack's weight as he slogged heavily along the muddy trail. He wondered why it always seemed to take four times as long to hike out as to hike in. He was sweating heavily despite the cold night air. His breath condensed ahead of him as he labored along under the load of his heavy pack. One lens of his glasses had completely fogged up. The other was inexplicably clear. Sweat appeared on his forehead, cooled, and ran in salty rivulets into his eyes, causing him to blink constantly. His back was soaked. The AA batteries in his tiny flashlight had given up long ago. The snow was patchy at this lower altitude, and it was difficult to keep on the trail in front of him in only the starlight. Mostly it was just a darker patch of ground stretching away in front of him somewhere between the trees. Rocks and roots were invisible, and he had tripped often. With the one lens fogged up, he had no depth perception whatsoever. The funny thing was that it was always the right lens that fogged up, never the left. It had been that way all his life. He had even tried hiking with his head sideways in the hope of letting some of the cold night air blow between his eye and the lens to clear it, but it hadn't worked. Of course, he could stop and wipe the lens with his shirt tail, but it would be fogged up again in less than a hundred yards. Besides, he wasn't walking very fast now. His ankle was killing him, and he had had to favor that leg considerably in the last few miles.

The cleated Vibram soles on his boots, which were so excellent for traction most of the time, were now clogged up with heavy mud. It felt as if each foot weighed at least ten pounds more than normal. Rod was bone-weary, and his legs felt like jelly as he slogged the last half mile to the car, which was always the longest.

Jamie was behind him somewhere. He had been right behind Rod until about fifteen minutes ago and then had dropped back. It had taken them much longer to hike out than they had anticipated. Without looking at his Timex, which in any case did not have luminous hands, Rod guessed it was nearly one in the morning. They were still hiking in the middle of the night because of the time it had taken for them to pick their way down the gorge and intercept the trail. It had been dangerous. The rocks had been slippery with new snow. They had finally found the trail right at dark, and it had been difficult to follow as it ran north along the flank of the mountain range for many miles. They should have made camp and continued in the morning. Rod had wanted to stop many times, but Jamie did not want to stop. He had been impatient to reach the car despite Rod's warning that he still intended to stop at the pay phone in front of the store in Crestridge.

Rod felt the trail begin to angle downward and widen between the trees. At last the parking lot should be only a hundred yards ahead. He stumbled over one of the logs placed across the trail by the forest service to stem erosion and then suddenly walked out of the trees to the clearing above the parking lot. The light was better here, and he could see his car parked exactly where he had left it. It was the only car in the lot. He made his way down the steps stiffly and shuffled across the gravel to it. He dumped the heavy pack next to it. He placed his hands in the small of his back and tried to straighten himself. He groaned. The night air felt cold against his damp shirt.

The car seemed unharmed as he fished in his pocket for the keys. He found the correct one, unlocked the driver's door, and opened it. He groaned again as he sat down sideways in the seat and stretched his legs out into the parking lot. His ankle seemed on fire. The bright interior lights hurt his eyes for a moment. The car had been covered with dust before the snowfall. It had melted that afternoon, causing small, muddy rivers to run down the finish.

Rod bent over and rubbed his aching ankle. Then he loosened the laces on his hiking boots and pulled them slowly off. He wiggled his toes as he stretched his legs out in front of him again and enjoyed the luxury of a soft place to sit.

He hoped Jamie would be along soon, and they could start back to Denver. He had left Jamie where the North Fork of the White Elk River had crossed the trail a mile or so from the parking lot. Despite the lack of a flashlight, Jamie had been determined to find the beer he had stashed there three days before. Rod had decided to continue on and hike the remaining distance to the parking lot. He had last seen his friend hopping from rock to rock in the dark, trying to salvage the six-pack.

Ten minutes passed and Rod began to feel the chill. He looked again at his Timex and was beginning to worry when he heard footsteps crunching across the gravel toward the car. Jamie came into the light carrying the beer, minus two cans. Jamie walked to the passenger side and slipped from his huge pack with a groan. Rod reached over and unlatched the door for him. Then he left his seat and stood stiffly in his sock feet looking across the roof of the Porsche. He frowned when Jamie leaned the metal pack frame against the car's front fender. Jamie opened the passenger door. Then he snapped one of the remaining beers off and handed it across the roof to Rod. Rod sighed and then carefully pulled his tab back.

Jamie took a large swallow and smacked his lips. "I didn't think I was going to find this shit. I was afraid the Boy Scouts had found it or something. I must have looked under a hundred rocks back there." He took another big swallow and playfully asked, "You ready to go? Will this piece of shit start?" He laughed and finished the beer. "Jesus, this stuff is cold!"

Rod replied testily, "Yes, it'll start." Then he walked stiffly around to the rear of the Porsche.

Jamie opened another beer, took a swallow, and set the can down right in the middle of the car's roof. He asked, "Hey, what're you so glum about?"

Rod looked at the beer can but decided he was too tired to complain. He opened the rear hatch and found the dipstick by feel. He held it in front of him as he tried to read the level from the light coming from the rear window. The level was only down a tiny bit despite the long drive from Denver a few days before. Rod fumbled in the dark trying to replace the dipstick. Jamie took the can from the roof and also walked to the rear of the car. Rod thought he had found the hole for the dipstick, but Jamie shoved his shoulder a little bit, causing him to miss. It was an old trick. Jamie laughed. "Hey, old buddy, you need some hair around that...remember that old joke?"

Rod found the hole and shoved the dipstick home. "Yeah, hardy-har-har. Real funny." He carefully closed the hatch.

"You still worried about that airplane up there?"

"Look," Rod said under his breath, "I'm tired, it's the middle of the night, and we've got a long drive to Denver."

"Hey, that's sounds like a line from that movie *The Blues Brothers* doesn't it. You know at the end, when they get ready to drive back to Chicago. Hey, I'll drive if you want."

Rod ignored Jamie's last comment and said, "What are you so up about anyway?"

"Well, old buddy, we're going to be rich as soon as I figure things out. Hell, we already have near a hundred grand—cash money, as they say." He added, "And some nice jewelry."

Rod corrected him, "Eighty-one thousand four hundred dollars to be exact, and I'm still calling the authorities just like I said up there." He walked to his pack where it lay by the side of the car and picked it up by the frame. He unlatched his seatback, pushed it forward, and carefully lifted it into the rear of the car behind the driver's seat.

Jamie finished his beer. He crumpled the can and threw it into the car onto the floor in front of the passenger seat as he walked by the open door to where his pack still leaned against the front fender. He began removing the climbing rope and hardware. He said, "I still think you ought to reconsider. Would you pop the front compartment for me, please?"

Rod finished stowing his pack, pushed the seatback in place, and reached under the dash to spring the latch. The lid popped open; Jamie raised it farther and began stowing the climbing gear in the front of the car. "Thanks."

Rod, still in his sock feet and carrying his heavy boots, tiptoed and half limped on the gravel to the front of the Porsche, where he sucked tentatively on his beer and stood waiting for Jamie to square the gear away. His ankle was still killing him. And the exertion of the hike was wearing off, causing him to shiver suddenly as the cold night air evaporated the sweat still under his clothing.

Jamie finished packing the hardware, and Rod positioned his boots to one side in the front. Everything had its place in the car. He would drive in his socks for a while on the way home until his feet felt better. He had a pair of old running shoes in the back seat for later.

Jamie looked at his friend and fantasized, "Think of what you could do with all that cash up there. We're still the only ones who know it's there. Hell, think of what we can do with forty grand apiece even."

Jamie never gave up, Rod thought, as he answered, "Yeah, and what if the rest of those suitcases just have dirty underwear in them? That airplane is totally unsafe sitting in that water. Are you going to risk your life again for some dirty underwear?"

Jamie was silent for a moment. The two men looked at each other. Jamie said, "Yeah, but I saw the money. It's worth a chance. And besides, what do I have to lose? Just let me do some thinking, okay?"

Rod mumbled something that sounded like, "You're nuts." Then he closed the front deck lid gently with a click and tiptoed back to the driver's side. He got in stiffly, fished for the key in his pocket, and inserted it in the ignition. He twisted it, and the engine cranked for a few moments before roaring into life and then idling smoothly. As Jamie grunted and positioned his pack next to Rod's on the tiny back deck, Rod quickly turned on the heater. Jamie pulled out his day pack before pushing the seatback forward and then climbed into the car. He slammed the door too hard in Rod's estimation before picking up the can on the front floor and tossing it over his shoulder. It ricocheted off the rear window. Rod winced.

The day pack was on Jamie's lap. He reached in, pulled out the damp packets of cash, and dumped them in his lap. He began idly thumbing through one of them.

Rod looked down at Jamie's muddy boots. "You could have taken them off, you know."

Jamie looked up from the money. "Huh?"

Rod nodded toward the floor. "Your boots."

Jamie looked over the money and picked one foot from the floor. He looked at it and said without interest, "Oh yeah." Then he thrust the packet of money toward Rod and thumbed it near his right ear. Rod grimaced and tilted his head away. Laughing, Jamie said, "I'll treat you to a car wash in Denver. Hell, I'll treat you to a whole new car."

Rod slowly let his breath out. The engine was sufficiently warmed up. He pushed in the clutch, carefully shifted into reverse, and backed out of the parking place. He switched on the headlights as the car moved forward.

Jamie dropped the money onto his lap. "Rod?"

"Huh?"

"I forgot to tell you that one of the Boy Scouts wrote 'wash me' in the dirt on my door." Then he went back to thumbing through the money with a smile on his face.

Leaving the gravel parking lot, Rod found that the formerly dusty road of a few days ago had been transformed by the fresh snow of the night before into a very slick, muddy track. This had been in the back of his mind as they had hiked out. He gritted his teeth as he slowly lowered the low-slung Porsche downhill from the parking lot on the forest service road toward the county road leading into Crestridge. The first few miles were going to be steep and slick. As a result Rod only used the first two gears as he let the engine compression brake the car. Progress was slow. Even using the engine compression, he had to frequently apply the brakes. When he did so, the car slid almost instantly. This required a deft touch on the brake pedal. Rod kept one tire on the shoulder and the other in the middle in an effort not to high center the car and to stay out of the ruts. The sounds of rocks and clumps of mud hitting the wheel wells could be heard over the exhaust. All four tires became large, mud-encrusted doughnuts in a few hundred feet.

Rod negotiated the first switchback and then the second. On the third turn, the last one before the road finally straightened out and the grade lessened, Jamie suddenly stiffened and yelled at the top of his lungs, "*Stop!*"

This so startled Rod that he instantly slammed on the brakes. It was too late by the time he realized his mistake. The silver Porsche slid sideways with all four wheels locked. The passenger side tires dropped down into a deep rut in the middle of the track while the driver's side tires went off the road in the brush. Before Rod could correct, there was a sickening thump and the sound of broken glass as the front left fender glanced off a large lodgepole pine near the side of the road. The turn signal and headlight were broken. Before the car finally stopped it slid along the tree. It made a squeaking sound as it dragged its rough bark along the paint. The outside mirror was pushed back just as the car stopped against the tree, rendering the driver's door unusable.

Jamie quickly opened his door and jumped out onto the muddy road.

Rod sat with his forehead against the steering wheel for a moment. His precious Porsche was ruined. Without looking up, he asked, "What did you yell for?"

Jamie leaned in and said, "I'll be right back." Then he jogged up the road, leaving the door open.

Rod switched off the ignition and sat in the sudden stillness. He looked at the big tree with the rough bark directly outside his window. Then he awkwardly slid over the gearshift knob to the passenger side. He got out of the car, forgetting he was still in his sock feet. The cold mud oozed around his toes as he made his way around the front of the car. He had to balance one hand on the right fender for support.

In the glare of the remaining headlight, Rod assessed the damage. The bumper was twisted at a funny angle. The turn signal was shattered. He saw the shattered pieces of amber plastic in front of the car. The headlight and chrome rim strip were also broken. The empty socket stared back at him. Steam rose from the hot filament. Rod worked his way around the tree. The fender from the bumper back to the driver's door was one large, crumpled scuffmark coated with sticky tree sap. The rearview mirror was pinned between it and the car. Rod also noticed in the sparse light that the door appeared to be buckled somewhat. He thought he would be soon in tears as he turned his attention back up the road.

Jamie arrived, breathlessly jogging up to the car and then walking around the front, where he joined Rod. Jamie assessed the damage, too. He sucked in his breath and put his hand on Rod's shoulder. "Hey, tough break. Doesn't look too bad though. We might have to pry some of the fender away from the tire. At least we're lucky the other headlight is still working."

Rod replied angrily, "Yeah, real lucky. Why did you yell so loud? I thought we were going to hit something in the road. And where did you go just now?"

"Hey, I wasn't the person who hit the tree. Don't worry about it. We've got enough money in the car to buy ten of these much less fix a little fender bender. C'mon, get in and start it up. I think we can get it away from the tree if you back and I push."

"You've destroyed my car. I haven't put a scratch on it in almost fifteen years."

Jamie took another look at the fender and bumper. He shook his head. "It's not destroyed, Rodney; it's just not a virgin anymore. Besides, like I've been saying, there's over forty grand on the front seat that belongs to you. Millions more if you want it. More than enough to buy a new fender and mirror. Now let's try to get this German piece of shit out of the bushes."

Rod walked back around the car. "You're not giving that money back, are you?"

"Hell no, and I'm trying to figure out a way to get the rest of it. C'mon, let's get going."

Rod crawled back over into the driver's seat, forgetting for a moment about his muddy feet. He picked up one of the packets of money Jamie had left on the front seat. He hefted it and felt the weight of the bills. How easy would it be now to fix the car? Pay off the engine rebuild? Or even buy a brand new one? For the first time, he truly realized just how much money was involved. He felt lightheaded. How easy everything would be with enough money.

Jamie braced himself against the fender. He yelled, "Now don't forget to put it in reverse!"

Rod threw the money back onto the front passenger's seat, started the car, and slipped the gearshift into reverse. He revved the engine and let the clutch out. The rear wheels spun in the mud. Jamie pushed and fought for footing on the slick road. Above the roar of the engine, rocks and mud rattled against the wheel wells and sprayed against the underbody. The Porsche began to inch backward, more from Jamie's effort than the engine. The tree slowly retraced its march along the car with its rough, resin-filled bark. The mirror was completely twisted from its mount and fell in the mud.

Jamie grunted and yelled, "Turn the wheel left! Turn it left, away from the tree!"

Rod followed his orders, and at last the car angled away from the tree. The rear jutted backward into some bushes, but the front was at least pointed in the right direction. It should be easy now to drive back onto the road.

Jamie bent down next to the damaged fender. It didn't appear to be rubbing on the tire. He then picked up the beheaded mirror, the pieces of headlight and turn signal, and walked around to the passenger side. He threw the mirror, glass, and amber plastic onto the floor, got in, and slammed the door.

Rod put the Porsche into gear and eased out the clutch. It didn't take much to get the car moving on the downslope, and soon they were creeping around the last bend. As the tension in the car lessened, Rod asked, "Why did you have me stop back there? Where did you go?"

Jamie answered, "The trailhead register. I had to rip out the page our names were on in case anybody investigates all this. That was close. I hope I didn't leave any more loose ends."

The twenty-odd miles into Crestridge took another thirty minutes. Neither man said much to each other. Each was lost in their thoughts. Jamie idly tried to tune into a station on the radio and was still trying to figure out a way to recover at least some of the money. The lake was as remote a spot as you could hope to find in the lower forty-eight states. The terrain was rugged. The airplane was balanced precariously on the bottom just ready to slide into some very deep water. He mentally juggled possibilities and logistics.

Rod realized for the first time the enormity of their find. But what were the risks? How much trouble could come their way? He had a family to think of.

Rod braked for the stop sign at the western edge of Crestridge, where the county road joined the state route that came north from Gunnison. For a few moments in the last thirty minutes, he had been almost swayed by Jamie's arguments. He continued straight into the sleeping town as the road became the main street. The tire was now making horrible rubbing noises against the fender. He would have to look at it. The tire was probably ruined, too. And those special tires were over forty dollars apiece.

He pulled up in front of the now deserted general store and stopped even with the gas pumps. The windows were dark. The old woman and the dog were asleep inside somewhere. The light in the top of the phone booth glowed blue behind the plastic panel and its modernized image of a bell. Rod switched off the engine, turned off the single headlamp, and tried to roll down his window. It would only go a third of the distance and made horrible squeaking noises. Three blocks east and one block south, music from the town's only bar could be heard dimly, even though it was far past the two o'clock closing time, but nobody was on the streets.

The two men sat in silence for a moment.

Finally Jamie said, "Look, I can't stop you from doing this, short of tying you up or hitting you over the head. Just think about what you're doing, okay?"

Rod tried to open his door. He had forgotten about the damage. It resisted. Metal creaked. He was only able to open it up some two inches.

He leaned into it harder, and it gave a little. Rod grunted. One more try and it swung open, accompanied by grinding and popping noises.

He leaned back into the car. "I've thought a lot about this. I've always gone along with you on everything over the years, but not this time." He hesitated. "I've got a family to think of…and it's just not safe for anyone to be around that airplane. I'll have to make the call." He looked up. The sky was clear. The stars were bright in the clear mountain air and high altitude of Crestridge. "Besides, with this good weather, they'll probably find the crash tomorrow."

Jamie sat grimly. "Yeah, sure." It was all he could manage. He fiddled with the radio some more as Rod walked over to the phone booth and folded back its door.

Rod closed the folding door. The overhead light illuminated again. He emptied his pockets of loose change and laid it on the shelf below the phone. He didn't have much money—maybe sixty-five cents.

Jamie opened the last can of beer and drained half of it.

His back to the car, Rod put the receiver to his ear, picked out a quarter, and dropped it into the slot. He dialed information, and soon a woman's voice came on the line asking what city he wanted. "Denver, ma'am."

"Yes, what number?'

"I'd like the after hours, emergency number for the FAA, the Federal Aviation Administration, please."

"One moment."

Then she continued quickly, "Here's that number, sir. Thank you for using AT&T."

A computer-generated voice started to read the number. Rod wasn't prepared. He had nothing to write with or on. He strained to remember the number. The voice repeated it twice. Rod mouthed the numbers to himself, trying to remember.

Jamie sat slumped in the car thinking hard while finishing the beer. He tossed the can in the back then selected the AM band on the car's radio. He ran the slide back and forth over the dial. There was a lot of static. Only one station. He stopped on that. He had come into the middle of a news broadcast, causing him to look at his watch: a little after two. A minute passed. The news announcer was talking about a fatal automobile wreck outside Gunnison the previous evening. Two drunken teenagers had been killed. Another one injured badly. Bridge abutment. He looked at his watch again. They should be in Denver by seven, seven thirty—right in time for the city's horrendous morning traffic jam. Now the bored announcer was talking about a new city sales tax somewhere. The announcer paused. Jamie watched Rod put another quarter in the phone. Jamie reached for the tuning knob, but the word *airplane* caught his attention. He sat up quickly in his seat and listened.

"Federal authorities and civil air patrol officials this evening reported no success in finding a twin-engine airplane missing since early Monday morning on a flight from Las Vegas to Denver despite improving weather conditions along the Front Range. The airplane, with two men aboard, belonged to the Forsyth Hotel chain. It was originally scheduled to land at the Gunnison airport but diverted to Denver because of the season's first winter storm. The search has been concentrated along the Front Range and in particular near the Breckenridge ski area in the vicinity of Hoosier Pass, where it was last seen on radar screens at the Longmont Control Center. The Summit County Sheriff's Department spokesman told reporters that the ground search will be intensified tomorrow. In an apparently unrelated incident, Edwin Forsyth, Jr., the president of the Forsyth Hotel chain and a longtime resident of this county, committed suicide this morning—"

Jamie snapped the radio off. It had to be the same airplane! Twin-engine, two men aboard. And the logo on the tail. Forsyth Hotels. Hell, he had stayed in one or two himself over the years. Now he remembered. The *F* and the *H* on the tail. But the authorities were looking a good eighty or ninety miles away as the crow flies from the actual wreck. Maybe closer to one hundred miles. Why the confusion over where the airplane had actually gone down? The authorities were not even close in their search if the location the news announcer had given was accurate. If this was so, then he and Rod were certainly going to be the only people who would know the actual crash site. No search would even come near it this winter, Jamie realized. And no one would hike into the lake until the middle of next summer. Soon the airplane would be completely covered by…That was the answer!

Jamie looked up. Rod stood in the phone booth with his ear to the receiver. He seemed to be talking to someone. "Shit!" he muttered under his breath. He opened the door and leaped from the Porsche.

Rod scooped the quarter from the coin return and put it back in the slot. He heard it clang its way through the phone's innards. He punched the O and waited. There was an annoying metallic tone, and a man's voice came over the line. "Operator, can I help you?"

Rod answered, "Yes, I'd like to call a number and charge it to my home phone."

"I can't do that. Do you have some sort of phone card?"

"Yes, but not with me. Look, this is sort of an emergency."

"I'm sorry, for that, simply dial 9-1-1." The operator hung up.

Rod looked at the receiver and silently cursed. He had left his card at home. Although he didn't want to, he dialed 9-1-1 for the first time in his life.

The phone rang twice on the other end before the sheriff's dispatcher picked it up while at the same time noting that the call was coming from a phone booth up in Crestridge. "Sheriff's emergency line, may I help you?"

Rod turned and was about to speak. He flinched as Jamie reached in, grabbed the phone from him, and hung it up.

"What the hell…" Rod said.

The phone rang immediately as the dispatcher called back.

Rod turned back to the phone.

"Don't answer it!" Jamie said breathlessly.

"Huh?"

"I've figured it out! I know how we are going to do it!"

"What are you talking about?"

Jamie answered, "Ice, old buddy!" He spelled it out carefully, "*I-c-e!*"

CHAPTER 25

Abandon Ship

P age 2
Walker County Eagle
Thursday, October 11, 1984

"Suspected Drug Airplane and Victim Found"
By Jolene McCarver
Eagle Staff

The Walker County Sheriff's Department is investigating the discovery of a mysterious drug-filled airplane and a bullet-ridden body. The aircraft was discovered at the Walker County airport twenty miles northeast of Beasley, Texas, on Wednesday morning. The airplane, believed to be a converted WWII bomber, was discovered in the rural area by a deputy on a routine patrol. The body was that of a Spanish American male believed to be in his early twenties. Walker County sheriff Jim Blackwell said a substantial amount of what investigators believe to be cocaine was also found aboard the airplane. Sheriff Blackwell declined to specify an exact value for the drugs, but he believed the amount to be worth "millions." An unidentified source put the amount of cocaine at 950 kilos. Federal authorities were also involved in the case and are working on the identity of the shooting victim. The pilot of the airplane has not been found, but authorities believe he might have been forced to land because of low fuel. The Walker County Sheriff's Department is also investigating the theft of a pickup truck from the airport's parking lot. Authorities declined to say if the theft of the truck was related.

CHAPTER 26

The Back Pages

P age 15A
The Denver Post
Thursday, October 25, 1984

"Hunt for Airplane Abandoned"

The Colorado Civil Air Patrol searched the Front Range area of the mountains west of Denver for the last time yesterday in an effort to find a twin-engine airplane lost almost three weeks ago on a flight from Las Vegas to Denver with two men aboard. The search had been hampered in the past two weeks by a series of unusual fall snowstorms and below-normal temperatures. A Civil Air Patrol spokesman, Kevin Douglas, doubted any more effort would be made to find the plane until late spring.

Said Douglas, "It is improbable at this time that there are any survivors. We've had as much as four feet of new snow in the high country of Colorado in the past three weeks, making it almost impossible to spot a white airplane. It is doubtful that if anyone had actually survived the crash that they would have survived the subzero temperatures that have followed."

Despite intense efforts by the Civil Air Patrol and ground searchers from the Summit County Sheriff's Department, no traces of the downed airplane were ever found.

CHAPTER 27

Landing on Skis

T he tiny, white Cessna 185 ski-plane circled high over the frozen lake and the jagged ridges in the pale afternoon sun like an eagle above its aerie, bobbing and dipping in the air currents. The pilot looked down as he circled in the thin air and tried to figure out the wind direction on the featureless white expanse. He had been here twice before, but conditions hadn't permitted even an attempt at landing.

Finally satisfied, the pilot of the small airplane flew east and gradually began to lose altitude. Minutes passed. He was now below the higher peaks as he made another turn back to the west. He read the altimeter and added power. He looked down past the wing strut, and the ski now pumped down under the tire. The ranch house and its circular driveway slid by far below. The log house seemed dark against the snow. There were no tracks on the drive and it appeared not to have been plowed in the last six weeks.

The airplane was now passing over the lower, darker forested slopes. Ahead was the cirque that held Hourglass Lake. In thirty seconds there would be no return, no room to turn around, no way to climb out. The pilot would be committed to land.

The Cessna entered the narrow gorge. The pilot reduced power and lowered the flaps to their first setting. The airplane slowed, and the airframe vibrated and rumbled. He checked the altimeter once more. Until the final turn, the way ahead was blind.

Midway the gorge twisted to the left. The pilot gently banked the Cessna. He added a bit more power and selected the second flap setting. He retrimmed the airplane. The airspeed read eighty knots. It seemed the wingtips must brush the jagged rocks on each side. The river was still hundreds of feet below.

The lake now lay directly ahead. A tiny, white landing area pinched in the middle by two sheer cliffs, any escape now blocked at the far end by a wall of unforgiving granite. The approach and landing had to be perfect. There would be no second chance. He was committed.

The Cessna shuddered in unseen but not unexpected turbulence. One wing dipped, but the pilot brought the airplane back to level.

As the lake neared, the pilot judged himself to be just above the frozen waterfall at its outlet. Actually there were three breathtaking ice falls to look at if he had been sightseeing. The lake's surface appeared to be untouched—a perfect surface of pure white. It was a bright December afternoon, but a high overcast blocked the sun. There would be no shadows or tracks to help him with his depth perception and judge his landing.

The pilot lowered the last flap setting. The Cessna slowed and then flashed over the narrow outlet, skimming the boulders there by mere feet. The pilot reduced the power to idle. The engine cracked and popped in the cold air. He knew he was just a few feet above the surface, but it was hard to judge. As the airplane sank toward the lake, he brought the nose up gently, causing the wings to gain their last small bit of lift. The stall warning horn began to blare just as the skis on the rugged landing gear kissed the snow. The airplane skipped once, settled firmly on its skis, and slowed rapidly. The perfect landing had required barely half the length of the lake.

The pilot added power and began taxiing slowly between the high rock walls on each side that pinched the lake together. The engine and propeller noise filled the cirque—a foreign, man-made sound that didn't quite belong.

The wreck sat rigid, its underside firmly encased in some twenty inches of ice and its nose and right wing still jutting toward the sky. Snow had drifted in along the fuselage, over the wings, and into the interior through the broken cockpit window. The pilot's body, now frozen, still slumped over the controls. The twin Cessna looked completely untouched.

The high nose of the Cessna ski-plane prevented the pilot from looking directly forward as he taxied toward the wreck. He had to turn from side to side and look through the propeller arc. As he neared the other airplane, he added power and rudder and spun the Cessna around on its skis so its nose faced the frozen outlet, his only direction for a safe departure. His prop blast spawned a small blizzard behind and blew snow against the wreck. The pilot pulled out the mixture control. The propeller rotated to a stop. He turned off the master switch and turned the ignition key.

The stillness crept back into the cirque once more. A puff of wind rocked the little airplane gently and moaned at the window.

The pilot picked his heavy gloves from the empty passenger seat and put them on. The outside temperature gauge above his head read five above zero. He pulled his parka's hood over his red hair and opened the door, catching his breath as the icy mountain air filled the cabin.

The Cessna sat high on its skis, and the pilot had to balance himself on the small metal step on the wheel strut before jumping down onto the dazzling white surface. As he landed, he sank to his knees in the powdery snow. The tiny grains sparkled in the light. He hoped that the takeoff would not be a problem. His dark aviator sunglasses were barely adequate for this type of light, and his eyes began to tear up as he squinted around at his surroundings.

He wallowed around behind the Cessna in the deep snow and slowly made his way over to the wreck, which sat about a hundred feet away. His feet made a small trench in the snow as he shuffled along. As he approached, the pilot saw that the cabin door at the rear of the airplane would be impossible to open. Barely a third of it was above the surface, the rest frozen tightly below the snow and ice.

He shuffled forward along the slanting fuselage and brushed some snow with his glove from the first window forward of the rear cabin door. He peered inside. The interior was dark. He took off his sunglasses and put his forehead against the window while cupping his hands around his eyes to block out as much sunlight as possible. Where water had once filled the steeply sloping aisle, there was now a solid surface of ice covered by a small amount of powder snow that had drifted in from the cockpit window. The passenger seatbacks stood above the cold surface like four tombstones. Toward the rear he could see part of a man's head and arm just above the ice, the rest of him presumably encased in the airplane like a wooly mammoth in a glacier from the last ice age.

Snow had drifted deeply behind the left wing, and the pilot moved with some difficulty to the trailing edge, the snow being almost waist deep at this point. He brushed snow from the wing and heaved himself up onto it.

He had noticed before as he had taxied up to it that the cockpit window was broken. No doubt, he believed, this had happened in the crash, although the front windows and the other side window were intact. He grasped the rear edge of the window for support and leaned in. The cockpit was a mess of broken gauges and tangled wires. He studied the other pilot's frozen body. The man had obviously been shot, judging from the head wound. He might have even survived the crash to be shot later. There was another bullet hole in the instrument panel adding to the mystery.

Tim smiled to himself. The wreck looked untouched. It was obvious that no one else had been here or even knew about the crash site yet. The millions inside were untouched. It wouldn't be easy though. He would have to chip the fortune free just like a gold miner working the mother lode. But he had time. To go farther, though, he would need the tools back in the other airplane.

He stood, slid down the wing, and jumped into the snow. He shuffled back to the Cessna along the track he had made and began to unload his equipment from the baggage compartment. Christmas was next week, and he wondered if they served turkey in the Cayman Islands.

CHAPTER 28

Collision Course

The Bell Jet Ranger skimmed over the sagebrush at what Rod thought was a suicidal altitude. He loved to fly, but flying at this altitude was ridiculous, he thought and he worried. And he had worried enough in the last week to last a lifetime—no, two lifetimes. Even through his noise-attenuating headset and ear plugs, he could plainly hear the whine of the turbine engine and the beat of the rotor blades over his head as they cast a flickering shadow over himself and Jamie. The view through the Plexiglas was almost hypnotic as the helicopter swept over the ground and blurred everything passing underneath them.

Jamie's voice filled Rod's earphones as he announced and pointed forward, "Another twenty minutes and we'll be there. Looks like the weather will finally hold for us."

Rod leaned forward and looked at the sky. There was a high overcast, but it was a bright day, and the White Elk Mountains stood out sharply to his left in the clear air as they flew north from Gunnison. The "mission," as Jamie called it, had to be cancelled twice before in the previous week because of bad weather. Rod had taken some vacation but now had had to extend even that. He felt his boss was wise to something but couldn't guess in a million—no—a billion years what his otherwise perfect, boring employee was up to this week before Christmas. His wife and son thought he was in Chicago at a weeklong training course for the company that had been extended another week. The lies hung on very slender threads. If his wife called the company for any reason, his goose was going to be cooked by both sides.

The Jet Ranger climbed suddenly to clear a small ridge. Rod was pushed down in his seat by the sudden increase in g-forces. Just as suddenly the helicopter dove down the other side, and he rose helplessly against his seatbelt and shoulder harness. Rod knew his stomach had to be just below his tonsils now. He remembered Jamie's confession about his depth perception problem and looked at the other man, wondering.

Jamie caught Rod's stare. He looked over and smiled. He sat casually in his seat. His fingertips caressed the controls. His feet danced lightly on the pedals. He was enjoying himself immensely. "This is the way we did it in 'Nam. Go in skimming the fucking trees, so they wouldn't have time to shoot at you. Then you'd see the smoke and LZ at the last second. Of course we only got sagebrush here."

With that the helicopter decelerated violently. The nose pitched up hard. Rod was thrown forward violently against his shoulder harness as Jamie suddenly brought the Jet Ranger into a hover above the sagebrush and then touched down gently in a small clearing not much wider than the helicopter itself.

He looked over at Rod and smiled, "See, that's the way it's done." They lifted off quickly, nose low, and were skimming the rangeland again.

Rod caught his breath. "Jesus, you could have warned me."

Jamie smiled and pointed forward with his free hand. "We're almost there."

Rod followed his finger. The snow-covered peaks of the White Elks range reared up in front of them in contrast to the lower, darker, forested slopes as Jamie changed his heading from north to west. The engine and whirling blades took on a new, more labored sound as they began to gain altitude.

Jamie hooked a finger over his shoulder. "Check on the gear once more, will ya. Make sure it's secure in case we get into a little turbulence."

Rod nodded and twisted in his seat. The small helicopter normally carried four passengers, but five could be squeezed into its interior in a pinch. Besides the two individual seats in the front, there was a small bench seat along the rear of the tiny cabin. The unneeded rear seat had been removed to help lighten the load and provide more room for their gear, which had been carefully loaded and secured with strong, nylon webbing. The tent, sleeping bags, tools, packs, and ropes were all in place. Rod's old hunting rifle also lay under the webbing on top of the gear in its vinyl case. It had not been fired for years, but Jamie had insisted they bring it along with a box of ammunition as part of their survival gear. He had planned at least two days at the wreck ferrying out the cash in multiple trips.

Rod faced forward. The whole plan was crazy of course, but here they were actually flying closer to the mountains. He started to feel the excitement build.

Jamie had explained the whole plan that morning two months ago after they had arrived back in Denver. He had laid it out over pancakes at the Perkins off I-70 near where Rod lived. Look at it as an adventure, Jamie had said. They would be just like the treasure hunters of yore, the gold miners in California in the 1840s, or even the men who dove in past years for riches from the Spanish ships which had sunk in the Caribbean. So what if it was an airplane in a lake instead of a sunken wooden ship laden with gold. So what if their airplane had been only lost two months instead of centuries. It was still treasure, wasn't it? Didn't they have the right to salvage, to plunder the money? Rod had tried to explain the difference—that most countries and states, like Florida, had laws governing treasure and that maybe the state of Colorado had laws involving removing goods from plane crashes in the high country, which were certainly felonies involving prison time. And besides, the owners of the gold on Spanish galleons were long dead, whereas the people who owned all that cash were certainly alive and looking for it and probably tough cookies. Jamie waved his hands in front of him and would hear nothing of it. Finders keepers, losers weepers—that was how he finally put it. Either you were in, or you weren't. It was that simple. He would go by himself if nothing else, but he sure could use some help. Rod had reluctantly agreed, more out of concern for his friend than for the money.

Jamie had departed for Louisiana the next night with a firm handshake and a conspiratorial wink at the airport. He had told Rod not to worry, that he would do all the planning. The plan was nothing Rod could have envisioned.

Two weeks ago Rod had told his wife about the required company training in Chicago. Last week he had packed his bag after secretly loading the Porsche up with the other supplies. He had told his wife that the car was finally going to the repair shop and that he would take a cab to the airport. Instead, he had driven himself to the Gunnison Airport in the battered car. That was the first lie: to his wife and kid.

He had requested a week's vacation for a personal emergency and then had it extended. That was the second lie: to his company.

Jamie had met him at the Gunnison airport as planned after the long drive from Denver over Monarch Pass. They had stayed at a nearby motel, the Mountain View, under assumed names. More lies. Rod had discovered the next morning that Jamie had a helicopter ready and fueled at the airport. Rod thought the registration number on the helicopter's tail looked very freshly painted. They had stayed in the Mountain View motel ten days now, and Jamie had paid cash for everything: the fuel, meals, and motel—with one hundred dollar bills.

The mountains were close now. Rod twisted forward in his seat and tightened his shoulder harness. The forested slopes were far below. The altimeter read almost twelve thousand feet. They were above the timberline and probably nearing the Jet Ranger's ceiling.

Rod said, "Everything looks okay."

"Great, we're almost there. Looks like we finally got some decent weather." Jamie looked down. "This sure beats walking in with heavy packs, doesn't it?"

Rod nodded and thought. This was a wilderness area. Landing the helicopter on the frozen lake was a crime. He shrugged. Just another felony to add to the others.

The Jet Ranger rushed into the gorge. The snow-packed, rugged rock walls rose steeply on each side. Tiny white avalanches cascaded from ledge to ledge, dislodged by the beat of the rotor blades.

Jamie made the final turn. The lake and the three frozen waterfalls were directly ahead. Jamie gained a bit of altitude as the helicopter bounced in unseen turbulence.

Rod looked down at the stream hundreds of feet below at his feet and tried to trace their path to the lake. A distance that had taken them hours was being swallowed up in minutes.

It was perhaps a mile from the outlet that Jamie spotted something on the ice. He leaned forward and raised his mirrored aviation sunglasses. He poked Rod's arm. Rod looked up.

Jamie pointed and asked, "What the hell is that?"

"Huh?"

"There, up ahead."

Then they both realized what it was.

Jamie spoke first. "Jesus, a Cessna on skis."

"Looks like." It was all Rod could manage. This was bad news.

Jamie slowed the helicopter and hovered over the outlet of the lake, just over the frozen waterfalls. They were only several yards from their campsite of two months ago and a half mile from the white Cessna at the other end of the lake.

The two men sat motionless in the Jet Ranger. Rod was puzzled. Jamie's anger began to build.

The crashed airplane was exactly as they had left it. There were tracks around both airplanes, but no one seemed to be around.

Tim had four suitcases free. They were very heavy, he had discovered. The bills had become waterlogged and then frozen. He had dragged two of them over to the other airplane and loaded them. The third and fourth were still inside and resting just behind the twin Cessna's cockpit. He almost had the fifth one free when he first heard the faint beat of the rotor blades. He stopped chipping and listened.

Until then only an occasional gust of wind and his chisel had disturbed the silence of the frozen lake. At first he had gone after the individual packets of money, but this had proved to be much harder work then he had expected. So he had decided to concentrate on the larger suitcases. He lay on his stomach with his feet extending into the cockpit. There wasn't much space between the ice and the ceiling, and he had alternated between kneeling and lying down. His heavy clothing and gloves had also made things awkward and had slowed his work. Despite them he was cold.

The beat of the blades grew louder, and now he could also hear the whine of the turbine engine. The helicopter was definitely coming his way. Maybe it would simply fly over. Tim crawled over to the first oval passenger window, the only one still entirely above the frozen surface, and looked out. The brightness caused him to squint, and he fished in his pocket for his sunglasses. His view was limited to the south side of the lake and the outlet, but he could see nothing. The sound grew louder still, but it was hard to judge direction as it bounced off the rock walls surrounding the lake. Then suddenly he saw it, hovering at the other end of the lake. A civilian Jet Ranger with its nose pointed directly at him a half mile away.

Tim cursed himself for leaving his weapons in the ski-plane and began backing out of the cabin when the helicopter began moving slowly toward him.

Rod squirmed in his seat and licked his lips, which had become very dry in the last few moments. This other airplane was definitely not in the script. He sensed this was trouble. He pushed his glasses up on his nose and cleared his throat.

"Uh, let's get outta here, okay? I don't feel good about this."

Jamie shook his head. "Jesus, someone else found my airplane. I'm going to find out who in the hell is messing around up here."

"Let's get outta here!" Rod pleaded once more.

Jamie ignored him. The nose dipped, and he began to edge the helicopter forward. He flew slowly, just a few feet above the snow. In a few minutes, they were fifty yards from the two airplanes. Jamie hovered there, watching. There was no sign of life.

Rod started to plead again, "Let's get—"

Before Rod could end his sentence, suddenly a man tumbled from the broken cockpit window. He slid off the wing and began to run in the deep snow toward the ski-plane. The man waved to them.

Jamie edged closer.

Tim knelt out of sight behind the dead pilot in the few minutes it had taken the helicopter to traverse the lake. It didn't seem to be any type of government aircraft. There were no markings. The paint job seemed to be civilian, and he noticed as it had gotten closer that it had a regular registration number. There were two men aboard, and they didn't seem to be in uniform. But who were they? Curiosity seekers who had spotted the aircraft from overhead? No, he decided, because he would have heard them fly overhead. These two had flown right up the gorge into the cirque just he had done three hours ago. They knew exactly where they were going. But whoever they were, there was no way he could let them out of the cirque alive. No one must find out about the crash. No one was going to come between him and all this cash.

With grim determination, Tim launched himself from the window. The Uzi submachine gun with a full clip was just behind the pilot's seat on the floor of the ski-plane.

The helicopter pilot hovered head on and slipped sideways as Tim hurried as much as possible along the path he had packed back and forth to the ski-plane. The helicopter pilot so far made no indication of landing. Tim began pulling off his heavy gloves when he was ten feet from the Cessna.

When Jamie spoke through the intercom, there was a sound of command in his voice that Rod had never heard. "Look, I don't know who this guy is but there're two of us and one of him. He's got to know about the money somehow or else he wouldn't be nosing around here inside the airplane. I'm going to back up a bit, and when I do, I want you to hurry and get that hunting rifle of yours out of its case. Then hand it to me after I shut down. You'll find another gun—"

The other man had reached the ski-plane and had pulled the small machine gun from behind the seat just as Jamie realized his mistake.

As Tim brought the submachine gun up, the helicopter turned violently to escape. It was broadside to him as he squeezed off the first burst.

Rod was caught completely by surprise by the sudden maneuver. Puzzled, he looked at the man next to the little Cessna and saw the sudden, bright muzzle flashes. He comprehended what had happened, a millisecond before the Plexiglas bubble in front of him disintegrated as thirty rounds easily bracketed the helicopter. In a reflex gesture, he threw his hands up in front of him as he heard additional bullets thump what seemed to be all around him against the thin aluminum hull of the Jet Ranger.

Jamie began to curse and yell while fighting the controls, which seemed to suddenly have a mind of their own. He managed to turn the Jet Ranger around as more bullets struck the rear of the helicopter.

Rod brought his hands down. He was cold, and he realized most of the Plexiglas in front of him was gone. What was left dangled above his head in a large jagged piece just below the whirling rotor blades. They were flying a few feet above the snow toward the other end of the lake. He smelled something burning. The small turbine screamed like a wounded animal as they staggered somewhat sideways through the air. Halfway down the lake, smoke began to fill what was left of the cockpit, and Rod knew they weren't going to make it. The rock walls on either side of the lake began to spin around them. The helicopter began to turn over on its back. Just before they crashed, Jamie put his arm in front of Rod as an adult might do in a reflex action to a child in the front seat of a car. Rod looked at his friend as the snow rushed up. He felt the impact and blacked out.

Someone was yelling his name. The voice was familiar. His shoulder and side ached. His cheek just below his right ear also was causing him pain. Somebody was pushing on his bad shoulder.

Rod slowly regained consciousness and was totally confused. He began to feel the cold air. Then he recognized the voice. It was Jamie, yelling his name. Suddenly he remembered and came to. The brilliant snow caused him to squint. He was hanging sideways somehow from his shoulder straps. He could smell jet fuel and oily smoke.

The Jet Ranger had crashed nose down and then had rolled slowly over. Rod's seatbelt and shoulder harness had kept him in place and saved his life. Besides his shoulder injury, his right arm felt somewhat numb, and his chest hurt on that side, too, as he drew in the frigid mountain air. The black nylon webbing was cutting into his neck.

Jamie pushed him again from below. Below? Then Rod realized the helicopter was on its right side.

Jamie yelled again, "Get the gun! He's coming! Get the fucking gun!"

Rod answered, somewhat confused, as he tried to shake the fog from his mind, "Huh? What?" He slowly became aware of a wetness on his neck and reached up with his free hand. He withdrew it and was horrified to see it covered with blood. Warm, slimy, red blood. His blood.

Rod screamed, "I'm bleeding!"

Jamie grabbed his arm. "You're not going to die; you've just got a bad cut on your ugly face from the Plexiglas." Then he grimaced from his own pain, which was considerable, and waited a moment before speaking again. His hand shook as he pointed down the lake. "He's coming to finish us off."

Rod pushed his glasses up and squinted into the distance. They had crashed roughly halfway down the lake just past the narrow portion. The crumpled helicopter rested on its side fifty yards from the northern precipice. One of the bent and broken main rotor blades lay in front of what was left of the cockpit. Rod saw a dark figure against the snow several hundred yards away making slow but steady progress toward them. It was the man who had shot them down. He was cradling his submachine gun in his arms. Rod forgot about the blood running down his neck. He tried to stifle the sour panic rising in his throat. He looked with wild eyes toward Jamie.

Jamie grimaced again against the pain in his back and leg. The crash had collapsed the right skid against the fuselage and cockpit. His leg was pinned between the small instrument panel and the side of the helicopter. His foot seemed bent at a funny angle to his leg, and a small but steadily growing pool of blood was forming near one of the twisted rudder pedals.

Rod began fumbling with the latching mechanism for his shoulder harness.

Jamie yelled, "Turn the thing clockwise...clockwise!"

Rod answered out of breath, "Yeah! Yeah!"

But he did as he was told, and the buckle clicked open. He immediately fell downward onto his friend, who tried unsuccessfully to fend him off with his free arm. Rod landed on top of him. Jamie clutched the thigh of his injured leg as the fiery pain shot through his body. He wanted to scream but caught his breath instead.

The man on the lake had gained another twenty yards in the thigh-deep snow.

Jamie and Rod lay twisted grotesquely together. Rod tried to find a foothold away from the crushed instrument panel. Jamie helped push, the pain almost overwhelming him. Rod found that he could stand on the now vertical edge of Jamie's seat and crouch under the helicopter's left front door which was now on top.

The man in the snow had gained another twenty-five yards. He was still out of effective range but quickly redoubled his efforts when he saw movement in the wreckage ahead of him.

Jamie clutched his battered leg in a vain attempt to free it. More jolts of pain shot up from his ankle and along his thigh. He cursed loudly and then was hit by waves of nausea as he almost fainted. It was no good. He was pinned solidly against the fuselage. The instrument panel would have to be pried away first, and it was just out of his reach.

Rod twisted the door handle and felt the door pop open. He pushed it upward easily with his shoulder and free hand. The door banged forward as Rod stood up, feet balanced still on the edge of Jamie's seat. He began to hoist himself up, bracing his arms against the door frame. He was still badly shaken, and his arms trembled. Rod rested for a moment on the door frame. His eye caught the muzzle flashes first. Then he heard the two bullets go over his head just before he heard the popping sound. His guts twisted, and he fell back into the helicopter. The panic began to rise again in his throat. His voice sounded unusually high and shrill as he crouched next to Jamie and pleaded, "Jesus Christ! Tell me what to do!"

The man had lowered the submachine and had gained another ten yards.

Rod grabbed Jamie's coat collar. Jamie jerked Rod's hand free and grabbed him by the front of his parka almost lifting him off his knees. He pinned him bodily against the tilted seatback. Jamie's voice became hard but also strangely calm. Rod had heard this tone only once before, over thirty years ago. He remembered the honeysuckle bushes near the fence line. The memory silenced him completely, and he listened.

"Stay calm. Whatever you do, stay calm. Take some deep breaths."

Rod did as he was told. "I'm okay."

"Sure?"

"Yeah."

"That's better. Now, he is still out of range with that little 9 mm popgun, but we have something better, don't we?"

Rod thought of his .30-06 hunting rifle with the telescopic sight just behind them. He and Jamie had gone elk hunting a few times before he had gotten married. The old Winchester rifle and sight had been purchased used from a pawn shop in Denver for a hundred bucks. He had only fired it a couple of times to sight it in, and that had been years ago. Jamie had insisted Rod bring it along—as a survival gun, he said. "Yeah, that's right!" He started to move up and out of the helicopter immediately, as Jamie gave instructions.

"Crawl between the seats into the back and get your rifle out. It should be right on top."

Rod pushed the door back and began to climb out the top of the helicopter.

Jamie continued to give instructions. "Make sure there is a round in the chamber and rest the rifle on the door frame. Then squeeze off a round in his direction. We'll see how tough he is after that. We've still got the range advantage on him, and he wouldn't be out in the open if he thought we were armed." Jamie grimaced but managed to laugh a little. "He's in for a surprise, isn't he?"

Rod was kneeling on top of the helicopter. He opened the passenger door and lowered himself into what had been the rear seating area. Their gear was still strapped in tightly and hung against what had been the floor. The nylon cargo webbing had done its job. The rifle case was in front of him. He was sweating despite the cold as he loosened the case from the rest of the gear. The smell of jet fuel was stronger. He thought of the possibility of fire again as he unzipped the vinyl case and removed the old Winchester hunting rifle. Jamie would be trapped. But first things first. There was a real, immediate danger a few hundred yards away.

The rifle hadn't been fired for over ten years; Rod remembered cleaning it once since, but that was almost three years ago, one snowy Saturday afternoon when he was housebound and trying to catch up on some small chores.

Rod knelt, cradled the rifle, and opened the bolt. There was no ammo! He worked the bolt again. Of course there was no ammo, he thought. You don't leave a loaded gun around with a kid in the house. Everybody knows that. How was he supposed to know he would need a loaded gun inside a crashed helicopter on a frozen lake? He started to feel the panic again. He was losing it.

He wailed, "There's no ammo; I forgot it was empty!"

Jamie tilted his head over his shoulder and tried to twist around to see the rear compartment between the seats but felt the numbing pain. He stopped. He knew his body would go into shock soon.

"Try to calm down and remember. You told me you had a box of ammo. Think about where you left it."

Rod stood still. Then he started to bite nervously on one of the fingernails of his right hand. He had to think straight. Then he remembered. The case! He had stuffed the box of twenty rounds down into the case when he had packed last week. He leaned the rifle carefully against the rest of the gear still secured against the floor by the nylon webbing and picked up the rifle case. The vinyl was stiff with cold.

He thrust his arm all the way to the bottom, wearing the case like a long, rigid gauntlet. His fingers closed around the small, rectangular ammo box.

He quickly pulled out the familiar yellow box with the big X on the side and dropped the case. The temperature had to be near zero, he knew, and his fingers were starting to feel the effect of the cold. His breath fogged around him in the small compartment.

He thrust the ammo box through the opening between the seats and yelled excitedly to Jamie, "I found it!"

Jamie answered quickly, "Great! Just great! But put some of them in the gun unless you want to just throw them at him."

"Okay, okay!"

Rod had trouble with the cardboard flap but finally opened it and pulled out the bright, shiny brass shells in their red, premolded plastic holder. There were indeed twenty of them. Ten on each side.

He picked up the rifle and opened the bolt. Then he delicately pulled two shells from the holder with what were almost numb fingers now. He crammed them down into the magazine and rotated the bolt shut smoothly, watching the top shell slide into the firing chamber. He unconsciously and automatically flipped the safety on and removed the round, black plastic covers from each end of the telescopic sight. His hands shook as he stood up in the door opening.

"Okay, I…I'm ready. What should I do?"

"Kill the bastard!"

Rod looked down the lake along the Winchester. The figure in the snow was still roughly two hundred yards away, an easy shot for a good marksman with a well-sighted-in rifle, but not one for a rifle that had spent the last decade in a closet and for an owner who had not pulled a trigger for a like amount of time. He was still making progress, although slower now. The snow appeared to be deeper—almost thigh deep. The man in the snow had probably underestimated that. It was evident he wasn't going to waste any more effort until he was right next to the helicopter, and then he would finish them off.

Jamie watched the man and then spoke over his shoulder to Rod, "Just rest it on the door frame and take your time. Line it up and squeeze one off."

Rod hesitated. He had suddenly discovered he had not shot at anyone in his lifetime.

Jamie asked, "Got that?"

"Yeah, sure."

But Jamie didn't sense any movement behind him. The smell of jet fuel had gotten stronger. He could smell the hot metal of the engine. His voice began to get hard again, and he knew what was wrong. "Squeeze a shot off!"

"I…I've…never shot at anyone. Here, you do it."

Jamie replied angrily, "I don't have a clear shot, for Christ's sake. It's him or us! Now do it! You have to take the shot!" He heard Rod switch positions behind him.

Rod rested the rifle on the frame and looked through the sight. The target was larger but still small in the telescopic sight. Rod pivoted the Winchester until the crosshairs rested somewhat in the middle of the man's chest. Even then he was nervous, and it was hard to hold them steady on the target. The man in the snow stopped and raised the submachine gun to his shoulder.

Rod pulled the trigger and flinched at the same time. The trigger mushed. The rifle remained mute. He moved his head and looked at his finger on the trigger. He squeezed again. Nothing happened.

A bullet ripped through the metal portion of the door just to one side of the window. The door flopped down onto Rod's head and left shoulder. A sharp report followed from across the lake. Rod saw with wonder that there was a neat bullet hole just six inches from his head. There was another pop from across the white expanse. Another bullet whizzed overhead.

Tears of frustration and panic began to well up in Rod's eyes.

Jamie yelled, "Shoot the asshole!"

Rod tried to find an answer. Of course! The safety was still on! He quickly flipped the small lever on the rear of the bolt. He had no time to take careful aim. The crosshairs danced all around the dark figure against the snow as he jerked the trigger.

This time the powerful hunting rifle exploded in the still mountain air with a sharp crack and a muzzle flash, driving the rear of its stock painfully into Rod's shoulder. He was knocked off balance and stumbled back against the rear of the cabin.

The bullet itself whined a good ten feet over its intended target's head followed by its sharp bark a fraction of a second later. It continued upward on its trajectory and finally pulverized itself against a boulder located midway up the rock wall at the western end of the cirque nearly a half mile away. The report roared from wall to wall.

Rod picked himself up. His ears were ringing. He rotated the bolt up and back then forward, ejecting the spent casing against what had been the ceiling of the helicopter and sliding the second cartridge into the firing chamber.

Jamie yelled and pounded the passenger seat above his head, forgetting the pain for a moment. "Atta boy, Rodney, he's on the run! That'll teach him to screw around with us, old buddy! Finish him off!"

Rod pushed the rear door open again and rested the rifle on the fuselage. Jamie was right. To his surprise, the man had fallen sideways in the snow and was just now picking himself up. Rod thought for a moment, maybe he had actually hit his target with a lucky shot. It would have been lucky indeed, because he knew he had had his eyes closed when he pulled the trigger on that first shot. But as he watched, the man in the snow began to shuffle perpendicular to them toward the shoreline and the cover behind the precipice on the north side of the lake.

This time Rod checked that the safety was off. He hesitated. The man in the snow was now moving to one side and not head on to them. This second shot would be much harder. This wasn't TV or a Dirty Harry movie. The target was over two football fields away. He tried to keep the crosshairs on the target by pivoting the rifle slightly on the door frame. Rod felt his heart pounding. His eyes were watering. His fingers were almost completely numb.

Jamie yelled again, "Shoot the bastard!"

Rod slowly took up the slack in the trigger. He wouldn't jerk it this time. He stopped breathing. The crosshairs danced around the man's torso. Rod tried to average his movements out and then squeezed the trigger just a little more. There was another sharp report and muzzle flash. This time the bullet went just a foot to the left of the running figure and buried itself in the snow.

Rod raised his head from the sight and pushed his glasses up on his nose. "Damn!"

Jamie yelled again in desperation when it was obvious Rod had missed, "C'mon, shoot him! Get him before he gets around behind the cliff!"

It was true. In a moment the man would be behind and around the precipice that narrowed the lake on the north side.

Rod cried back, "I'm out of ammo! Jesus, where's that box!" He stooped over and picked up the empty gun case while still holding the rifle in his free hand. The familiar yellow box of ammunition was underneath it. He propped the rifle to one side, opened the box, and pried two more shells from their plastic holder. He picked the rifle back up and slid open the bolt as before. Then he crammed the two brass cartridges into the magazine, trying not to hurry and trying to keep his hands from shaking so much. He rotated the bolt shut like before, straightened up, and aimed the rifle across the lake. The man in the snow was almost to the shoreline and would disappear from view in seconds.

Rod braced himself again. He knew he had one more chance. Surprisingly, he felt calmer, the rifle felt steadier, and the crosshairs didn't move around as much. Well, he thought, chalk it up to experience. And someone was actually running from him. He was actually trying to kill this unknown person. How very weird, he thought, as he carefully squinted through the sight. He stopped breathing. He would be more careful this time. This time he would nail the asshole.

Three, maybe four giant steps would see the man behind the wall. Well, he wouldn't make it that far. Too bad, thought Rod, as he gently squeezed the trigger.

But the man in the snow dove forward simultaneously. The bullet struck the granite just above him and then ricocheted toward the other side of the lake. The shot again echoed back and forth between the walls and then quickly dissipated with a muted roar. Rod couldn't believe it. He had missed the third time. It was just plain bad luck. He muttered something inaudible to himself and lowered the Winchester.

The man in the snow was gone.

Rod stared at the frozen lake and its stark landscape. It was empty now except for the three aircraft. One still flyable and two ruined.

Tim pulled himself to his feet and leaned against one of the large boulders along the shoreline. He brushed most of the snow from his parka and pants then pushed the hood back from his head before removing the blue stocking cap from his head. He tried to catch his breath. His heart was still pounding from the exertion in the deep snow, and he took deep gulps of air in the thin, high-altitude atmosphere. The sunlight was taking on a distinct purple hue, and he thought he might faint for a moment. Despite the cold he wiped the sweat from his forehead before replacing the stocking cap and pulling the bottom edge over his ears.

Tim kept a wary eye on the shoreline and took stock of his situation. He didn't think they would come after him immediately. He was sure there were just two men in the chopper, and one appeared to be injured or trapped or both. He thought the one with the rifle would help the other one first rather than come after him now. He also realized how incredibly stupid he had been to just wade down the lake like that, expecting the men in the helicopter to be dead or unarmed. He had been caught out in the open with his pants down. That last shot had almost nailed him.

He had perhaps fifty rounds of ammo left. Twenty or so rounds in the clip still in the gun and one more full thirty-round clip stashed in his waistband under his coat. He wished for more ammo. But who could have foreseen a battle going on at this deserted and lonely place? He should have concentrated his first volley on the occupants instead of the chopper's engine.

He had good shelter in either airplane, and that was good because he really hadn't planned on being on the lake for more than a few hours. He also had a clear field of fire should the man with the rifle decided to come after him. Tim looked up at the sheer walls surrounding the lake, shielding his eyes from the low winter sun. Yes, the other man would have to come up the lake, sticking as close as possible to the boulder-strewn shoreline for cover.

Tim shouldered the machine gun and began working his way back to the ski-plane. His breathing had slowed although he could feel his pulse racing at his temples. His vision had lost the purple tint. In an hour or so, the sun would slip behind the western rim, and darkness along with extreme cold would follow. He wondered how well prepared the men in the helicopter were. And who were they? How did they know about the wreck in the ice? Tim was sure of two things. First, the two men could not be left alive. No one else could know about the crash. He would have to eliminate them. Secondly, he had the only way out—the Cessna ski-plane.

CHAPTER 29

Bivouac

J amie tried to silently curse his predicament as Rod gently helped lower him onto the snow at the edge of the ice. He was obviously in a great deal of pain and had fainted twice so far, even though he seemed conscious and lucid for the moment. Rod helped him move back a few inches, so his back rested against one of the boulders that made up the shoreline in the summer. Jamie was a tough customer, that Rod certainly knew, but even so, all the color had drained from his face and his breathing had become shallow and labored. Ice crystals had begun to form in his beard and eyebrows.

Rod hooked his hand under the Winchester's leather carrying strap and lifted the rifle off his shoulder and over his head. He placed the butt end in the snow and leaned the barrel carefully against the boulder right next to Jamie's head. It was fully loaded now with five cartridges. The remaining eleven were loose in his parka's right front pocket.

Rod looked nervously down the frozen lake to the other end, then knelt wearily in the snow and steeled himself to see just how bad Jamie's leg was injured.

Jamie reached out and tried weakly to push him away. "Shit, Rodney, don't worry about me right now. Go after the gear. We got to shelter ourselves, or we're both going to die tonight." Then he coughed uncontrollably before catching his breath. He took a couple of big gulps of air. He pointed at the demolished helicopter fifty yards away. "You've gotta get the gear. We can't survive long up here without it."

Rod turned. The Jet Ranger, their only way out, rested on its side like some kind of large, very dead insect. Thank God there had been no fire after all. But the machine would never fly again. Slowly the implication of that fact began to seep into the outer edges of Rod's consciousness. He looked down the lake again. The winter sun was fading. A vision of a man with a submachine gun lurking behind the precipice who wanted to kill them both danced in his head. He had had enough gunfire to last a lifetime. It was time to retreat. But how?

Rod turned to Jamie and stammered, "What if he is just waiting for me out there. Just waiting for the dark?"

Jamie's words came slowly, "It's a chance…you're…no, we're going to have to take. Either way…We're dead. I don't think I'm in any shape… to walk out." He tried to laugh but instead ended up coughing. Then he continued, "Besides…old buddy…he's just plum afraid of you and old Betsy. You've got the edge on him. He…doesn't know how much ammo you…have left…or other surprises." He leaned back against the rock and closed his eyes for a moment. He bit on his lower lip and became very still.

Rod began to feel the panic. "Jamie?" He bent, looked closely at Jamie, and then was relieved when he saw his chest rise and a small amount of vapor emerge from his nose and mouth. God, he thought for a moment that…But he had just fainted again. He touched his neck. Wasn't that how they did it in the cop shows? The pulse was there. Not strong, but there. Jamie was right about the equipment. Death from hypothermia was more of a factor at this moment than a bullet.

The smashed instrument panel had been relatively easy to pry away from Jamie's leg. All that was needed was some leverage in the correct direction. The hunting rifle's stock had worked despite the scratches that had been made in the wood and metal. Then he had used the rifle butt to break out the rest of the Plexiglas bubble in front of him. The real difficulty had been struggling across the lake in the deep snow, trying to give support to Jamie and his injured leg and ribs. Jamie weighed nearly two hundred ten pounds, much more with his heavy clothing and boots.

Jamie suddenly opened his eyes and focused on Rod. He was puzzled. How long had he been out that time? A few seconds? A minute? He blinked and looked around. "Where's the gear? I'm cold."

"Huh? Oh yeah, I'm going. You've only been out a few seconds." Rod nodded at the helicopter. "What if that thing blows up or something?"

Jamie closed his eyes again and mumbled something.

Rod asked, "What?"

Jamie opened his eyes again, "Huh?"

Rod asked again, "What'd you say?"

"When?"

This was getting confusing, thought Rod. "Just a second ago."

Jamie blinked, "I said: no guts, no air medal."

"What's that supposed to mean?"

Jamie didn't answer.

Rod picked up the Winchester and brought the bolt back gently an inch or so. He nervously checked for the twentieth time that there was indeed a cartridge in the firing chamber. He flicked on the safety again; no use shooting yourself, he thought, and then slipped the leather carrying strap over his head. He looked nervously down the lake once more. From this location along the shoreline, he couldn't see the two airplanes at the far end. He also didn't like the idea of going back to the helicopter. The ruined jet engine had certainly cooled by now though. Most of the jet fuel should have leaked into the snow by now, too. The environmentalists wouldn't like any of this one bit, he thought. The danger of fire had certainly passed. What if the man at the other end of the lake had somehow sneaked around behind the helicopter?

Rod swallowed. He felt edgy as he followed the path they had made in the snow coming from the other direction. He had gotten ten feet when he heard Jamie cough and call his name.

Jamie beckoned with one hand. "Leave the rifle here; I'll cover you."

Rod hesitated. He almost went back, but it was apparent now that Jamie was lapsing in and out of consciousness and that he was also starting to suffer from the effects of shock and pain. That leg would have to be attended to quickly. No, thought Rod, he couldn't trust him now.

Rod raised his hand. "Just lie still. I'll take care of things." Then he hiked the rifle up higher on his shoulder and turned. It was the first real decision he had made.

In a minute he was back alongside the Jet Ranger. He cast a nervous eye down to the far end of the lake again. There was no movement. The ski-plane seemed deserted. He felt vulnerable standing there in the middle of the frozen lake as he lifted the rifle off his shoulder. It would be too cumbersome in the tight confines of the cabin. Idly, he wondered just how thick the ice was under him as he leaned the Winchester against the chopper's belly. Plenty thick to take the impact of the crash he knew.

Rod climbed up the shattered nose until he knelt on the front passenger door. He lifted the rear door again, eyeing the neat bullet hole, and let himself down inside the rear compartment. He began to unload the gear by unlatching the upper part of the cargo netting first. Packs, duffel bags, freeze-dried food, sleeping bags, the first aid kit, and the tent went up, out, and over the door to land on the snow beside the belly of the wrecked helicopter.

Jamie had thought out this expedition well. That he had packed accordingly for some days on the ice was evident as Rod unloaded the helicopter. There was a large, new expedition level tent. He recognized both the brand and model from the dozens of catalogs that came to his house in Denver. It was highly prized by mountaineering experts—and expensive, too: at least five hundred dollars for the three-man model. There were fancy aluminum expedition boxes of food. Two full-length, three-inch foam pads for sleeping. The sleeping bags themselves were thick, warm, arctic models insulated with the latest and best man-made fibers, which could stand up to both the wet and the cold. There was a stove and spare fuel canisters. Cooking pots and utensils.

As Rod dug lower, he came to an assortment of tools including two ice axes and shovels. There were also hundreds of feet of mountaineering rope and climbing hardware.

He found what he wanted near the bottom: a large, blue-and-white first aid kit. The box was lightweight, molded plastic. Knowing Jamie's thoroughness, he hoped it contained some kind of painkiller not bought off the shelf in any drugstore.

But the surprise was at the very bottom, underneath the first aid kit.

Rod lowered the kit and reached for the weapon. He picked it up delicately as if it might explode in his hands and then turned it over and over. Then he placed one hand under the forestock and the other near the rear, close to the trigger. He whistled softly to himself admiring its deadly, completely functional lines and the forward curved banana clip. Although Rod had only seen one of these on the evening news, anyone would have instantly recognized it. You usually saw it in the hands of some desperate, third world guerilla fighter in tattered fatigues. But no matter where in the world it was seen, it was known to be a copy of the famous, Russian assault rifle, the AK-47. Not the prettiest weapon—in fact rather cheap looking—it was known to be simply one of the finest, most rugged, reliable firearms in the world.

The one Rod held had seen better days. Its wood stock was pockmarked and bruised. Many of the metal parts were worn smooth and shiny. The leather strap was frayed. But, of course, it was no sportsman's firearm to be hung on a wall and admired and cherished.

It was made instead to take large doses of punishment and keep firing. Rod had no doubt it would work well. He just had to find out how it worked. And he was curious about its origin, although he could guess where it had come from: Vietnam.

Rod brought the bolt back a fraction of an inch and looked inside the opening left in the submachine gun's side. The action felt stiff and resisted his efforts. There appeared to be no round in the chamber, although he guessed the clip was probably full. He let the bolt go. It slammed forward with a metallic click.

He turned the assault rifle over in his hands. It felt slightly lighter than his Winchester hunting rifle. There had to be a safety somewhere, but he could figure it out later. There was some kind of selector switch on the side. There were also funny symbols and foreign writing etched into the metal on its side. He shrugged and hooked the leather strap over his shoulder so it hung on his back muzzle down just like he had seen the guerrillas in Afghanistan do on the news years ago.

Then, as he bent down for the first aid kit, he saw another clip lying under the little bit of gear still left inside. He picked it up and turned it over in his hand. A stubby brass cartridge lay in the top opening, and from the weight he had no doubt that the clip was also full. He stuffed the spare clip into one of his parka's large front pockets, picked up the first aid kit, and climbed hurriedly out of the helicopter.

He froze in the door and stared across the lake. Could it have been him? Had he just seen movement in the distance from the corner of his eye? He thought he had seen the door to the ski-plane close. Rod pushed up his glasses and squinted down the lake. He was almost sure the door had been open before. Now it was closed. It meant the other man had to be in the airplane right now. He had to have been crossing the lake from the shoreline while Rod had been fooling around inside the helicopter with the gun and first aid kit.

He felt his heart pounding again at his temples. There was a familiar knot growing in his stomach. Rod remained frozen in the opening. The Winchester, the gun he knew how to use, was out of reach in the snow. He surveyed the white expanse. The lake seemed deserted again except for the two airplanes at the other end.

There was a sudden metallic clank from behind him. Rod jumped and twisted. Had the man somehow worked his way unseen around behind the helicopter? Was he at this very moment crouched there and waiting? Rod froze.

Nothing moved. He began to shiver and breathe heavily through his mouth. It was probably a broken part in the tail or the engine that had shifted suddenly. That had to be it.

Rod jumped into the snow from the helicopter. It was not a graceful leap. He landed heavily on all fours and picked himself up. The Russian assault rifle slapped him hard in the small of his back. Rod picked up the first aid kit and stumbled in the packed snow in front of the helicopter. He worked his way around the Jet Ranger, grabbing the Winchester with his free hand and dropping the first aid kit. There was no one behind the wreckage. There were no tracks to be seen as far as the outlet of the frozen lake hundreds of yards away where they had camped only weeks earlier. Rod heard nothing but the wind. His imagination had been playing tricks on him. He was suddenly angry.

There was another metallic clank, and Rod jumped. He caught his breath and turned slowly. This time he saw the source of the noise. One of the broken rotor blades was striking the fuselage in the rising wind.

Rod breathed deeply. He lowered the Winchester. He bit his lower lip and cursed. He told himself to get it together. Then he walked back to the gear. As he bent down, a shadow swept over him. The wind was becoming colder. He looked up as he picked up the first aid kit. The sun had been covered by some ominous, feathery clouds, which seemed to be spreading out rapidly. The sky was rapidly changing from a whitish blue to steel gray.

Rod ferried the gear as fast as possible from the helicopter to the shoreline. The job took another twenty minutes. Although he had taken the first aid kit over first, Jamie still refused any help until the task was done and the tent and gear was organized. It was evident he was still suffering badly. The work had warmed Rod up considerably. On the second trip, he had removed his red down parka and spread it over Jamie. Each time over to the helicopter, Rod had carried the Winchester. Jamie would have to explain how the assault rifle worked.

The tent was not easy to set up in the growing winter darkness. It was the heavier, expedition model designed for at least three men and their gear, possibly four. There was a bewildering array of fiberglass poles that had to be inserted into nylon sleeves, which ran in cross patterns. But the result was a low, wide tent resembling a geodesic dome.

The weather could always change very fast in the Colorado Rockies in the winter, and by the time the tent had been set up and most of the equipment had been stowed inside, the clouds had lowered around the peaks, and the first big snowflakes were being blown across the lake in the ever-increasing wind. Visibility was rapidly being reduced.

Now that the work was done, Rod began to feel the cold again as his sweat evaporated. He pulled his stocking cap down over his ears and crunched over to Jamie. He pulled his parka from him. He had expected some cussing or a reply of some kind, but he got none. This was puzzling. He pulled the parka on and drew the hood around his head. He leaned over the other man. Jamie seemed to be sleeping. His face was white as a sheet. Rod feared the worst until he saw his chest rise and fall. He should put that thought out of his head. Jamie was a tough customer. They would get through this mess somehow.

Rod gently shook him, and slowly Jamie came back to some sort of consciousness. He looked up through eyelids coated with snow and said weakly with a half-smile, "Hey, what's going on?" He looked around and asked, "It's getting dark?"

Rod reached down. "C'mon, give me your arm, and I'll help you into the tent. Let's go."

Jamie grimaced and said in a still weak voice, "Damn, old buddy, I'm really hurting. I think I might've busted some ribs along with the leg." He coughed. "There's some stuff in the first aid kit for pain. Goddamn, I'm cold."

With Rod's help, Jamie struggled to stand on one leg but found it difficult to maintain his balance. He had to put most of his considerable weight onto Rod, and both men struggled the twenty feet or so to the tent. Rod lowered him gently to the snow. The pain must have been great as he helped him slide into the tent. Jamie cried out twice. Finally he was settled onto one of the three inch thick foam pads. Rod unzipped one of the thick red sleeping bags and threw it over him. It was finally time to have a look at the broken ankle. Rod reached up and zipped the door shut.

Tim sat in the left seat of the Cessna. Despite the sleeping bag he had wrapped around him, he shivered and cursed the sudden storm. He should have been a multimillionaire by now. The wind suddenly shook the tiny airplane, and large snowflakes danced around the curved Plexiglas windshield. He couldn't remember being so cold in all his life as he took a bite of a hard Snickers bar. He pulled on the stiff nougat center until it snapped.

The sleeping bag was not much good. It was obvious now that the clerk in the hardware store had ripped him off. The man had raved on and on about the "miracle" man-made fibers and its advantage over goose down. Well, the asshole wasn't sitting in an airplane on a frozen lake at over eleven thousand feet when he had flapped his lips. Tim looked up. The outside temperature gauge in the upper left-hand side of the windshield read just about zero, or even a degree or two below.

Another gust rocked the Cessna. Tim worried about the wind. He had no way of tying the airplane's wings down. Too strong a wind, and the little airplane could end up on its back. He reached down and pushed the small, red rocker switch to on. The gyro-driven instruments in front of him began their characteristic whining sound as they sluggishly began to spin in the cold. He briefly switched on the landing light, which was located on the leading edge of the wing. A bright, white beam of light shot out only to be stopped dead in less than twenty-five feet by the swirling snow. Trying to save the battery, Tim turned off the light and cursed again.

He had wanted to finish off the two men that night as quickly as possible. He had watched just one of them unload the helicopter. This no doubt meant that the other one was injured somehow. After it had gotten dark, he had started out across the lake again. Then the snow had started in earnest. He was still amazed at the suddenness of the storm. He had barely found his way back to the ski-plane in the whiteout. It was now out of the question to try to find anything in the dark in this weather. It would be too easy to get lost without any visual references in these conditions. And to get lost in this weather would be fatal. No, it would have to wait until first light. He felt the cold steel of the Uzi cradled in his lap. Hopefully, the storm would blow itself out by then.

Tim finished the candy bar. He tried to draw the sleeping bag closer around him. He turned sideways in his seat in an attempt to get more comfortable and hoped the two men were worse off than he was at the moment. No, if he couldn't get to them, he decided, then they couldn't get to him.

A wind gust rocked the airplane yet again and both control wheels tried to twist despite the gust lock. Tim cursed himself again. As soon as the weather lifted, he'd get the both of them.

Rod was still nauseous and felt like throwing up. Jamie's repeated request didn't help settle his stomach. He knelt on his foam pad under the low tent roof and made some final adjustments to Jamie's thick red sleeping bag. He pulled the bag up around the other man's shoulders. With each small movement, Jamie bit his lip, despite the morphine. Rod felt guilty causing his friend so much pain. But his color was better, and the shivering had lessened as his body had warmed under the thick insulation.

Rod's bent figure was silhouetted against the green-and-tan tent fabric by a small butane lantern near the door. Outside the storm raged. Sharp gusts caught at the outer fly and caused the fiberglass support poles to flex downward and then spring back when the wind abated. It was a superb design, spilling the wind to either side and over the top. The tent simply shrugged off the blasts of air and the snow accompanying them. In any other circumstances, he would feel safe and snug in such a tent.

Jamie asked again for a little more painkiller, but Rod felt he must follow the directions.

Another gust tried to uplift the tent causing the outer fly to snap and the poles to quiver.

Rod picked up the lantern and moved it closer to the first aid kit. He made an attempt at repacking the box. His heart wasn't in this anymore, and he tried vainly not to think about the next few hours. He simply did not know what to do. There was no 9-1-1 to call here. Their situation, he knew, was dire.

Jamie's ankle and shin had been the most gruesome thing he had ever remembered seeing. The break had been much worse than he had dreamed when he had finally cut the pants away and begun tending to the injuries. The skin was bruised and discolored. He had a hard time even looking at the jagged, white bone sticking out from the gaping wound. Jamie's foot was bent around in an unnatural way, like a puppet's. The wound oozed blood. Rod gagged more than once and had to look away several times before he finished with the sterile dressings and secured the plastic splint around the break. Then he had gone over the rest of Jamie for other injuries. There seemed to be broken ribs all right and lots of bruises, and Rod feared his friend had serious internal injuries as well. It had taken a long time to maneuver the big man into the sleeping bag. It had taken even longer to get his nerve up to give Jamie the shot of morphine, all the while hoping there were no air bubbles in the syringe. He had done it exactly as he had seen it done in the movies.

They were so far from any help. A sense of doom swept over him as he continued to neaten the tent. He thought of his family. Why had he gone along with this get-rich scheme? It had seemed so easy. Sure, just fly in and scoop up the money. All problems solved after that. But they were stuck real good, now weren't they? They had outsmarted themselves, hadn't they? Nobody was going to come to their rescue. The helicopter's ELT antenna had snapped off in the crash. Nobody even knew where they were. There was no way to call for help. Jamie was hurt very badly and needed a doctor and hospital immediately. And to top it all off, there was another man at the other end of the lake, barely a half mile away from where he was kneeling at this very moment in the tent, who was going to try and kill them and would probably succeed. He probably would have done so by now except for the sudden snowstorm. Skiers all through the state were rejoicing at this sudden change in the weather while he sat on death row. Worst of all was the certain knowledge that he would have to abandon his lifelong friend just before first light and go for help. It was the only viable plan he could come up with. He would have to somehow climb down next to the frozen waterfalls, on ice encrusted rock, without a safety rope; and if he lived through that, make his way down the gorge solo, in conditions that would make the hike out a few weeks ago seem like summer picnic. How deep the snow would be when he made the tree line was anybody's guess. Could he make the big ranch down below in one day or two? Or three? Or at all? He had no snowshoes or skis. And then the awful nagging questions: What would become of Jamie? Could Jamie defend himself? Was he really going for help or was that an excuse? Was he abandoning his friend for good? Should he stay and defend Jamie and himself? Did he have the courage to do so? These questions surged through his mind over and over as he knelt in the tent, feeling the wind against the nylon fabric as if it were a living being pushing from the outside. Still the tent held fast.

Jamie mumbled something then, but Rod missed it against the wind noise and his thoughts. Rod turned and knelt over the other man. He asked, "What did you say?"

Jamie answered softly, "I said...when we get out of this mess...I'm suing you for your half of the money...medical malpractice...that shot hurt."

Incredible, Rod thought, Jamie still had the money on his mind.

"You'd better get a good lawyer."

Jamie smiled.

"I'll give you another shot in a while."

"Okay."

"You doing okay?"

"Yeah, feeling a little better. You did a good job." Jamie closed his eyes.

"Thanks."

Rod remembered for the first time that day that neither of them had eaten since breakfast that morning in Gunnison. Some food for both of them was the next order of business. As Jamie rested, Rod started going through the equipment and stores in order to see what they had. He had just located the small but powerful butane stove when he heard Jamie mumble something else. He turned around.

"What?"

The wind ripped at the fabric.

Rod bent over him. "What did you say?"

Jamie had pried one arm from the sleeping bag and was trying to focus on his large Seiko chronograph. "What time is it?"

"Just early evening yet. We've got all night to sit this out before I have to get ready to leave."

Jamie became agitated and tried to raise his voice. "What do you mean *leave*?"

Rod was puzzled. Was Jamie starting to talk out of his head? He answered him, "You know, start out to get help in the morning."

"Are…you…nuts?"

"What do you mean by *nuts*?"

Jamie was getting drowsy with the painkiller. "What…about the money? Have you forgotten…why we're up here in the…first place? What…about the asshole on the…other end of the lake? We can't stop now." Jamie stopped and coughed. He caught his breath then continued, "Jesus, besides the money, we've…got to get even. There's some honor here…at stake."

Rod answered hotly, "I can't believe you're still thinking about that money. Because of it, we almost got ourselves killed!"

"Not…just the money. We've got to get even."

"You keep saying that. So what?"

"So what? The asshole…shot us down. In all my flying, even in 'Nam, I never…personally put a scratch on any aircraft, much less…" He pointed outside. "Totaled one…we gotta pay him back."

Rod knew what was coming next. He sighed though and said weakly, "I'm going for help first light. It's our only option. Case closed."

Jamie had a convincing argument and used it to his advantage. "You can't leave me here, old buddy. We…never…left wounded behind… ever."

Rod didn't answer. The question of leaving Jamie behind had been nagging him, but he couldn't think of any alternative.

Jamie was silent for a moment, too. "Another...thing. We owe about one hundred fifty grand...on that pile of junk outside the tent."

A gust of wind caught at the fabric. The roar was like a locomotive. The tent poles flexed.

Rod was lost in thought and didn't think he heard Jamie correctly. He looked at him in horror. "What do you mean? Did you say one hundred and fifty thousand dollars? And what do you mean 'we'? I didn't have anything to do with it!'

Jamie coughed. "Your name is on the registration."

"I didn't sign for anything! This is your idea!"

"I signed...for you." Jamie's words were becoming slurred.

Rod began to sweat despite the cold in the tent. "I don't suppose it was insured."

"No."

"Yeah, I didn't think so somehow." Rod slumped down on his sleeping bag and asked weakly, "What do you think we should do?"

Jamie was resting easier. He closed his eyes. "Don't worry, I have a plan."

CHAPTER 30

Night Patrol

Rod zipped the tent door shut. He leaned back against the boxes and supplies he had stacked behind him and pulled the thick sleeping bag up around his shoulders in the dark. He left the bag partially unzipped so his arms would be free. He squirmed back and forth, trying to get comfortable, but couldn't. It was no good; he hadn't been able to get a wink of sleep. He picked up the assault rifle and laid it across his lap. His breath clouded in front of him. He watched the tent door for any movement. His ears were alert for the telltale crunch of boots in the snow just outside.

The wind had decreased significantly in the past hour. It still seemed to be snowing lightly. The entire lake was enveloped in thick fog now. He had gone outside an hour ago to relieve himself, and the air still felt very sharp on his face. He estimated it must still be hovering around zero.

Rod tried hard to will away the next eight or ten hours ahead of him to no avail. The plan still bothered him.

The inside of the tent was in total darkness. It seemed very quiet now that the wind was no longer buffeting it. Rod turned but could barely make out Jamie's bulk. Thank goodness he was sleeping now. He was resting easier and snoring softly in his painkiller-induced state.

Rod sighed and brought his arm up. Jamie's large Seiko dangled loosely from his wrist. Jamie had insisted he take it because it could be read in the dark, whereas Rod's Kmart special couldn't. He read the luminous hands—just a little after midnight. About a half hour to go. He would give Jamie another shot and leave.

Rod closed his eyes and wished it was over. He had never felt such absolute despair. Jamie had told him to watch for that feeling. It always came eventually to losers who were overwhelmed by it. He remembered the words and tried to shake it, but couldn't. He decided to wait another five minutes before preparing to go. His stomach felt unsettled—the trepidation. He thought this must be what it was like to be a Marine before an amphibious landing. An astronaut before the launch. A soldier in a trench afraid to go over the top but more afraid of his own officer's pistol behind him. The whole plan dangled from a very slender thread.

Rod studied the watch again. The hands seemed to be moving with alarming speed. He decided the time was close enough. He put the AK-47 assault rifle to one side, unzipped his sleeping bag, and crawled out of the warmth into the frigid atmosphere of the tent. There were no choices left now.

Rod knelt on his foam pad and ducked below the low nylon ceiling. He extracted his boots from inside the sleeping bag, still warm from his body heat, and hurriedly threw the bag aside. He sat back against the supplies, placed his feet inside the boots, and proceeded to lace up each one. The added wool socks made the boots somewhat tighter. Besides extra socks, Rod was also wearing Jamie's dark gray heavy wool pants and sweater. Although too big for his small frame, when worn over his own clothes and sweater, it didn't seem too bad. Rod decided to leave the stocking hat, mittens, and navy blue parka off until he was out of the tent. He laid these near the door along with the assault rifle and the backpack with his climbing gear. Rod withdrew a small flashlight from his pocket and flicked it on. He shielded the beam. Then he reluctantly reached over and gently shook Jamie's shoulder. He whispered, "Jamie, wakeup. It's time." There was no response. He shook him harder the second time and raised his voice. "C'mon, wake up."

Rod felt uneasy. He was beginning to become strangely nervous as if behind schedule. Perhaps now that he had actually put this thing into motion, he wanted to get it over with.

Jamie slowly opened his eyes and rolled over slightly, so he was flat on his back. He stared up at the tent roof. He blinked a few times, slowly coming back to consciousness. There was a dull throb in his leg and guts. The painkiller was wearing off sooner than he expected. He began to feel nauseous again and strangely lightheaded, detached from his surroundings. He tried to take some deep breaths. His chest hurt, and he felt he couldn't get enough air. He tried to form a clear thought and asked, "What time is it?"

Rod tried to answer lightheartedly, "Sorry I had to wake you. It's time for your sleeping pill."

"Huh? What…sleeping pill?"

"I'm only joking. You know, how in the hospital the nurse wakes the patient to give him a sleeping pill."

"Sure, I get it. Heh-heh." Jamie's head cleared a little more, and he asked again, "What time is it?"

"It's a little after midnight."

"Is everything ready to go?"

Rod held the small AA flashlight in his mouth, fished in the first aid kit, and found the red plastic box containing the remaining syringes. He removed one and latched the lid. He turned and knelt next to Jamie. He removed the flashlight from his mouth and answered, "Yeah, everything's set. How are you feeling?"

Jamie swallowed. "Really lousy. My insides hurt. I feel kind of sick again. I must have really clobbered my guts when we hit the lake…but it's not too bad yet."

Rod put the flashlight back in his mouth, took the cap from the syringe, and squirted some of the liquid from the needle. "You're going to have to tell me all about it someday." At least that was what he intended to say. His words were jumbled by the flashlight. He reached out and mumbled again, "Here, give me your arm."

Jamie apparently understood what he was saying. There was a rustling of the red nylon fabric as he slowly brought his arm out of the sleeping bag. Jamie asked weakly, "You don't remember that part? The crash, I mean?"

Rod shook his head negatively in answer to the question as he reached for the other man's arm. He guessed you could get used to anything, as he jabbed the needle into Jamie's arm. This one was easy. Why had he been so squeamish before? He released the morphine and pulled out the needle in one neat motion.

Jamie flinched, "Ouch! You're the ugliest nurse I've ever seen." Then he began to relax as the drug took effect. "Shit, my...lawyer will be in touch...with your lawyer in...the morning."

"Yeah, get in line, sucker," Rod said in a tougher voice that had strangely come from somewhere, as he squared away the first aid kit and emptied syringe.

Both knew the jokes were like whistling as you walked through the graveyard.

Next Rod turned and picked up the large, gray rucksack leaning against the supplies behind him. He had carefully packed it some hours ago. It was heavy, and it took some effort to swing it around and place it near the door next to his parka, assault rifle, and down mittens. As he set it down, the climbing equipment on the outside jangled back and forth. A new multicolored climbing rope was tightly secured in loops under the pack's flap. The pack now rested on its back near the door. He picked up the battered but deadly AK-47 with its full thirty-round banana clip by its leather strap and leaned it against the pack.

Next he reached to one side and lifted up the Winchester hunting rifle. This he lay alongside Jamie with its barrel pointed toward the door. It was fully loaded also.

Rod stopped for a moment and sucked on his lower lip. He laid his hand on the hunting rifle and thought for a moment. He might never see his friend alive again. He spoke softly, "There's one round in the chamber. The safety's on. There are four more in the magazine. Are you sure you want the Winchester and not the other gun?"

"No, you...take the AK. I'll be okay...with the rifle. You might need the firepower more than me."

Rod hesitated for a few awkward moments. "Jamie, I'm scared to death—that's the truth. I don't want to go."

"I'm not...feeling too good about...all this either."

"Really?"

"Yeah, never more petrified in my life. We're in a tough...spot. Toughest... I've ever been in. It's up to you...old buddy. Remember how I told...you that you just...get caught up in events sometimes. Do your...best."

Rod reached over next to the stove and picked up an opaque plastic water bottle. It felt almost three-quarters full and stiff. He squeezed it with both hands. An inch of ice near the top broke into pieces with a cracking sound. He reached over and tucked the bottle into Jamie's sleeping bag.

"Here's the rest of the water. I have another bottle with me in the pack. Do you want any food or anything?"

Jamie smiled weakly. "No, I'm not hungry. Don't worry about me; worry about yourself."

Rod sat back on his heels. His head just grazed the tent roof. The lump in his stomach rose suddenly into his throat. His eyes watered as he sputtered, "I...I don't want to leave you here. I just can't leave you here by yourself. I...I'm staying. We'll face this guy together."

Jamie's left arm shot out of the sleeping bag. He grasped Rod around his right wrist. The grip was surprisingly hard. Rod winced. Jamie's voice was still weak but took on an edge. "Look, we discussed this hours ago. This is the only chance for both of us." He had put extra emphasis on the word *both*.

"I…I just don't think I can go through with this…I wish I was the one who was hurt…I always trust you to know what to do." There it was—plain and simple.

Jamie had released his grip. "Quit thinking you have a choice—you don't. No fucking choice whatsoever. Like I said, events have overtaken you. There is only one way out…remember that over and over…one way out…either him or you…Harden yourself."

Rod took a deep breath. "Yeah, you're right. We're going to be okay, right?"

Jamie released his grip and gave Rod a thumbs-up. "That's the way to think, old buddy." Then he slapped Rod's arm. "Now go to it."

Rod twisted the knob on the lantern, and its light quickly faded. He crawled on his hands and knees to the tent's low door and unzipped it all the way around. Then he picked up the AK-47and checked the safety once more. He held it to one side and manhandled the large rucksack outside onto the snow followed by his parka and mittens. Using the assault rifle for support, he crawled through opening himself. He turned and looked in the door, but it was really too dark to see Jamie at the far end. He grimaced and zipped the door shut.

The brief snowstorm had been intense and Rod was not surprised to find five inches of fresh snow. It was the light, fluffy powder usually associated with very low temperatures.

He leaned the rifle against the tent, stood, and turned to look toward the upper end of the lake. His eyes slowly adjusted to the dark. It was perfectly still. Ice crystals seemed suspended in the air around him by the billions. His breath added more. Visibility seemed to be about ten yards or less. That was good. The overwhelming illusion was that of being lost in a dark, smoky void.

Rod turned and looked over the dim outline of the dome tent toward the lake's outlet. He stood still and breathed slowly. The sharp, cold air penetrated his lungs. He listened intently for a few minutes. The stillness was complete.

Rod wondered if he suddenly yelled at the top of his lungs, would the other mystery man in the Cessna ski-plane hear him? Maybe they could arrange some kind of truce. But he knew it wouldn't be possible. Whoever the other man was, he wouldn't negotiate. Grimly, he knew there would be only one winning side today.

Rod stooped and picked up the parka and mittens. The rustling of the nylon seemed loud as he put the coat on, the zipper even louder. He bent down and hefted the pack up over his head and down onto his shoulders. He shrugged once to settle it. The weight didn't seem too bad as his bulky clothing spread the pressure of the straps. He picked up the assault rifle and brought the strap over his head and hung the AK-47 in front of him.

As he faced the tent, the shoreline should be to his left. A flashlight would be useless in the restricted visibility. He shuffled through the snow in the dark and almost immediately stumbled into the rocks. He could barely make out the difference between the smooth, white lake surface and the darker boulders along its side. Still, using what he could see as a guide, he turned right and began walking in the direction that would eventually take him to the lake's outlet and the frozen waterfalls.

CHAPTER 31

The Night Climb

Rod shuffled along. He really couldn't take steps; the snow was up to his knees. He left a deep track behind him in the dark. In a minute he stopped and turned.

He was absolutely alone now. The tent was lost in the ice fog and darkness. The only sound was his own breathing and the occasional creak of the rucksack's straps as he shifted the weight on his feet. The thought that the other man might be out there trying to find *him* worriedly crossed his mind. The man in the Cessna ski-plane could be fifteen feet away from him at this very moment, and he wouldn't see him. That the only thing he would see before he died might be the orange muzzle flashes from the other man's gun also occurred to Rod, and he shivered.

With some difficulty, Rod checked Jamie's Seiko. They had figured in the tent that it would take roughly a half hour to reach the outlet end of the lake. It had been only five minutes since he left the tent.

Rod turned and resumed his shuffling walk. He relied on his sense of direction and occasional brushing against the large boulders just to his left to ascertain he was indeed headed in the right direction. If he left the shore, he could wander for hours in circles out in the middle of the lake. He suddenly wished he had a compass, something Jamie had forgotten apparently. Maybe he could have removed the compass in the helicopter somehow if he had been thinking.

Rod tried to visualize the lake and its surroundings as he inched forward. He counted his steps and walked what he estimated was about three hundred yards. He stopped and turned—nothing but a dark void and the white lake surface at his feet.

Again, he set off in what he believed was the correct direction and almost immediately stumbled into the rocky shoreline, which was now different than back near the tent. The rocks were smaller, and the area surrounding them seemed flatter. He also didn't sense the high granite wall immediately behind them. He stopped to catch his breath and again tried to visualize what the lake had looked like on their trips past. He must be nearing the outlet.

Rod heaved himself up on the rocks. The pack was hard to balance, and he almost toppled onto his side. He walked forward in the darkness and then stopped. This was different than shuffling along the smooth lake surface, and he brought the small AA flashlight out. He flicked it on. The beam went barely five feet, but it was enough for him to see the ground immediately in front of him. The snow didn't seem as deep as out on the lake. The area was littered with small boulders, interspersed with broad flat areas seemingly blown clear of snow, which made walking much easier. The top of the first waterfall should be somewhere to his right.

He walked forward thinking of the drop of more than one hundred feet somewhere just ahead of him when he heard the water. It was muted, gurgling somewhere under the ice. He took some tentative steps forward and began to hear the muted roar of the waterfall under the ice. In a few moments, he recognized the beginning of the large crack in the ledge in which he and Jamie always finished their climb from down below. He skirted around its upper end and worked his way carefully over the ice and snow-covered rock, shining the small flashlight beam almost directly at his feet. He took a couple more tentative, shuffling steps on the slick surface. The sound of water under the ice seemed to be right next to him.

Almost before he realized it, the small yellow beam of the flashlight edged into a void. He knew he was standing within inches of the top of the precipice and the gorge beyond. Rod turned carefully from the edge and followed the sound of water, simultaneously playing the beam along the snow and ice to his left. The gurgling of the outlet got louder at one point, and he continued to play the beam back and forth until he found an open hole no more than a foot in diameter through which he could see the icy water run downstream the last ten yards before tumbling over the edge under the ice encased waterfalls. Although he had a water bottle with him, he was thankful he had found this open spot. He slipped off the pack and rifle, removed his mittens, and knelt at the hole, drinking deeply with both hands. The lake water was so cold it hurt his mouth but tasted wonderful nonetheless. Although he knew the temperature was probably at zero or a little below, Rod felt warm, his clothing adequate for now. Two more mouthfuls and he put the mittens back on and stood.

He hefted the pack and then the assault rifle back over his shoulders and turned back up the lake. In a few yards, he gained the rocky shoreline again and hopped up on the closest rock, then the next higher one. Slowly he began to climb in the dark up to the ridge above. With each step higher, he felt the weight on his back sag more heavily onto his shoulders. The easy part was over.

CHAPTER 32

The Descent

Rod stopped and tried to catch his breath. He took big, heaving gulps of the thin air. His heart was racing, and his legs felt like the cheap rubber bands that wrap newspapers. He bent forward and tried to shift the weight on his aching shoulders. The pack and assault rifle seemed twice as heavy as just a few hours ago down on the lake. He glanced at the luminous face of Jamie's Seiko. First light would be soon. He had been pushing himself hard and was still behind schedule.

Rod looked around. The moon over his shoulder was bright, and he could clearly see the Collegiate Range some forty miles away as they jutted above the clouds, which seemed to fill the entire park to just a few hundred feet below his boots. The landscape around him stood out in stark bluish whites and dark in the moonlight. Mt. Grant rose just to his left, and he felt he could reach out and touch the summit in the sharp, clear air.

He had not really stopped since his climb began down near the frozen waterfalls and the going had been tough. The rocks and boulders that led up to the ridge above the lake had been slick with a thin covering of ice, and there had been pockets of deep snow between them. This had greatly hampered his efforts to find a good foothold. At times it seemed that for every foot he gained he slid back two. Twice the weight of the pack and assault rifle threatened to pull him over backwards.

But finally he had gained the top of the ridge and started the long uphill hike along its spine. The gradient had been easier, less steep, but it had been impossible to maintain a straight line. Unlike summer, large, deep snowfields blocked his path. He had to skirt these, picking his way around them on the rockier, windswept tundra. At one point just below the boulder field that guarded the summit of Mt. Grant itself, he had not been able to make a detour and had been forced to slog his way through deep snow, which at times came up to his waist.

It had taken almost an hour and a half to negotiate this snowfield in the dark. The effort was doubly hard because he was now at an altitude of over thirteen thousand feet. The thin air lacked oxygen. He had been exhausted upon finally reaching the boulder field. He could have walked the distance on a summer day in few minutes.

But two factors continued to favor him, considering his exposure on the ridge. The wind had been calm, practically nonexistent during the remainder of the night, and he had climbed up out of the cloud, which lay heavily in the cirque. Without the wind, and with the physical effort, he had been able to keep warm in the subzero temperatures, and, without the cloud, he had been able to keep his directions straight in the moonlight, avoiding the sheer drops of several hundred feet on each side of him. Even now as he removed the pack and AK-47, he shuddered at what it would have been like trying to negotiate that distance before the storm had blown itself out earlier, hampered all the way by strong winds and poor visibility.

Rod leaned the assault rifle and pack against a convenient boulder. He unzipped his parka and withdrew his water bottle kept warm by his body heat. There wasn't much left, maybe three big gulps. Exhausted, he sat down heavily next to the pack. He absentmindedly stuffed the rigid, empty plastic bottle back into his coat and zipped it back up. The sky seemed perceptibly lighter to the east, or was that his imagination? The surrounding peaks seemed just visible now, or were his eyes just adjusting? There was still no telltale yellow glow over the Collegiate Range, but dawn was nearer now. The sky was slowly turning from black to dark blue it seemed. He must not delay any more, he knew, but it felt so good just to sit for a short while.

Below, the white cloud layer still engulfed the entire cirque and spread out in an even blanket over Elk Park. It would be a spectacular perch from which to watch the sunrise, if only he could have stayed. Rod rested for another twenty minutes. Gradually, some strength began to seep back into his legs.

The eastern horizon lightened even more, and the stars began to fade. Soon the horizon would take on a yellow glow, and he must be back down on the lake behind the airplanes by that time. Surprise was a must. Maybe, just maybe, he would catch the other man off guard, or even better, asleep.

He shivered. Suddenly he was cold, sitting still after all those hours of exertion. Rod stood with a groan, his legs and shoulders stiffening with the inactivity. He heaved the pack over his shoulders and then the assault rifle. With a sigh, he slowly and carefully began to inch himself downward from the rounded crest of the ridge. He told himself once again to quit thinking about all this, perhaps for the thousandth time since leaving the tent and Jamie. Hadn't he gotten this far? That would prove to anyone he had at least some toughness. Not just anybody could have gotten even this far if they didn't know what they were doing. Just do it, he thought suddenly.

He worked his way slowly around the first rock outcropping, and the pitch increased. Ice covered the bare rock surfaces, and snow had been packed between them by the winds. The lake was at least three hundred feet below him. This would be the most dangerous part, and the slowest, as he worked his way down to the final precipice above the airplanes.

Within ten minutes Rod had descended into the fog again. But visibility seemed to be increasing as the sky lightened more. The billions of ice crystals were a mixed blessing. They made him invisible from below but hindered his progress. They had planned for him to make his descent in the dark, but obviously both had underestimated the time required to get even this far. The fog was now his friend, but he must be all the way down before it burned off or the wind began to pick up again. If the visibility suddenly increased to more than a few hundred yards, he would be a sitting duck with no shelter to shield him.

Thirty minutes later Rod hopped onto a ledge and found himself at the edge of the final drop, exactly at the very spot from which he and Jamie had climbed down back in October. It seemed like a lifetime ago.

In a straight line, he was barely one hundred yards from the two airplanes just below. The wreck was closer; the ski-plane just beyond. The descent to this point from the top of the ridge had gone surprisingly well. He had slipped once midway down but had been able to catch himself. Maybe, after having come this far, he thought, this plan just might work after all. The thought cheered him, and he felt strangely optimistic for the first time since they had left Gunnison in the Jet Ranger.

The same large boulder around which he had secured the climbing rope weeks ago was just behind him. He took the pack from his back as quietly as possible and then leaned the assault rifle against it. He was so close now that dislodging a rock and alerting the man in the ski-plane could be fatal. He knelt at the edge of the precipice and peered into the fog still enveloping the entire lake. He could hear his pulse, blood racing through his temples. It was lighter now, almost dawn, and he must make his move. He thought he could now actually begin to see the outline of the wrecked airplane in the ice. This was not good. Nothing definite—there were no distinct features, just a shadow, but now that dawn had come and the night would no longer cover him, the visibility had increased to a dangerous level for his rappel down the cliff face, the point at which he would be most vulnerable. He knew he must hurry with his preparations. Still, he was cautious and took one more look around the area below him. The deep snow between himself and the airplanes remained unbroken. At least no one had come this way.

Rod bent and undid the rucksack's straps. He pulled the climbing rope from the pack then looped the rope around the boulder, at what he thought was the middle, and heaved the remaining two halves over the edge. It fell in quick jerks but did not tangle and finally straightened out beautifully. As he looked down, Rod saw that his estimation was not off by much: one end dangled ten feet higher than the other. He adjusted the difference by pulling up one end of the rope and bringing it around the back of the anchor rock. Still, as he looked down again, he was dismayed to see that the two ends just barely touched the rocks below. This rope had to be a good fifty feet shorter than the one he and Jamie had used last fall.

Rod dug into the pack and began to lay out the hardware he would need for the rappel. Two carabineers, one with a brake bar. He dug deeper into the pack. Shit! Where was the sling made of nylon webbing? He dug some more in the pack. He had completely overlooked the webbed nylon sling necessary for the rappel. Damn! The other hardware was totally useless! He stared into the pack for a moment. There was another way to do this. Sure. He had learned it during his first climbing lesson back at the university in Boulder. He had tried it once or twice. Although it worked, it wasn't all that comfortable or safe. He would have to let his body act as the brake and create the all-important friction by wrapping the rope first between his legs, then up around his waist, and then over one shoulder. A climber could create some nasty burns this way if he wasn't careful. Rod decided that all his extra clothing should help that aspect of the rappel. He would also descend as slowly as possible.

To save time Rod decided to rappel with the pack and assault rifle on his back instead of lowering each separately. He stood and hefted first the pack over his shoulder then the rifle but decided that his parka made things too bulky when combined with the AK-47. He took the pack and rifle off once again, removed the parka, and stuffed it into the rucksack. He felt the chill immediately but felt better about maneuvering the rope around his body. Once again he hefted the pack and rifle over his shoulder then straddled the doubled rope with his back to the cliff and frozen lake below. He reached down behind himself and picked up a section of the rope, brought it around his right thigh and then draped it over his shoulder. The rope now trailed down his back and over the edge. With his left hand holding the rope in front of him as a guide, he yanked hard on it twice. It seemed firmly anchored around the rock in front of him. He felt extremely unprotected without a safety rope and a climbing partner belaying him, but that could not be helped this time. He felt strangely guilty breaking this rule, like running a stuck red light.

He bent at the knees with some effort due to the pack and rifle and, grasping the rope behind him with his right hand, which would act as a brake, began slowly walking backward, paying out rope as he inched toward the edge. The rope quickly tightened around him like a python. It would be worse once his entire weight was supported by it. Three more steps and he was at the edge. He glanced once more over his shoulder. The light and visibility had improved. The Cessna ski-plane was visible.

Rod hurriedly leaned out over the drop, breathed deeply a few times, and put one foot on the vertical rock. This is it, he thought. If the other man saw him now, he would be completely vulnerable. He brought the other foot onto the cliff face and let some more rope pay out through his right hand. His weight quickly shifted entirely to the rope, and he felt it tighten around him just as he had expected. Rod began to walk down the cliff face to the frozen lake below. After a few steps, he began to feel surer about his control over the descent, but even so there would be no neat, rope-singing jumps down the rock this time as there would have been if the carabineers and brake bar were creating all the friction. Roughly a third of the way down, he stopped and, with some difficulty, looked over his shoulder. He had to keep both feet planted on the rock in front of him to keep from spinning, or worse, turning upside down and falling out of the rope.

The area was brighter, the sun surely just above the horizon now. The visibility seemed the same. The ski-plane was visible although indistinct. With luck he wouldn't be seen. With luck the other man would not think of looking in his direction, expecting someone instead from the other end of the lake. A lot depended on luck.

For the hundredth time Rod thought of Jamie back in the tent. Was he even alive after all these hours?

He faced the rock wall and continued his slow, careful descent. He estimated he had forty feet or so to go when he felt the rope slip a second later. It was just a tiny movement, really no more than an inch or so, but it had slipped. Panic began to creep up in his throat again for the first time in hours. Probably the rope had settled into a crack at the base of the boulder he had anchored it to.

Rod froze. There was no safety rope belaying him this time. He tried to visualize the rope's hold on the boulder. It must have worked its way toward the top. He continued the rappel hardly daring to breathe. He paid out the rope slowly. One step, then two. He nervously looked above, vainly trying to inspect the rope. At step five, he dared to breathe normally again. The rope seemed to be holding fast. He prayed in general: just give me ten more minutes. Another twenty-five feet. At step six, the rope slid up and over the boulder. Rod fell.

He went over backwards and felt that queer weightless sensation in his guts, the kind he remembered when he jumped off the high board the first time at the municipal swimming pool. He saw the rope snake over the edge and follow him downward. He didn't yell or scream like the movies. Instead he shut his eyes tight.

He landed hard on his back on the snow-covered rocks below with a thud. The AK-47 flew from his shoulder against the cliff face. The last four inches of its stock was broken off like a kitchen match. He felt the breath being violently knocked from his lungs and then blackness. The rope fell heavily upon him.

CHAPTER 33

The Firefight

T im twisted in his seat and shivered. It was time to go. He felt sluggish. Probably the cold, he guessed. He glanced at his watch and was surprised to find that an hour had gone by since he had first decided to get out of the airplane. It was getting light, and he had wanted to start out in the dark. Visibility was improving with every minute. The crashed airplane was in the clear to the right, and even now some sunshine seemed to be finding its way through the opaque sky and dancing on one of the propellers.

As he was about to turn back in his seat, Tim sensed movement behind him. He twisted further in his seat. The cliff behind him and the rocks at its base were in plain view now, but he saw nothing.

Tim shrugged and thought maybe it must have been a small avalanche from above. He twisted around again and faced the instrument panel. Let's get going, he thought. With great effort he brought one hand out of his sleeping bag and plucked his sunglasses from the top of the panel. The metal felt very cold for a moment on his ears and nose. He squinted at the airplane's thermometer at the top left edge of the windshield. The needle had crept up since first light. It now was a relative balmy five degrees Fahrenheit. Not a heat wave yet, but better than the five below it had read most of the night.

Tim willed himself to unzip the sleeping bag. He was only mildly concerned about the lack of feeling in his toes and fingertips. He was confident they would warm up once he began walking. He struggled with the bag for another minute and finally extracted himself from it. He piled it in on the floor in front of the right seat. Why did things seem to take too long?

Tim picked the Uzi off the front seat, checked that the safety was still on, and popped the pilot's door open. He jumped down into the deep snow. His feet felt like lead weights.

He stood and listened. The silence seemed to be total. Overhead the sky was a whitish blue, promising a final burn-off of the fog, which had enveloped the cirque all night, and relative warm sunshine soon.

Shuffling through the new snow, he walked to the front of the Cessna and stood under its high nose and propeller. He shielded his eyes and looked down the lake. The sheer cliffs on either side were growing more solid by the minute.

Tim walked back to the airplane, pushed the door shut, and latched it. He turned slowly and walked under the left wing then began shuffling through the snow toward the rugged shore. He didn't wish to expose himself like last time. He would skirt along the rocks before coming around the final curve of the cliff on the northern side of the lake and coming into view of the other men's camp.

Jamie lay at the open tent door and fought hard to remain conscious. His sandy beard and eyebrows were covered with white frost. Only his legs were still encased in the red nylon expedition sleeping bag. The rest of the bag was unzipped and lay draped around his shoulders. His red stocking hat was pulled down over his ears. The painkiller had worn off hours ago. He thought he would become more alert, but somehow this wasn't happening. His mind just didn't seem to focus anymore.

The sun was climbing higher in the sky. Most of the fog layer had burned away, leaving the entire cirque bathed in brilliant morning sunshine. At this altitude the sky was a deep, beautiful blue. With the new snowfall the previous evening, the effect of the sun on the frozen lake was dazzling as billions of snow crystals sparkled in the light. Jamie's eyes watered as he squinted and tried to focus on the other end of the lake.

In a reflex motion, he reached for his large aviator sunglasses, which he always kept in his right shirt pocket. He withdrew them and slowly put them on one earpiece at time. Even the smallest task seemed to take forever. Their mirrored outer surfaces reflected the peaks around him. He noticed one lens was cracked from his impact with the instrument panel, and frowned. He had had these glasses since Vietnam.

He lay still for a while so that his breathing slowed. Any exertion that caused him to breathe harder, take deeper breaths, hurt his chest.

Jamie reached out the tent door, scooped up a handful of snow, and pressed it to his lips. He tried to suck on the dry, fluffy snow. His lips were dry and cracked now. The snow didn't contain much moisture.

Movement in the distance caught his attention immediately. He looked up and tried to focus once more. With one hand, he pawed at his eyes under the sunglasses in an effort to clear his vision. There it was again. Someone was moving slowly near the north precipice.

Jamie reached back along his sleeping bag and felt for the Winchester hunting rifle. His hand closed on the cold steel barrel, and he dragged it up to the tent door with some effort. He tried to roll onto his stomach and bring the rifle to his shoulder but couldn't. Pain shot up his leg and into his guts. His vision blurred, and then seemed to turn purple. Jamie fainted.

The pain started at the base of his spine and wound its way to the very top of his head like a lightning bolt. Rod groaned and tried to move. He also tried to focus on his surroundings. Nothing helped—everything seemed vague and fuzzy. He came around some more. He seemed to be lying on something hard with his head below his feet. He seemed to be in the shade, but the sky in the crack over his head was a deep blue. He instinctively brought his arm up over his head to shield his eyes. Jamie's large Seiko dangled from his wrist. He studied it with curiosity.

His mind cleared a little more of its cobwebs. Blue sky...rocks... Jesus! It all came roaring back suddenly. The fall! How long had he been lying here? Rod brought his head up and studied the watch. He just couldn't seem to focus on it. He brought it closer still until it was just inches from his face. The crystal was cracked, but it was slowly ticking off the seconds one by one. He had been out for almost a half hour.

Something still seemed wrong as he pushed the heavy climbing rope from his chest and groaned. His glasses! Shit! He muttered to himself. His glasses were gone. And the gun. Where was the gun?

Rod climbed out from under the climbing rope and turned over. He had been lying head-down on the steep back side of a large boulder right next to another larger one, which slanted overhead by the shore of the frozen lake. He struggled to come to his hands and knees. The rucksack pulled him backwards, and he rolled to the base of the rock in a heap. He finally was able to let the pack slip from his shoulders and came to his knees.

Rod felt stiff and sore. He checked himself over. Besides some torn clothing, some superficial cuts and bruises, and a sore back, everything seemed to be working okay. Nothing felt broken.

He turned and squinted at his surroundings. Everything at a distance of ten feet or more was hopelessly out of focus. But he had been lucky. He had landed on his back, glancing down the side of the boulder, and the parka he had stuffed into the rucksack had padded the fall enough to save his life.

The panic began to creep in to his guts. Was he too late?

Rod began crawling around on his hands and knees, his head close to the ground, desperate to find his glasses, and hoping they were still somewhat intact. He lifted the pack and felt around in the snow. The glasses weren't there. He worried that they had left his face during the fall. They could be anywhere. But no, he remembered seeing the end of the rope come over the edge clearly. He was sure they were on his face when he hit the ground.

Rod continued to search the area. He found the AK-47 first, just ten feet to his right. He picked it up, held it close to his face, and inspected it. The stock was broken but the metal parts seemed intact. At least nothing seemed bent.

He leaned the assault rifle carefully against a nearby rock and continued to search, delicately feeling in front of himself with both hands, his head down. The area seemed loaded with all kinds of nooks and crannies. The task seemed hopeless, but they had to be somewhere.

The next object he came across was his left mitten. This surprised him. In his haste and panic, he hadn't realized one hand was bare and the other covered. He took the other one off and tossed both over next to the pack.

He continued to crawl around on his hands and knees, feeling for his glasses in the snow. He searched every crevice. He shifted through patches of snow. He reached under the larger boulders. His pants were wet with melting snow. His fingers stung from the cold. And all the time, he looked over his shoulder and worried about the man in the ski-plane.

Finally, as he was about to give up, with tears of frustration welling up in his eyes, his numb fingers closed around a familiar object at the base of a boulder far to his left. His glasses apparently had been thrown off his face much farther than he would have ever guessed. He held his breath and pulled them gingerly from beneath the rock, hoping they wouldn't slip further into the crevice.

Rod held them to the sky and inspected them just a foot from his face. One earpiece was bent, and a chunk of the plastic lens about the size of a dime had been chipped from the left side. Otherwise they were intact.

He tried to straighten the bent earpiece a little bit with both thumbs, trying desperately not to break the cold, brittle metal. He was able to get it somewhat straight and usable although wavy. It was the best he could do; there was no Lens Crafters around the corner here. He put the glasses on and the world came into focus. They hung on his face crookedly, but he could see clearly once more.

Rod crawled over to the pack and the AK-47. He picked up the assault rifle, testing it in his hands. Although the stock was now a useless, jagged piece of splintered wood, he could still hold it fairly well by the pistol grip near the trigger with one hand and the wooden forestock under the barrel with the other. He pushed the combination safety lever and fire selector on the side of the receiver down two clicks to the fully automatic position and then back to safety. He slid the bolt back a half inch, satisfied that a round was still chambered, and let the bolt snap forward. The rifle was probably still functional, he decided. He slowly and cautiously stood up alongside the large boulder that was between himself and the lake. As he straightened his legs, he was aware of a sharp pain in his right knee for the first time and groaned aloud. He tested it gingerly and was satisfied that it would hold his weight.

The sun now reflecting off the dazzling white surface of the lake hurt his eyes. They began to water, and he had to squint for a few moments as he tried to adjust to the brilliant scene. Both airplanes were in plain view: the wreck just offshore where it had always been and the ski-plane just beyond and behind it. The sky was a deep blue; the jagged peaks guarding the cirque wore a sparkling mantle of new snow. From his vantage point, however, the wrecked airplane partially blocked his view of the ski-plane. He couldn't detect any movement but neither could he see its entire cabin.

Rod cursed to himself, muttering under his breath, and wished for his compact pair of binoculars. They would be very handy right now. But they were safely back in his desk drawer on the forty-second floor in the heart of Denver, while he was stalking around a frozen lake with a machine gun. Unbelievable.

He crouched behind the rock and waited. Still nothing moved. He looked at the unbroken snow between his hiding place and the wreck. It seemed a great distance now, even though Jamie had swum it in a few minutes. He licked his lips. His mouth was suddenly dry. Jamie had told him to keep the wrecked airplane between himself and the other Cessna for cover—his only cover. That had seemed like a good idea last night in the tent, but not now. Airplane aluminum was very thin, he knew.

He tried to climb up and over the large boulder, but his legs wouldn't move. Instead, he turned, slid back down to its base, and ended up sitting safely next to the rucksack with his back against the boulder.

He just couldn't do it. He just couldn't will himself to expose himself out on that lake. He pounded the ground with his fist and wanted to yell, but knew he didn't dare. The sound might expose his hiding place.

So this is what it is really like, he thought, to really face death. Face to face with the grim reaper. But what was the alternative? Freezing to death? Whimpering behind some piece of granite? No, he had to go out there on the lake. He knew it. He had to see this through; he had no choice. So this is what it is like, he thought. Maybe there aren't any heroes, just people with no choice. Like Jamie said, people caught up in the event with no real way out of it.

Rod grabbed the AK-47, clicked the safety off and the lever down to the full automatic fire position, and crawled up the backside of the boulder. He slid down the side facing the lake and jumped onto the flat rock on which he had stood when Jamie had swum out to the wreck.

He boldly jumped down onto the frozen surface into the knee-deep snow, cradling the assault rifle in front of him, and began taking large, exaggerated steps. His right knee hurt every time he placed weight on it; his ankle seemed on fire now; his insides throbbed, and he suspected a broken or bruised rib; and he was rapidly developing a headache and fear of a concussion.

He waded through the snow fifty feet. He was halfway there. He was totally exposed on the ice now. Still there was no movement that he could see either around the wreck or beyond in the ski-plane. He held the assault rifle in front of him, his finger now on the trigger.

Seventy-five feet and he felt he would make it at least to the wreck. He was breathing hard from the exertion, and his glasses were beginning to fog up. The AK-47 seemed heavier.

Suddenly he was there. The wrecked airplane's nose rose up above him as he crouched by its side. He listened, his heart pounding. His breathing slowed gradually. There was nothing but the wind as it lightly blew some ice crystals in a tight circle near his feet. He listened carefully. No sound, no footsteps.

Rod knelt and then crawled around the nose to the area between the fuselage and the left engine, which he used for cover. He reached up and ran his left hand along one of the propeller blades and read the manufacturer's decal. Incredible, he thought. This was the closest he had been to the machine that had caused him all this trouble in the first place. He suddenly became curious about the interior and wanted to peer inside. Instead, he rolled over on his hands and knees then cautiously reared up until his forehead and eyes were just above the wing's dull black deicing boot. He fully expected to be shot between the eyes.

Some one hundred feet away, the other airplane appeared to sit empty, its skis covered by new snow. Rod rose up cautiously and aimed the AK-47 at the Cessna. Funny, he thought, no one in sight. The other airplane seemed deserted. The fresh snow, though, seemed to be disturbed on the far side of the ski-plane. Someone had been around there recently.

A mild warning signal began to sound in the back of Rod's consciousness. He stood up and began to slowly work his way around the silent engine and wing. He held the assault rifle in front of him as he quickly covered the distance between the two airplanes. It was the bravest thing he had ever done.

He walked around the tail of the ski-plane and into the shade of the left wing. He literally held his breath as he gingerly stepped up onto its landing strut and peered inside, still fully expecting the other man to jump up out of the back seat. But except for the two front seats, a crumpled sleeping bag, and some gear in the back with two large, brown leather suitcases, the airplane was empty.

Rod was at first relieved then puzzled. Where had the other man gone? Then the realization came upon him like a freight train. He turned from the airplane and jumped down into the snow. The tracks! The tracks led from the airplane down the lake toward Jamie. Shit! While he had been out cold and then screwing around finding his glasses as it got light, the other man had been making his way down the lake toward their camp.

Rod shielded his eyes and looked down the lake. It was empty as far as he could see except for the helicopter wreckage in the distance, just visible outside the cliff. There was no sign of life. Nothing moved.

Rod's breath started coming in huge, chest-heaving gulps as he realized what was happening. At this moment, the other man was either near their camp or at it.

He had heard no gunfire. Surely Jamie would put up a fight. But maybe he wasn't even conscious anymore. Rod felt the nervous sweat begin to form under Jamie's too large sweater. He willed his legs to move. He couldn't run in the deep snow. He was too late. He knew it and felt it. The inside of his mouth began to taste coppery, an unpleasant metallic taste.

Tim was one hundred feet from the tent when he saw the big man in the door move for the first time. He leveled the Uzi and walked forward carefully. The man in the tent groaned then he was still. Tim continued toward the tent.

He had watched the area from a distance for a good half hour before deciding that the injured man was alone. He had finally decided that the man at the tent door was either dead or unconscious. The other one had probably gone for help, he thought.

Tim walked closer, the submachine gun trained on the tent, the safety off, the selector on full auto. For the first time, he noticed fresh tracks behind the tent leading in the opposite direction, confirming his suspicion that, indeed, the other man, the smaller one who had shot at him from the helicopter, had gone for help. Well, he's too late, Tim thought, as he now stood over the injured man in the tent door. He held the Uzi loosely at his side and looked down at him.

He lay on his side with the red, nylon sleeping bag wrapped around him. The man in the tent moaned again and rolled to one side. Then his hand began groping next to him for the hunting rifle with its telescopic sight.

Tim laughed out loud. It was pathetic. He didn't stand a chance, but Tim sadistically decided to let him go a little farther before he blew him away.

Jamie's hand found the Winchester's cold, steel barrel. He tried to drag it out in front of him but was too weak to move it more than a couple of feet. Then Tim suddenly stepped on the other man's wrist, pinning it, and laughed. Next Tim reached down and pulled the rifle away from him. Jamie tried to grab the rifle as the other man picked it up, but the man easily shook Jamie's hand free and it flopped back onto the tent floor. Tim held the Uzi in one hand and flung the hunting rifle far out into the snow.

At the same time, Rod came around the north precipice and saw the man standing in front of the tent. He tried to run faster but couldn't. The deep snow tugged at his legs. It was the classic bad dream with everything happening in slow motion. As he tried to run, his lungs began to burn, and his legs felt rubbery. But he was still too far to risk a shot.

Tim leaned down and softly touched the muzzle of the Uzi to the side of Jamie's head, slowly pushing him down onto the tent floor. Jamie was lucid for a few moments and caught sight of Rod in the distance as he was forced to turn his head toward his killer. He hoped there hadn't been a flicker of recognition on his face to make the other pilot turn and give his friend away. He somehow had to stall for a few more minutes and try to stay conscious.

Tim leaned closer. His finger tightened on the trigger ever so slightly, and he smiled. "Nothing personal, you understand." He studied Jamie's face above the sleeping bag. Frost clung to Jamie's eyebrows, mustache, and beard. Then there was the red nylon expedition sleeping wrapped around his shoulders...the mirrored aviation sunglasses...the red stocking hat...

Suddenly Tim jerked back like he had been hit by an electric shot. Later, Jamie would tell Rod he thought Rod had gotten off a lucky shot and had waited for the distant report.

But Tim was still very much alive as he turned and looked at the helicopter wreckage and then back to Jamie. The dream. He suddenly heard the pounding of the Huey's rotor blades again, felt their wind, and smelled the rancid, warm water in the rice paddy. The realism of the vision, of the dream was overwhelming. Again, as he turned back toward the Jet Ranger's wreckage, he saw the crew in the rescue chopper. The elves, the antlers, the pilot dressed in red…

He turned back to the tent, screamed, and grabbed Jamie, "Tell me who you are!"

Jamie fought to remain conscious as the other man shook him. "I…I…I…" He fought to answer the sudden madman in front of him.

"Vietnam! You flew in Vietnam, didn't you!"

Jamie half spoke and half gargled, "Two…years."

Tim continued to scream, "You're Santa Claus. Tell me you were dressed as Santa Claus one day!" Then Tim let go and stood up. He dropped the Uzi.

The memories came flooding back to Tim in a sudden flashback. The stinking jungle, the heat and humidity, the small men in black pajamas.

Tim stopped, stood up, and caught his breath. He turned. The flashback was complete. There was one of them now with an AK-47 now not a hundred feet away across the rice paddy.

Tim turned and reached down for the Uzi.

Rod stopped and leveled the AK-47. He yelled across the ice, "Please, don't do it, mister!"

Tim picked up the submachine gun and whirled around.

Rod pulled the trigger and held it down. The assault rifle jumped and bucked in his hands. It reared up like something alive, spewing empty cartridges out one side. In an instant, ten shots pounded the air, in a roar that reverberated off the stone walls and almost sounded like one.

Tim had not completed his turn when three of the bullets ripped into him. The first one was low. It ripped through his leg and then the tent fabric near Jamie's head. He began to fall. The second one struck him in the midsection and pulverized his spine. As the AK-47 continued to ride up in Rod's hands, the third bullet struck Tim in the throat pushing him over backwards into the tent. The remaining bullets went harmlessly over the tent and crashed into the rocks high along the shore.

The Uzi dropped from Tim's hands and slid into the snow as he died, wide-eyed and spread-eagled against the blue, nylon fabric. At first the tent poles absorbed his weight by flexing, but they suddenly sprang back, shrugging the body into the snow, which began to turn crimson. His right arm twitched once, then twice, and then he was still.

As the sound of gunfire roared through the cirque and then diminished, Rod stood frozen, mouth open and wide-eyed, for a few moments not believing either what he had done or the scene in front of him. He was astonished at the destruction he had caused in a few short seconds. He looked down at the assault rifle in his hands. Small wisps of smoke rose from the barrel. The smell of burnt gunpowder was strong for a moment, a scent he would never forget.

Jamie groaned loudly.

Rod was stirred from his spell suddenly. He threw aside the AK-47 and tried to run the remaining distance to the tent. All he managed was a fast shuffle through the deep snow. Finally he was at the tent's door and collapsed on his knees next to Jamie. He gently rolled him over. His hands were shaking badly as he fussed with the sleeping bag and tried to bring it around his friend's shoulders. Jamie groaned again. He looked like death itself, pale and ghostly.

Rod asked with a quaking voice no louder than a whisper, "Are you alright? Jesus, you look bad."

Jamie tried to smile and looked at the body next to him. "Not as bad…as that guy. He almost pulled…the trigger. You saved my life, old buddy."

"Yeah," Rod answered weakly while he tried not to look at the body next to them.

Jamie chuckled weakly. "That'll teach him not to mess with Rod Coleman, won't it?" Then he coughed. His ribs hurt. His leg was on fire.

Rod looked at Jamie and said in a suddenly hard, cold voice, "Look, let's drop the subject and worry about getting out of here, okay? Do you need another pain shot?"

"Yeah, I'm feeling lousy. If...you...move me around...I'll need something." Then he asked, "Where...in...the hell...were you? You sure took your sweet...time."

"Jeez, bitch, bitch, bitch. It's a long story. I'll tell you all about it someday soon." Rod crawled past him into the tent.

Jamie asked weakly, "Are you going...to be able to fly that Cessna?"

Rod answered, "You'd better hope so. I think I can remember enough from all those lessons years ago. Besides, what is your alternative? I hate to break the news, Jamie, but you don't look so good. You need a hospital as soon as possible. Yeah, I'll try and fly it out." In reality Rod felt weak inside but didn't want to show it to his friend. That was the last thing both of them needed right now. He figured it was a fifty-to-one shot that he could actually fly the Cessna on skis. What was the alternative? That he hike out? Jamie would surely die. And he might not make it out, too. Nobody, not a living soul, actually knew where they were.

Rod crawled back alongside Jamie a moment later with a syringe. He held it in the air. "Here, give me your arm. This is the last one."

Jamie weakly picked up his arm. Rod stuck him quickly in the forearm like an old pro. He released the morphine and pulled the needle out. "There, you should be able to relax in a few moments."

Jamie felt the effect of the drug immediately. He replied, "Thanks, old buddy." Then he continued, "Funny thing about that guy, though, whoever he is. He was yelling something ridiculous about Santa Claus and me being in Vietnam. Then he went berserk when he saw you."

"Yeah, I heard him yelling. What'd you think he meant?"

Jamie's speech began to slur. "I don't know exactly...my crew and I volunteered...once to go to a big orphanage...on Christmas Day...We were going to do things up right...land in the courtyard...do things up right...surprise them...Shit...we went the whole nine yards... Someone borrowed the costumes...my crew as elves...me as...wait a minute...Santa Claus...even had a pillow under my big, black belt... Hell, someone dug up some antlers...We wired them to the Huey's nose." Jamie drifted off.

Rod began making preparations to leave. "Sounds like fun to me."

Jamie answered drowsily, "Yeah, it would have been...but we never made it...Halfway there, we got a report of a downed pilot...and diverted...We were close...found the SOB wandering around near the tree line in a rice paddy...He had already iced five or six of them... picked him up...heavy enemy fire....my Silver Star."

Rod still refused to look directly at the man he had killed. "Do you think it was him?"

Jamie made an effort to rise up and look around Rod at the body. He settled back down. "I...don't know...You kind of disfigured him... talk about your irony..."

Rod had been fighting an increasingly queasy feeling since he had let go of the trigger. He crawled to the other side of the tent and vomited.

CHAPTER 34

The Rescue

Rod sat and tapped his finger on the Cessna's shiny, black control wheel. He glanced at Jamie's Seiko dangling beneath his wrist and worried about spending another night on the lake. Jamie lay slumped in the rear seat, either unconscious or just sleeping. He couldn't tell. The breathing seemed shallow and difficult. At least he was still alive. You had to hand it to him, he was tough.

Rod thought about what Jamie had said, what they had argued about while he had still been conscious. The butane stove hissed and sputtered.

He would make another attempt at starting the engine in about fifteen minutes. The lake was not giving them up without difficulty. How many times had he tramped between the airplane and their tent in the last hours? Over four...he couldn't remember just how many. A glaze was forming over his mind, caused by the events of the last twenty-four hours, fatigue, and lack of sleep. He was literally becoming numb. If the next attempt failed, they would probably sit here and freeze. He suddenly remembered the movie *Flight of the Phoenix*. Jimmy Stewart had been the pilot and had faced the same dilemma. One more try at starting the engine. Only Jimmy Stewart had been stuck in the desert.

It had taken the better part of two hours to get Jamie from the tent to the ski-plane on the sleeping bag. Rod had thought that the end might be in sight, only to discover the ignition key wasn't in the airplane. He had walked back to their camp on what was becoming a well-worn path to face the unpleasant task of finding the keys on the other man's bullet-riddled body. Rod had tried not to look at him, but curiosity had crept in, and he had found himself hurrying back to the Cessna trying hard not to gag again. The dead man's eyes seemed to stare directly at him, somehow accusing him of his death.

Upon returning to the ski-plane, Rod's nagging fear had been confirmed when he found the airplane's battery had barely enough electrical power to spin the propeller slowly—not fast enough to start the cold-soaked engine with its heavy aviation oil in the tank. He had tried twice to start the engine and had suffered a moment of dark despair before coming up with what he thought was a brilliant solution.

It had meant one more trip back to the tent and the dead man again. This time to salvage the butane stove, spare canisters, and the down sleeping bag for Jamie.

It had taken him twenty minutes to remove the lower nose cowling from the Cessna with his Swiss Army knife, a tough job in the cold. The special fasteners had fought him every bit of the way. His fingers stung against the cold metal.

Now, the stove was using up its last dwindling supply of fuel to warm the engine and the battery. Rod had it stacked on some of their gear directly beneath the oil reservoir. He also had draped some tarps he had found over the nose and down each side to direct all the heat upward.

The battery was low. There were no more butane fuel canisters. He had one more chance.

As the stove roared, Rod thought about the takeoff. He was trying to remember all those lessons years ago, when the hissing stopped. It caught him by surprise, and he straightened in his seat. There was no more stove fuel left.

Pushing the cabin door open, he placed one foot on the step on the wheel strut and then jumped down into the snow. He walked around the left ski and stood next to the engine. Pulling a portion of the tarp back, he took off a glove and tentatively placed a bare hand on the oil tank. He held his breath. He was relieved to feel the metal was actually warm to his touch. Almost hot. A good sign, but with every second that precious heat was radiating out into the frigid air that surrounded the airplane on the lake. Although the bright sunshine reflecting off the snow made it seem warmer, in actuality the air temperature was hovering at just ten degrees above zero.

Hurriedly Rod threw the spent stove aside and then the stack of gear it had rested upon. He made sure everything landed well clear of the skis. He debated whether to try and put the cowling back on but decided against it. Valuable time would be lost struggling with the fasteners again, and it looked like a two-man job.

Rod threw the cowling aside as he ran around the wing strut in the packed snow. He jumped up into the left seat. The Cessna, he thought, was just a larger version of the trainer he had flown years ago. He quickly set the controls to start the engine.

He pushed the mixture control with the red knob all the way forward and then back out a little. This should now let fuel into the engine cylinders. He would have to watch this control and maybe pull it out a little more to compensate for the high altitude. After all, the lake was over twelve thousand feet above sea level, and, despite the cold, the air was very thin. He wouldn't want to flood the engine. The propeller governor control was a new one to him. The trainer he had flown those years ago didn't have this control, but Rod knew it should be pushed all the way forward to its high RPM setting. He confirmed the fuel tank selector was on both tanks and not in the off position.

Rod pushed the throttle about a half inch. He pulled the primer out and then slowly pushed it forward. He could feel pressure and heard fuel being sprayed into the engine cylinders. He did this twice. He hoped he was not flooding the engine, and at the same time, he hoped he was adding the right amount of fuel. He then placed his right hand back on the throttle and his left hand on the key underneath the control yoke. He held his breath and took a quick look over his shoulder at Jamie. His friend seemed to be stirring a little although his chin was resting on the red sleeping bag.

Rod took a deep breath. This was it. He turned the key to start.

The starter whined in protest, but this time the propeller spun much faster than before as the warm and therefore thinner oil was circulated into the engine. One cylinder fired immediately, then two. Rod worked the throttle in and out. More cylinders fired. The propeller spun faster. Then the engine quit.

"Shit!" Rod muttered.

He primed the engine once more and then turned the key. The engine coughed once, but this time it roared to life. The Cessna moved forward on its skis as the tail lifted. Rod throttled back, and the engine settled into a throbbing idle. He turned the red mixture knob counter-clockwise a full turn, and the engine idled a little faster with the leaner mixture.

Rod decided not to press his luck any more with the mixture control. Sure, it was a fact that the cold air was denser than in the summer, but the elevation was still twelve thousand feet above sea level. The engine on the Cessna was running, and he decided not to mess with it and keep it that way. They should have some precious heat soon.

Rod looked once more at the instrument panel. The gas gauges showed half full. Plenty of gas for what he now had in mind. The needles on all the engine gauges all seemed to be in the green arcs except for the oil temperature gauge, but even it had now come off its peg. The battery was charging.

Rod reached over near Jamie and pulled out the heater control. Nice, warm air began to come out from under the instrument panel. It was the first heat he had felt in some twenty-four hours and felt good. Optimism about their situation began to seep in just like the warm air. They just might make it.

But something nagged at him. Rod turned and looked over his shoulder through the Cessna's back window at the other airplane caught in the ice. Its row of oval windows disappeared beneath the white surface. Snow still covered its wing and engines. The bent propellers stuck up at odd angles. The Cessna's cabin was warming.

Jamie stirred and mumbled something, but Rod couldn't hear him over the sound of the idling engine and propeller. Rod leaned closer. Jamie's eyes suddenly were open despite the pain he must be suffering. He looked around the cockpit and then at Rod. Rod put his ear near Jamie's lips and yelled, "What?"

Jamie gulped once and asked in a hoarse whisper, "You're not thinking of flying us out are you? You haven't flown for years. You'll kill us for sure."

Rod answered, "No, don't worry. I thought about it." But he said almost jovially to his friend, "Hey, *I've* got a plan. I'm going to let them find us."

Then he remembered what had nagged him after the engine had started a few minutes ago. He had been preoccupied with warming the oil and hoping the battery had enough juice. He had to find and turn on the ELT. That was the next thing. The emergency locator transmitter. It would send its distress signal to an overhead satellite or another airplane listening to the correct frequency. He had to locate it.

Rod scanned the cockpit for a switch for the ELT. No switch that he could see. Then he suddenly remembered something from his flying lessons long ago. The ELT was located in the tail of those Cessnas.

Although it would activate by g-forces, there should be a manual switch at the base of the tail behind a spring-loaded trapdoor.

Rod opened the Cessna's door, put one foot on the wing strut, and jumped down into the snow. Now that the interior of the Cessna was warming, the outside air felt sharp and cold. He shuffled through the snow to the tail of the airplane. Nothing on the left side. Rod leaned over the fuselage. There! On the right side where the tail joined the fuselage was the ELT hatch. Rod shuffled around to the other side of the airplane. He bent over and pushed the little square door open. It was spring-loaded. Rod peered inside. There was the switch, simply labeled ON-OFF.

Holding the door open with one hand, Rod pulled the glove off the other hand with his teeth. Okay, here goes, he thought, as he flipped the little switch up to the on position.

There was no beeping or flashing red lights. That was for the movies. Rod knew he would have to climb back into the Cessna's cockpit and tune one of the comm radios to a frequency of 121.5.

He shuffled around the tail and climbed back up into the warm cockpit. Pulling the door shut behind him, Rod turned on the top comm radio in the stack of radios in the middle of the instrument panel and hurriedly tuned the correct frequency into the little window. Immediately a loud whooping noise came from the overhead speaker. The ELT was working! Rod knew that very likely a satellite or passing aircraft was instantly picking up this signal and relaying their location to the authorities.

In fact, the captain of a passing airliner, who thought it was simply a good idea to monitor the emergency frequency and who was now over central Colorado flying from Los Angeles to Minneapolis, was speaking to Denver Center about the ELT's signal he had suddenly heard at that moment. An orbiting satellite had also picked up the ELT's signal instantly.

Jamie stirred and simply asked, "The ELT?"

Rod turned and nodded.

Jamie closed his eyes again, but Rod noticed there was a slight smile on his lips.

The Cessna's engine was running beautifully. The fuel tanks were still half full. The cockpit was warm. Even if rescue came tomorrow, they still should be okay. Rod looked over at Jamie and sighed. He opened the Cessna's door and climbed down into the snow once more. Although he felt that rescue was on the way, he knew that it would probably take some hours to organize. He had time.

Rod walked around the rear of the Cessna again, shielding himself from the prop wash. He shuffled up to the right door of the Cessna. The four heavy, brown leather suitcases still lay in the snow where he had pushed them when he had helped Jamie into the airplane.

What the hell, he suddenly thought, as he hefted the first suitcase up onto his shoulder and started to walk wearily in the deep snow across the frozen lake to the far shore.

When he had returned the last time out of breath, Rod had covered the distance between the idling Cessna to the rocky south shore four times. In the hours before rescue, he figured the wind should eventually cover his tracks to the inaccessible, steep south side of the lake.

Rod shuffled over to the wreck. He scrambled up onto the slick, snow-encrusted wing and made his way carefully to the broken cockpit window. He was conscious of the ski-plane's idling engine as he bent over and peered inside the demolished cockpit. After all the danger and trouble, he realized he had never actually looked inside.

Rod caught his breath. The frozen pilot was still hunched over the controls. His skin was bluish white. A good deal of his head was missing. There was frozen blood everywhere. Rod's stomach swirled. Snow had drifted into every nook and cranny. A good amount of snow lay between the top of the instrument panel and the front windshield.

Trying to ignore the dead pilot, Rod squeezed through the window with some difficultly. As he brushed the dead pilot, he wondered how Jamie had gotten through but then Jamie had been naked and not wearing a puffy down parka. It was creepy. The dead man was very solid to the touch. Like a tray of ice cubes.

Once in the cockpit, Rod stooped between the pilot seats and faced rearward into the cabin. He let his eyes adjust to the relative darkness. It was obvious that the other pilot, the man he had just killed hours before, had done some work before he and Jamie had surprised him with their helicopter. There were some tools scattered about near one of the seats on the left. A large pile of frozen money, still banded, lay on the floor to the right. A lot of money, Rod thought.

Large and small piles of ice were also piled near the rearmost area of the cabin, where the frozen surface met the sloping ceiling. Undoubtedly, the ice had been thrown there by the ski-plane's pilot as he frantically tried to uncover all the money. And there were more brown, leather suitcases.

As his eyes adjusted from the brightness outside, Rod gaped at the sight of yet another man's forehead and two hands protruding just above the icy floor much like a swimmer treading water. Just like the pilot up in the cockpit, the dead man's forehead had a milky blue tint to it. It was weird, but Rod noticed that his oily, jet black hair was still neatly in place.

Rod decided to go, but his attention was drawn to one of the large, brown leather suitcases lying between two of the passenger seats on the left side. It was identical to the ones he had found in the other airplane. It looked as if for some reason this suitcase had not been encased in the ice but had ended up after the crash on the forward seats as had the others. Maybe it had been thrown there by the impact. He and Jamie had obviously surprised the ski-plane pilot after he had taken the first four suitcases to his airplane and was preparing to remove the fifth easy one and then the rest with more difficulty still encased in the ice inside the airplane. Removal of these five suitcases would have been easy compared to the rest; Rod noticed there were at least five or more of them still almost totally submerged in the ice inside the wrecked airplane.

What he didn't know was there were still more of them in the luggage bins behind each engine.

Rod heard the ski-plane idle get rough and then smooth out. Time to go.

He turned to leave then hesitated. He bit his lower lip. Why not the other suitcase, too? He probably had time. No, he left it just where it was and then scrambled back into the cockpit.

With some effort Rod climbed headfirst over the dead pilot again onto the wing. He slid down into the bright snow. He squinted and came to his feet while brushing the snow off himself. And then he shuffled a final time back to the ski-plane and up into the warm cockpit. Jamie looked up, smiled, and gave him a weak thumbs-up.

A few hours later, the wind picked up once more and completely covered all his tracks across the frozen lake's surface to the rugged south shore. Rescue came late that afternoon in the form of a loud Colorado Air National Guard Huey helicopter—the same model that Jamie Anderson had flown in Vietnam.

CHAPTER 35

Aftermath

It became known as "The Airplane in the Ice Case." The US Forest Service, FAA, DEA, Customs, FBI, US Air Force, Las Vegas Police Department, and the Gunnison County Sheriff's Department were all eventually involved. The news media from all over the nation immediately picked up the story. The government agencies tried to stonewall them at first, but the facts gradually leaked out. After all, it wasn't every day that an airplane was found encased in ice with millions in drug money aboard and two dead men.

Rod and Jamie were helicoptered to the hospital in Gunnison that night and transferred to a hospital in Denver the next day. Rod had escaped unscathed except for cuts and bruises, but Jamie had serious injuries. His prognosis was pronounced guarded but good. A police guard was placed at their doors. They were under arrest. This caused Jamie no end of good humor.

The feds really didn't know what to do with both of them. It was determined that they really hadn't broken any big laws, and it was proven quickly that they hadn't been involved in any drug smuggling either. They were model citizens really. Rod Coleman had a good, honest job and a family. Jamie Anderson was a very highly decorated war hero. An adventure of sorts had gotten out of hand.

Rod was finally sent home under house arrest with charges supposedly pending. Jamie continued to recover in the hospital after surgery on his leg, and the police guard was eventually removed. He became well known among the female nursing staff.

Before spring arrived the government launched an extensive cleanup at Hourglass Lake. The Cessna ski-plane was fueled and flown off the lake by an expert pilot from Alaska. It was secured in a large hangar at the Gunnison airport along with the wreckage of the helicopter and the twin-engine Cessna, which had to be jack-hammered out of the ice. The DEA seized the money, and it disappeared into government coffers somewhere, never to be seen again. The exact amount was never released to the public. The bodies of the three men were eventually returned to their families. Finally, all charges were dropped against Rod Coleman and Jamie Anderson that spring.

CHAPTER 36

Sighting

The following December, a lone cross-country skier traversing the White Elk Range reported to the US Forest Service two days after returning to Gunnison that he had seen a lone, noisy civilian helicopter with two men aboard enter the gorge leading into the Hourglass Lake area a week earlier in probable violation of the Wilderness Act and leave by the same route thirty minutes later. The skier was unable to provide a registration number for the helicopter. A follow up to this report was never filed, and it was forgotten.

CHAPTER 37

August 1986
Kismet

I t was a glorious Colorado summer morning. Not a cloud marred the deep, blue sky. A slight breeze ruffled the streamside willows at almost regular intervals. The woman concentrated on the ghostly, dark shadow at the base of the riffles just where the river tumbled into the long, dark pool. Her back was to the road at the moment, and she didn't notice the big, silver Mercedes approaching from the south. Although over fifteen years old, its large V-8 engine whispered, and the gravel crunched under its premium tires as it slowed, pulled off the road, and parked opposite and above her. She made another careful cast but still the large brown trout ignored her expertly placed fly. The blond man with the gray-flecked beard powered his window down and watched with interest as she made another cast.

Today was the second day of her well-deserved vacation. She had been working practically nonstop, seven days a week, for the past almost two years since her brother's death. The takeover bid had been successfully thwarted. It had taken a dozen lawyers and six months in court, but the business was hers now. The plans for the new hotel in Mexico City were advancing rapidly. Construction was slated to begin in three weeks, and she would have to fly down there to turn the first spade full of dirt. The revamping of the flagship hotel in Las Vegas was also going very well. In line with the current trend, the Las Vegas hotel and casino were being given a more family-oriented theme. In fact, she was even thinking of demolishing the original hotel and building a still larger, more modern hotel and casino on the same spot. Strangely she thought her father would have approved. The business overall had even shown a small profit in the last quarter. And, more importantly, the entire hotel chain was clean now and slowly gaining back the good reputation her father had been responsible for in the early days. All the law enforcement agencies had focused on her dead brother and had left her alone for the most part; although they knew she had had a hand in things, somehow they couldn't prove it. But those agencies, along with some important local politicians, had decided in back rooms that it was better for everyone—from the thousands of employees to the taxman— to keep the hotel chain in business and so had officially cleared her of any wrongdoing.

The man in the Mercedes opened his door and unfolded himself from the cracked leather seat. He was tall and gaunt with the lean, pale look of someone who had been sick for a long period and had lost weight. His clothes hung slack from his frame. Before shutting the door, he reached inside and lifted a cane from the rear seat, hesitated, and decided to leave it in the car.

He favored one leg as he walked slowly down to the stream's edge. He stood behind and to one side of the woman and watched as she made another cast. He made an appraising look and found her very attractive, even in her old wool shirt and waders.

She brought back her rod for still another cast to the stubborn brown trout. As she turned her head for the cast, she was startled to see him standing there and jumped. He was smiling, and she thought she detected a certain mischievous twinkle in his eyes. But she had hesitated a little too long, and her fly had snagged a willow behind her.

As she backed out of the stream to retrieve her fly, she asked not unkindly, "You do know this is private property, don't you?"

Jamie extended his hand to help her up the bank.

Upon closer inspection, she decided his eyes were the bluest she had ever seen.

Leaving his hand extended to her, he motioned with his other hand at the distant mountains. "Don't tell me you're the one who owns all this?"

As he spoke, she noticed that merriment in his eyes again. The crow's feet radiating outward from them were magnificent.

Debbie laughed and smiled back at him. "Maybe I do; maybe I don't; maybe I'll have one of my hired hands ride down here and string you up from one of the barn rafters."

Then she reached up and took his hand. She could not help noticing instantly the large emerald ring he wore. It had a unique style, and she knew she had seen either it or its twin someplace.

Jamie hoisted her up onto the bank easily. When they stood together, he nodded toward the river behind them. "You know, old Mr. Brown just might take a weighted nymph down deep instead of that dry fly you're using."

Debbie lifted her polarized sunglasses from her eyes and stuck them in her hair, which was tied back in a ponytail. Jamie couldn't help but notice the way the sunlight reflected attractively off the silver strands that were beginning to show here and there in her auburn hair.

She asked him, as she walked over to the willow stand to retrieve the fly, "What makes you the fishing expert?"

Jamie grinned at her. There was that twinkle again.

He said, "Years of experience. Why don't you let me show you?"

Debbie nodded up the road a half mile toward the log house. "I've got a better idea. I've been up since before sunrise. It feels almost like lunchtime to me. Why don't you give me a ride up to the house, we fix a couple of sandwiches, and we talk fishing. Then I just might give you permission to try and show me how to catch Mr. Brown."

They turned toward the old Mercedes.

As Debbie wound the line back onto her reel, she asked, "Have you ever shot trap before? I was going to practice some this afternoon."

"I'm one of the best shots in the world," Jamie quickly replied.

Debbie stopped next to the car. She turned and sized him up again. "You wouldn't want to put some money where your mouth is, would you?" She realized that neither knew each other's name yet, and they were acting like old friends.

Jamie pulled a crumpled hundred dollar bill from his pocket and held it up. "How about this?"

She took the hundred and examined it. "This bill looks kind of like it's been through the washer, but you're on."

Debbie settled into the sumptuous, worn leather passenger seat. Jamie started the engine. As he put the Mercedes into gear, she suddenly remembered where she had seen that ring. She shook her head. That would be impossible, except…

As they drove up the ranch road, Jamie found himself studying the high peaks of the White Elks to the west.

CHAPTER 38

September 1986
Airborne

T he slipstream roared around the man and the boy as the small, red-and-white biplane dove toward the ground and accelerated rapidly at the end of the loop. The little boy in the front seat yelled with delight and spread his arms wide to catch the wind. The man slowly brought back pressure on the stick between his legs and the nose rose higher until the sturdy little airplane flew level once more.

Rod glanced at his watch. The four diamonds mounted on the black face sparkled in the Colorado sunshine. Reluctantly, he banked the tiny Pitts Special back toward the foothills and the Boulder airport. He had barely two hours to land, squeeze the little airplane back into its hanger, and make it to his first class of the fall term at the university.

The boy turned around in his seat and held up one finger, indicating he wanted to do it one more time. Rod shook his head and pointed to his watch. Rod Jr. understood and turned back around in his seat. He put both hands against the fuselage and let the wind force its way up his sleeves.

In a few minutes they reached the airport, but, still needing to lose altitude, Rod circled lazily over the city. He flew over the university and then their new home snuggled up against the foothills in the pines. The house had cost over $100,000. He circled twice. Except for the old silver Porsche, the driveway was empty. Ann had mentioned she was going to Denver that afternoon to look at some more antique, 1940s furniture. It was expensive, but it was her passion at the moment, and besides, the account in the Caymans was certainly more than up to it.

It had been more difficult to gain admittance to graduate school than Rod had initially expected. The competition these days was fierce, but he had been accepted into the fall semester thanks to the influence of an old professor friend.

2032 AD
Ashes

The sun had set, and the living room was now in shadows as Jamie finished talking. Both men sat in silence. Jamie leaned back in the sofa and stretched. Junior, lost in his thoughts about his father, idly flipped through a packet of the old, green one hundred dollar bills he had taken from the vintage leather suitcase an hour ago. The sudden quiet was ended by the sound of a car door shutting. The two men's short reverie was broken. Jamie reached to his right and turned on a table light while Junior rose and approached the front door.

Deborah Forsyth had kept her maiden name after the marriage forty-five years ago to Jamie Anderson but was just known simply as Deb by her friends and employees. She walked purposefully to the front steps.

She was now a fit woman in her late seventies and, like her husband, a noted and famous businessperson. She had become an icon and role model to other women over the past decades, as an example of what could be achieved through intelligence, hard work, and good humor. For the memorial service, she had acquiesced and worn pearls to go with an expensive black dress and shoes by a noted designer, more for the benefit of the photographers than herself. Her salt-and-pepper hair was pulled back in her trademark ponytail. A pair of stylish aviator sunglasses was forgotten above her forehead. She wore no makeup. Not one for pretension, she was known for her comfortable casual dress at the headquarters and the ranch: usually a pair of jeans and a sweatshirt advertising one of her charities.

Junior held the door open as Deb squeezed past. He noted the perfume and, as always, the absolute beauty and class. Junior shut the door and turned.

Deb turned and gave Junior a sudden hug. Her voice broke a bit. "I'm so sorry about your dad."

Junior simply nodded and lowered his head.

Deb dropped her arms and held one of Junior's hands. Then she turned and looked at her husband. Jamie nodded. She turned back to Junior. "Well, what do you think of all that?"

Junior blurted, "You actually shot a guy?"

Deb smiled and turned back to her husband. As she held his eyes, she brought up her free hand and mimicked a pistol aimed at him. She let her thumb fall and said with a wink, "It's what happens when a man wrongs me, Junior."

Jamie Anderson chuckled. Junior thought he caught a small bit of nervousness in the other man's laugh.

***

His godparents had certainly shanghaied him. Junior thought about this as he prepared to take only the second helicopter ride in his life. The first ride had been three days ago in this same sleek helicopter.

At that time, to his surprise, the three had finished up quickly at the house in Boulder, put his Honda next to the Porsche in the garage, and locked up the house. The old suitcase with the money had been casually placed in the Lincoln's trunk.

Next, Jamie had driven them to the Denver hotel on the top of which sat the helicopter. They had spent the night there in Denver. Junior was given a VIP room, and they had eaten a delicious meal in the immaculate hotel dining room. It was evident to Junior, from the way the employees reacted to his hosts and the way they treated him as a very special guest during his brief stay, that everyone adored Jamie and Deb. There were lots of laughs that evening, and mostly first names were used.

The next morning the three had flown to their White Elk Ranch near Gunnison. For the next two days, the weather in the mountains to the west just hadn't cooperated, and they were apparently grounded; although grounded from what, Junior had no clue. There was a lot of secrecy going on around him. Then he had begun to understand.

This morning the weather had broken, and it had dawned clear over the mountains to the west of the ranch. And here he was in the helicopter once more, clutching his father's urn on his lap. He sat behind Deb, who was now in the front left, or copilot's, seat of the helicopter. Jamie sat in the right front seat, which Junior had gathered was the pilot in command's seat. Both wore dark aviator-style sunglasses. All three were dressed in heavy clothing. Colorful, thick down parkas had been discarded on the remaining passenger seats as the interior warmed. Deb, to Junior's surprise, was also a rated helicopter pilot, and the two had been in different seats for the flight from Denver. She had been the one to fly them smoothly from the hotel rooftop to the ranch.

Junior listened to the muted roar of the twin Pratt and Whitney turbines to the rear as they came up to temperature in the still frigid morning air, and realized it was the sound of money. He was now apparently going to become a relatively wealthy man himself of course. At the couple's urging, he had even quit his job two days before. He had never guessed his father had accumulated so much. Rod Sr. had made what were excellent but conservative investments over the years with his share of the money. But as Rod Jr. took in his present surroundings, he knew that he was seeing only a tiny part of really big money. In fact, he thought everything around him oozed wealth: first, his sumptuous leather passenger seat; then this sleek Sikorsky helicopter itself, with the familiar *F* and *H* scrolled on the rear fuselage; the classic log house just behind them with its servants watching from the front windows; the antique gun collection—some legal, some not; the classic silver Mercedes sedan in front of the house parked next to the early 1940's Cadillac convertible, both cars restored to perfection; and, of course, the thousands upon thousands of acres of land surrounding them. And this was just the tip of the worldwide iceberg.

Now Jamie and Deb were consulting their final checklists. They were certainly a team these past four decades, Junior had decided.

Jamie leaned back and asked, "Seat belt fastened?"

Junior gave him a thumbs-up. Jamie indicated for him to put on the headset, which would facilitate communication between the three. As Junior did so, he heard the sound of the twin turbines increase as the rotor blades above them began to rotate faster and faster.

Jamie moved the controls, and the helicopter moved a little back and forth, hesitated, dipped its nose, and rose up and forward. Junior looked forward through the cockpit windows as the helicopter gained altitude. He saw Deb reach forward and retract the landing gear at Jamie's command. He had been at the ranch a few times with his father as a child and once about fifteen years ago. But as the helicopter at first followed the renowned trout steam downstream, he tried to imagine it over four decades ago as he now knew the story.

To his left was the ranch road. Yes, it was straight for over a mile before it turned and climbed the hogback. A perfect airstrip. He could imagine the old WWII bomber touching down and taxiing up to the log house now disappearing rapidly behind them.

Jamie banked the helicopter to the right and flew west, still gaining altitude. The White Elk Mountains loomed majestically in the distance before them, framed this December day by a vivid, blue sky.

Soon they were over the first foothills, and the sagebrush gave way to the first ponderosa pines. Jamie climbed higher. Snow became visible between the trees. Junior now saw the gorge and part of Hourglass Lake nestled at its head in its cirque.

They skillfully entered the gorge. Jamie maneuvered the left turn, and the snow-covered lake with its majestic cliffs on each side was directly ahead. Jamie began to slow the helicopter as Deb reached ahead and lowered the landing gear.

Now moving forward slowly, they passed over the frozen waterfalls, then the rocky campsite beyond on the lake's edge.

Jamie hovered over the lake just above the surface. He picked a spot somewhat clear of snow. The blue ice glimmered in the sunlight. Some helicopters would have trouble doing this even in the cold air at twelve thousand feet, but with the powerful engines of this latest model, the altitude was no problem.

They slowly touched down, once then twice. Jamie was testing the ice, Junior thought. On the third landing, he let all the weight settle onto the ice.

Jamie reached over and cut both engines. The turbines wound down, and there was silence as the rotor blades came to a halt.

Deb was the first one out. She popped her door open and climbed down onto the bare ice; frigid air poured into the interior. She walked a few feet to the rear and opened the passenger door for Junior.

Jamie opened his door on the other side and also climbed down. On his side of the helicopter, the snow was a few inches deep.

Junior grabbed his yellow parka and his father's urn and climbed down. He quickly zipped the coat, balancing the urn under his arm.

Deb followed him around the front of the helicopter, quickly donning her blue parka and carrying Jamie's red one. She handed it to him, and he shrugged into it. All three looked at the lake in its breathtaking setting.

Finally Deb broke the silence with a whisper, "Better than any cathedral."

Jamie pointed to his right and began to speak. "About one hundred meters up the lake, Junior, on the right is where your dad and I crashed the chopper." He continued, "Up behind there is where he climbed up to the far ridge. A brave thing to do. It was pitch black. Then he came around on the ridge and climbed back down to the upper end of the lake, trying to get behind the other guy. Over thirteen thousand feet. I was hurtin' and in and out of it. And it was cold. Colder than it is now, and it's zero right now."

Junior took in the scene. It was one thing to be told the story, but to glimpse the cirque firsthand was much more than impressive.

Jamie gently took the urn from the other man and unscrewed the lid. His voice broke. "God, this is going to be hard."

With that he walked forward across the ice to the tiny campsite at the outlet of the lake and began to gently shake the urn and sprinkle his friend's ashes out onto the snow. He stepped back and handed the urn to Junior who did the same; then Deb, who emptied the rest.

Now standing together, Jamie said, "This is what Rod wanted. He told me years ago that he wanted his ashes scattered up here at his favorite place in all the world." Jamie took his wife's hand. "He saved my life. I owe him for all the wonderful things that came after." Then he took a breath and said, "C'mon, we gotta go before those engines cool too much."

With that the three friends climbed back aboard. One turbine caught, then two. In a few minutes, the rotors began to turn, and they lifted off the ice. Jamie flew slowly to the upper end of the lake and turned around not fifty feet from the surface. He flew slowly down to the outlet. He hovered for a moment at the gray area on the snow, then dipped the nose in a salute before turning and accelerating down the gorge and home.

THE END